# DANGER AHEAD

OTHER BOOKS AND AUDIO BOOKS
BY BETSY BRANNON GREEN

KENNEDY KILLINGSWORTH MYSTERIES
*Murder by the Book*
*Murder by Design*
*Murder by the Way*

HAGGERTY MYSTERIES
*Hearts in Hiding*
*Until Proven Guilty*
*Above Suspicion*
*Silenced*
*Copycat*
*Poison*
*Double Cross*
*Backtrack*

HAZARDOUS DUTY
*Hazardous Duty*
*Above and Beyond*
*Code of Honor*
*Proceed with Caution*

OTHER NOVELS
*Never Look Back*
*Don't Cross Your Eyes*
*Foul Play*

# DANGER AHEAD

*a novel*

## BETSY BRANNON GREEN

Covenant Communications, Inc.

Cover image: *Spy* © Lorado, courtesy of istockphoto.com

Cover design copyright © 2014 by Covenant Communications, Inc.

Published by Covenant Communications, Inc.
American Fork, Utah

Printed in the United States of America
First Printing: October 2014

20 19 18 17 16 15 14     10 9 8 7 6 5 4 3 2 1

ISBN: 978-1-62108-891-2

To Harrison Michael Farrer, my first grandson, who stands for the right—truly a warrior in God's army!

# ACKNOWLEDGMENTS

I OWE SO MUCH TO SO many people. Thanks first and foremost to my husband, Butch, for putting up with me throughout this very long creative process (it's not easy being married to someone who has a whole cast of characters living in their head). Thanks also to my children for being so perfect that I almost never have to worry about them (or my grandchildren). Thanks to Little Caesars (who feeds my family as often as I do when I'm working on a book). A special thanks to Stacey Owen for her editorial expertise (and for not giving up on me). A huge thank-you to all my readers who have waited patiently for this sequel (and even to those who have been impatient). And as always, I'm thankful to Covenant for letting me be a part of their "team."

# PROLOGUE

BROOKE CLAYTON FOLLOWED CORPORAL HUNTER Ezell through her parents' kitchen toward the garage where his car was parked. They were holding hands, and he was basically pulling her reluctantly along.

"Why do we have to go?" she asked as they reached the back door.

Hunter led her down the steps into the dimly lit garage. "You know why. The DA said he needs us to sign some statements, and your uncle told him we were on our way."

Brooke wrapped her arms around his waist. "We could just forget about the DA's statements and leave town. We could go back to the Civil War resort or," she whispered into his ear, "we could elope!"

Hunter looked uneasy. "Brooke . . ."

She rolled her eyes. "I'm just kidding about the eloping part—for now anyway. But I wouldn't mind skipping the trip to the DA's office."

"Mr. Shaw is expecting us," Hunter replied logically. "And some of Hack's guys are waiting to follow us there."

"I'm having a hard time making myself care about any of that," she murmured. In fact, there in the semidarkness with Hunter standing so close, she found it hard to think about anything but him. "What should I call you?"

He frowned. "I thought we had settled on Hunter."

Her arms snaked up around his neck. "I mean, when I'm introducing you to my family or friends or even strangers. Saying you're my boyfriend sounds so juvenile. But you're not my fiancé—at least not yet."

He reached up and loosened the fingers she had wrapped around his neck. "Can we worry about that later?"

She shook her head. "It might come up at the DA's office. I could call you my 'significant other.'"

"Please don't," he said with an air of desperation.

She laughed as he opened the passenger door. "Or my sweetie pie."

"Just tell them I'm your bodyguard." As he settled behind the wheel, his phone rang. After a short conversation, he returned the phone to his shirt pocket and told her, "That was one of the guys assigned to follow us to the courthouse. There are some Nature Fresh protesters in front of your parents' house. We'll have to drive by on our way out, and he just wanted to warn us."

"Nature Fresh protesters?" Brooke repeated. "What are they protesting against?"

"You," Hunter replied.

"Me?"

"Well, Joined Forces," he amended. "They've lost their jobs because of the fire at the chicken plant, and I guess they want someone to blame."

"But protesting outside my parents' house?" she whispered. "That's so . . . personal."

"To them it is personal." He opened the garage door and eased his car down the driveway. "Look straight ahead," he advised. "Try not to make eye contact."

She did as he suggested, but she was peripherally aware of a small group of people gathered on the road. They were wearing Nature Fresh uniforms and holding signs that looked hastily made. She felt their collective gaze following Hunter's car.

By the time they were on the interstate headed for downtown Nashville, Brooke had recovered her equilibrium. "They should be mad at the owners of Nature Fresh. If they hadn't been doing illegal things, none of this would have happened."

He shrugged. "I guess it's easier to blame you."

The air conditioning was going full force to combat the humid summer heat. Brooke lifted her hair and leaned forward so the cool air could reach her neck.

"Do you think they'll protest at my apartment too?"

"Probably."

She dropped her hair and grabbed his arm. "Thank goodness I have you to protect me!"

Hunter kept his eyes on the road. "Hands to yourself while I'm driving. You'll make me have a wreck."

She laughed and released her hold on him. "I'll try, but I can't promise that I won't touch you again before we get to the courthouse." She swiveled in her seat so she could address his profile. "After we sign these statements for the DA, maybe we could plan our first real date. Remember, you owe me dinner."

"You want me to go into a restaurant looking like this?" He pointed at the bruises and cuts on his face.

Guilt assailed her, and she stroked his cheek. "Oh, Hunter, I can never apologize enough!"

"No touching," he reminded her. "And don't apologize. You didn't beat me up."

"Of course not, but if it wasn't for me, you wouldn't have been kidnapped or beat up. But if you hadn't had to protect me from those Nature Fresh guys, we might not have fallen in love."

His tone softened. "That was worth at least a few bruises."

Brooke was pleased. "I'm going to turn you into a romantic after all."

He gave her a little half smile. "I wouldn't count on that. I'm just saying this whole crazy thing had some positive side effects, like us getting together and your decision to leave Joined Forces."

Her good mood faded slightly. "I don't have to leave Joined Forces—it's self-destructing. With no leadership and no money, there's not much chance the group will survive."

"Good," Hunter muttered as he weaved in and out of traffic.

"I know I should be relieved, but I can't help feeling a little sad," she admitted. "At one time our group did help a lot of mistreated animals."

"You can still help abused animals," he said.

"I know, but this is the end of a chapter in my life. I always find endings a little sad, don't you?"

He risked a glance at her. "I never thought about it."

She laughed. "Something else I could learn from you! Now, what about our date?"

They still hadn't come to a decision about dinner when Hunter pulled into the parking deck near the courthouse.

"Don't think I'm letting you off the hook," Brooke said as he opened the door for her.

"I would never think that," he replied. "Now let's get this over with."

She clutched the fingers of his good hand more tightly in her own. The crisis with Nature Fresh was over, and except for Hunter's bruised face and broken arm, they were unharmed. They were in love and looking forward to a future together.

They walked hand in hand to the elevators with the bodyguards trailing a few feet behind. When they reached the fifth floor, the entourage stepped out into a small waiting room.

A well-dressed young woman with a haughty smile greeted them. "My name is Yolanda, and I'm Mr. Shaw's assistant," she told them. "If you'll have a seat, I'll notify him that you have arrived."

Brooke and Hunter settled on a small couch while the bodyguards sat across the room facing them. Brooke rifled through a stack of magazines looking for something that might interest their bodyguards. Based on the men's massive size, she assumed they were serious eaters, so she chose two recent issues of *Bon Appétit* and extended them toward the men.

They both shook their heads, declining in unison.

Brooke returned to the magazines to the stack and selected one called *Decorating on a Dime* for Hunter. "You might see some ideas you could use to fix up your apartment."

He stared at the magazine blankly. "I doubt it."

With a shrug, she tossed the decorating magazine back onto the stack and chose a copy of *Field and Stream* for herself. She thumbed through it until the assistant returned.

"Mr. Shaw is ready for you," Yolanda said. "Follow me, please."

Brooke and Hunter stood, and their bodyguards did the same.

Then Yolanda held up a hand. "I'm sorry, but your . . ." she waved toward the two huge men, floundering for the right word and finally settled on, "*friends* can't come into Mr. Shaw's office. The statements you'll be signing are confidential."

This didn't seem like a point worth fighting over, so Brooke flashed the bodyguards a charming grin. "Stay here, guys. We'll be right back. And if we need you—we'll scream!"

She heard Hunter sigh again as the men exchanged an uncertain glance. Then reluctantly, Hack's men returned to their seats. Before they could change their minds, Brooke grabbed Hunter's hand and followed the assistant down the hallway.

They made several turns, and Brooke noted that as they walked, the offices got bigger, the carpet got plusher, and the décor got pricier. Finally they reached a wood-paneled wall. Above the huge double doors were the words *Davidson County District Attorney* spelled out with individual brass letters.

Brooke took a deep breath and stepped into the district attorney's spacious inner sanctum. Mr. Shaw was sitting behind a massive wooden desk, but he stood as they entered the room.

"Thank you so much for coming," he drawled. Then he waved toward two pieces of paper arranged on his desk. "We've prepared statements for each of you to sign."

Anxious to take care of this and get on their way, Brooke found the document with her name printed under the signature line and signed quickly.

Hunter also approached the desk, but instead of just signing, he insisted on reading his statement first. He sat down in one of the chairs in front of Mr. Shaw's desk. Brooke settled in the other and watched him read.

Although she was anxious to leave, watching Hunter do anything was a pleasure, so Brooke didn't mind too much. His long, tanned fingers contrasted pleasantly with the stark white paper he was holding. His green eyes skimmed along each line the same way he did everything—seriously.

There was a knock at the door and then a quiet whoosh as it opened behind them. Brooke was too enthralled with Hunter to even glance up. She assumed it was Yolanda returning to do more of her assistant duties. But Hunter did look toward the door and then sprung to his feet. The statement he'd been reading dropped from his hands and floated to the floor as he charged the door.

"Hunter!" Brooke cried in surprise. Then she jerked her head around to see Sperry, the man who had tried to burn them in a forest fire. Brooke gasped, and Mr. Shaw looked annoyed.

Hunter tackled the man and held him on the ground. "Call the police!" he instructed over his shoulder. His good arm was wrapped around the man's neck.

Mr. Shaw spoke into the phone. "I have a situation in my office. Send security at once! But tell them to come around the back way. There are a couple of bodyguards sitting in the lobby that we don't want involved."

Brooke heard Mr. Shaw hang up his phone, but she kept her eyes on Hunter. He was balanced on Sperry's back with his cast-covered arm held up high like a rodeo rider. Whether this was for balance or to keep it out of harm's way, she couldn't be sure.

Sperry's eyes bulged as he clawed at the arm across his neck.

"I think you might be strangling him," Mr. Shaw said.

Hunter didn't relax his grip.

Brooke took a step closer. "Is there anything I can do to help?"

"Just stay back."

After what seemed like an eternity, the security guards finally arrived. They burst into the office and charged toward the men scrabbling on the floor. As they reached down, Hunter released his hold to facilitate the prisoner transfer. But instead of grabbing Sperry, the security guards grabbed Hunter and wrestled him into a chair.

With quick, experienced movements, they duct-taped his mouth, arms, and legs. It was over in seconds, and Brooke stared at Hunter, who sat before her bound and gagged. But she did not scream for the bodyguards in the lobby.

Instead she addressed the DA. "Tell them they've tied up the wrong person! They were supposed to get him!" She jabbed a finger toward Sperry, who was cowering in the corner of the room, as far away from Hunter as he could get without leaving.

Hunter's eyes watched her. He was angry about being tied up, of course, but she could sense his confidence that this was a mistake and could easily be fixed.

Mr. Shaw dismissed the security guards and then said, "There was no reason to restrain Mr. Sperry. He didn't attack anyone."

"He tried to kill us by the Nature Fresh plant!" Brooke pointed out heatedly.

"I wasn't trying to kill anyone!" Sperry insisted. "They promised me nobody would get hurt!"

"Mr. Sperry was just doing the job he'd been hired to do." The DA's eyes narrowed. "Although I don't know why I'm explaining this to you, Miss Clayton, since you were well aware of the plan."

Hunter's intense gaze was now confused and concerned but still trusting.

"I never approved any plan that involved Hunter being kidnapped or the two of us being tied to a tree." Brooke disclaimed what she could. Then she waved toward Sperry. "He should be in jail."

"Well, he shouldn't be here at least." Mr. Shaw gave the man a severe look.

Sperry hung his head. "Sorry, I just—"

"Apology accepted," Mr. Shaw interrupted. "Now leave and don't ever set foot in my office again. If you do, the charges I just dropped will be reinstated."

"But I . . ." Sperry's eyes drifted over to Brooke. She glared back at him, and he turned away. Then he walked to the door and slipped into the hall.

After the door closed behind him, Brooke said, "I can't believe you're letting him go!"

"We can't risk the public scrutiny that would come with a trial," Mr. Shaw replied evenly.

"You had no right to make that decision without my approval!" Brooke shot back.

"You're not the only one who could go to jail if the authorities learn the truth." Mr. Shaw's tone was still calm, but his eyes were angry. "I was hired to protect Joined Forces, and I had to protect myself as well."

Brooke decided it wasn't worth the trouble to argue this point. Sperry was gone, after all. And she couldn't worry about the increasingly alarmed looks Hunter was giving her. Once they were alone, she could explain. But the important thing was to get him out of that office. "I want Hunter untied immediately."

Mr. Shaw shook his head. "The corporal now knows enough to be very dangerous to me and to you and to Joined Forces in general. So until we can decide how to silence him, he stays taped to that chair."

Brooke understood the implied threat and had no doubt that it was real. With Sperry just minutes away and a security force at his disposal, Mr. Shaw could be very dangerous. She leaned across the desk and said with authority, "You will not arrange for anyone to hurt him!"

"No," he agreed. "If that's the decision we reach, you will have that privilege—just like you arranged for the fire that destroyed the Nature Fresh plant."

Brooke felt Hunter watching her, waiting for her to deny it. She wanted to be the girl he loved and trusted. But that girl didn't have the power to save him. So with a heavy heart, she told the DA, "You work for me, not the other way around. And if you aren't careful, I'll arrange for someone to hurt *you*."

"I'm not scared," he claimed, although he looked a little nervous. "And regardless of who hired who, you are in *my* office. If necessary, I'll call security again."

"That won't be necessary."

"I'm glad to hear that." He walked over and plucked Hunter's phone from his shirt pocket. Turning it off, he asked Brooke to do the same to hers.

She complied—not because she felt obligated to obey but because the phone was worthless. Outside help couldn't arrive in time to help Hunter.

The phone on Mr. Shaw's desk rang, and he said, "Excuse me while I get this, please." He pushed a button on the phone console and said, "Hello? Major Dane?"

Brooke's heart ached, and she saw Hunter tense as they heard the familiar voice.

"I'd like to see Nature Fresh pay for the things we think they've done—even if it's just through a denied insurance claim," her uncle was saying. "But I really want Hunter and Brooke to be safe. So please make sure that their names are not mentioned on anything. In fact, I'd prefer that their statements be shredded."

"I'll destroy their statements if that's what you want." Mr. Shaw sounded sad.

"Do you have any idea when they'll be through?" Uncle Christopher asked. "We're waiting on them before we head home."

"They left a few minutes ago." Mr. Shaw raised an eyebrow at Brooke, almost daring her to contradict him. "They asked if there was a faster way to get to the parking deck than going through the lobby. So I showed them the back elevator."

He was making it seem as if they had ditched their bodyguards—again—and gone off without notifying her family. Hunter fought against his restraints, but Brooke remained silent. Her uncle couldn't get here in time. She would have to handle things without his help.

Her uncle's voice sounded as hollow as she felt when he said, "Thank you."

As Mr. Shaw hung up the phone on his desk, Brooke clasped her hands tightly together and forced herself to look at Hunter. She knew she had been sufficiently convincing in her role as Joined Forces leader when she saw the loathing in his eyes. With a shudder, she turned away.

"Well, that worked out perfectly," Mr. Shaw declared with a complacent smile. "And no one will ever doubt your dedication to the cause, Miss Clayton."

# CHAPTER ONE

FOR MONTHS NOW BROOKE HAD been doing what she *had* to do at the expense of what she *wanted* to do. She had hoped that the past was finally behind her, but obviously, she had been wrong. Based on the look in Hunter's eyes, she had ruined any chance of a happy future with him. Defeat threatened to overwhelm her.

But when she thought about all the people who would pay the price for her failure, she knew she couldn't give up, even with the odds stacked against her. She might lose in the end, but she would fight until the last speck of hope was gone. So she reached for the tape that bound Hunter's good arm.

"I told you not to untie him!" Mr. Shaw objected strenuously.

"I guarantee that Hunter won't tell anyone what he's heard here today."

"How can you possibly guarantee that?"

Brooke forced herself to look into Hunter's hostile eyes and told the simple truth. "Because he loves me. And if he tells the police that I helped burn down that plant, I'll go to jail."

Hunter's expression didn't soften, but after a brief pause, he tipped his head in a little nod of acknowledgment. She smiled sadly and went back to work on the tape.

The DA pinched the bridge of his nose as if he were getting a headache. "You people are impossible to reason with. I don't know why I ever agreed to help you in the first place."

"You wanted campaign contributions, and you were willing to break the law to get them."

Mr. Shaw fixed her with an unfriendly gaze. "As a Joined Forces arsonist, I don't think you're in a position to throw any stones, Miss Clayton."

Brooke continued pulling at the tape. "You won't have to put up with my unpleasant company any longer. As soon as I get Hunter loose, we're leaving, and I promise we won't ever come back."

"You aren't going anywhere," the DA stated flatly.

She looked up and saw that he was holding the phone.

"I'll call security back if necessary," he said. "The corporal remains in restraints until your boss gets here to take responsibility for you both."

"My *boss?*" she repeated in confusion. Joined Forces had no leadership beyond herself. It was a rudderless ship, sinking fast.

As if on cue, the office door opened, and a voice she'd hoped never to hear again said, "Well, well, if it isn't Miss Brooke Clayton."

Reluctantly Brooke turned to face him. "Rex."

He looked about the same as he had when they parted ways—tall and thin with longish dark hair and intense brown eyes. He was tan now, after months in the California sun, and he was better dressed than he'd been during their shared past. In the old days, he'd worn jeans and faded T-shirts. Today he had on khaki pants and a button-down oxford shirt with a little emblem embroidered on the pocket.

"What are you doing here?" she asked.

"I'm here to save Joined Forces and clean up the mess you've made of things," he replied.

"But you moved to California." She knew this was not the most intelligent comment, but her mind hadn't had time to catch up with this sudden turn of events.

"I moved to California, but I never 'left' Joined Forces." *I only left you.* The unspoken words fairly echoed in the large office. "I've continued to recruit new members and—more importantly—new donors from what you might call a supervisory role. I'm sure Freddo told you I was advising him."

Brooke shook her head. "No."

"Typical Freddo, trying to take all the credit for himself." Rex lifted his shoulder in a little shrug. "The organization's in shambles, so I had to come back. Aren't you happy to see me, Brooke?"

"Not particularly," she replied, keeping her voice flat and devoid of emotion. "But you're right about Joined Forces. Things are so bad I see no choice but to disband."

"Things *were* bad," he corrected. "But now I'm here, and soon Joined Forces will be stronger than ever."

She tried to hide her disappointment but knew she'd failed when she saw his cruel grin.

He took a step closer and lifted a lock of hair from her shoulder. "So you went blonde."

She endured the contact with distaste. "It was a disguise—part of this whole thing with Nature Fresh."

"I like it. You should keep it this way."

In that moment she determined to return to her natural color as soon as possible. She took a step back, and her hair slipped from his fingers as a painfully thin young woman with huge eyes and short brown hair walked into the office. She looked between Brooke and Rex and then put a proprietary hand on his arm.

"Brooke, meet Millicent." Rex patted the young woman's hand.

Millicent regarded Brooke critically, as if sizing up the competition.

Brooke wished there was some way to reassure the girl that there was nothing she wanted less than to resume her former role as Rex's girlfriend.

"And this beat-up young man is Brooke's current love-interest." Rex gestured vaguely toward Hunter.

Millicent's eyes skimmed over Hunter. She was apparently uninterested in his presence and unconcerned about the fact that he was bound to a chair.

"I've hired Millicent to be the new personnel director for Joined Forces," Rex continued. "For now she's also doubling as our public relations director. Eventually there will be a whole board, but that'll have to wait until we can get some revenue coming in."

Brooke wasn't sure what surprised her most—the fact that Joined Forces would have an official board or that they would be hired. The leadership of Joined Forces had always consisted of college kids who volunteered their time.

"Millicent is very talented." Rex smiled down at the thin girl. "She's designed our new logo, written a very moving mission statement, and is now working on a jingle for our first commercial."

Brooke couldn't hide her astonishment. "Are you serious?"

Rex nodded. "Completely."

"But a jingle and commercials sound so . . . unradical."

"We don't have to be radical to help animals," Rex replied in his signature I'm-so-much-smarter-than-you tone. "We just have to get our message out. And don't feel too bad about dragging me away from sunny

California," he added as if Brooke had apologized. "We needed a place to test our new business model, and Nashville will work just fine."

"Business model?" she repeated. Then the full implications of what he'd said dawned on her. "You're moving back *here*?"

"Just for a while," he said, obviously enjoying her discomfort.

Millicent spoke for the first time. "We're opening a call center here in an old bankrupt church that Rex bought for almost nothing. The grand opening is on Saturday. We're calling the event "Dinner and an Auction"—kind of a play on dinner and a movie."

Brooke tried to look like she was paying attention, but her mind was searching for a plan that would get herself and Hunter out of the DA's office and as far away from Rex as possible.

Rex said, "One of our most enthusiastic new members is a coin collector, and he donated some coins for the event. He asked a few of his fellow collectors to do the same, and *voilà*! We have an auction. The buyers get rare coins, we get to keep the proceeds, and the donors get a tax deduction."

"It's so sophisticated!" Millicent gushed.

"It's genius," Rex corrected. "A coin auction attracts a richer class of people, which is why the governor has agreed to put in an appearance. It's a chance for him to rub elbows with potential campaign contributors with deep pockets."

"The governor," Brooke repeated in dismay. Her hope that Joined Forces was in its death throes was growing dimmer by the minute.

Rex nodded. "His presence gives the whole event . . . clout. Don't you think?"

Before Brooke could respond, Millicent pulled on his arm. "Speaking of the new call center, I need to get back there. My employment interviews begin in an hour."

Rex passed her a set of keys. "You go on and take the rental car."

"You're not coming with me?" Millicent glanced from Brooke to Rex, as if she was afraid to leave them together.

"I have to handle this little situation first." He twirled his finger between Brooke and Hunter.

Millicent persisted. "But I can't do all the interviews myself."

"I'll be there as soon as I can," Rex assured her with an edge of impatience.

Millicent didn't look happy, but she took the keys from his outstretched hand and walked out the door.

Once she was gone, Rex turned back to Brooke. "Now, where were we?"

"You were telling me that you're here to save Joined Forces and take over everything," she provided. "Which is actually a huge relief since I'm busy trying to finish my last semester of school. I don't have time for anything else—including Joined Forces."

Rex wagged a finger back and forth in front of her face. "Oh no. You're not going to create this public relations nightmare and then just walk away."

"You don't need me, Rex. Let me go." She couldn't make herself add please.

He studied her for a few uncomfortable seconds. Then he said, "You really want out—permanently?"

She nodded. "I still love animals, but I don't have the time or the energy to be a member of Joined Forces anymore. I need to concentrate on school and my personal life." She risked a glance at Hunter. He was staring straight ahead.

Rex surprised her by saying, "Well, since you asked me so nicely, I might consider accepting your resignation after we've turned this crisis around."

Encouraged, Brooke asked, "How do you plan to do that?"

"I've set up a few publicity spots for you on some local talk shows. No big deal, just a way for us to put a positive spin on everything that's happened and get some free publicity for the call center's grand opening."

"I want to help Joined Forces, but I don't want to do any interviews," she said carefully. "I've told enough lies already."

Rex was unmoved by this argument. "Then a few more won't hurt you. And we're already committed, so I can't cancel now. It's just one radio interview today and two TV spots tomorrow. You can handle it."

"So if I do these three interviews, you'll let me leave Joined Forces?"

Rex laughed. "Certainly not! I've got a grand opening here on Saturday, and I'm going to need your help to pull that off. But if you do these three interviews, I won't schedule any more."

Brooke was profoundly disappointed, although she knew she'd been foolish to hope that Rex would let her off so easily. "Okay," she agreed because she had no choice. "I'll help you until after the grand opening on Saturday, and then I'll give you my resignation."

With a self-satisfied smile, Rex walked over and stood behind Hunter. "Now we have to decide what to do with your friend. Mr. Shaw's in favor of shooting him."

Although Brooke was pretty sure Rex was joking, her heart pounded painfully.

"I have no preference about the silencing method," the DA corrected. "I'll leave that up to you folks, as usual. I just want to be sure the corporal doesn't go around saying things that could ruin me."

"Oh, we'll make sure the soldier boy doesn't spread any tales," Rex assured him.

"His name is Corporal Hunter Ezell." Brooke clasped her hands together so Rex wouldn't see that they were trembling. "And he won't repeat anything he's heard here."

"Because he loves her," the DA provided.

Rex raised an eyebrow. "Is that true, Corporal?"

Hunter gave a brief nod. Brooke felt love and guilt in equal measure.

"Well then, we have nothing to worry about." Rex's tone was flippant. "Go ahead and release him."

Brooke finished unwinding the tape that bound Hunter's arms. Once his good hand was free, he reached up and ripped off the tape that covered his mouth. Then he untaped one leg while Brooke did the other.

Mr. Shaw stalked over to Rex. "You're not really going to depend on *love* to keep him from going straight to the police?"

"Actually the corporal looks like the type of man who keeps his word," Rex murmured. "But even if his love for Miss Clayton wanes, he won't go to the police."

"How do you know?"

"Because he has no proof," Rex replied. "To make wild accusations would be pointless."

"I won't talk," Hunter said stiffly. "To protect Brooke."

She felt both grateful and humiliated.

"But I don't want her to do any publicity spots about the Nature Fresh fire," Hunter continued. "She's already got people from Nature Fresh protesting at her parents' house. If she antagonizes them, they may do more than picket."

Rex waved this concern aside. "You'll be there to protect her."

Hunter stood his ground. "It's too big a risk. Brooke can't make any television or radio appearances."

All vestiges of humor left Rex's face. "Let me be clear, Corporal. I'm opening a call center here in a few days. Many rich and influential people, including the governor, are scheduled to attend. If we don't turn this Nature Fresh fiasco into good publicity, these people may decide they don't want their names or their money associated with Joined Forces. I won't allow that to happen. Brooke *will* do the interviews."

Hunter turned to Brooke. "Tell him you're not doing them."

She didn't want to further alienate Hunter, but she couldn't cross Rex. So she said, "I'll do the interviews that are already scheduled but no more."

Hunter looked incredulous. "You don't care that he's risking your life for publicity?"

Rex raised his eyebrows. "I believe you're being a little dramatic, Corporal."

"I'm being cautious," Hunter shot back. "And you should be too."

"I just want to do what is best for everyone," Brooke said.

Hunter's jaw was clenched. "The interviews are only good for him!" He hooked a finger toward Rex. "It's a foolish, unnecessary risk," Hunter said tightly. "I advise against it."

She nodded. "I know, and I hate to go against your advice, but I have to do the interviews."

Hunter stared at her, seething.

"Don't feel too bad, Corporal," Rex said. "You win some, you lose some."

"It will be okay," she whispered softly. Then she turned to Rex. "It's only a matter of time before my uncle sends people to look for me, so I should call him and avoid an all-out search. He'll probably insist on sending my bodyguards back, which should help alleviate some of Hunter's security concerns."

Rex scowled. "That means those goons will be tagging along with us to the media interviews?"

This was an essential part of her hastily formed plan. The presence of the bodyguards would protect Hunter as well as herself. "Yes. You know how my uncle is. He'll have people follow me anyway, so it might as well be at our invitation."

Rex relented ungraciously. "I guess there's no way to prevent it, so I'll approve a security presence. Just tell them to be discreet."

Relief washed over her. She glanced at Hunter and saw he was watching her, a cold, hard look in his eyes. He was safe, but there would be a price. She had no doubt about that. Before Rex could change his mind, she pulled out her phone, waited for it to turn on, and dialed the familiar number.

Rex was watching her closely. "Put it on speaker so we can all hear everything."

She complied, and a few seconds later, her uncle's voice blared from the phone.

"Brooke! Where *are* you?"

"Hunter and I are at the courthouse. We went out into the parking deck to talk for a few minutes. When we came back for the bodyguards, they had left."

"They left to search for you! Why did you and Owl sneak away and then turn off your phones?" Her uncle used Hunter's nickname out of habit.

"I'm sorry about that." There was only one excuse Brooke thought might work. She knew Hunter would hate it, but it was all she had. "Hunter and I were having a fight—kind of a lover's spat—and we needed a private place to work things out."

"You couldn't have told the bodyguards first?" Her uncle did not sound appeased.

"We could have, and we should have," she agreed, infusing her voice with remorse. "But in the moment when emotions were running high . . . Well, we just didn't use our best judgment. Love can do that to you."

Hunter kept his expression blank, but his cheeks turned pink, and she regretted that she had to embarrass him.

She averted her eyes to maintain her focus on the task at hand. "You remember how it feels to fall in love, right?"

There was a brief pause, and then he said, "I do remember."

"So you forgive me?" Brooke cajoled.

"I'll forgive you," he said. "But with these Nature Fresh protesters, I don't want you going around without protection. So I'm sending the bodyguards back. And I know I don't even have to say it . . ."

"I won't lose them again," she promised.

"So are you two headed back home?"

"No, actually Joined Forces is opening a new call center in Nashville on Saturday, and they've asked me to do some publicity spots on a few local radio and TV shows. We can't pass up the free publicity."

"You can if it puts you in danger," her uncle disagreed.

"It's my final contribution to the cause," she explained with a pointed look at Rex. "But my appearances might annoy the people at Nature Fresh, so the bodyguards are appreciated."

"It would be wiser to skip the publicity appearances altogether."

"Please, Uncle Christopher. This is important to me."

"It's your decision." His disapproval was clear. "Now let me speak to Owl."

She held her phone out, and Hunter accepted it with obvious reluctance.

All the indulgence he had extended to Brooke was gone when her uncle addressed his team member. "How could you let Brooke talk you into leaving Hack's men behind?"

"I'm sorry, sir."

"And you turned off your phone so we couldn't contact or locate you!"

"It was inexcusable, sir."

"You have disobeyed more orders in the last few days than in all the time I've known you," her uncle continued the berating Hunter didn't deserve. "I'm starting to think Brooke is a bad influence."

"Yes, sir," Hunter replied.

Brooke knew she had no right to be offended by this, but she was a little.

"I want you to stay with Brooke around the clock until further notice. I have to know two things—that she is secure and that you will answer my calls."

"I can guarantee both, sir."

"I was going to dismiss the team and head back to Virginia, but we'll stay in Nashville for a few more days to be sure this new publicity doesn't cause new problems."

"Yes, sir," Hunter replied.

"Call me if you notice any suspicious activity."

Before Hunter could add another "Yes, sir," they all heard the distinctive click. Uncle Christopher had ended the call.

Hunter looked a little shaken as he handed the phone back to Brooke. She had so many regrets, but getting him in trouble with her uncle was toward the top.

Rex grinned. "Well, that was fun! And the best part is that your uncle is determined to keep the corporal with you 'around the clock.' If only he knew that Corporal Ezell poses as much of a threat to you as Nature Fresh. Maybe more since he *knows* you're guilty, and he could be *forced* to testify against you. He's your worst nightmare! Oh, I love irony."

"I've already said I wouldn't go to the police," Hunter muttered.

"But what if you're subpoenaed? Will you lie under oath?" Rex pressed.

Hunter stared back at him. "I'll make sure I don't get subpoenaed."

"I wouldn't expect Hunter to lie under oath for me," Brooke said without much conviction.

Rex laughed. "You say that now, but if you were really facing prison, I think your courage would fail you. If you want to limit what he could be forced to say against you in court . . . maybe you can convince your soldier friend here to marry you!"

Brooke saw the appalled look on Hunter's face and wanted to cry. "Please, Rex, stop."

"A little teasing never hurt anyone," Rex claimed. Then he asked Hunter, "Is this the first time you've been on the wrong side of the law?"

"Rex," Brooke's tone was a little firmer this time.

He held up his hands in mock surrender. "Okay, okay. I'll stop.

Mr. Shaw said wearily, "I hate to be rude, but I really need to get back to work."

Rex looked amused. "So you're asking us to leave?"

"Yes, the sooner the better. But before you go, I'll have Yolanda draw up a statement for the corporal to sign implicating him in the whole Nature Fresh fire plot. It's not that I don't believe in love, but I'll feel better knowing that if he changes his mind and talks to the police, he'll go to jail too."

Rex nodded. "That sounds reasonable to me. As long as it won't take much time."

"A matter of minutes," the DA promised.

"You don't have a problem with that, do you, Corporal?" Rex asked.

Hunter shook his head.

"That's fine then," Rex told Mr. Shaw. "And will you return the corporal's phone please? If his commanding officer tries to reach him again and finds it turned off, he might have to face a firing squad or be forced to walk the plank."

"Rex, you promised to stop teasing," Brooke said as Mr. Shaw gave Hunter his phone.

"What can I say?" Rex replied. "I'm incorrigible." He stepped out into the hallway and then stopped suddenly. "I just realized I don't have transportation. I loaned my rental car to Millicent." He looked at Hunter. "Can we go in your car?"

Hunter shook his head. "It's too small."

This was not precisely true, and Brooke held her breath, waiting for Rex's response.

Rex narrowed his eyes suspiciously but didn't challenge this. Instead, he turned to the DA. "Mr. Shaw, can you drive us to the interview at the radio station? It's just a few blocks up the street."

The DA did not look pleased. "Can't you get another rental car?"

Rex shook his head. "That will take too long. Think of the free airtime you'll get to push your reelection campaign!"

"Since you put it that way, I'll be happy to have my assistant reschedule this morning's appointments again."

Rex ignored the DA's sarcasm. "Perfect."

Mr. Shaw frowned as he ushered his increasingly unwelcome guests into the reception area.

Rex took Brooke's arm. "We'll wait by the elevator while you and the corporal take care of that little matter of business." Then he propelled Brooke forward, leaving Hunter and the district attorney behind.

As they walked he checked his watch. "I wonder how long it will take your bodyguards to return. We don't want to be late to your first interview."

"I'm sure they'll be here soon. They haven't had time to get far." They came to a stop by the elevator, and Brooke pulled away from his grasp.

He seemed amused. "Are you afraid I'll make your boyfriend jealous?"

"No." Unfortunately she really wasn't worried about that.

"He seemed upset that you were complicit in the Nature Fresh fire."

She looked over at Hunter, who was waiting patiently by Yolanda's desk while the assistant prepared his false statement. "He's an honest person, and it was hard for him to find out that sometimes I'm not."

"So is it *true* love?" Rex asked derisively.

Brooke knew she had to use extreme caution. Hunter could not become a weapon for Rex to use against her. "He thinks so."

Rex's smile was malicious. "You're using him!"

"I prefer to look at it as he's helping me."

"Until you don't need him anymore."

She shrugged. "I'll let him down easy when the time comes."

Rex looked pleased. "That's a mature attitude. Love and sentimentality have no place in a logical world."

"I learned from the best," she muttered.

Rex seemed to take this as a compliment. "I'll admit I wasn't too happy when I found out you had a soldier boyfriend," he told her. "It was a complication to an already volatile situation. But when we're doing television interviews, the corporal's battered face might turn out to be a big asset—something to feed the American collective morbid fascination."

Brooke couldn't consider Hunter's injuries in any positive way. "I feel terrible that he got hurt. I presume you're the one who changed the plan to include his kidnapping?"

"I did change the plan," he confirmed. "I thought having some near-victims would make the case against Nature Fresh much clearer. Using Sperry, who they had previously employed to do their dirty work, was a stroke of genius. You have to admit."

There was an evil wisdom to hiring Sperry, so she gave him the slightest of nods. "And why wasn't I consulted before changes were made?"

Rex grinned. "Because you never would have approved the changes."

She had no argument for that. "I guess it's a good thing I'm leaving the group since I'll never be able to trust you again."

He laughed out loud at this. "Like you ever trusted me!"

"I did . . . at first," she countered.

"You poor little fool," he said with a smile. "Well, you're a big girl now with a mature outlook on life. So neither trust nor love will be an issue for us anymore. And I hope you'll reconsider leaving Joined Forces. This is the wrong time to be getting out. Nashville is just the beginning. Soon we'll have call centers all over the country, hundreds of employees, six-figure salaries, and maybe even a private plane!"

"How could Joined Forces afford to buy a plane?" Brooke had seen the bank statements, and there was barely enough to pay for a plane *ticket*.

"See, you're thinking small," he scolded her mildly. "You're thinking about the old Joined Forces. But once we're bringing in millions of dollars in nonprofit revenue, a private plane will pay for itself. And we might not even have to buy one. These wealthy people are always looking for tax write-offs, so one of them might donate a plane to the cause. But one thing is for sure, you can't run a successful business if you're dependent on airline schedules."

Rex sounded even more pompous and overbearing than usual. And Brooke was personally opposed to just about everything he'd said. Joined

Forces was a charity, not a business. It was run by volunteers, not employees. A year ago most of its members didn't even own cars, let alone a plane.

"And the perks don't end with private jets," Rex bragged. "You remember that Haitian businessman I visited a few times? The one who owns an entire coastal town?"

Brooke searched her memory. "Vaguely. You were trying to get him to make a donation."

"Well, I finally succeeded. He gave us a very generous contribution, and what's more—he's invited me to vacation there anytime as his guest. I plan to take him up on that offer in a few weeks. You could come too if you want. I'll even let the corporal come, if you haven't dumped him by then."

Brooke controlled a shudder. "Thanks, but I can't think about vacations until after I graduate from college."

"Well, when you're ready for paradise, just let me know," Rex said.

Brooke was saved from a reply by the arrival of Hunter and Mr. Shaw.

"Looks like we're ready to go." Rex leaned over and punched the elevator button.

Brooke eyed the elevator warily. She half expected to see Sperry or another thug on the elevator when the doors opened, but the elevator was empty. And when they stepped out into the crowded lobby, Brooke knew any opportunity for foul play had passed. Hunter was safe now. She had protected him from her mistakes. And there was some satisfaction in that.

# CHAPTER TWO

THE GROUP MOVED FROM THE elevators to the thick glass doors at the front entrance. Rex suggested that Mr. Shaw get his car from the parking deck and pull it around.

"That'll save us a little time," Rex explained. "And time is about to become an issue."

Mr. Shaw left, and Rex paced impatiently until Brooke's bodyguards returned.

"At least your uncle didn't fire them for dereliction of duty," Rex teased. "Well, not yet anyway."

Mr. Shaw parked his sleek Acura sedan behind the bodyguards' car, and Rex instructed them to hurry. When they reached the Acura, Hunter opened the back passenger door for Brooke with his good arm.

Rex seemed to find this amusing. "So it's true! Chivalry isn't dead in the South!"

"Good manners shouldn't be dead anywhere," Brooke replied in Hunter's defense. Then she climbed into the backseat and slid over to make room for him. He sat close to the door, keeping as much space between them as possible. She didn't know if he was punishing her or just couldn't stand to be near her. Either way, it hurt.

Once everyone was settled, Mr. Shaw merged into the Nashville traffic with Hack's men following close behind. As they rode through the crowded streets, Rex talked about the new call center. Brooke wasn't interested in their conversation, and since Hunter was pointedly ignoring her, she turned and looked out the window.

Dark rain clouds had settled low over the city like a pall. It seemed that even the weather was expressing disapproval.

Just as they arrived at the building where the first interview was to be conducted, fat raindrops slapped against the windshield.

"Can this day get any worse?" Mr. Shaw muttered as he parked at the curb.

This time Brooke didn't wait for Hunter to open the door for her. She pushed the door open herself and ran through the steady drizzle to the entrance. An enthusiastic intern wearing a name tag that said "Shelley" waved her in.

"Come out of the rain!" she encouraged.

Brooke squeezed past Shelley into the small lobby. Seconds later Hunter, Mr. Shaw, Rex, and the two bodyguards followed.

Shelley frowned. "We were only expecting Miss Clayton and Mr. Moreland."

Rex gave her what he probably thought was a charming smile. "Well, then this is your lucky day. In addition to myself and Miss Clayton, you'll have the honor of interviewing Mr. Kirk Shaw, Nashville's district attorney, and Corporal Ezell, who was with Miss Clayton during the Nature Fresh fire. As you can see by the bruises on his face, the corporal took the brunt of the attack."

Brooke winced inwardly, and Hunter's lips pressed into a hard, angry line.

Oblivious, Rex waved toward the bodyguards. "These other guys are just here for security."

Shelley's glance skipped over the bodyguards and lighted on Hunter. "Too bad we're just a radio station. Those bruises would hypnotize a television audience."

"He's a regular hero," Rex praised with false sincerity.

Shelley continued, "We are honored to have you all here, but space in our studio is very limited, and I'm afraid there won't be room for everyone."

"The security guys can wait here in the lobby," Rex offered as a solution.

"Since your audience won't be able to see my face, I'm not much good either," Hunter added. "So I'll skip the interview too."

Shelley rewarded his helpful attitude with a smile. Then she turned to Hack's men. "You fellows make yourselves at home. This won't take long."

As Shelley led them down the dark, narrow hallway toward the studio, Rex leaned over and whispered, "This interview is live, so keep your answers brief and to the point. Mr. Shaw and I will do most of the talking."

"That's fine with me," she assured him. "The less I talk, the less I'll have to lie."

He glanced meaningfully at Shelley's back. Duly chastised, Brooke fell silent.

They were ushered into a room that was, as Shelley had warned, very small. Shelley introduced them to the radio-show host. Then she rounded up another folding chair to accommodate Mr. Shaw while Hunter hovered in the doorway. The interview was blessedly short. Brooke answered the questions concisely, as she had been instructed. Most of Rex's comments could have been classified as a commercial for the grand opening of the Joined Forces Nashville Call Center. And Mr. Shaw filled in the gaps with careful legalese.

When they were finished, Shelley returned them to the lobby where the bodyguards were waiting.

"Great job!" she praised. "And good luck with your grand opening auction thing."

"Thank you." Rex gave her a business card and a calculated smile. "Tickets are still available for the dinner. Call if you'd like to come and help the mistreated animals of Nashville."

Shelley stared at the card for a second. Then she pulled a five-dollar bill from her pocket and extended it toward Rex. "I can't afford a ticket to the dinner, but I do want to help. I can skip lunch today for such a good cause."

Rex accepted the girl's lunch money without a qualm. "We'll put this to good use."

Shelley held the door for them, and they walked outside. With rain pelting their backs, they hurried to the waiting cars.

"What did I tell you?" Rex asked Brooke as they piled into Mr. Shaw's Acura. He rubbed the five-dollar bill between his thumb and forefinger. "Joined Forces is money in the bank."

His phone rang, and she was grateful she didn't have to reply.

While Rex talked on the phone, Brooke and Hunter resumed their previous positions on opposite sides of the backseat. They both stared at the dreary rain.

When Rex ended his call, he said, "Millicent has been overwhelmed by eager job applicants and needs my help with the preliminary interviews. I need to get to the call center quickly. Can we impose upon you for a ride?"

Mr. Shaw didn't look pleased, but he nodded.

Brooke leaned forward. "Will you drop Hunter and me off at the courthouse, please?"

Rex frowned at her over his shoulder. "You're supposed to come to the call center and help out."

"We'll come," she promised. "But we need to pick up Hunter's car and change clothes first."

"Don't take too long."

"We'll be there as soon as we can," she assured him.

As they approached the courthouse, Rex looked at Brooke. "Remember we can track you using GPS. If your phone is disabled or if you fail to show up at the call center, there will be consequences."

Hunter looked defiant, but Brooke said, "I told you we'll come help, and we will."

Rex gave her a soulless smile. "I just wanted to be sure we're on the same page."

Mr. Shaw pulled the Acura to the curb, and Hunter climbed out. Brooke slid across the seat and did the same.

"See you soon!" Rex called with a wave.

Brooke nodded and closed the door.

Hunter waited for one of their bodyguards to get out of the other vehicle, then he started walking across the concourse toward the parking deck. He was moving fast and with no apparent interest in whether or not Brooke was keeping up.

As they rushed past a little stone alcove, Brooke's eyes lingered. Wrought iron benches circled the exterior edge. Flowering trees joined their branches above to provide lovely, fragrant shade. It was both romantic and private—exactly the place she needed for a serious talk with Hunter. Privacy was a necessity, and she figured the romantic atmosphere couldn't hurt. So she ran a few steps to catch up to Hunter and grabbed his arm.

He stopped and looked down at her hand.

She removed her hand. "We need to talk for a minute. How about here?" She pointed to the alcove.

He followed her finger to the quiet spot. "We can talk in the car."

"That's probably not the best idea." She stepped closer and whispered, "Rex let us go, but he doesn't trust us. He probably bugged your car."

Hunter's eyebrows shot up. "I didn't realize Joined Forces had surveillance capability."

She shrugged. "We used to bug people all the time. It's cheap and easy."

"It's also illegal." He paused. "But I guess breaking the law isn't a problem for you and your group."

She looked away. "I've broken the law several times to help the animals. I'll make you a list of my crimes later if you'd like, but right now I just want to talk."

He nodded with obvious reluctance. "I'll let our bodyguard know we're taking a little detour." He pointed to the huge man a few feet behind them.

Brooke watched as Hunter walked over to the bodyguard, and after a short conversation, the man nodded and took up a position a few feet from the sitting area.

Hunter returned to Brooke and motioned toward the bench at the far side of the alcove. They sat on opposite ends, close but not touching. Hunter's eyes were focused on the flowering bush over her shoulder.

"I'm not going to make excuses," she began. "But I would like to explain or at least apologize."

He lifted his shoulder in a gesture that might indicate he didn't care what she said, but she chose to believe it was his way of conveying passive permission.

"Most of what I told you before is true," she began. "I became a member of Joined Forces partly because I'd always wanted to make a difference in the world and partly because I was infatuated with Rex. I loved the meetings and the rallies and the protests. I even liked the fact that the group was a little radical. In my mind it seemed like the more I sacrificed, the more I cared."

She waited for him to respond, but when he didn't, she continued. "In the beginning my role was just secretarial. I would take notes at meetings, print flyers, answer the phone, and make the occasional plane reservation. Gradually I became more incorporated into the decision-making process until, finally, I was one of the leaders. I helped to formulate all our plans, including the one to shut down the Nature Fresh plant."

She took a deep breath and pressed on. "It was a setup from the start. I didn't really have car trouble, and I didn't 'discover' the environmental infractions by accident. We knew about the sewage pipe and the inhumane chicken coops, but we had no proof. When Nature Fresh offered to let some activists tour their renovated facility, it was the opportunity we had been looking for. I went with the group. Afterward, I disabled my car and left it in the woods. Then I circled back along the creek and took pictures from behind the plant."

"Why did you go to all that trouble to take pictures if you were going to burn the plant?"

"The fire was our backup plan—in case the legal route didn't work. I never thought it would come to that, and I guess at the time I didn't care. Nature Fresh was willfully mistreating animals, polluting a creek, and misleading the public. I thought they deserved it. And after they sent those goons to threaten me and my family, I actually hoped it would happen."

He gave her a disapproving look.

"I didn't think about people losing their jobs, and I certainly didn't know the whole forest would burn down." His expression didn't improve, so she moved on. "When you offered to take your own pictures and testify at the hearing, the fire was no longer necessary. I called Freddo and told him to cancel it—or at least postpone it until we could see if the DA would press charges. But instead of canceling the fire, Freddo skipped the country with most of our money."

"Rex ordered the fire?"

"Yes. And he also expanded the original plan to include Sperry kidnapping you and luring me into the woods."

He raised his eyes to meet hers. "So when we were tied to that tree and Sperry was pouring gasoline around us, you didn't know it was Joined Forces carrying out the backup plan?"

She shook her head. "No. I might have been suspicious if Sperry hadn't been there. But he'd threatened me before, as an employee of Nature Fresh, so I thought it was just like he said. They were going to burn down their own plant and blame it on us. They'd collect the insurance, and we would get a lot of bad press. I didn't know it was Joined Forces until today."

"But in the DA's office, it seemed like . . ."

"In there I had to act like one of them to make sure they didn't kill you. I didn't know Sperry was working for Joined Forces when he burned down the plant."

He considered this for a few seconds. "Why didn't you tell me all this before?"

"I hoped you'd never have to know," she answered honestly. "I was afraid if you knew, it would change things between us. Which it has." Unable to bear the wounded look in his eyes, she glanced away.

"Why did you agree to the media interviews when I advised you not to?"

"I'm doing the interviews to protect . . ."

"I don't need your protection," he interrupted.

"Not just you," she said solemnly. "The baby too. Rex is so arrogant he assumes that I followed his instructions and had my pregnancy 'taken care of.' As far as he knows, there is no baby. But if I give him any reason to want revenge against me, he might dig into the past, and well, I can't risk him challenging the adoption."

He was quiet for a few minutes and finally said, "In addition to excellent vision, I also have better-than-average hearing. So I heard most of your conversation with Rex by the elevator—about how you were planning to break my heart gently when my usefulness ends."

Tears sprang into her eyes. "Oh, Hunter, that *was* a lie! I misled Rex about our relationship because I think he's jealous of you."

"He has no reason to be jealous of me."

The implication was clear and painful, but she pressed on. "I should have been completely honest with you about the whole Nature Fresh thing. In the beginning I had an excuse—since I didn't know you. But when we were hiding in the mountains, I should have told you every lousy detail. I wish I had."

"I wish you had too."

"Would it have made a difference in how you feel now if you'd known then?" she asked.

"I don't know," he admitted. "But it makes a difference now that I didn't know then."

She spread her hands helplessly. "I'm sorry."

"Me too." They were both quiet for a few seconds, and then Hunter said, "One of the many things I can't understand is why you didn't just ask your uncle for help. He had the resources to protect you and your family. It makes no sense that you tried to handle it alone."

"I know it sounds stupid, but I really did think I had it under control. And I didn't want my uncle to know that I'd been involved with something dishonest."

"You're right," he muttered. "That does sound stupid."

"I guess you've never made a mistake?"

"I've made plenty of them," he said. "But if I was in trouble, your uncle would be the first person I'd tell."

"If I could do it all again, I'd ask for his help. And I'd tell you the whole truth even if it meant you'd leave me before instead of . . ." She couldn't make herself add "now."

"There's nothing we can do about the past," he said.

"I love you, Hunter."

"I know," he acknowledged without reciprocating.

She pressed her trembling lips together for a few seconds and then added, "I want us to have a future together."

"We'll discuss that later, but right now we just need to concentrate on making it through the next few days. If Rex keeps his word and lets you out of Joined Forces after Saturday, then that's fine. If not, we'll have to get your uncle involved."

There really wasn't any choice, so she didn't argue.

He stood. "Now we'd better change and get to the call center before Rex sends Sperry after us—again."

Brooke nodded, wishing she thought that was a joke. She followed him across the concourse at his customary up-tempo stride. And as usual Brooke had to semi-trot to stay with him.

As they walked, a slight movement caught her eye, and she turned. A figure was standing in the shadows, and she was pretty sure it was Sperry. "Hunter!" she reached out and touched his arm.

He turned and stared at her fingers splayed on his arm.

"Sorry." She moved her hand. "But I think Sperry is watching us." She pointed behind them.

The shadows were still there, but Sperry wasn't.

"He must have left when he realized I'd noticed him," Brooke said.

Skepticism had joined the other negative emotions reflected in Hunter's eyes.

"Maybe Rex assigned him to watch us," she suggested.

"The DA said he'd press the old charges if Sperry came around again."

"Rex does what he pleases without consulting anyone else."

Finally Hunter shrugged. "I guess that's possible. Or maybe you were just imagining things."

"I really saw him. You have to believe me!"

"I don't have to believe you," he corrected. "Not anymore." He frowned. "Let's get out of here." He turned and continued his faster-than-necessary pace toward the parking deck.

Once they reached the parking deck, Brooke followed Hunter to the elevator while the bodyguard who'd been trailing them climbed into the car with his partner. Hunter pushed the up arrow, and Brooke used their wait time to catch her breath. When the elevator doors opened, they stepped in, and Hunter pushed the button for level D. But before the door could close, a man slipped inside. It was Detective Napier from the Nashville police.

"Hello, Miss Clayton," he said pleasantly. "I've been waiting for you."

The elevator moved upward for few seconds. Then the detective pushed another button, and the elevator came to a shuddering halt between levels. "There," Detective Napier said. "Now we can talk privately."

"What do we need to talk about?" Brooke asked.

"And why are we talking in an elevator?" Hunter added.

The detective addressed Brooke. "Your mother called me about some protesters that have set up in front of her house. I sent a couple of uniforms over to keep them in line. I assigned some officers to your apartment too, assuming there would be a similar group there. And there is."

"We know about the protesters." Hunter dismissed this. "We have Brooke's security covered."

"If you'll stop interrupting me, I can explain." The detective looked a little cross. "While the officers were in the manager's office at your apartment building, watching the protesters on the security cameras, they saw a man leave your apartment. He had on gloves, the kind you wear when you don't want to leave fingerprints."

"A thief?" Brooke asked. Oddly that seemed like the best possibility.

Detective Napier shook his head. "Based on the wrappers he put in a Dumpster down the street, he was installing surveillance devices—mostly audio but a few little cameras too."

"He was bugging the apartment," Hunter said with a quick glance at Brooke.

Brooke didn't even try to look astonished.

"Did your guys arrest him?" Hunter asked the policeman.

"No," Detective Napier said. "They thought it would be wiser to follow him, and because of that decision, we know who he was working for." He paused to raise an eyebrow at Brooke. "I assumed it would be your enemies at Nature Fresh. So imagine my surprise when the man left your apartment and drove straight to the new Joined Forces call center downtown."

Brooke lifted her shoulder in a casual shrug. "My relationship with Rex Moreland is . . . complicated. He's come back to run Joined Forces and expects a power struggle. He doesn't trust me. I'm annoyed that he bugged my apartment, but it's not a big deal."

"Now I'm even more surprised," the detective claimed. "I thought you'd be quite upset—enraged even."

Hunter looked enraged, but he didn't voice his feelings about Rex. Instead he asked the detective, "Can you get the bugs out of the apartment?"

"If that's what Miss Clayton wants."

"Don't remove them," Brooke said. If the surveillance equipment was Rex's insurance against betrayal, she could live with that.

Detective Napier nodded as if her response was what he had expected.

"Why not?" Hunter asked her.

"It will make Rex feel . . . comfortable if he thinks he's monitoring my every move," Brooke tried to explain without saying too much in front of the detective. "We'll be careful what we say and do. It's just for a few days."

"If that's how you want to play it." He turned to Detective Napier. "Well, thanks for the tip. Now will you please let the elevator go up?"

"Oh, I didn't come to talk about the surveillance at Miss Clayton's apartment." Detective Napier seemed amused. "That was just kind of a side issue. The real reason is much more serious."

"What's the real reason?" Brooke was fairly sure she wouldn't like the answer.

"While I was trying to imagine what would cause Joined Forces to invest their time and resources to spy on one of their own, my captain stopped by my office. He told me that the owner of Nature Fresh, a guy named Jimmy Van Wagoner, wants us to reopen our investigation into the fire at his plant. He claims that he is an innocent victim and that you, Miss Clayton, are the guilty party."

Hunter answered before Brooke could. "The Nature Fresh guy says *he's* the victim? Do you see my face?"

"It's obvious that someone beat you up," the detective's tone was neutral, "but Mr. Van Wagoner says he had nothing to do with it. He alleges that you and Miss Clayton, along with other members of Joined Forces, burned down his plant and then conspired to make it look like he set the fire. On the surface his claims seemed . . ."

"Ridiculous," Hunter provided.

"I was going to say far-fetched," the detective amended. Then he looked at Brooke. "But after going through the file again, I realized that his account makes as much sense as yours."

"He just wants to divert attention from the laws his company has broken," Hunter said with impatience.

The detective kept his gaze on Brooke. "You hate poultry companies in general and Nature Fresh in particular. Sometimes people get carried away with good causes and do things that are wrong. If there's something I need to know about you and that fire, this would be a good time to tell me."

"I did not burn down that plant," Brooke stated flatly.

Hunter said, "You're not taking this Van Wagoner guy's wild accusations seriously?"

"I have to take his accusations seriously, wild or otherwise, because my captain has ordered that the whole case be reexamined. And I'm not sure Miss Clayton's story will hold up under further investigation." The detective smiled humorously, exposing his coffee-stained teeth. "Which prompted this elevator chat. If you know something incriminating about Rex Moreland, this would be a good time to tell me that too."

Brooke folded her arms and looked away. "I have nothing else to say."

Detective Napier narrowed his eyes and asked, "Have you ever heard of a man named Lyle Carmichael?"

Brooke was glad to be able to honestly deny something. "No, I've never heard of him."

"Carmichael is a wealthy man with many businesses across the country. The FBI is convinced that he's connected with organized crime and that some of those businesses are fronts for laundering illegal revenue. Recently he's taken an interest in Joined Forces, a *big* interest."

She had no trouble believing that Rex would recruit a criminal, but she kept her expression blank.

"Brooke said she doesn't know Carmichael." Hunter shifted his weight from one foot to the other impatiently. "So what's the point of talking about him?"

Detective Napier's pleasant expression didn't falter. "Carmichael is important because he might provide Miss Clayton with an opportunity to square herself with the law."

Hunter took a deep breath and opened his mouth for another indignant denial, but the detective forestalled him with a raised hand.

"Enough, Corporal. I'm not a fool. I don't know exactly what Miss Clayton's role has been in recent events, but I'm confident that a thorough investigation will not be a good thing for her, especially if Joined Forces decides to make her their scapegoat as the surveillance suggests."

That possibility seemed to take the fight out of Hunter. He slumped against the elevator wall.

"What do you want from me?" Brooke asked.

"You've misunderstood my purpose here," the detective said earnestly. "I'm trying to help you."

"How?" Hunter wanted to know.

"What Miss Clayton needs is legal leverage," the detective said. "That will come in very handy if any charges are leveled against her. And I think Lyle Carmichael can provide that leverage."

"Go on," Brooke invited. Hunter flashed an irritated look at her, but she ignored him.

The detective continued, "I have a contact at the FBI, an Agent Gray. He's an expert on organized crime and very familiar with Mr. Carmichael. In fact he says they suspect the grand opening for the Joined Forces call center this weekend is really a cover."

"A cover for what?" Hunter asked.

"Carmichael deals in drugs and racketeering, like most other crime bosses," the detective explained. "But his passion is rare coins."

"Coins?" Brooke whispered, keeping her eyes lowered so the detective couldn't see her panic.

Napier nodded. "He's obsessed with them, and, according to Agent Gray, his collection is rumored to be full of items that can't be purchased legally. I guess when you're rich enough to own anything money can buy, you start to crave things you *can't* buy. Apparently there are many collectors who are willing to purchase stolen coins, but the transactions are risky. So the sellers have to find creative ways to display their wares."

"Like an auction for a nonprofit group?" Brooke said.

Detective Napier nodded. "Carmichael and some of his cronies have donated a few legitimate items that will be auctioned to benefit Joined Forces. But illegal coins will be available as well, sold privately, and the proceeds will benefit only the owners. It's a pretty sweet setup."

Hunter said, "I'm guessing the FBI doesn't have any proof of all this or you wouldn't be questioning us in an elevator."

"If they had proof, there would be no opportunity for Miss Clayton."

"What kind of opportunity?" Hunter asked suspiciously.

"Miss Clayton is a Joined Forces insider. She could get the proof the FBI needs, and in turn they can give her immunity from prosecution—in the event that she needs it."

Hunter shook his head. "Brooke isn't getting between a crime boss and the FBI. That would be way too dangerous. If any accusations are made, we'll deal with them some other way."

"There is a very small window of opportunity here," the detective warned. "Once the coin auction is over, Miss Clayton won't be in a position to make a deal."

"We're not interested," Hunter said.

"What would I have to do?" Brooke asked.

Hunter turned to stare at her, his expression a mixture of disbelief and frustration.

"I'm not saying I did anything wrong," she added quickly, "but I am worried about Rex trying to frame me."

The detective nodded. "It's always wise to plan ahead. And as far as your contribution to the FBI's cause, it would be as simple as taking a few pictures. A large shipment of coins has already been delivered to the call center. You would need to determine where they are being stored and take a few pictures. One illegal coin is all they need to get a search warrant."

"No way," Hunter refused for her. "You're asking Brooke to risk her life."

"We'll provide officers to protect Miss Clayton while she's taking the pictures."

"We've declined your offer," Hunter said. "Now unless you want to take us to the police station for an official interview, this little elevator visit is over." He pushed the button for level D again, this time with more force than necessary. The elevator jerked and slowly resumed its journey upward.

The detective handed Brooke a card. "I can always be reached at one of these numbers if you change your mind." He leaned close and whispered, "A clear conscience is a wonderful thing."

She looked away.

"And as a show of goodwill, I'll assign a couple of police officers to watch you for the next few days. Sometimes just the sight of uniforms will discourage people who are up to no good."

Brooke was about to decline when Hunter said, "Thank you."

It was her turn to give him an irritated glance as the elevator stopped.

The doors slid open to reveal a maintenance man. He was standing on the parking deck, holding his toolbox. "Heard the elevator was broken," he said.

"I don't know anything about that," Hunter replied as he walked by with Brooke right behind him.

"It seems to be working fine," the detective added. Then he punched a button, and the elevator doors closed in the man's face.

* * *

As they approached the car, Hunter stopped and waved for Brooke to join him near the stairwell. "I need to talk to you, and I don't want to do it in the car just in case it is bugged."

She nodded.

"I don't agree with everything Detective Napier said, but I think he's right about Rex using you as a scapegoat. If the new police investigation turns up evidence against Joined Forces, they won't hesitate to let you take responsibility for the Nature Fresh fire. And if they subpoena me . . ."

"Your testimony will convict me."

"I'd lie under oath if I had to."

"Oh, Hunter, you can't!" It wasn't just a desire to protect him that prompted this plea. "You're a terrible liar! They'd convict us both."

He thought about that for a few seconds and finally nodded. "You're right. So there's only one way to keep us out of jail. We're going to have to take your old boyfriend's advice."

She frowned. "What advice?"

"We're going to get married."

She had dreamed of this moment but never under these cold, calculated circumstances. "Married?" she managed around the lump in her throat.

"We'll have it annulled as soon as the danger to you is over," he said. "But in the short-term, a marriage provides you with the highest level of legal protection." Hunter regarded her steadily.

She forced a light tone. "That's probably the worst proposal in the history of the world."

"It wasn't a proposal," he said. "This is a legal necessity."

"You're serious?" she asked, though she already knew the answer. Hunter was always serious.

"Yes."

"My parents are going to be sad they missed the wedding."

"They'll never know about it," he replied, stepping back. "Now let's hurry. We've got to give your bodyguards an excuse for going back into the courthouse and then get a marriage license."

With a heavy heart, she followed after him.

* * *

The county clerk's office was manned by a bored-looking older woman with a bad perm who gave them an application to fill out. Brooke and

Hunter had to corroborate some to complete this paperwork, but there were no secret smiles or longing looks shared by this bride and groom. Once the application was complete, they returned it to the woman at the desk.

She skimmed the form and checked their drivers' licenses. Then she informed them, "The fee is $99.50, but you can get a $60 discount by participating in a premarital preparation course. When you have your certificate of completion, just bring it up to us, and we can process the application at the discounted price."

"That's okay," Hunter said in a tone not much more enthusiastic than the clerk's. "I'll pay full price." He took out his wallet and removed a hundred dollar bill.

"If you take the course later, you can bring your certificate of completion, and we'll refund the sixty dollars."

"I don't mind paying full price," Hunter reiterated.

The woman shook her head. "Well, I guess it's up to you, but the course is very helpful for a long and successful marriage."

This marriage was doomed from the start—nothing could make it successful. Sadness welled up inside Brooke, and she turned away.

The frizzy-haired clerk took the money from Hunter. She returned a few minutes later with the marriage license and two quarters for his change.

"This license expires in thirty days, so you have to use it before then," she said.

Hunter nodded. "Can you tell us someplace that performs marriages around here, like a wedding chapel?"

The woman handed him a neon-pink flyer. "Here's the most current list." Then with a victorious gleam in her eyes, she added, "And most of them teach the marriage classes too, just in case you change your mind."

Hunter took the flyer without comment and headed toward the door.

"Thank you," Brooke told the woman.

She nodded, and her hair billowed. "Good luck." She didn't add, *You look like you need it*, but Brooke read it in her eyes.

Once they were in the hallway outside the county clerk's office, Hunter and Brooke studied the flyer.

"Wedding Chapel, packages starting at thirty-nine dollars," she read aloud. "That's what I call starting married life off right."

"We've just got to get someone to marry us before the Nashville PD or your old boyfriend or the Mafia try to stop us," he said.

Brooke pointed to the Aloha Ice Hut. "That's close—just one block over."

"The Aloha Ice Hut it is then." Hunter folded the flier and put it in his pocket.

# CHAPTER THREE

THE ALOHA ICE HUT WAS a free-standing establishment on wheels, basically a large cart. The owner-operator was a redheaded man named Chuck who had a plentitude of freckles and was almost certainly not Hawaiian.

Hunter explained the purpose of their visit and handed Chuck the marriage license.

"You got here at the perfect time," he said. "Right before the afternoon rush."

Chuck pulled out a laminated fee chart and showed them the available options. Hunter chose the Thrifty Man's Special for $49—one step up from the economy rate of $39.

"Good choice," Chuck praised him. "It's worth an extra ten bucks for your bride to get a real bouquet." He pulled a little bunch of wilted flowers out of the cart's pint-sized refrigerator and placed them on the counter covered with faux palm leaves. Then he slipped on a black jacket with a priest's collar that fairly screamed Party City. "Do you want the Bible version or the civil text?"

Brooke said, "Civil."

At the same time, Hunter said, "Bible."

Chuck smiled. "Uh oh. Marital discord already?"

Hunter looked embarrassed. "I just thought because you're religious . . ."

Brooke was surprised. She hadn't thought of herself in those terms for a long time. "Let's just keep it simple," she suggested.

"Civil text," Hunter told Chuck.

The man handed Brooke the flowers. "I've got a veil you can use if you want." He pointed to a slightly discolored tulle creation that might have been stylish in the fifties—but probably not.

Brooke shook her head. "No, thank you."

With a shrug Chuck said, "You're the bride." Then he stretched out his hands and bellowed, "Friends! Fellow Nashvillians! Come watch now as I join this couple in legally sanctioned matrimony!"

Much to Brooke's mortification, a small crowd gathered instantly.

Chuck continued, "We are here today to unite"—he referred to the license—"Hunter and Brooke as husband and wife."

There was a smattering of applause from the impromptu guests.

"Hunter, Brooke, please take your places here at the love altar." Chuck waved toward the leaf-covered counter.

They did as he requested, standing side by side in front of the Aloha Ice Hut. Chuck commandeered two strangers as witnesses. A homeless man pulled out a harmonica and started playing something mournful.

And then the ceremony began. Chuck went on for several minutes, making questionable observations about love and misquoting poetry. It was too terrible to be sad, and Brooke found herself fighting giggles.

When Chuck pronounced them husband and wife, the crowd insisted on a kiss.

Hunter's reluctance was obvious.

"He's shy," Brooke offered as an excuse.

"Come on, Hunter. You have to make an exception on your wedding day, man," Chuck encouraged. "The crowd isn't going to let you go until you do it."

Brooke held out her arms. "Just get it over with."

Hunter narrowed his eyes but leaned down and kissed her quickly. The crowd booed his lame effort.

"Well, let's hope Hunter's kissing gets better with practice," Chuck murmured. Then he put a plastic cup on the counter and said, "If any of you want to give a little something to the happy couple, feel free!"

"No, please," Hunter tried to decline as the departing guests dropped money in the cup.

Brooke couldn't say anything. The giggles had finally won out.

"Let me take your picture," one of the witnesses offered.

"We don't need a picture," Hunter said.

The woman looked scandalized. "Of course you do."

Hunter handed over his phone to the stranger. Brooke stopped laughing and leaned close to her temporary groom as the woman snapped the picture.

"There. Now you can remember this day." The volunteer photographer returned the phone.

"Thank you." Brooke wiped her watering eyes and whispered to Hunter, "How in the world could we ever forget it?"

Chuck dispersed the crowd and then gave Hunter the signed license and a handwritten marriage certificate. "Take this back down to the clerks' office and file it. They'll mail you an official certificate in a few weeks." Finally he added, "And that will be forty-nine bucks."

Hunter paid their fee, and Chuck put the money in his shirt pocket.

"It was a pleasure doing business with you. Would you like a Hawaiian shaved ice to celebrate? They're half price for the bride and groom."

"No, thanks," Brooke replied.

Hunter just shook his head.

Chuck wiggled his eyebrows at Hunter. "Looks like somebody is anxious to get to the honeymoon."

Hunter's expression was something between mortified and murderous.

"And don't forget your wedding gift!" Chuck pressed the plastic cup that contained a few dollar bills and some change into Hunter's hands.

Afraid that Hunter might actually die of embarrassment, Brooke said, "Let's go get our marriage license recorded."

She took him by the hand and pulled him along the sidewalk toward the courthouse. As they walked past the homeless man with the harmonica, Hunter handed him the cup of money and Brooke's wilted flowers.

The man looked up, confused by his sudden good fortune.

"Thanks for the music," Brooke said.

"Aloha!" Chuck called after them. "Have a happy life!"

Brooke turned back to give him a quick wave. "Aloha!"

As they continued toward the courthouse, she found that she was strangely content. It wasn't the wedding of her dreams, but she was legally, if not permanently, married to Hunter. Which meant that even after the risk to her life was over, he would be forced to deal with her. Hopefully during that time she'd be able to convince him that she was worthy of his love and trust.

Based on his stiff posture, she could tell that Hunter was not so optimistic about the future. In fact, he seemed thoroughly traumatized.

\* \* \*

They filed their license with the curly-headed woman in the county clerk's office and left the courthouse as husband and wife. But this change in marital status had not brought them closer. If anything, Hunter seemed more distant than ever.

Before they returned to the car, which might be bugged, Hunter said, "We've got to get someone to scan your apartment and tell us where the devices are located. If they put anything in the bedroom or bathroom, it will have to be disabled."

"Then Rex will know we found them."

"Not if they do it right. Hack has some guys who dress up like pest control people and take out a device by spraying it with something that ruins it but it looks like a mistake."

Brooke considered this for a second and then nodded. "I'll make the call. I don't want you to have to lie, and I have nothing to lose in that department."

She dialed her uncle's number, and when he answered she explained the situation, using the same excuse she'd given Detective Napier for Rex's disloyalty.

"I'd advise you to have all the devices removed and cut your ties with Joined Forces immediately," her uncle said.

"I will after the dinner on Saturday night," she promised. "But I can't until then."

"I don't like it."

"I know."

"But if you and Owl can live that way, I'll ask Hack to go over to your apartment and take care of it."

"Thank you," Brooke told him. "And maybe you could keep this quiet. I don't want my parents to worry."

There was a long pause before her uncle said, "I don't want them to worry either. But you be careful."

"I promise," she said. She ended the call and nodded at Hunter. "Hack's going to take care of it."

* * *

As they drove toward her apartment, Brooke tried to think of something she could do that would help to heal the rift between them. She'd already tried to explain. She'd apologized for being dishonest and asked for his forgiveness. There really wasn't anything left to say. So they rode in silence.

When they got to her apartment building, a Nashville PD squad car was parked in front, as Detective Napier had promised. There was also the group of Nature Fresh protesters, and they had been joined by a Channel 7 news van.

Hunter parked by the curb close to the entrance and said, "When I get out, I'm going to open the trunk. I need the suitcase I bought for the Civil War resort so I'll have clean clothes."

Brooke raised an eyebrow. "Those clothes actually fit you?"

He frowned. "Of course. Why would I buy clothes that don't fit?"

"I thought you just bought that stuff so we wouldn't show up looking like hobos."

"I did," he acknowledged. "But I got things in my size. They'll do until . . . well, at least until this assignment is over."

She nodded, wishing he didn't sound so anxious to be done with her.

"Wait in the car until I have the suitcase out. I'll come around and open your door. Then we'll walk up the entrance. Hack's guys will be there to provide a barrier between us and those people. There's nothing we can do about the news cameras, but if they ask any questions, we have no comment."

She nodded again.

Satisfied that he had covered all the bases, Hunter opened his door and walked around to the trunk. Within seconds he had the suitcase out and was standing by her door. She pushed it open and got out of the car.

She expected the news people and protesters to rush them, but instead they waited like spiders by the entrance.

Hack's men and two police officers formed a protective line between the car and the door. Hunter took her elbow and rushed her toward the door. The protesters chanted insults, and the news people called out questions.

"Miss Clayton!" The reporter shoved a microphone toward them. "Is it true that the police have reopened their investigation of the fire at the Nature Fresh plant and now consider you a suspect?"

Brooke paused, wanting to defend herself. Hunter put some pressure on her arm, propelling her forward.

"No comment," he said.

They stepped into the lobby, and one of Hack's guys followed them inside.

"My partner is going to watch the people out front and your car," he said. "I'm going to stand right outside the apartment door."

"We're just here to change clothes, and then we'll be headed back to Nashville," Hunter told them.

"Thanks for the notice," the bodyguard said. "We'll be ready to follow you."

"We'll try to make this assignment as easy as possible," Hunter assured him.

The man risked a doubtful look at Brooke.

She raised her right hand like she was about to take the witness stand. "I promise not to run off without you."

The bodyguard didn't seem particularly reassured as they hurried to the elevator. Hunter looked inside first and, after making sure it was empty, waved for her to get in. The bodyguard stepped in last, and they rode up in silence.

When the elevator doors opened, they found Hack waiting for them. He was wearing an ill-fitting khaki shirt with *Dino* embroidered on the pocket. His long braids were brushing his shoulders, and his gold tooth glinted when he smiled in greeting. "Well, I'm glad you two decided to come out of hiding again."

"Sorry about that," Brooke said with an apologetic smile. "The next time we have a fight, we'll let you know where we are."

Hack raised an eyebrow. "Already planning a next time?"

Brooke shrugged. "It's inevitable. You know how ornery Hunter is."

Hack grinned at his comrade over Brooke's head. "Yeah, he's a royal pain."

She tapped the name on his pocket. "Nice shirt, Dino."

"It's a cover we use fairly often, but this shirt must have shrunk in the wash." Hack flexed his pectorals against the tight fabric. "I wore it so I could check your apartment for bugs."

"And I presume you found some?" Brooke said.

"Oh yeah," Hack confirmed. "There are three cameras—one in the kitchen, one in the living room, and one in the bathroom."

"Perverts," Hunter muttered.

"I destroyed the one in the bathroom with my pesticide wand." Hack lifted a canister with a sprayer attached to the top. "It should look like an accident by a clumsy pest control guy."

She nodded. "We can't have a camera in the bathroom, obviously."

"A listening device in the bedroom met the same fate," Hack continued. "But I left all the stuff in the living room and kitchen."

"So we can talk safely as long as we're in the bedroom or bathroom?" she asked.

Hack moved his hand from side to side in a "maybe" gesture. "I can't guarantee privacy anywhere in that apartment. The listening devices didn't seem very sophisticated, but they might be able to pick up sound in the next room. That's why we're having this conversation by the elevators instead of near your apartment door. If you need to have a private conversation, I suggest you do it outside or in the bathroom with the shower going full blast. The sound of the water will drown out your voices, and the steam will fog up any cameras I might have missed."

"We'll do that," Hunter said. "But please tell Major Dane about that precaution so he doesn't think we're really . . ." he paused, and his cheeks turned pink, "showering."

Hack grinned again. "I sure will tell him."

"I guess you should scan us too—and my car," Hunter suggested, refusing to meet Hack's eyes. "Just to be sure they didn't plant anything on us."

Still grinning, Hack scanned them both. Finally he pronounced them clean. "I'll check your car on my way out, but the safest thing to do is assume they're listening. Now let me look at your phones to make sure Brooke's untrusting friends didn't put anything on them."

He checked Brooke's phone quickly and returned it. "You're good." Then he scrolled through Hunter's. After a few seconds, his finger froze, and he looked up at them. "What's this?" He turned the phone around and showed them the picture the pushy lady had taken at their wedding.

Brooke laughed. "Oh, that's one of those photo booth things."

Hack pointed at the little bunch of flowers in her hand, and Brooke was thankful she had declined Chuck's offer of the ugly veil. "Why are you holding flowers?"

"Hunter bought them for me from a street vendor." That much was true. "He's so romantic. But they wilted, so we gave them to a homeless guy."

Hack looked between them suspiciously. "Well, I'm glad you're getting along better."

"If you don't mind texting that to me," Brooke requested as Hack returned the phone to Hunter. "I mean, it's just a silly picture, but I'd still like to keep it."

Hunter nodded curtly. "I'll send it to your phone. Later."

Hack picked up his spray canister and pushed the down button on the elevator. "I'll head out now." He glanced at his employee, who had been standing a few feet away. "If you think you can keep up with them this time."

The man nodded. "Yes, sir."

Brooke sighed. "I've promised that I won't sneak away again."

"And I'm going to trust you *again*," Hack said. He waved and added, "Call if you need me." Then he stepped onto the elevator.

Hunter led the way down to her apartment door and waited while Brooke unlocked it. She stepped inside, and Hunter came in behind her. It was uncomfortable knowing they were being watched.

While he locked the door, she stared at the huge old piano that dominated the small room. It had been a gift from Hunter—a very grandiose and romantic gift. It reminded her of the earlier days of their relationship, when Hunter both loved and trusted her, a time when they had a future together.

After securing the door, Hunter walked around the piano without looking at it. He checked every room and then came back to where she stood. "All clear," he whispered. Then in a louder voice, he said, "Why don't you go ahead and change clothes in the bathroom."

She leaned close and felt him stiffen as she said, "I need to talk to you."

"Later," he replied softly with a meaningful look around the room.

She put her arms around his neck and said, "I'm all hot and sweaty. Let's go take a shower."

His horrified expression would have been funny under any other circumstances.

"It's important," she mouthed. "Trust me."

His jaw tensed, and she regretted her choice of words.

"Please, just one more time."

He reached back and loosed her hands from behind his neck. "I guess we have time for a quick shower." Then with obvious reluctance, he allowed her to lead him down the hall.

Once they were inside the bathroom, she closed and locked the door. The room was small, and he took up more than his share of the space, making it feel a little claustrophobic.

She turned on the shower as hard as it would go, and they stood silently for a couple of minutes, close but not touching. Then she whispered, "I think that's enough steam to fog up any cameras that might be watching us. Not that we'll be doing anything we wouldn't want someone to see."

He sighed the way he used to when they were falling in love. "So what is it that you so urgently need to tell me?"

"Lean down so I can talk directly into your ear—just to be on the safe side."

He did as she requested.

She watched tendrils of steam circling his head. He seemed almost magical, like a handsome, heroic fairy. Reaching her hand up, she touched his face. He drew back, reminding her that he was a real man who happened to be unhappy with her at the moment.

After clearing her throat to help regain focus, she said, "We have to make peace. We know Rex is watching us, and he'll never believe we're a loving couple if you're always scowling at me."

His shoulders sagged. "I'll try."

"At least when we're in front of the cameras, you have to act like . . . well, the way you did before." Her voice trembled a little.

"I'm not much of an actor."

"You've had some practice. Just remember the resort."

"I remember," he said softly.

Their eyes met and held for just a second before he looked away. "Think of the Mengenthals." She hoped the memory of the newlyweds at the resort, who couldn't take their eyes off each other, would inspire him.

"I could never be that ridiculously romantic," he replied.

"Then I guess it's hopeless."

He grimaced and said, "Okay, I can pretend we're a happy couple as long as we don't have to be over the top with it. So are we done here?"

"No," she said. "We still haven't made peace."

"I agreed to act happier."

"I know, but I want you to really be happier. I want you to forgive me. I want another chance."

"I'll agree to a cease-fire—that's the best I can do."

She decided to consider this progress. "I know you think I'm a total liar, and I'll admit I have a tendency to stretch the truth. But I never lied about my feelings for you. I do love you, and I'm sorry I wasn't honest with you." She was thankful for the steam that hid the tears pooling in her eyes. "Can you just love me now and learn to trust me again as time goes on?"

"Love and trust are closely related. I'm not sure you can have one without the other," he said. "But what bothers me the most is that I can't tell when you're lying and when you're telling the truth. Like even now this might all be a show."

She looked away. "I wish there was some way I could convince you."

He nodded. "I know."

"And about what Detective Napier said . . ."

He shook his head. "I'm not willing to even consider that unless we bring your uncle in on it. Are you ready to make a full disclosure?"

"You know I'm not," she said. "I can't."

"Then there's nothing to discuss." He turned off the water. "This shower has gone on long enough—even for a very loving couple. And if we don't get to the call center, there's no telling what Rex might do."

She nodded. "Since we were supposedly taking a shower, I guess we should look a little wet when we walk out." She leaned over the sink and turned on both faucets. Then she put her head under the stream of water. When her hair was soaked, she stood and flipped it back away from her face.

"Do you want to bring your clothes in here and change while it's still steamy?" Hunter whispered.

She shook her head. "I'll change in my room. I have a walk-in closet, and I'll keep the light off just in case Hack missed a camera—which I doubt."

"I'll change in here then," Hunter said.

With a nod she opened the door and walked into her room.

* * *

Brooke was surprised when they arrived at the church that was being converted into a call center for Joined Forces. It was not the lovely old building she had expected. It had probably been built in the sixties, and the architecture was painfully dated. The exterior bricks were a pale pink and formed a lattice pattern. The front entrance was a modern stainless-steel and glass combination, and it led to a small lobby.

Rex, with the faithful Millicent at his side, met them at the door. He eyed Brooke's hair, which by now had dampened the back of her shirt and the lower half of her jeans. He asked, "Why are you all wet?"

"We took a quick shower," she explained with a smile at Hunter.

He looked back, obviously embarrassed.

Rex seemed annoyed.

"So what is our assignment?" Brooke asked.

"There's a lot of cleaning to do," Millicent provided.

Rex glanced from Brooke to Hunter and then said, "I thought I'd give you a tour of the place before we put you to work."

She shrugged. "Whatever, we're just here at your command."

He gave her a little smirk and then went into tour-guide mode. "We replaced the front door to let in some natural light."

"And because the old one was hideous," Millicent contributed. "It was heavy wood carved in Mediterranean style—like that was ever appropriate for a church in *Tennessee*."

"We raised the ceiling on this whole main level to give the illusion of more space." Rex waved both hands, showcasing the area. "We refinished the hardwood floors with a darker stain, and I picked the paint color for the walls. It's called soothing sage."

"It's a nice color," Brooke admitted.

"I wish you could have seen this place before we started renovations," he said. "It's really impossible to appreciate what I've done without the 'before' comparison. It looked worse in here than it does on the outside— if you can imagine that."

She couldn't, but she didn't give him the satisfaction of saying so.

"How long is this guided tour going to take?" Millicent asked a little petulantly. "We need to sort through today's interviews." She was obviously reluctant to leave Rex.

"I'll hurry," Rex replied. "You can make it without me for a few minutes, I think."

Millicent gave him a little smile. "Just a few, I guess." She backed down the hallway, maintaining eye contact with Rex until she had to turn a corner.

The minute she was out of sight, Rex sighed. "What is it with women? You give them a little attention, and they think they own you."

Brooke instantly felt sorry for Millicent. Rex would discard her as soon as she was no longer necessary to him. Brooke had been in that position herself and knew the pain that awaited the girl. But there was nothing she could do. She followed Rex as he stepped forward and threw open a set of wooden double doors, exposing what had once been the chapel area of the old church. Hunter followed silently behind him. His disdain for Rex was almost palatable.

The big room was crowded with various tradespeople intent on completing their part of the building's overhaul.

"They had those gorgeous wood beams covered with ceiling tiles." He waved toward the exposed rafters that had been stained to match the floors. "The lighting was terrible, and the room was full of clunky wooden pews with worn gold velvet cushions." He paused for a shudder. He pointed at a large wooden podium. "We wanted to take this out, but it's filled with concrete and tied into the foundation. Can you believe that?"

"Maybe they wanted to be sure it was secure when the preacher pounded on it," Brooke said.

"It would be secure if the preacher wanted to stand on it," Rex remarked. "Anyway, it would have cost a fortune to remove, so we decided to leave it. This room will be used for employee orientations, community education, and fundraising events like the one on Saturday night. And sometimes a podium will be useful."

He led them through a door on the side into a room filled with rows of identical cubicles. Each partitioned area held a desk and a computer. "This was where they held Sunday School. Now it will be the heart of our call center. Imagine it filled with well-trained, highly-motivated telemarketers." He sighed audibly. "It can't happen soon enough."

They proceeded down some stairs and into an open area with a kitchen on one end. "Unfortunately there was nothing we could do about these low ceilings." Rex reached up and touched the tile above him. "Since it's not presentable enough for the public, we made it into an employee lounge." He walked to the refrigerator and opened it. "Fruit anyone?" he asked as he removed an apple.

Hunter shook his head.

Brooke was starving but felt she had to follow Hunter's lead. "No, thanks."

Rex closed the refrigerator door and took a bite of his apple. Then he waved the fruit toward the back wall. "The door on the left leads to a nice-sized mail-processing room. The door on the right is a storage room."

Brooke stared at the shiny door. If Detective Napier was correct, then that storage room contained stolen coins that would be illegally sold during the Dinner and an Auction on Saturday. It was a little frightening to be standing just a few feet away from stolen goods. And knowing the location of the coins made her feel guilty for not helping the FBI.

Rex didn't seem to notice her discomfort. "The mail room is almost as important as our telemarketers," he was continuing. "Once a pledge is made, we send a thank-you note with a return envelope for their payment."

"That sounds more like a bill," Brooke murmured.

Rex smiled. "Clever, don't you think?"

Brooke couldn't tell him what she really thought, so she just nodded.

"We also include a pamphlet showing other ways they can help the cause. It's very professional and effective. And now, the last stop on our tour is our administrative suite."

They climbed a second set of stairs on the other side of the room and walked into a hallway lined with offices. Millicent was standing in front of one of the doors with an iPad—obviously ready to interview the next potential employee. Rex winked at her as they passed, and she blushed.

Rex walked to the end of the hall and unlocked a door. Then he shoved it open with his shoulder and ushered them into a large office. Unlike the rest of the building, it didn't seem to have been touched by improvement or renovation.

"This used to be the preacher's office," Rex informed them. "So I've claimed it for myself."

"Why do you need an office here?" Hunter asked. "Aren't you going back to California?"

Rex turned to Hunter. "We're headquartered in California, but I'll be spending quite a bit of time in Nashville—at least until we have this call center running smoothly."

Brooke did not consider this good news. It would be more difficult to cut her ties with Joined Forces—and Rex—if he was living in Nashville.

"You seem a little nervous about holding on to your girlfriend with me around, Corporal," Rex added slyly.

"Rex," Brooke said. "You promised not to tease."

Rex laughed. "That's it for the tour. What do you think?"

"You've utilized your space wisely, and well, I think it will make a great call center."

He smiled. "That's what I wanted to hear. Now let's put the two of you to work. How do you feel about painting?"

"Painting?" Brooke repeated. "Hunter has a broken arm."

"You just need one good arm to paint," Rex pointed out.

She shrugged. "It's your call center. If you want a one-armed man and a girl who has never lifted a paintbrush working on your walls . . ."

Rex frowned at her. "There's always cleaning up construction garbage."

Brooke surrendered. "Show us to the paint."

\* \* \*

All the hired workers left at five, but it was almost seven before Rex and Millicent came out of his office to "release" the volunteers for the day. Millicent requested that everyone return the next morning at eight for the final push to get the call center ready.

While she was addressing the rank and file, Rex sauntered over to the corner where Brooke and Hunter were haphazardly stacking the cans of primer. He seemed pleased by the paint splatters on their clothes and skin.

"You weren't kidding when you said you couldn't paint," he said to Brooke. "You've even got some in your hair."

"It will wash out." She hoped that was true.

"I'll come by and pick you up in the morning at six thirty for the television interviews," Rex continued as Millicent joined him. It was more of an instruction than an offer. "You're still in the same apartment, right?"

"Right."

"I'll call up when I get there." He sent a sly glance toward Hunter. "Or I could just let myself in, unless you've changed the locks since I lived there."

"I changed the locks. We'll be waiting in the lobby at six thirty."

She and Hunter walked outside. It had been a long, stressful day, and the evening air felt good. As they climbed in the car, Brooke asked if they could stop and get some groceries. "I haven't been home in a while, and my cabinets are pretty bare."

"We can't go anywhere like this." Hunter held out his paint-splotched arm.

"We could stop at a drive-thru."

He shook his head. "We need to get this washed off as soon as possible. We'll just eat what you have."

She didn't know if he was really concerned about their ability to wash off the paint or if he was starving her as punishment for her dishonesty. But either way, being hungry made her cranky, and she was very hungry.

They rode in silence to her apartment. The contingent of protesters was still in place. She recognized a few, but most of them were unfamiliar, and all looked angry. At least there was no news van. Hunter herded her inside with the help of Hack's guys and the police officers.

When they got to the door of her apartment, Hunter put a finger to his lips, reminding her about the surveillance equipment inside. She nodded and opened the door.

They took turns in the bathroom, scrubbing off paint and changing into clean clothes. Brooke was standing in the kitchen when Hunter walked out wearing another pair of new jeans and a plaid, button-down shirt.

After turning on the television a little louder than normal, Hunter joined her in the kitchen. He leaned close and whispered, "We may have to let people monitor us, but that doesn't mean they have to hear every word we say."

She nodded and opened the refrigerator. The few items inside had expired.

Hunter stood beside her and surveyed the limited options. "It looks like we're going to have to find time to go to the grocery store tomorrow—even if we're covered in paint again."

"Yes, I'd say groceries are an emergency." She didn't add, *I told you so,* but she wanted to. "We may have to order pizza."

He shook his head slightly. Apparently pizza would be a security risk. She was so hungry she wanted to cry.

"Let's see what we've got to work with." Hunter pulled a few cans from the cupboard and lined them up on the counter. Chili beans, corn, and Spanish rice.

She stared at the assortment suspiciously. "What can you do with this?"

"My mother used to take leftovers and mix them together. She called it goulash."

"I've eaten goulash, and it wasn't made with leftovers."

He stiffened. "I didn't say it *was* goulash. It's just what she called it."

Brooke regretted her comment. He'd shared something personal with her, and instead of enjoying the moment, she had corrected his culinary terminology. She knew she couldn't regain lost ground, but maybe she could keep from losing more.

"So we can make our own version of goulash with this stuff?" She waved at the line of cans on the counter.

"I don't think we have much choice."

She got a pot from the cupboard while he opened the cans. Then she stood beside him and watched as he combined the ingredients. Once the concoction was hot, he added a few spices and carried it to her small kitchen table.

"We'll need bowls," he told her. "And that bottle of ketchup in your refrigerator—just in case this is terrible."

It wasn't terrible. It was hot and filling, and Brooke actually wanted a second helping, but she pretended to be full so Hunter could have the rest. He ate every remaining kernel, grain, and bean.

"What kind of stuff did your mother put in her goulash?" Brooke asked, casually trying to return to the topic of his childhood. "Not that I'm complaining about your version."

"Roast, mashed potatoes, green beans, spaghetti."

"I was okay until you got to the spaghetti."

"Some versions were more successful than others," he admitted. "But my father didn't allow any complaining around our table."

"Your father sounds like a hard man."

"He lived a hard life," Hunter said. "He wanted me to have more than he ever did, but he also wanted me to appreciate where I came from."

"That's fair."

"After my mom died, he did the best he could," Hunter said. "And his parenting style prepared me to be a soldier."

"I'm sure he'd be very proud of you."

Hunter frowned, and Brooke was afraid that she had overstepped her bounds.

Finally he said, "I hope so."

Brooke felt a new wave of guilt. Hunter had never had much tenderness in his life. He should have found it with her, but she'd betrayed his trust. He might never reach out again.

They cleaned up in silence, not completely companionable but not at odds either. When they were through, he asked if she was ready to go to bed.

"It's a little early," she said. "Maybe we can watch TV for a while."

So he walked into the living room and sat stiffly on the couch.

She was following him when her phone rang. It was her mother.

"Are you okay, honey? These protesters are such a nuisance."

"I'm fine, Mom. The protesters don't bother me at all." This wasn't completely true, but she wanted to reassure her mother. "I've got Hunter here with me. Hack's guys are guarding the door and the lobby. And there are policemen outside. I'm perfectly safe."

"That does make me feel better," Neely admitted. "But I saw that horrible Nature Fresh man on television making all kinds of accusations against you and your friends at Joined Forces. I told Dad we should sue him for defamation of character."

Brooke laughed. "Daddy has enough legal problems as it is."

"That's exactly what he said," Neely muttered.

"Well, thanks for checking on me, Mom."

"I guess you need to go."

After several assurances that she would keep in touch, Brooke ended the call and walked into the living room. She couldn't help looking around, wondering where the hidden camera was placed. It was like being on display, and she found it unnerving.

Settling down beside Hunter, she whispered, "You should probably put your arm around me. It's what loving couples do."

Slowly he lifted his arm and rested it ever so lightly across her shoulders.

Even though she knew it wasn't real, she snuggled close and enjoyed this limited contact. There was nothing she could do about the future now. So she decided to enjoy Hunter's company while she could and pretend that tomorrow would never come. Unfortunately she was getting good at that.

They watched *Wheel of Fortune*. She guessed at all the puzzles and was often wrong. He never guessed, just sat awkwardly beside her.

As the game show ended, she looked around and said, "Now that we're roommates, we'll have to buy some manly stuff to decorate this place."

He gave her a blank look. "Why?"

"So it won't be all girly," she explained. "I'm sure you miss the things you left behind at your apartment at Fort Belvoir—army medals, sports paraphernalia, hunting trophies . . ."

"I don't have any decorations at my apartment. I'm hardly ever there, so it's just a place to store extra uniforms, tax records, that kind of thing."

"Still, that says something about you. You're neat and minimalistic. And you have a healthy respect for the IRS."

He watched her warily—unsure if he was being teased or not.

Brooke continued, "If we at least put away some of my stuff, maybe you'll be more comfortable here."

He looked around the apartment as if he were seeing it for the first time. "It's fine the way it is."

She gave up on engaging him in a meaningful conversation or learning more about his personal life. "Okay, then. I guess it's time for bed."

Without any argument he used the remote to turn off the television, and they stood. She held out her hand, and he looked at it for a few seconds before wrapping his fingers in hers.

She led the way to her bedroom. "We need our rest. Tomorrow is going to be a long day."

# CHAPTER FOUR

BROOKE WAS SPRAWLED OUT ON her bed wearing her flannel Christmas pajamas and staring at the ceiling. She had offered Hunter the other half of the bed, and she couldn't imagine him looking any more horrified if she'd suggested he drown a litter of newborn puppies.

"What will Rex think if Hack missed a camera in here?" she had whispered.

"He'll think I take your safety seriously," Hunter had replied softly. Then he made a pallet for himself on the floor right in front of the door. The fan was blowing, more to drown out any noise they made than for comfort. And his phone was playing ocean sounds—also a precaution.

She closed her eyes and tried to sleep, but she couldn't relax. So she hung her head off the edge of the bed and whispered over the sound of crashing waves, "Are you awake?"

"Yes," he replied.

"I can't sleep."

"It might help if you don't talk."

She smirked toward him through the darkness. She could just make out his shadowy form. "Rex is picking us up at six thirty. Should I set an alarm?"

"I'll wake you up."

"Are you sure you don't want to move closer to me in case those protesters outside try to break in?" she teased.

"Hack's guys will handle any invading protesters."

"What if I decide to ditch them again?"

She heard him sigh.

"I'm just kidding."

"I know."

"Let's talk about tomorrow," she suggested.

"What is there to talk about?" he asked. "In the morning, we'll perpetuate lies to benefit a Joined Forces call center that is run by criminals. And after that we'll do menial labor for your ex-boyfriend."

She winced. "That does sound grim. I guess the trip to the grocery store will be the highlight of our day."

"We do have to go to the store," he agreed. "We don't even have the ingredients for goulash."

"And after Saturday night, we'll never have to go to the call center again. We'll be finished with Rex. The protesters will disperse, and I'll be safe without you." That was a sad thought. "I'll go back to school, followed from class to class by some of Hack's oversized bodyguards, of course."

"Of course."

She stared at his shadowy profile. "And you'll go back to flying military VIPs around?"

"Yes."

"And you'll annul our marriage."

It wasn't really a question, and he didn't answer it.

Into the darkness she whispered, "And we might never see each other again."

"Let's not worry about all that tonight," he advised softly. "Now stop talking and go to sleep."

"I'll stop talking," she said. "But I can't promise I'll go to sleep."

She turned over and burrowed into her pillow, trying not to cry. She was in trouble and Hunter was protecting her, but they weren't a team anymore. She was a job again.

* * *

When Brooke woke up the next morning, Hunter and his homemade bed were gone. She knew he hadn't abandoned her, so she stood and stretched. It wasn't quite six and was still dark outside.

Yawning, she walked out of the bedroom. Hunter was in the kitchen. His short hair was damp, and he was wearing more of the new, stiff clothes from his resort suitcase.

"You're going to look nice on TV today," she told him.

"It doesn't really matter what I wear," he replied. "All people will notice is my beat-up face."

She had no response for that. "I'm going to get ready now." She returned to her room for fresh clothes then went into the steamy bathroom and turned on the hot water. Once she had it so foggy she couldn't see an inch in front of her face, she undressed and bathed quickly.

Since she was going to be on television, she took a little extra care with her makeup. She tried to do the same with her hair, but the extreme humidity in the bathroom made it curl wildly. She would straighten one section, only to have it spring back into unruly ringlets as soon as she moved to the next clump of hair. Finally she gave up and walked to the living room.

Hunter was leaning over the piano rubbing a brownish cloth across the aged surface. He raised both eyebrows when he saw her hair.

"I know I look like an overgrown Shirley Temple, but I can't do anything with it in that steamy bathroom," she explained.

He looked away. "It's fine."

"What are you doing?" she asked curiously.

He seemed embarrassed. "I looked up some information online about how to restore the finish of an old piano. The first step is to wash it with a mild detergent and determine how bad the original finish is. Based on my work so far, the finish on this piano is pretty bad."

She laughed and tucked a curl behind her ear. "So what's the next step? For finishes that are beyond soap and water?"

"Wood stripper and sandpaper. I figure we can get some of both while we're grocery shopping today."

Brooke liked the idea of working on a project with Hunter, and she loved the idea of having her piano refinished. "Thank you." She reached up and gave him a quick kiss on the cheek. "Just for the camera," she whispered.

He stepped back and cleared his throat. "I made you an omelet."

"Well, that was sweet of you." She walked into the kitchen and sat down at the table. "Where did you get the eggs?"

"Hack sent one of his guys to get us a few things to hold us over until we can get to the grocery store," he replied.

"An errand of mercy." Brooke took a big bite of her warm, cheesy omelet. "This is delicious!" she said with her mouth full.

"It's better than goulash anyway."

"I don't know about that." She shoved in another big bite.

Hunter continued to wash the piano while Brooke ate her breakfast. She had just finished when her phone rang.

"This will be Rex," she told him.

Hunter put down the cloth with a sigh.

She picked up her phone and answered the call. "Hello."

"We're parked at the curb," Rex informed her. "Hurry downstairs. We can't be late."

"We'll be there in a minute," Brooke promised. She ended the call and put one more bite of omelet in her mouth. Then she moved toward the door, where Hunter was already waiting. "Maybe they'll have a professional who can redo my hair when we get to the television station."

He frowned. "Why? You look fine."

She twirled a stray ringlet around one finger. "Just fine?"

Realizing that he'd been tricked into complimenting her, Hunter gave her an impatient look and nodded. "Just fine."

"Well," she said as she sailed past him into the hallway, "I'll have to try a little harder next time."

She nodded at Hack's sentry by the door and walked on to the elevator.

There was just a small group of protesters in front of the building and no TV crews, but Hunter made her stand inside the lobby until Rex pulled up in his rental car. Then Hack's men escorted them to the curb.

Millicent was in the front seat talking on her phone. She gave them the briefest of nods as Brooke opened the back door and slid in. Hunter was close behind her.

"What took you so long?" Rex demanded. "I'm going to have to drive like a maniac to keep us from being late for our first interview."

"Long shower," Brooke said. "And you always drive like a maniac, so we should make it with time to spare."

Rex glared at Brooke in the rearview mirror. Then his eyes widened. "What is wrong with your hair?"

She raked the curls back from her face. "Steam from the shower," she told him. "And there's nothing I can do about it now."

Millicent ended her call and laughed. "You look like a poodle!"

Many responses came to Brooke's mind, but none of them would help her get away from Rex and Joined Forces. So she pasted a fake smile on her face. "Thanks."

Millicent blinked, unsure how to respond.

"She's teasing you," Rex told her. "Brooke knows her hair is a mess."

"Oh." Millicent sent Brooke a glare and then turned her full attention to Rex. "I can't believe you made me reschedule all my interviews just so I can come to these silly pseudo-news programs. Especially with her looking like that!" She jabbed a finger toward Brooke.

Rex laughed. "Maybe her hair will win us some sympathy points with viewers. And we are appearing on these morning shows because lots of little old ladies who own pets watch them. When they see us with their favorite talk show host, we'll gain instant credibility—which will translate into increased donations."

Brooke cringed at this blatant admission of greed. And she didn't have to look at Hunter to know he was scowling with disapproval.

Millicent gave Rex a pretty little pout. "Well, I guess it's worth it then. But why do you need me?"

Rex flashed her a condescending smile. "I need you with us because you explain the donation process better than anyone else. And your pretty face will sway even the stingiest penny pinchers."

Millicent fell for his manipulation. "I guess that's a decent reason. But I don't understand why *he's* here." She poked a finger at Hunter. "It's a big risk having him be a part of the interviews. He's not even a member of Joined Forces. We don't know him, and I certainly don't trust him."

Rex glanced in the rearview mirror. "Corporal Ezell has good reasons to be trustworthy. If he says or does anything that could cause legal problems for Joined Forces, we'll have him in jail with so many charges even Major Dane and the US Army can't help him."

Millicent smiled and Brooke felt sick. Now that she wasn't under Rex's spell anymore, it was easy to see him as a self-important egotist. He was very smart, if amoral, and for her and Hunter, he posed a very real threat. She controlled a shudder and glanced at Hunter. He was staring straight ahead, seemingly unconcerned by Rex.

Finally Hunter spoke. "Since the owner of Nature Fresh has publicly accused Brooke of burning down his plant, I thought you might reconsider these interviews altogether."

Rex shook his head. "Van Wagoner is the reason we have to do these television interviews. People believe what they hear on TV. We can't let Wimpy Jimmy convince everyone in Nashville that he's the victim. We have to fight back."

"Not that Jimmy Van Wagoner can put up much of a fight now that he's broke," Millicent said without a trace of sympathy. "He sunk all his money into reinventing his company's image."

"And all for naught," Rex contributed.

Rex and Millicent shared a smile.

Brooke was ashamed to be associated with them. And now she had to feel guilty about Jimmy Van Wagoner too, since she was partly responsible for his woes. If there was a limit to the amount of guilt one person could feel, surely she was close to it.

"He deserves everything he gets," Rex was saying. "He's been torturing animals for years. Losing his fortune just means he won't be able to finance more chicken slaughter."

"But he doesn't seem willing to go broke quietly," Brooke pointed out. "He's trying to take me and possibly Joined Forces down with him."

"You're risking Brooke's safety," Hunter said.

"The cause is bigger than all of us," Rex said loftily, as if they were really supposed to believe he would sacrifice himself for anything. "And Brooke has plenty of protection." He looked out the rear windshield, where Hack's man and a police car were following. "In fact we look like a parade."

Millicent glowered at Hunter. "I don't know why you're making such a big deal. It's just two interviews."

Hunter looked at Brooke, silently willing her to stand up to them. But she couldn't, so she shook her head. He turned away in disappointment as they arrived at the television station. It was modest and nestled between a hair salon and a dry cleaner.

"Wow, this is underwhelming," Millicent said as they parked at the curb.

"This is Nashville," Rex reminded her. "You aren't in San Fran anymore."

"How could I forget?" she replied.

"Nashville has plenty of things San Francisco doesn't," Brooke said in defense of her hometown. "It's the country music capital of the world!"

"Are you trying to prove my point?" Rex opened the car door and climbed out.

Brooke clenched her teeth and followed him onto the sidewalk. Then they walked into the station that Rex and Millicent found so unimpressive.

The interior wasn't much better, and Brooke saw them exchange an amused look.

A middle-aged woman wearing too much makeup greeted them. She had on a suit jacket with a bright floral scarf at her neck and wore jeans at least one size too small. She looked like two halves of separate people stuck together.

"You're the folks from Joint Forces?" she asked.

"*Joined* Forces," Rex responded.

She waved blood-red fingernails. "Whatever. I'm Joy-Lynn. I own this independent television station, and I'm the host of *Rise and Shine Nashville!* I do mostly upbeat stories, but I made an exception in your case at the request of a friend who happens to be one of your contributors."

"We appreciate the invitation," Rex told her in a sickeningly gracious tone.

"I hope I don't regret it," Joy-Lynn replied. "Now follow me back here to the set, and we'll get to work."

Rex and Millicent seemed equally appalled by Joy-Lynn. Brooke couldn't tell whether it was because of the woman's appearance or the lack of respect she was showing toward them.

When Brooke glanced at Hunter and saw his smirk, she had to control a nervous laugh.

Joy-Lynn led them to a small room, and when she flipped on the lights, she illuminated a grouping of dated furniture. She took a seat behind the desk, and with her heavy, denim-clad hips hidden, she looked younger, more attractive, and surprisingly professional.

"Have a seat," she invited, pointing a red-tipped finger toward the couch. "The fire victims first, you other two on the far end."

"I'm Rex Moreland," Rex explained. "I'm CEO for Joined Forces."

"Good for you. Far end of the couch." Joy-Lynn arranged some notes on the desk.

Put firmly in his place, Rex retreated to the end of the old couch. Brooke sat closest to their host with Hunter beside her. Millicent sat by him leaving Rex such a small space that he had to perch halfway on the arm in order to sit. He looked annoyed, which Brooke found very satisfying.

"Do we need to put on more makeup for the cameras?" she asked Joy-Lynn.

Their host shook her head. "That won't be necessary."

If heavy makeup wasn't necessary for the cameras, Brooke wondered why Joy-Lynn was wearing orange pancake foundation and more eyeliner than Cleopatra. But apparently, almost inconceivably, this look was just her cosmetic preference.

Trying not to stare, Brooke listened as Joy-Lynn gave them instructions.

"Once the camera technician arrives, we'll be ready to start on the hour. This is live TV, so if you make a little mistake, just press on and don't worry about it. I'll guide you along."

"What's the lead-in for your show?" Millicent asked. "*Good Morning America*?"

Joy-Lynn blinked her heavily painted eyelids twice before she responded. "This is an independent station, so we don't get network syndicated shows. But we follow an episode of *The Golden Girls*."

"Wow," Millicent sounded truly shocked. "I think my grandma watched that show when she was a kid."

"It's very popular with our viewers, and so this is a coveted spot," was Joy-Lynn's tight-lipped response.

Millicent gave her a weak smile.

Joy-Lynn turned to Brooke and Hunter. "After I introduce you, I'll ask a few questions about your ordeal. Then we'll show a short clip of the fire. After that you two," she tipped her head at Rex and Millicent, "can close up with your pitch for contributions."

Joy-Lynn didn't wait for any of her guests to confirm that they understood her instructions. Instead she pulled a small mirror out of a desk drawer. She quickly assessed her appearance and was apparently satisfied with what she saw since she put the mirror away without making any adjustments.

A timer sounded, alerting everyone that they had one minute until showtime. A technician walked in and took his place behind the camera.

Joy-Lynn gave the man some last-minute instructions. "Be sure and get several close-ups of the bruises on this young man's face." She pointed at Hunter. "Since we're covering a depressing story, we might as well go all the way with it."

"Yes, ma'am," the cameraman agreed. "Everybody ready?"

They all nodded with varying degrees of confidence.

"You'd better be!" he said. "Three, two, one, and go!"

Joy-Lynn smiled at the camera and welcomed her viewers. She made a little small talk that included a brief discussion of the weather and a description of her grandson's fifth birthday party. Then she began the introduction of her guests. "Today our show is a departure from the norm," she informed them. "Visiting our set is Miss Brooke Clayton and her friend Corporal Hunter Ezell. They are members of an animal rights group, and a few days ago, they were nearly killed in a forest fire near the Nature Fresh plant."

Brooke saw the camera swing toward them and zero in on Hunter's damaged face.

"Corporal Ezell was attacked by Nature Fresh employees and seriously wounded."

On the monitor Brooke saw Hunter's grimace. She wasn't sure what he objected to more—the misrepresentation of who tried to kill them or Joy-Lynn's portrayal of him as the loser in a fight.

Joy-Lynn said, "Now why don't you tell us what happened?"

Brooke didn't want Hunter to have to lie anymore than absolutely necessary, so she answered this question. "Nature Fresh claimed that their new plant was humane and environmentally friendly, but they were hiding parts of the plant, like old, horrible chicken coops and a drainage pipe that was polluting a nearby creek."

"So Nature Fresh was misleading the public."

Brooke nodded. "And breaking the law."

"And they knew that the two of you were aware of their misdeeds?"

"Yes," Brooke said. "Hunter was going to testify for the district attorney. So they beat him up and kidnapped him. Then they tricked me into coming to the woods. They were going to make it look like we burned down the plant."

"And eliminate you as witnesses?" Joy-Lynn directed this toward Hunter.

"Yes," he replied.

Brooke was so nervous her responses sounded canned even to her own ears. And if anything Hunter was worse. Joy-Lynn seemed relieved when it was time to cut to the fire footage. After that she gave Rex and Millicent a few minutes, as promised.

Brooke hated to admit it, but they were much more natural on camera than she and Hunter had been. They seemed relaxed and sincere and genuinely concerned about protecting animals and the environment while Hunter, the most honest of them all, had appeared almost suspicious. She grimaced. So much for truth in broadcasting.

"That was torture," Hunter muttered as they left the station.

"That was nothing," Rex corrected him. "You should see what it's like to be interviewed by someone who's hostile."

"The worst part was looking at that horrible host!" Millicent chimed in. "She must have learned to apply makeup in clown school!"

Rex chuckled. "You'll never have to see Joy-Lynn again," he told Millicent. "And just one more interview to go."

"Thank goodness," Brooke said with relief.

Hunter didn't comment.

They climbed in Rex's rental car and headed toward their next stop.

The studio for Channel 12 in downtown Nashville was a little more impressive. As they stepped through the smoked glass doors into the cool, quiet lobby, Brooke's phone vibrated, indicating that she had a text. She pulled the phone out and checked the screen. It was from her mother.

*"Saw you on TV. I like your new hairstyle, but you looked pale. Please get more sleep and eat regularly."*

"Do I have time to call my mother?" she asked Rex.

He checked his watch. "Yes, but hurry."

She called the number. "Hey. I got your text."

"Are you feeling okay?" Neely asked with worry in her voice.

"I'm fine," Brooke assured her. "I had to get up early this morning, so that's probably why I looked tired. And I can thank the steam from the shower for my hair."

"I like it," her mother insisted. "How many interviews do you have to do?"

"Just one more, and then I'm through," Brooke replied.

"Oh, that's good." She could hear the relief in her mother's voice. "Maybe you and Hunter could eat dinner with us on Sunday."

"Maybe," Brooke hedged. She didn't want to bring danger near her parents. "I've got to go. It's time for the next interview, but we'll talk later."

"Good luck!"

"Thanks, Mom."

The second interview took a little longer but was otherwise much like the first. Brooke felt like a fraud. Hunter looked miserable, and she knew he felt the same way she did, maybe worse. But at least he was there because of his assignment to protect her. She had no excuse.

A few protesters had gathered outside the studio by the time they left, along with a news crew from a Knoxville station. Hack's men and the police were there to keep them at bay, and Brooke assumed that they would hurry to the car and get out of sight as soon as possible. But Rex told Millicent to take Brooke and Hunter to the car. Then he went over to the waiting crowd and held a mini press conference, milking the situation as much as he could.

While Rex was handling the protesters and the news people, Brooke watched through the windows. The protesters were chanting but more for the TV cameras than at her.

Millicent pulled out a compact and checked her makeup. "Van Wagoner is probably paying them to come out and protest. It's just a ploy to gain public sympathy."

Finally Rex trotted over to the car. Millicent unlocked the door for him, and he slid in under the wheel. "Wow! That was exhilarating!"

"You must have done well," Millicent said. "My phone is blowing up with people asking for interviews."

"Local or national?" Rex wanted to know.

"Local, so far," Millicent reported. "But it's only a matter of time before we get some attention from a bigger market." She pointed at the news van. "Knoxville is already here."

"Brooke is done," Hunter reminded them. "That was our agreement."

Rex nodded. "If we decide to do more media, I'll handle it with Millicent's help. From this point on, we want to downplay the past and focus on the future."

"And getting contributions?" Hunter added sarcastically.

Rex was not offended. "Exactly." Then he turned to Millicent. "Keep a list of the offers that come in, and we'll go over them tonight."

Millicent immediately started making notes, anxious to do his bidding.

Brooke felt sorry for her. She remembered how it felt to want Rex's approval. And how impossible it was to get it.

"Even if Brooke doesn't appear personally in future interviews, if you talk about the fire, it could still mean added danger for her," Hunter said.

Rex flashed him a smile. "Well, it's a good thing she's got you to protect her then, isn't it?" He merged his rental car into the flow of traffic. "Now, how about breakfast?"

Millicent shook her head. "Remember, we have interviews starting in a few minutes."

Rex gave her a disappointed look. "I hope I don't starve to death because of my dedication to the cause!"

"I put some fruit in the refrigerator yesterday," she replied. "That should tide you over until lunchtime."

Rex looked at Brooke in the rearview mirror. "So are you two up for some more painting?"

"I can't think of anything I'd rather do," Brooke muttered.

* * *

Brooke and Hunter painted for a while, and then they were switched to cleanup duty. "I actually prefer this," Hunter said. "At least you don't get paint on your clothes."

"I hate it just as much as I do painting," Brooke told him. "Maybe if we leave to get some lunch, they won't notice if we don't come back."

"It's worth a try," Hunter agreed.

But this plan was ruined when Rex came out of his office and called all the workers and volunteers together. He announced that lunch was being provided by Trixie's Designer Sandwich Shoppe.

"What's a designer sandwich?" Hunter asked as they joined the line of hungry workers.

"I'm not sure," Brooke admitted.

A few minutes later, they were each handed a paper plate. Centered in the middle were two small, round rolls filled with vegetables and blue cheese. Two blueberries and a plump strawberry completed the "meal."

"I guess *designer* means you're still hungry after you eat." Hunter popped one of the little sandwiches into his mouth.

She smiled. "I guess."

It only took a couple of minutes to finish their lunch, and they were about to go back to work when Rex spoke from the podium again.

"If I can have everyone's attention!"

"For someone who wanted that podium removed, he sure uses it a lot," Hunter muttered.

Brooke covered her mouth to prevent a giggle as Rex continued.

"We hope you enjoyed your lunch, and we want to thank Trixie's for providing the meal." He waved to the people who had served the sandwiches, and there was a smattering of grateful applause. "Now please return to the task you were working on before lunch. And as you complete a job, see Millicent for a new one."

Millicent waved wildly at the crowd.

"We can't let up now," Rex added. "We're close, but we have to push hard until we're done. So everyone plan on working late tonight."

There were groans from the crowd, but Rex didn't seem to notice.

Brooke collected their paper plates and put them in a garbage can while Hunter walked over to their paint paraphernalia. When Brooke joined him, he was studying the walls they'd painted. "I'm looking for any spots we might have missed."

"I don't see any," she said. "I think we're through here."

"I guess that means we have to ask Millicent for a new assignment," Hunter said without enthusiasm.

Brooke looked over where Millicent stood with a long line of volunteers waiting to talk to her. "It might be a while."

"I'm in no hurry to get back to work." Hunter sat on the top of a paint bucket.

They had a few minutes of peace before Rex found them.

"All done?" he asked, surveying the walls.

"Yes." Brooke gestured toward Millicent. "We were waiting for the line to die down."

Rex glanced at Millicent and then back to Brooke. "Well then, this would be a good time to show you the virtual tour of our future call center in San Francisco. An architect made it for me, and once it's built, it will put this place to shame." Then he shrugged. "But you've got to start somewhere." He put a hand on her elbow and pulled her toward the hallway. "Come on. It's on the laptop in my office."

Brooke didn't want to spend time with Rex, and she really didn't want to see a call center he planned to build with dirty money. But she gave him her best impression of a smile. "Sure."

Hunter stood and walked beside her protectively.

Rex dropped his hand from her elbow. "You're coming too, Corporal?"

"Where she goes, I go," Hunter replied. "Those are my orders."

Rex smirked but didn't object. "Follow me." He turned and led them down the hall to the preacher's office.

When they passed Millicent, she turned away from her line of volunteers to ask, "Where are you going?"

"I want to show Brooke the virtual tour of the future San Francisco call center."

"But aren't they supposed to be painting or cleaning or something?" Millicent gestured vaguely at Brooke and Hunter.

"I won't keep them away from their work for long," Rex replied.

"Can you wait a few minutes?" Millicent requested. "Once I get these volunteers assigned, I can watch it with you."

Rex shook his head. "You've seen the virtual tour a thousand times." Without waiting for a reply, he moved on.

Brooke could feel Millicent's eyes boring into her back as they walked down the hallway. When they reached his office, Rex pulled a handful of keys from his pocket and unlocked the door. "Every door in this place has its own key—can you believe it?"

"That is inconvenient," she acknowledged.

"I can't wait to have the whole building rekeyed so I won't have to carry this bulky ring around with me everywhere."

Rex unlocked the door and then used his shoulder to force it open. Once Brooke was inside, he turned back to Hunter. "You stay here, soldier. Some of this is for real Joined Forces members only. But you'll be able to see her at all times so her safety won't be compromised." He exaggerated his voice for this last part, indicating that Hunter's presence was ridiculous.

Hunter looked at Brooke, obviously waiting for her to overrule his exclusion from Rex's office.

But she just shook her head slightly and said, "I'll be fine."

Hunter's normally solemn expression deepened into a frown of deep disapproval.

Brooke gave Hunter a pleading look before following Rex into the office.

Rex flipped on the light switch and hung the cumbersome key ring on a hook beside another equally bulky set of keys. Then he hauled a chair over to his desk, adding more scars to the old wooden floor. "Have a seat," he invited her.

As she sat down, she checked to be sure Hunter could see her from his position by the door. Rex noticed and seemed amused. He settled in the desk chair and turned on his laptop. She tried to keep as much distance between them as possible. It was hard to believe she ever thought she was in love with him. Now he made her skin crawl.

He pointed at the screen. "Okay, before I show you the virtual tour, I want you to see a training video we put together. Our contribution collection system is much more sophisticated now."

The face of an attractive young woman filled the screen. She introduced herself as Kinsley and said she was going to demonstrate how to solicit donations. Then Kinsley called an elderly woman who expressed interest in Joined Forces but because she lived on a fixed income declined to make a contribution.

Kinsley skillfully kept her on the phone by sympathizing over her tight finances. Then she asked about pets. Unfortunately for the money-strapped woman, she had a dog. Kinsley used her love for the dog to convince her to donate ten dollars a month.

"You won't even miss it!" Kinsley assured the old woman. "And think of what you'll be doing for animals just like your cute little doggie all across the country!"

Brooke thought about the private plane Joined Forces was planning to buy and wondered if the old woman's monthly ten dollars would help to support that as well.

As the clip ended, Rex asked her, "So what do you think?"

Obviously she couldn't be completely honest, but she refused to endorse blatant extortion. "I don't love the idea of taking money from poor old ladies. Can't you concentrate on a wealthier segment of the population?"

"We have specialized training videos for all types of potential donors," Rex said. "People in every income bracket can help fund the cause. We can't just depend on rich donors."

At a loss for words, she just nodded.

Rex glanced toward the door, where Hunter was standing. Then he lowered his voice and whispered, "I can't get over the change in you. You're so much more mature now. Remember how you followed me like a lovesick puppy?"

Her dislike for him solidified into something else, something worse. "Please try to forget that. I certainly have."

He laughed. "Okay. Here's the virtual tour I promised you. You're about to see the future of Joined Forces."

She watched as the front of a modern brick building with beautiful landscaping and the San Francisco skyline as a backdrop filled the laptop screen. It was impressive, so she was even able to muster a "wow."

Rex seemed pleased. "Wait until you see the inside."

He tapped a few keys and led her, via the computer, through the imaginary call center. Floor by floor, he pointed out various features. The architecture was stunning and the furnishings tasteful. Apparently no expense would be spared to create a beautiful and functional building that would certainly make a statement. She just wasn't sure the statement would have anything to do with mistreated animals.

One good thing about the call center was its location. If it was in San Francisco, Rex would be there too. Brooke couldn't say that, but she knew she had to say something. She finally settled on, "This will cost a fortune."

"Millions," he confirmed.

She frowned. "How much money does Joined Forces collect from little old ladies who love their dogs?"

This seemed to amuse him. "We've done very well with donations lately, but we haven't collected enough to pay for something like this." He pointed at the laptop. "We'll have to depend on large corporate donations from people like Mr. Carmichael to build the San Francisco call center."

"Mr. Carmichael? The man who's donating coins to the auction?"

"One and the same," Rex confirmed. "Mr. Carmichael is an animal lover and an environmentalist."

*And a criminal,* Brooke thought to herself. "And all these contributions are legal?"

Rex shrugged. "More or less. That's why we have lawyers and accountants, to make sure everything is on the up and up." He leaned close and lowered his voice. "Or if it's not, to make sure no one ever finds out about it."

Brooke gave him a fake smile, but she felt sick.

"You'll meet Mr. Carmichael tomorrow night at the dinner and auction."

"That's something to look forward to," she lied.

"Maybe Mr. Carmichael can convince you to stay with Joined Forces and take a full-time position after you graduate. I need an assistant to schmooze potential donors, and you'd be perfect."

She controlled her revulsion and rolled her eyes. "I'm not much in the schmoozing department."

"Oh, we can train you to be a schmoozer," he said with certainty. "I'd start you out at a generous salary and lots of fringe benefits."

"Like free tropical vacations?"

"Exactly." He winked.

"I'll think about it," she said, even though she wouldn't. She stood. "Since we've finished our painting, can Hunter and I take a little break?"

Rex raised an eyebrow. "You want to leave?"

"Just for a few hours," she said carefully. "Hunter is used to eating a bigger lunch, and we need groceries. You've got so many people here now we're tripping over each other."

He thought about it for a few minutes and then said, "Okay. I guess we can do without you for a few hours."

Brooke was so happy for the reprieve she had to steel herself against feeling grateful to Rex.

"But be back about five," he added. "That's when I have to let the construction guys go in order to avoid paying them overtime. So we'll need lots of free labor to clean the place up if we're going to have a chance of being ready for the dinner tomorrow."

"We will be here at five," she promised.

He closed his laptop and followed her to the door.

"I've trusted you with some sensitive information," he said. "Obviously none of this can be repeated."

"Obviously."

He had a smug expression on his face as they walked out into the hallway. He had complete confidence that she would keep his dirty secrets. And that bothered her.

"Corporal," Rex said pleasantly to Hunter as he walked by.

Hunter stared after him with an annoyed expression. He had the same look when he turned to Brooke.

"You know I have to keep him happy," she whispered.

"I know you think you do," he replied.

She decided not to get into a discussion of Rex or her relationship with him at the call center where people could overhear. So she let that go. "I have some good news and some bad news," Brooke told him. "Which do you want first?"

"The bad news, of course."

"Of course." She smiled. "The bad news is that we will probably be here until late tonight. But the good news is . . . we get the afternoon off! We're leaving right now and don't have to be back until five."

His surprised expression made her laugh.

"We're leaving? Now?"

"Right now!" She took his hand, and they headed for the door.

And they almost made it out before Rex caught them. "Brooke!"

She stopped and turned around to face him.

"Do you need a ride home?" he asked a little breathlessly.

Hunter shook his head. "No, we'll ride with the bodyguard Brooke's uncle assigned to us."

"Having an overprotective uncle must be so tiresome," Rex murmured.

"I'm not complaining," Brooke said. "With Mr. Van Wagoner making accusations and his employees protesting against me, I'm grateful for the protection."

"Well, all right then," Rex said. "See you at five."

They walked outside. The air was thick and heavy with the smell of honeysuckle and gardenia. Brooke held out her arms, embracing the Nashville afternoon. "I love this!"

"You love hot and humid?" Hunter asked.

"I love freedom," she told him. "Even if it is temporary."

"It is nice to be away from Rex," he agreed. "And that snooty Millicent."

Brooke laughed. "So, do you still want to go to the grocery store?"

Hunter nodded as he led the way toward the car where one of Hack's men was waiting. "Whether I want to or not, we're going. There's no food left in your apartment, and I'm starving."

"You're always starving," she said with a smile.

"A grown man can't live on a couple of fancy sandwiches the size of a quarter."

"There was also a strawberry," she reminded him. "And *two* blueberries!"

He scowled. "That lunch was a joke."

# CHAPTER FIVE

As Brooke walked down the aisles of the Walmart supercenter, filling her basket with food, she felt lighthearted. There were still plenty of problems in her life, but she was done with the publicity interviews and almost free of Rex and Joined Forces. Hunter was staying with her for a few more days. She wasn't optimistic enough to believe that she could convince him to make their marriage more than a legality. But maybe he would at least agree to a date. And in the meantime, they were going to be restoring her beautiful antique baby grand together.

Once they had enough groceries to feed a small army, they went to the hardware department for wood refinishing supplies. There they met a young man so helpful she wondered if he worked on commission. He seemed knowledgeable, and Hunter accepted all his recommendations.

As they left the hardware department, Brooke surveyed their basket. "Are we buying one of everything?"

"Better too much than not enough," Hunter responded.

"I'll take that as a yes." She steered their basket toward the home goods section.

Hunter looked around at the towels and toothbrush holders with a frown. "What do we need here?"

"I thought we could get you some masculine stuff, like brown towels or a clock shaped like a football—something that would make you feel more at home in my apartment."

"I don't need to get comfortable at your apartment, Brooke," he said. "I'll only be there for a few more days."

That was not the response she was hoping for, but at least he said it nicely.

He continued, "And all the towels in my apartment are army green."

She looked over at him. "Was that a joke?"

He raised an eyebrow. "What do you think?"

"I think you don't know how to tell a joke, and you really do own only army-drab towels."

He nodded, not offended in the least.

It was hard to work with someone who didn't even *want* to have a sense of humor. She picked up a stack of green towels and added them to their basket.

"I don't want those," he said.

"They're not for you—they're for me," she told him. "I'll be more comfortable if you're more comfortable."

He stared at the towels for a few seconds and finally said, "We'd better get out of here before you decide you want army-green sheets too."

She rolled her eyes. "Like that would make you more comfortable since you sleep on the floor."

He ignored this and pushed the basket toward the checkout area. Brooke offered to split the cost of their purchases, but Hunter insisted on paying for everything.

"Business expenses," he said.

"The supplies to refinish my piano and my green towels?"

He shrugged as they walked into the parking lot. "That part is a gift."

"First you give me a piano and now all this! You're such a romantic!" She reached up and kissed him on the cheek.

He looked down at her. "A lot of things have changed since I got you that piano."

"And some things haven't," she whispered into his ear. Then she climbed into the backseat while their bodyguard helped Hunter unload their purchases into the trunk.

\* \* \*

Just as they pulled up to the curb in front of her apartment, Brooke's phone rang.

"It's Rex," she told Hunter.

His lips pressed into a hard line. "Wait until we're in the lobby to answer it."

Hunter and the bodyguard grabbed the groceries and then ushered Brooke quickly past the protesters. As soon as they were inside, she raised the phone and said, "Hello."

Without wasting time on a friendly greeting, Rex jumped right in. "I just had the strangest call from a Joined Forces member who works at the Davidson County Courthouse. He said a marriage license was issued for you and the corporal yesterday. Would you like to tell me about that?"

There was no point in trying to hide the truth now, but she didn't want the bodyguard to know since he might feel obligated to share the news with Hack. Then he would tell her uncle, and that would be disastrous. So she walked over to a corner of the lobby where she would have some privacy. "I don't really want to tell anyone about it."

"I thought it must be some kind of mistake." Rex sounded stunned. "Yesterday you told me that your relationship with the corporal is just temporary. Then a few hours later you married him!"

"We decided to take your advice." She was careful to keep her tone light and emphasize the fact that it was his idea. "Like you said, we posed a danger to each other if anyone ever decided to hand out subpoenas."

"I can't believe something so monumental happened in your life, and you didn't even mention it to me." He acted like his feelings were hurt—as if he had any.

"Our relationship is temporary, and so is our marriage," she said softly. "It's more like a limited partnership."

"That's it?"

She watched as Hunter crossed the room to stand beside her. "That's it. But if it means this much to you, the next time I get married, I promise I'll warn you first."

He laughed. "It doesn't mean anything to me. I was just caught by surprise."

"It's not like we planned it," she said. "And please don't tell anyone else. I wouldn't want it to get back to my parents. When this is over, we'll have it annulled, and no one will ever know." Saying the words made her sad.

But they seemed to cheer Rex considerably. "My lips are sealed," he promised. "See you in a couple of hours. Do you want me to pick you up?"

Hunter shook his head.

"No, we'll drive ourselves."

When she had ended the call and her phone was back in her pocket, Hunter spoke. "You handled that well."

"Yes, we've established that I'm a good liar."

He frowned. "But you told the truth."

She looked away. "I hope that was my biggest lie ever."

* * *

The bodyguard helped them carry the Wal-Mart sacks up to Brooke's apartment.

"Any activity?" Hunter asked the other guard, who was standing by the door.

The man shook his head. "Been quiet all day—no reporters or Nature Fresh protesters up here. Easiest assignment I've had in a while."

"I hope it stays that way," Hunter said.

After they took the groceries inside, Hunter made himself two ham sandwiches and ate half a package of Oreos for dessert. Then they turned their attention to the piano.

Hunter arranged the refinishing supplies on the kitchen table and asked, "Are you ready?"

She took a deep breath and nodded. "I can't wait."

"According to the Internet, this is a tedious and unpleasant task," he warned.

"The actual work might not be fun, but I'm anxious to return the piano to its former beauty." She leaned close and whispered, "I'm hoping it's symbolic of our relationship—something that can be restored."

"I guess we'll have to see about that." He handed her a can of wood stripper and roll of steel wool. "And since the stripper can eat through your skin, you have to wear these at all times." He passed her some gloves.

Her eyes widened at this dire warning. "Seriously, holes in my skin?"

"I think that skin holes occur only after prolonged exposure," he said. "But better safe than sorry."

"Definitely," she agreed.

He went to work on one side of the piano, and she took the other. The task *was* tedious, but she didn't find it unpleasant. Of course, the fact that she had Hunter in her line of sight didn't hurt.

As she worked, her mind drifted. For a while she fantasized about a future with Hunter. They would be living in Washington, DC, so he could continue to fly for military VIPs. And it would be quite a challenge to decorate their apartment tastefully while limited to a color palette of army drab and brown. But gradually her thoughts turned from pleasant possibilities to grim reality. She needed a way to bridge the gap between the person she was and the person she wanted to be. The only thing she could think of was Detective Napier's proposal.

If she helped the FBI arrest and convict Rex and Lyle Carmichael, she might be able to live with herself. And Hunter might be able to forgive her. And she would be free of Joined Forces permanently. Her heart pounded with a mixture of fear and hope. She was in a position to do it, but the auction was the next evening. It was now or never.

Up to this point, she had been too afraid of Rex to cross him. But his power to hurt anyone would be severely limited if he was in jail. All the possibilities and consequences and benefits rolled around in her head. Finally she put down her goopy steel wool pad and looked at Hunter. "I need a shower."

He frowned. "Now? We've only been working for a few minutes."

She walked around the baby grand and took his hand. "And you need a shower too."

He didn't resist as she pulled him into the bathroom and closed the door. She turned on the water, and they waited in silence until steam was billowing around them.

Then she said softly, "Do you think it's safe to talk?"

He nodded. "Now what is the purpose of this pretend shower?"

"I've been thinking about what Detective Napier told us—specifically the stolen coins at the call center and the spare set of keys I saw in Rex's office today. Rex is determined to turn Joined Forces into a corrupt organization. He's recruiting criminals and taking money from poor people to support a multimillion-dollar call center and a private plane. It's wrong, and he needs to be stopped. So maybe I should help the FBI."

"Brooke, it's too dangerous—"

She held up a hand. "Hear me out."

He sighed. "Okay, but hurry. It's sweltering in here."

Encouraged, she began. "We'd have to lure Rex away from the call center somehow and get the keys to the storage room out of his office. You could be my lookout while I go into the storage room and take some pictures with my phone. Then the FBI will arrest Rex and Carmichael. Simple."

Hunter put his hands on her shoulders and tried to tamp down her enthusiasm. "You make it sound simple, but if you become part of an FBI investigation, you might have to testify at a trial—against a *crime boss*. Imagine what it would be like to have Carmichael as an enemy. You'd be looking over your shoulder for the rest of your life. Is that what you want?"

"No, but I'm not sure I can go on living this way either," she told him, "feeling like a coward and constantly worrying that I might be arrested. I don't think I'd have to testify at a trial since the pictures are just a way to get the warrant. The evidence will be collected during the dinner. And the FBI might not get another opportunity like this."

"What if you get caught taking pictures?" he asked.

"I'll make up a convincing lie. You know that's my forte."

Hunter was not amused. "These aren't the kind of people who forgive and forget. If you're really serious about this, we'll have to get help from your uncle. That means telling him everything."

She shook her head. "I agree that we'll need my uncle and the team, but I can't tell them everything. Not about the baby. That conversation deserves its own moment. It can't just be a side part of something else."

Hunter tipped his head slightly in acknowledgment. "We can leave that out."

"And we can't tell them anything incriminating," she continued. "That would put them in a position of having to testify against me if charges are ever issued. And there's a limit to the number of people I can marry."

He sighed. "What's left?"

"I'll tell them the pictures I took at the chicken plant were all part of a setup. That means I trespassed and lied to the police. That puts me at odds with the law and explains why I would be willing to take a big risk to square myself."

He thought about this for a few seconds and then nodded. "Okay, we'll make only a partial disclosure now. But later, after you've been given immunity, you have to tell your uncle everything. And if you don't—I will."

She stood a little straighter and looked him in the eye. "I know I have to face my mistakes in order to put the past behind me. If I tell my uncle after I've successfully helped the FBI take down a crime boss, it might soften the blow. And I might even regain a little self-respect."

Hunter considered this for what seemed like a long time, his face growing more solemn by the second. Then he said, "I don't like it. There's too much personal risk involved. But if you're determined to do it, I'll help you."

Clasping his hands in hers, she told him, "I have to do this, but you don't. I'll ask my uncle to relieve you of your bodyguard duties if you'd rather not be a part of it. And you can go back to flying planes, and I'll take pretend showers with someone else." She held her breath, waiting for his response.

"I guess I'd better keep this guard detail," he said finally. "There's no point in one of the other guys having to marry you too."

She smirked. "I don't marry all my bodyguards. Just you."

He seemed conflicted, which she considered a major improvement over distrust and disillusionment. She wanted to kiss him and make him admit that he loved her. She longed for that connection they'd developed while hiding out at the Civil War resort. But she knew she couldn't push too hard. If he was going to trust her again, it would have to be in his own time.

So she smiled and said, "There's always a chance Uncle Christopher will strangle me when I tell him about my checkered past, and then I won't be anyone's problem."

"He won't strangle you—although he may feel like it."

"How reassuring," she murmured.

Hunter was frowning. "There's a lot that needs to be arranged before the dinner tomorrow night for this to work. Maybe too much."

"Are you kidding? There's no challenge too big for my uncle and his team."

Hunter ignored this. "Step one is to invite ourselves over to your parents' house so we can put together a plan."

"That will be easy enough." She turned off the water. "All right, soldier, shower time is over."

\* \* \*

Brooke called her mother and asked if they could come over. "We have a little free time and wanted to visit."

"Your timing is perfect!" Neely said. "Uncle Christopher and his team are leaving tonight, so I cooked them a farewell lunch, and there's plenty left over." She lowered her voice. "But hurry, I can't guarantee that the food will last much longer."

Brooke laughed. "We'll get there as fast as we can." She ended the call and told Hunter, "The good news is we're invited. The bad news is you're going to have to eat lunch for the third time."

He rubbed his stomach. "That's not bad news. I'm already starting to feel a little hungry."

* * *

When they pulled up in front of her parents' house, Hunter said, "It looks like the protesters took the afternoon off."

"Maybe they think a presence in front of my apartment is enough," Brooke said.

"Or maybe Hack scared them away."

"That's more likely," Brooke agreed.

As they started up the sidewalk, the front door swung open, and her mother stepped out to greet them. "Welcome!" she cried as she gave them each a hug.

"Thank you, Mrs. Clayton," Hunter replied.

"Call me Neely!" her mother insisted.

"My mom always acts like it's been months since she's seen me." Brooke explained the enthusiastic greeting to Hunter.

"Usually it *has* been months since I've seen her," Neely told him. Then she turned back to her daughter. "But it's always good to have you here."

"How's Dad?" Brooke asked. "Is everything going to be okay with his business and all?"

"I can't promise that his company will survive, but we're going to be fine." Neely led them to the dining room, where everyone was gathered around what was left of the farewell feast. "Look who's here!"

Uncle Christopher was sitting at one end of the table with his wife, Savannah, and her daughter, Caroline. His team members were seated in various chairs around the table. They all looked up when Brooke and Hunter stepped into the room.

"Well, well!" Steamer called out. "It's the lovebirds."

Brooke saw Hunter's cheeks turn pink and stepped in front of him to draw away the unwanted attention. She threw her hands out and said, "Ta-dah!"

She knew she'd been successful when Steamer made fun of her hair. "I see you're trying a new hairstyle. What's it called, the lion's mane?"

She pulled on a stray ringlet. "It's called 'too much steam from the shower,' but I have to admit, 'the lion's mane' is catchier."

Caroline jumped out of her chair and hurled herself at Hunter. He caught her in midflight and swung her up into his arms.

"I missed you!" Caroline told him fervently. "We haven't played Scrabble Junior in forever."

"I've missed you too," he replied without a trace of the embarrassment he'd shown when accused of being Brooke's co-lovebird.

"Why haven't you come to play with me?"

"I've been taking care of Brooke," he explained.

Caroline frowned. "Why? She's big."

He laughed, and the sound was so rare and beautiful that Brooke was transfixed.

"Even big girls need to be taken care of sometimes."

Caroline turned to Brooke.

"Sorry I've been keeping Hunter to myself," she said, feeling uncomfortably jealous of a six-year-old.

"It's okay." Caroline looked back at Hunter. "You're here now, and we can play. I'll get the Scrabble board."

"Maybe later." Hunter put her down, and Caroline looked disappointed as she trudged back to her seat.

Hack demanded, "You didn't lose your bodyguards, did you?"

"Not yet," Brooke replied.

Hack was not amused. "Security is nothing to joke about."

"Sit down," Neely invited them, waving toward the two empty seats. "There's still some food left."

"We have a little business we need to go over with the team," she told her mother gently. "It's important, and we don't have much time, so would it be okay if we talk first?"

"It's so important that it can't wait until after you eat?" Her mother's voice was full of anxiety, and Brooke accepted a little more guilt onto her already overburdened shoulders.

"Yes, it's that important, but it won't take too long." Brooke felt Uncle Christopher's wary gaze.

Neely acquiesced graciously. "Well, of course then. Go straight into your father's office."

Uncle Christopher stood. "All team members in Raleigh's office." He looked down at his wife. "That includes you, Savannah. Neely, will you keep an eye on Caroline?"

Neely nodded. "She can help me put together the strawberry shortcakes for dessert."

Caroline perked up a little at this.

Brooke turned toward the hallway, her heart pounding. Hunter took her hand and urged her forward. She wanted to thank him for the gesture of encouragement, but it took all her concentration to breathe. So she just clutched his fingers, drawing strength and comfort from their steady warmth.

Uncle Christopher sat behind her father's desk. Savannah perched herself on the arm of his chair. Doc, the unassuming team medic with thick glasses, sat on the couch. Steamer, a real estate agent and lawyer from Las Vegas, turned a wooden chair backward and sat with his chin resting on the top rail. Hack leaned against the wall near the window. And they were all watching her with a mixture of curiosity and concern.

Her uncle pointed toward an empty chair. "Have a seat."

Brooke shook her head. "I'll stand."

He looked as if she'd just confirmed his deepest fear. "So tell us."

"Make it quick," Hack added. "We're leaving for the airport in an hour."

Brooke felt panicked. Making her confession was going to be bad enough without having to rush through it.

"Take your time," Hunter whispered. He had positioned himself behind her but remained within her line of sight. She understood that he wanted to provide support without being intrusive.

"I need help from the whole team, but before I ask you about that, I owe you an apology. There are a few details of the Nature Fresh fire that have been misrepresented . . ."

"Brooke," Hunter prompted.

"Okay, I lied," she admitted. "I lie a lot. It's one of my few talents."

"You lie a lot?" Savannah was obviously perplexed.

Uncle Christopher frowned. "I thought you outgrew that."

"I didn't," she said. "I just got so good at it that no one can tell when I'm lying."

His frown deepened. "What did you *misrepresent* recently?"

She clasped her hands together and faced these people who had trusted her. "We—Joined Forces—I mean I knew about the sewage pipe and the old chicken coops when I went on that tour of the Nature Fresh chicken plant. The tour was our opportunity to get onto their property and take pictures so we could expose them. The picnic, the car trouble, the walk up the creek bed to get help—all that was made up."

Hack cursed under his breath.

"I told you there was something off about that story!" Steamer cried.

"Shut up, Steamer," Hack told him.

"Nature Fresh is a terrible company," she hurried on. "They were breaking the law and polluting the creek and senselessly torturing helpless animals. We wanted to stop them. We thought if we had pictures, the district attorney would prosecute and the bad publicity would ruin them. I wanted to put them out of business. I thought that was the right thing to do."

"But you knew it wasn't right to obtain evidence illegally and then lie about it," her uncle pointed out.

"Yes, I knew that." She forced herself to face him. "I guess I thought that what they were doing was worse."

Her uncle said, "You shouldn't have lied to anyone, but you certainly shouldn't have lied to us."

She nodded. "I know."

"Mr. Shaw is involved too," Hunter told them. "He knew the evidence was obtained illegally, and he helped them cover it up by dismissing the charges against the guy who set the plant on fire."

"I'm disappointed in Mr. Shaw," Savannah said. "He seemed so nice."

"You can't trust anybody these days," Hack muttered.

Brooke forced herself to continue. "And this wasn't an isolated incident. I've broken the law for Joined Forces on several occasions. I don't want to give you specific details because I don't want you to be put in a position of having to testify against me."

The room was silent for a few seconds.

Finally Doc said, "All the members of this team have stretched the truth a time or two. And we've certainly broken laws for a good cause."

Uncle Christopher took exception to this comment. "What we do is sanctioned by the US Army."

"Most of the time," Savannah murmured.

"All the time," her husband responded. "If we have to make a plan adjustment in the field that breaks a law, we do it under blanket authority from General Steele. And once we get back, he gives our actions specific approval."

Savannah raised her eyebrows. "Except that one time when you broke the law, and he left you languishing in prison until I came to get you out."

He gave his wife a long look. "Yes, except that one time."

Brooke knew Savannah was trying to help, but she didn't want to be responsible for a rift between her aunt and uncle. "I recognize my mistakes, and I take full responsibility."

Steamer said, "Your biggest mistake was getting caught."

Uncle Christopher frowned at Steamer and then turned back to Brooke. "I wish you had told us sooner, but it took a lot of courage to come here today, and I respect that."

Unshed tears stung her eyes. "Thank you."

"I understand your desire to help animals," her uncle continued. "But you have to work for change within the confines of the law."

"And if you decide you have to break a minor law, you need a good cover story," Hack chimed in. "That one was awful. Even Steamer saw through it."

"Hey!" Steamer objected.

Her uncle ignored them. "As has been mentioned, sometimes our team breaks the law, but it's always a last resort."

Steamer smiled at Brooke. "Your heart's in the right place, but being a hero isn't as easy as we make it look."

"Enough about everything Brooke did wrong," Hunter interrupted. "She wants to put things right, and she needs help from the team."

"So, I guess I should cancel the plane reservations?" Hack asked.

Uncle Christopher nodded. Then he asked Brooke, "You're going to talk to the police?"

"I already have, sort of." She told them about the elevator meeting with Detective Napier, his disclosures, and his offer to help her work out a deal for immunity.

Her uncle interrupted. "So this Rex is your old boyfriend? The one you're in a power struggle with over the leadership of Joined Forces?"

"Rex is my ex-boyfriend, but any power struggle is just in his mind. I don't want a leadership role in Joined Forces," she assured them. "I don't even want to be a member anymore. But I have to be careful how I sever those ties since I don't want Rex and Joined Forces to haunt me the rest of my life. So that's why I'm allowing him to think he's monitoring me."

"Go on," her uncle said.

She explained about Lyle Carmichael, his connection to organized crime, and his illegal coins. "The FBI believes that the Dinner and an Auction is a cover for an illegal coin swap and that at least some of the stolen coins are already being stored at the call center."

"And this call center is where?" Uncle Christopher asked.

"Downtown Nashville, a few blocks west of the library. Rex bought an old church, and they're renovating it."

"Detective Napier said he could work out an immunity deal for Brooke if she takes pictures of the coins for the FBI," Hunter contributed.

"Everybody wants me to take pictures!" She laughed nervously. "I guess I should have majored in photography."

Hunter didn't acknowledge the joke. "If they get proof that just one coin in that storage room is stolen, they'll get a warrant and arrest all the people involved at the dinner tomorrow night."

"I didn't accept the detective's offer because," she glanced at Hunter, "we thought it would be too dangerous for me to help the FBI get evidence against a crime boss."

"You got that right," Hack muttered.

Heads nodded in agreement all around the room.

"But after some consideration, I've decided it's worth the risk."

Arguments were presented immediately.

"Are you crazy?" Hack demanded.

"I hate to agree with Hack." Steamer really did look regretful. "But I'm from Vegas, baby, so I know about organized crime, and you do *not* want to get yourself in the middle of that."

Brooke held up a hand to stop them. "My pictures will just be used to get the warrant. I won't have to testify at a trial because they'll collect more than enough evidence when they crash the dinner."

"And Rex and Carmichael will be in jail," Hunter added.

"Jail don't stop crime bosses," Hack said.

"We can make my cooperation conditional on total anonymity," Brooke assured him. "And by doing this, I'll not only protect myself from prosecution, I'll be helping to stop something illegal. It won't make up for what I've done in the past, but it's a step in the right direction."

"It's a very brave plan," Doc said. "One that sounds like it has a good chance of working."

"And since your deal would be with the Feds, you won't have to worry about the crooked DA undermining you," Steamer said.

"When would you get the pictures?" her uncle asked.

"Tonight," she said. "That would give the FBI time to get their warrants and set up the mass arrest tomorrow night."

"How do you plan to get into the storage room?"

"Rex keeps an extra set of keys hanging on a hook in his office. If we can come up with an excuse that will get him away from the call center, I can use the extra set of keys to open the storage room. But it won't be easy to get him out of there. We'll need something flashy that he won't be able to resist, like dinner with the governor."

"That's flashy," Steamer agreed.

"And unlikely," her uncle murmured. "Especially at this late notice."

"I could probably set up dinner tonight with some members of the local press," Savannah suggested. "He could make his pitch for contributions and advertise the auction dinner."

Brooke smiled at her aunt. "All that publicity would be irresistible to Rex."

Savannah made a note in her phone. "I don't have much time, so if you'll excuse me, I'd better start making some calls."

"Do you really think you can pull it off so quickly?" Doc asked.

Savannah flashed him a smile. "It won't be fancy. I'll just reserve a party room at a local restaurant and let the guests order off the regular menu."

"You've also got to convince members of the local media to change whatever plans they had for tonight and attend this little dinner."

"It's probably better that my name isn't associated with the invitation," Savannah said. "So I thought I'd call my old producer in DC and ask her to do the inviting."

Uncle Christopher pulled Savannah onto his lap. "It's a good thing you're a celebrity with friends in high places."

Savannah rolled her eyes. "It's been a long time since I did any real work on television, but I do have good friends in all kinds of places."

"It's barely been a year. Who could forget your beautiful face?" Uncle Christopher teased.

Savannah laughed. "Everyone, but thanks for the vote of confidence."

He seemed hesitant to release her even though he knew she needed to go. "Are you feeling okay?"

She held up a Gatorade bottle. "I've got Steamer's magic anti-nausea elixir to combat morning sickness. So I'll be fine."

Uncle Christopher released Savannah and watched as she walked out of the room with her phone to her ear. Then he turned his attention back to Brooke. "Once Rex and Millicent are gone to Savannah's dinner, then what?"

"I'll need an excuse to be in Rex's office so I can get the keys," Brooke said. "As he's leaving, I'll say I have a headache and ask if I can lie down on the couch in his office."

"And he'll agree because . . . he's still in love with you?" Doc asked doubtfully.

"No." Brooke couldn't bring herself to admit that Rex had never loved her. "He has definitely moved on. But he's such an egotist he can't imagine that anyone could move on from *him*. Anyway, I think he'll agree to let me use his couch."

"We've established that Brooke is an accomplished liar," Steamer interrupted. "She fooled everyone but me with that hiking in the woods story."

Brooke knew she deserved that and tried not to be offended. "If Rex doesn't give me access to his office, I have a backup plan. His office door sticks. Old wood, settling building—I don't know why, but he has to shove it open with his shoulder. So when they leave, I just need to make sure it doesn't close all the way."

"Both of your plans sound kind of sketchy to me," Hack told her.

"If neither plan works, Hunter can pick the lock on the office door and get the keys," Doc solved the problem.

Brooke nodded, remembering how quickly Hunter had picked the lock at a house in the mountains near the Civil War resort. "Yes, I've seen him work, and it's very impressive."

"It's nothing," Steamer told her. "We can all do that. Lock picking is Super-Soldier 101."

Hack said, "But picking a lock can leave traces, so we'll use the keys if possible."

"How much danger would there be for Brooke if she goes into the storage room to take the pictures?" Her uncle addressed this question to Hunter.

He shrugged. "With Rex Moreland and Millicent out of the building, not too much. As long as I'm inside and we have a few guys on the outside to step in if something goes wrong."

Hack shook his head, slinging his long braids from side to side. "If there really are valuable coins in that storage room, I'll guarantee you that Carmichael has people there. We'll need more than just Owl inside. I'd say two from the team and a couple of my guys for good measure."

"The electrical panel is downstairs, so Doc and Steamer could pose as inspectors," Hunter suggested. "That will give them an excuse to be near the storage room door for an extended length of time. It would also give them the authority to ask anyone else to clear the area."

Hack said, "As long as they arrive after five o'clock, any wise guy who decides to check them out will just get an answering machine at city hall."

Steamer puffed out his chest. "I like the idea of being an inspector."

"Two inspectors is overkill. Doc will be the inspector; you'll just be his sidekick," Hack decided, earning a glare from Steamer.

Uncle Christopher asked, "Once you're in the storage room, you'll be hidden from view?"

Brooke nodded. "The only risk is when I'm going in and out."

Hunter added. "There are two staircases going down to the basement floor where the storage room is located, one from each side of the chapel area. Doc will need to position himself near one staircase, and Steamer can watch the other one."

Uncle Christopher turned to Brooke. "It goes without saying that you'll need to work fast."

She nodded again.

"Now we need to figure out how to provide security during the dinner tomorrow night," Hunter said.

Her uncle frowned. "I thought once she took the pictures, she'd be done with Rex Moreland and Joined Forces."

"We'll have to attend the dinner," Brooke said. "If we suddenly back out, Rex or Lyle Carmichael might get suspicious."

Her uncle rubbed his temples. "And you said the governor is going to be at this dinner too?"

Brooke nodded. "He's giving a speech."

He glanced at Hack. "We'll need to take that into account. The governor will have his own security detail, and we don't want to shoot each other. And the FBI team that makes the arrests will need to know about our presence for the same reason."

"Got it," Hack confirmed.

Her uncle continued, "Hack and I will stay outside and monitor things from a vehicle. I want Steamer and Doc inside, along with a few of Hack's guys. We'll just have to make sure they don't look like the inspector and his assistant anymore."

"I went to culinary school for a few months, so you could put me in the kitchen," Steamer suggested.

"You think you can pass as a chef because you've taken a couple of cooking classes?" Hack scoffed. "I say we make Steamer a janitor since he likes everything neat and tidy."

"There's nothing wrong with cleanliness!" Steamer defended himself.

"I like the idea of Steamer and Doc working with food service but probably as waiters since that gives them the opportunity to walk freely through the crowd," Uncle Christopher intervened.

"Or busboys." Hack shot a look at Steamer.

"Hack," Uncle Christopher said in a warning tone.

The big man nodded. "I'll work on that."

Doc pushed his heavy glasses back up onto the bridge of his nose. "What's our next step?"

"I think our next step should be to call Detective Napier," Brooke said. "He'll need to work out my immunity deal with the FBI."

Uncle Christopher frowned. "I trust Detective Napier, but we're not getting the FBI involved yet. We'll wait until you actually have pictures. The fewer people who know that you'll be inside that storage room tonight, the better."

"You're suspicious of everybody," Brooke tried to tease him.

He didn't smile. "It's a trait you should develop."

"She can work on that later," Doc said. "What's the next step?"

"We need to get the layout for the call center and the surrounding area and then secure it with as many people as that takes," her uncle replied. "Owl, can you draw me a sketch of the place? It doesn't have to be perfect, just the basic layout."

Hunter picked up a legal pad and pen from the desk. Then he started drawing a neat sketch of the call center.

"I've got it on Google Earth," Hack said without looking up from his laptop. "I'll print some pictures of the neighborhood."

A second later the printer behind her father's desk whirred, and Brooke watched as several satellite pictures slipped out onto the printer tray. Uncle Christopher removed the pictures and shuffled through them.

"We need to get some cameras on the perimeter and listening devices inside the building so that nothing happens in that place without us knowing about it. Brooke doesn't go in again until we have the whole area secure."

Hunter looked up from his sketch. "There are so many construction people and volunteers all over the place it should be easy to get surveillance equipment inside and to maintain an exterior presence as long as our guys dress the part. And the vehicles we use should be older model pickup trucks with lots of tools in the back."

"I'll get us a couple of vehicles that will fit right in." Hack resumed typing.

"And there's no guard at the storage room door?" Uncle Christopher asked.

"There wasn't one this morning when Rex gave us the tour," Brooke replied.

"What about security cameras?" Hack wanted to know.

"Rex didn't mention any, and it would be unlike him to miss an opportunity to brag," Brooke said.

Hack made a note of this. "I'll have a few of my guys wear the pest control costumes and do a thorough sweep. If they find any cameras, we'll figure out how to deal with them then."

"What kind of camera will you use to take the pictures?" Uncle Christopher asked.

"I'll just use my phone," Brooke replied.

He nodded. "That's simple enough."

"Once you have the pictures, give the phone to the detective and let him download them directly at the police station," Hack instructed. "If you try to text or e-mail them to him, the transmission could be intercepted."

"But Rex said I have to answer my phone whenever he calls," she told them, feeling foolish and a little cowardly.

Hack scowled. "Tell him you lost it and that he can contact you on Owl's phone."

She felt relieved. Rex would think her silly, but he would believe that she could irresponsibly misplace her phone.

Her uncle said, "Okay, we have a plan for securing the call center. Hopefully Savannah will soon have a plan to remove Rex from the area during the time Brooke's taking pictures. What else?"

"My pest control guys are on their way over to look for bugs and plant a few," Hack announced. "We'll be able to monitor camera and audio feeds from here using my laptop."

Uncle Christopher nodded. "Steam and Doc, find out what a city electrical inspector and his assistant would wear so you can dress accordingly."

Hack handed Doc a piece of paper. "There's a pickup truck waiting for you at this address."

"Don't start your inspection until you see Rex and his girlfriend leave." Uncle Christopher walked them to the office door. "While you're waiting, you can check out the area, identify escape routes, and all the stuff we normally have days to do before an operation."

"Yes, sir!" Steamer clicked his heels and saluted.

Doc just nodded and put the piece of paper Hack had given him into his shirt pocket.

"And Steam?"

"Yes, sir?"

"Assistant electrical inspectors probably don't wear $200 shoes."

Steamer's face fell. "Why can't I ever impersonate someone with good taste?"

Uncle Christopher patted him on the back. "Check in every thirty minutes."

He returned to the desk and addressed his remaining team members. "We have a lot to arrange in a very short time." He checked his watch. "Brooke, please call Detective Napier and ask him to come here immediately. Make it sound like you have concerns about the Nature Fresh protesters, just in case anyone's listening."

Brooke pulled out her phone and made the call. After a brief conversation, she reported, "Detective Napier is on his way."

When Savannah walked back into the office, Uncle Christopher asked, "Well, how did it go?"

"Bunny issued the invitations and has twelve confirmed for tonight, including Rex and his new girlfriend, Millicent. I've reserved the Performing Arts Suite at the Capitol Grille, and the dinner will begin at seven o'clock."

Uncle Christopher gave her a quick hug. "Good work."

Savannah looked up at him. "And the best part is that Bunny's coming here to host the dinner personally."

"Can she make it in time?" he asked.

"She's headed to the airport now. I tried to talk her out of it." Savannah's eyes looked a little misty. "She's too busy to drop everything and rush down here. But she insisted."

"I told you that celebrity mystique would come in handy."

Savannah smiled. "Good friends come in handy."

He kept his arm around his wife's shoulders but included the others in his next comment. "Now let's go eat strawberry shortcake and make arrangements for Caroline."

"What kind of arrangements?" There was dread in Savannah's voice.

Brooke felt a new wave of guilt. Caroline was being uprooted again because of her.

"I thought we could have Neely stay with her at my parents' house for a few days," he said.

Savannah pressed a hand to her chest. "I thought you were going to send her to Colorado."

He gave her a small smile. "She doesn't have to go that far this time."

"Once you have it arranged, I'll take them," Hack said. "And I'll leave some guys there just as a precaution."

Uncle Christopher said, "If you go personally, it will mean I won't have you at the call center tonight."

"If I don't take them personally, none of us will have any peace of mind," Hack pointed out.

Her uncle shrugged in acknowledgment. "You're right."

"I'm always right," Hack replied with a gold-toothed grin. "I'll leave my laptop so you can monitor the surveillance devices we're putting inside the call center. And I'll be back by midnight to help make security plans for the dinner tomorrow."

Uncle Christopher nodded and waved toward the door. "Let's go eat."

"Best idea you've had lately," Hack returned. Then he led the way to the dining room.

"Is everything okay?" Neely asked once they were all settled around the table eating dessert.

"Everything's fine," Uncle Christopher answered. "Brooke is going to do a little favor for the police. It involves an ongoing police investigation, so we can't discuss it, at least not now. But don't worry. I'll take care of her."

Neely still looked nervous, but she nodded and asked her brother, "So you're not leaving this afternoon like you'd planned."

"No, we'll have to stay here a little longer," her brother confirmed. "But I need you to take Caroline to visit Mom and Dad for a few days. Hack will drive you as soon as you're packed."

Neely paled. "It's that serious?"

Uncle Christopher shook his head. "It's just a precaution. You know how I like to overdo things security-wise."

"I'm helping the team with a couple of things, and it will make things simpler if Caroline is occupied elsewhere," Savannah added. "There's nothing to worry about."

Caroline looked up from her shortcake. "I'm going to visit Grandma and Grandpa Dane with Aunt Neely?"

"Yes," Savannah confirmed. "We'll get you packed just as soon as we eat our strawberry shortcakes."

"And after I play Scrabble Junior with Hunter," Caroline amended. "He promised."

Hunter nodded. "We'll work in a few minutes for Scrabble."

With a smile, Caroline dug a fork into her dessert.

Neely was not smiling.

"You trust me, right, Crybaby?" her brother murmured.

"I trust you," she said.

"Then stop worrying," he added.

When dessert was over, Caroline ran upstairs to get the Scrabble board ready for her playdate with Hunter. After she was gone, Uncle Christopher instructed the team to meet back in Raleigh's office. Brooke and Savannah offered to help clear the table and help clean the kitchen, but Neely declined.

"I'll take care of this," she insisted. "You go do . . . whatever."

Brooke gave her mother a quick hug. Then she joined the others in the office.

Before a meaningful discussion could begin, Caroline yelled from upstairs. "Hunter!"

Savannah turned to her husband and said, "If Hunter doesn't go up there for at least a few minutes, you'll have a real crisis on your hands."

Uncle Christopher deferred to her wisdom. "Owl, go play with Caroline. We'll call you when Detective Napier arrives."

Hunter stood and moved toward the door. Brooke wanted to go with him, but since she hadn't been invited, she stayed in her seat. It was as if there was another woman complicating her already-strained relationship with Hunter.

# CHAPTER SIX

THEY WERE DISCUSSING THE JOINED Forces dinner scheduled for the next night when Savannah and Hack both got phone calls at almost the same moment. Savannah walked to the corner of the room, and Hack stepped into the hallway. Once they were alone, Uncle Christopher pinned Brooke with a piercing look. "What's the deal with you and Owl?"

"He loves me, but he doesn't trust me, so he thinks we can't have a future together. I'm trying to convince him otherwise." Her lips trembled, but she didn't cry.

"You're learning the hard way that there are real consequences for your actions. I'm not judging you—as my team so clearly pointed out, I've made a lot of questionable decisions myself—but you have to accept the fallout."

She nodded.

"Don't give up. It may take a while, but if he loves you, he can learn to trust you again."

Brooke looked away. "I hope you're right."

Savannah ended her call and announced, "Bunny is boarding her plane and will be here in two hours. Since the dinner doesn't start until seven, she'll have time to spare. And she's now getting calls from media people in Nashville that she didn't invite begging for an invitation!"

"I'm glad your party is going to be such a success," he told her.

Savannah took the compliment in stride. "Miracles do happen. And you're lucky I have such great friends."

His voice sounded a little odd when he replied softly, "I am lucky. I won't argue with that."

\* \* \*

When Detective Napier arrived, Neely ushered him into the office. "I'll send Hunter down, and then I'll help Caroline pack while you have your meeting."

"Thank you," Uncle Christopher said with a wink.

They got the polite greetings out of the way while waiting for Hunter. When he walked into the room, Brooke savored the sight of him. He looked more relaxed after spending some time playing Scrabble, but he tensed as soon as he saw Detective Napier.

Once Hunter was seated, Uncle Christopher waved toward Brooke. "My niece has decided to assist the FBI in exchange for legal immunity in the event that any charges are brought against her related to her membership in Joined Forces."

Detective Napier nodded. "I assumed that was the case when she called and asked me to come over immediately."

"We are setting things up now, and she plans to take the pictures tonight."

"Your team will provide security for her?"

"Yes," her uncle confirmed, "both tonight and tomorrow night during the dinner. But here's the thing—I don't want the FBI to know about Brooke's involvement until the pictures are already taken."

The detective raised an eyebrow.

"In fact, I don't want anyone within the Nashville PD to know except you."

"Can I ask why you want such extreme secrecy?"

"I just learned that Joined Forces bribed the district attorney. And there could be others who have been compromised, including people within the police department and FBI. Brooke will be at her most vulnerable when she's inside the call center. So I'd rather keep this just between us until the pictures are taken and she's safely out of there."

"I can see the wisdom in that," Detective Napier agreed. "That's a shame about the DA. I thought he was a good guy."

"I'm not sure there are any good guys anymore," Hack muttered.

"There are some good guys left," Savannah said with conviction. "I'm looking at several right now."

"Thanks for the vote of confidence, Mrs. Dane." Detective Napier turned back to Uncle Christopher. "So, how are you going to handle it? That is, if you trust me with that information."

"You wouldn't be here if we didn't trust you," Uncle Christopher replied. Then they filled the detective in on the basic plan.

When they finished, Detective Napier said, "Just make sure you remove whatever surveillance devices you put in. Carmichael probably has any place he goes swept, and you don't want to give them any reason to suspect that something's up. These are the kind of people with long memories and unlimited resources. Even from prison, Carmichael could cause problems."

Hack sent Brooke an I-told-you-so look. Then he told the detective, "I'll make sure Steamer and Doc remove any devices we put inside."

"Brooke's pictures will be used only to get a warrant, right?" Uncle Christopher asked. "We don't want her to be called as a witness during the trial."

"I understand your concern, and I'll make sure her pictures are only used for the warrant," the detective promised.

Uncle Christopher checked his watch. "Brooke and Owl are supposed to be back at the call center by five. Savannah has arranged a media dinner at seven o'clock that will take Rex Moreland and his girlfriend away and give Brooke the chance to take her pictures."

"I'm worried that Brooke's presence at the call center after hours might draw attention," the detective said.

"There's a lot do before the grand opening," Hunter explained. "Plenty of volunteers will be there late tonight."

The detective shrugged. "Then I'm out of objections."

Her uncle turned to Hunter. "Both of you go into the storage room, but I want you to do the actual photography. I wish we could leave Brooke out of it altogether, but her presence is necessary to get in. After that, though, I want to limit her involvement as much as possible."

Hunter nodded. "Yes, sir."

Brooke shook her head. "Absolutely not. This is my problem, and I'm handling it. Besides, if I get caught, they're less likely to shoot me."

"They will most likely shoot *anyone* they catch," Hunter pointed out.

Uncle Christopher didn't acknowledge this comment. "Owl is trained for these types of situations; you aren't."

"As a seasoned petty criminal, I'm better trained for this type of situation than you might think." Brooke stood her ground. "And I won't let Hunter take the risk for me. Not again."

"I want to," Hunter said. Then he looked embarrassed.

Brooke and her uncle ignored him, their eyes locked in a battle of wills.

"I won't negotiate this point," she said. "If we go in, I'm taking the pictures."

She saw his silent fury, but she wasn't afraid. She was right, and she knew it.

Finally Hunter interceded. "I'll follow her step for step, and we'll both take pictures. We can cover more ground faster that way. And if we get caught, they'll have to shoot me to get to Brooke."

Her uncle considered this and then said, "I'll agree to that if you will."

Brooke nodded. "I can't stop Hunter from taking pictures if he wants to, and that will get us out quicker."

"How long before the call center is secure?" Uncle Christopher asked Hack.

"My guys are about to go inside now. They should have cameras and audio in place within thirty minutes."

"It's a little after four," Uncle Christopher told Brooke. "That gives you about thirty minutes to reassure your mother before you have to leave for the call center. When you get there, try to keep a low profile. Watch for signs that Rex is about to leave and, right before he does, give him your headache story."

Brooke and Hunter nodded in unison.

"Wait a few minutes after they leave to be sure they're really gone, then get down to the storage room. You'll see Steamer and Doc posted near the door. If they give you the all clear, get in there, get your pictures, and get out."

"Yes, sir," Hunter said.

"When you leave the storage room, give your phones to Steamer or Doc, whichever one is closest to the door. They'll take them to Detective Napier."

Hack shook his head. "Hunter can't 'lose' his phone too. Moreland would have to be an idiot to believe that."

Uncle Christopher gnawed his lower lip for a few seconds. Then he said, "That's true. Owl, on the way in to the storage room, switch phones with whoever's by the door. On the way out, switch back." He turned to Brooke. "But if anything goes wrong, abort the mission. We can find another way to square things with the police if we have to. It's not worth your life."

"We won't take the pictures if we run into a problem," Brooke promised. "And thank you."

"Promise you'll follow my directions."

She smiled. "To the letter!"

He frowned. "Do I need to make sure you don't have your fingers crossed?"

She held out her hands so he could see that all her digits were completely straight. "But I'll let you in on a little trade secret . . ."

He raised an eyebrow.

"Only amateurs cross their fingers when they lie."

\* \* \*

During the drive back to Nashville, Brooke was anxious to have it over but not really nervous. Once again she was taking pictures of criminal activity. Once again betrayal was involved. But this time Hunter and her uncle and the law were on her side. She could take comfort in that.

When they arrived at the call center, Hunter parked beside a nondescript pickup truck.

He opened his door, and she did the same. Then together they walked slowly toward the building. She saw his eyes taking in everything. Apparently he didn't see anything suspicious.

They had barely walked through door when Rex rushed up to them. "It's about time you got here! So how was your time off?"

If he had been monitoring the cameras in her apartment, then he knew about their trip to her parents' house. And if her parents' house was under observation as well, he knew that Detective Napier paid a visit while they were there. So she decided to give him an explanation that covered all the bases.

"It didn't turn out quite like I'd planned," she said. "We went to visit my parents, and while we were there, a detective from the Nashville PD came over to talk about the Nature Fresh protesters."

"Those protesters are harmless," Rex said dismissively.

"I think so too, but my uncle doesn't take anything for granted."

"Except that his niece is a sweet little thing who would never dream of doing anything illegal," Rex taunted.

Brooke sighed. "Yes, except for that."

"Well, too bad about your afternoon," Rex said without a trace of sincerity as he led them into the former chapel. "But I'm glad you're back.

Millicent and I have been invited to a special dinner tonight with the local newspeople, and I need you to get things finished up around here while we're gone."

Brooke looked around at the scaffolding against the back wall, the stacks of materials scattered everywhere, the wires hanging from gaping holes in walls. She shook her head in dismay. "A magician couldn't get this place finished by tomorrow night."

"*Finished* was the wrong word," Rex corrected himself. "In fact, an air of incompleteness works to our advantage since it will help people see the need for additional donations. We just have to get it passable."

Brooke had doubts that even "passable" could be achieved in the time they had left, but she kept this thought to herself.

"Corporal," Rex continued, "you're back on paint duty. The baseboards need a touch-up."

Painting baseboards would be backbreaking work and particularly difficult for Hunter because of his broken arm, but he didn't complain. He just picked up a can of paint and a brush.

Brooke shot Rex an annoyed look, but he didn't seem to notice. "Millicent will tell you what to do," he told her.

Brooke wasn't thrilled that she and Hunter would be working separately.

"Just remember, we have to stay in the same room so I can keep an eye on her," Hunter reminded him.

"Oh yes, we don't want to bring the whole US Army down on us!" Rex said as Millicent walked up. He turned, pointed at Brooke, and said, "Here's your replacement."

Millicent's eyes widened, and Rex laughed.

"Just while we're gone to the press dinner," he clarified.

Millicent nodded, but she didn't smile.

To smooth things over, Brooke said, "I'm at your service. Just tell me what to do."

Rex started backing away. "Since you ladies have things covered, I'm going to go put together some facts and figures so I can impress everyone at dinner tonight."

Millicent nodded vaguely. Brooke ignored him.

Once Rex was gone, Millicent led Brooke to the front of the old chapel near the podium. She waved toward a corner where round tables and folding chairs were stacked.

"The tables and chairs we rented for the dinner were delivered this afternoon, and they need to be set up." She stepped onto the raised area behind the podium. "We're going to need six chairs set up about here for the dignitaries."

"Six chairs," Brooke repeated to show she'd been paying attention.

Millicent extended two pieces of paper toward her. "This first page is the things that still need to be completed, listed in order of importance. When volunteers come to you for another assignment, give them the next unassigned task. Be sure to write their name beside it so you won't give the same job to more than one person."

"Okay." Brooke tried not to be intimidated by the lengthy list.

"The other page is a diagram of how I want the tables arranged. I'll assign a couple of volunteers to help you set them up. Once the tables and chairs are in place, you can put on the tablecloths. They are up here in what used to be the choir-robe closet." She walked to a large wooden door and pulled the handle. It didn't budge.

"It's locked?" Brooke guessed.

Millicent made a face. "Apparently. When you're ready for the table-cloths, get the extra set of keys from Rex's office. You'll only have to try about a hundred keys until you find the one that fits this door."

Brooke stared at the young woman who had unwittingly played right into her hands. It looked like she wouldn't need to fake a headache after all. Brooke felt an almost uncontrollable desire to hug Rex's girlfriend—but she resisted.

Meanwhile, Millicent was saying, "We ordered green and blue tablecloths to match the new Joined Forces logo. Just alternate the colors evenly."

Brooke cleared her throat and tried to concentrate. "That sounds easy enough."

Millicent pursed her lips. "I don't see how you can go wrong as long as you follow my diagram. But if you need me, I'll be in my office until I have to leave for this dinner Rex is making me attend. I told him I have too much to do here, but he insists the publicity is like money in the bank."

Brooke gave her a sympathetic smile. "You know Rex, always working a money angle."

"That's what it's all about," Millicent said.

Brooke couldn't help but say, "I thought it was all about helping animals."

Millicent shrugged. "Then you're naïve. We can't make a difference if we don't have money."

"In the old days, we didn't have money," Brooke disagreed, even though she knew she shouldn't. "We still made a difference."

"You would have made a bigger difference if you'd had more money," Millicent responded tartly.

Brooke hated to let Millicent have the last word, but arguing with her was counterproductive. She needed the girl to go with Rex to the press dinner. And she needed them to leave soon. So she clamped her lips shut, preventing an outburst, and pretended to study the table diagram.

Millicent commandeered a couple of volunteers to help with table setup. Then she returned to the podium where Brooke was standing.

"One more thing—I need dinner choices for you and your . . ." she glanced over at Hunter, "your whatever, so I can give the caterer our final numbers. The menu options are vegetarian or chicken."

Brooke was stunned speechless. Finally she managed, "Joined Forces is serving *chicken* at the call center's grand opening dinner?"

Millicent gave her a bored nod. "Mr. Carmichael requested it."

"But I thought vegetarianism was, well, obvious."

Millicent shrugged. "We're not just about saving chickens anymore. We help a lot of different animals, and many of our new donors—like Mr. Carmichael—aren't vegetarians. Chicken is just an option. No one will be forced to eat it."

Brooke couldn't get her mind around the concept. A nonprofit organization founded to eliminate animal cruelty—particularly in the poultry industry—serving chicken at a fundraiser. It was such a complete contradiction.

"Well?" Millicent demanded impatiently.

"Vegetarian plates for both of us," Brooke said. Even though Hunter was a meat eater, she knew he would want to stand by her on principle.

Millicent nodded and hurried off toward her office.

Brooke was watching her leave when four young men walked over and asked where she wanted them to put the tables. Brooke introduced herself and thanked them for their help. Then she instructed them on the placement of each table, following the diagram exactly. Soon round rental tables dotted the big room in Millicent's carefully planned pattern. Then they put eight chairs around each table, also per the diagram.

"Now what?" one of the young men asked once the last chair was placed.

"Now it's time for tablecloths, and I can handle that," she told them. "Let me check Millicent's list and give you another assignment."

Once she had them sweeping construction debris in the parking lot, she rushed over to Hunter and whispered, "I'm about to pull out the tablecloths that are locked in that closet." She pointed behind her. "Millicent said I'll have to get the extra set of keys from Rex's office." She wiggled her eyebrows. "What do you think about that?"

He stopped painting and looked at her. "It's almost too good to be true."

"Don't you believe in luck?"

He shook his head. "No, not really."

She rolled her eyes. "I need to hurry and get the keys before they leave." She started toward the door. "I'll be right back."

"Wait, I'm coming with you." He balanced the dripping brush on top of the paint can and followed her to the hallway.

When Brooke reached Rex's office, she knocked on the open door. He looked up from his laptop in surprise.

"Sorry to bother you," she said, "but Millicent sent me to get a set of keys. The tablecloths are locked in the closet." It was slightly misleading— implying that Millicent would be in possession of the keys instead of Brooke—but not untrue.

He motioned toward the hooks on the wall. "Help yourself."

She walked over to the keys and asked, "Does it matter which set I take?"

"Take either one. They're identical."

Her hand closed around the set she'd seen him hang up there earlier. "I'll bring them back as soon as we're through putting out the tablecloths."

Rex nodded vaguely, still focused on the laptop.

Grateful that he was distracted, she walked out of the office and into the hall where Hunter was waiting. She opened her hand just enough for him to see the cluster of keys. "Like taking candy from a baby," she whispered.

His mouth turned up slightly at the corners, which further accelerated her heart rate. He opened the door to the old chapel, and they walked in together. Hunter went back to spot-painting baseboards, and Brooke sorted through the keys until she found the one that she needed. The closet was much larger than she'd expected, with shelves on the side walls and a rack full of choir robes along the back. Each tablecloth was wrapped in plastic and piled into neat stacks on the side shelves.

Brooke removed the tablecloths one at a time, making this particular job last and thereby delaying the moment when she would need to return the keys.

While she worked, Brooke noticed her eyes straying toward Hunter; their gazes met often. She noticed he wasn't getting much painting done. Whether that was because he was constantly watching her or because he didn't want to help Rex and Joined Forces in any way, she couldn't tell.

She had just finished covering the tables when Hunter walked over. "I got a text from Hack. Rex and Millicent drove away five minutes ago. It's time to take pictures."

Brooke's hands started to tremble, and she was surprised by this sudden case of nerves. She was usually calm under pressure, but the stakes had never been this high before. She wasn't about to trespass or inflict minor property damage. She was about to cross a dangerous crime boss. The next few minutes could determine whether or not she spent time in jail. And whether or not she had a future with Hunter.

Taking a deep breath, she said, "I have to find someone to pass out assignments for me."

Hunter nodded. "I'll wait here."

She found a girl on the washing windows crew and put her in charge of the job-assignment sheet. "I'm going downstairs for a little break," Brooke explained. "I'll come and relieve you soon."

The girl said, "Don't hurry. I'd rather hold this list than wash windows."

Brooke hoped she hadn't chosen someone *too* smart. "I won't be long, really. I just need something to eat."

Then she took Hunter's hand, and they walked down the stairs to their left. "I feel like part of the *Mission Impossible* team," she whispered as they descended.

"You've got to be serious about this," he replied.

"I'm completely serious," she assured him.

When they reached the lower level, they saw Doc. He was dressed in neatly creased black pants, a stiff white shirt, and a boring blue tie. He was standing near the kitchen, pretending to inspect an electrical panel. Steamer, wearing baggy gray coveralls, was close to the storage room door. Brooke couldn't help glancing down at his shoes. No Gucci loafers this time. He was wearing a pair of Nikes so battered she could barely make out the signature swoosh.

It should have been funny to see the fastidious Steamer dressed in dirty and unstylish attire. But Brooke just felt guiltier, defying what she'd thought was her self-recrimination limit.

"We need to hurry," Hunter said, shaking her from these unpleasant thoughts.

Hunter switched phones with Steamer, and Brooke started trying the keys on the storage room's new steel door. There were a lot of keys, and the ring was small, so it was difficult to keep track of which ones she'd already tried. As the number of untried keys dwindled, she started to worry that the key for the storage room was not there. Maybe only Mr. Carmichael had a key and that was why there were no cameras and no guards. Then, just when it seemed that all hope was gone, she slipped a key into the lock, and it turned smoothly under her hand.

"Bingo," she whispered to Hunter.

He nodded calmly, but she saw the anxiety in his eyes. He was a trained soldier, brave beyond the norm, so she knew he was not afraid for himself. He was worried about her. It wasn't an admission of love exactly, but it was close.

"It's going to be okay," she tried to reassure him. "The guys will let us know if there's a problem."

With a slight nod, he pushed the storage room door open, and they slipped inside. He closed the door behind them and used the flashlight feature on Steamer's phone to locate the light switch. When he flipped it on, the room was instantly suffused with hard, bright light.

Brooke held up a hand to shield her eyes while they adjusted to the glare. The room was larger than she had expected, with concrete floors and cinder block walls. Several metal posts dispersed at regular intervals helped to reinforce the low ceiling.

One side was crowded with various items that had at one time belonged to the now-defunct church. There were velvet covered pews in need of repair. Several file cabinets lined one wall with labels like "Choir Music," "Vacation Bible School," and "Donations" on the drawers. There were crates filled with utilitarian dishes and dusty hymnals.

The other side of the room was lined with long folding tables. On each table were stacks of thin black boxes. Hundreds of thin black boxes. Daunted, Brooke looked up at Hunter.

"It could take hours!" she whispered.

"We don't have hours," he dismissed this outright. "We'll just photograph a sampling from each stack. It's all we can do." He pulled two pair of latex gloves from his pocket and handed a pair to Brooke. "Put these on before you touch anything and give them to Steamer or Doc on the way out. Neither one of us can have anything incriminating on us in case we're searched."

Brooke's heart beat a little faster, but she nodded.

Hunter pulled on his gloves and moved toward the first table. "We need a system. Let's do every fifth box just to make it simple. As you finish with each stack, put them back in order and make sure they're straight. It has to look just like it does now when we're finished."

Brooke put on her gloves as she walked to the table beside him. Following his lead, she removed the box from the top of the stack and lifted the lid. Inside were twelve coins, neatly separated, labeled and encased in plastic. She took two pictures with her phone, careful to get the coins and the labels. Then she replaced the lid and set the box aside.

Glancing over at Hunter, she saw he was already on his second box. Anxious to keep up, she removed the next four boxes, careful to keep them in order, and pulled out the fifth. The coins inside looked much the same as the ones in the first box. She took two pictures, replaced the lid, and put the box back in its place. Then she counted down four more boxes and removed the fifth.

Once she'd finished with the entire stack, she lined them up just as they'd been when she started and moved on to the fourth table. Hunter was already working at the third one.

They continued their systematic progress down the left side of the room. Brooke was so intent on getting a good sampling that she lost track of time. A crash from upstairs brought her back to reality. She froze and saw Hunter do the same. There was some yelling and the sound of something heavy being dragged across the floor. But no one approached the storage room door, and after a few seconds, they resumed their picture taking.

But Brooke had lost her rhythm. The nervousness had returned, and she felt sweat gathering along her hairline. It wasn't hot in the storage room, but the air felt stale—like a coffin. Her hands trembled, and the box she was holding fell to the floor.

She gasped, and Hunter looked up sharply.

"It's not broken," she whispered, feeling foolish.

"Just pick it up and keep going," he encouraged.

Fighting the urge to run for the door, Brooke did as he'd instructed. Time seemed to crawl. Each time she finished a stack of coins, there was no sense of satisfaction. There were too many coins and not much time. The possibility of failure hung over them like a thundercloud.

They were at the end of the second row when Hunter got a text. She paused in her photography while he checked Steamer's phone. Then their eyes met over the stacks of coin boxes.

"We have to leave now." Hunter returned the phone to his pocket. He closed the box he'd been working on and stacked it neatly.

Brooke looked down at the many tables that they hadn't gotten to. "What if those are the stolen coins, and this has all been a waste of time?"

He shrugged. "Nothing we can do about that now."

She followed him to the door. When they reached the light switch, Hunter scanned the room quickly, looking for any sign of their presence. Apparently satisfied, he turned off the light in the storage room and cracked open the door to make sure the coast was clear. Then he slipped out with her following close behind.

"Moreland and his girlfriend just turned onto Church Street headed back this way," Doc informed them softly.

"Why?" Brooke cried in alarm.

"We don't know," Doc replied. "But you two need to be upstairs when they get here."

Brooke removed her gloves, and Hunter did the same. Then he swapped phones with Steamer while Brooke gave hers to Doc. Hunter grabbed Brooke's hand, and they started for the stairs.

Suddenly Brooke stopped, pulling him to a halt. "Wait!" She let go of his hand and ran to the small kitchen. She opened the refrigerator and removed an apple from the fruit tray inside. Then she closed the refrigerator and hurried back to the stairs.

Holding up the apple, she said, "I said I was coming down for a snack."

He gave her a rare look of approval before hauling her up the stairs.

Hunter reclaimed his paintbrush, and Brooke relieved the window-washer of Millicent's volunteer to-do list just as Rex strode into the room, looking angry.

Brooke didn't have to fake a startled reaction. "Rex!" She put a hand to her chest. "I thought you were at the press dinner!"

"Millicent was supposed to bring free tickets to the grand opening to give away at the dinner, and she forgot." He crossed the room, and Brooke followed right behind him. "That girl is an idiot."

Brooke agreed, but not because of forgotten dinner tickets. She didn't voice this opinion.

"How could she possibly forget the tickets?" Rex ranted on. "The only reason we're attending this dinner is to publicize the grand opening!"

Brooke continued to follow him and noted that while Millicent was being held responsible for the forgotten tickets, they were apparently located in *his* office. She waited a few steps back while he unlocked the door and then shoved it open. Then while Rex walked to his desk and opened the middle drawer, Brooke casually returned the keys to the hook on the wall.

"I'm done putting out the tablecloths, and I think the room looks really nice." Her hands were shaking, so she shoved them in the pockets of her jeans.

Rex was still focused on Millicent and her dinner-ticket failure. "That's good," he said absently as he pulled a stack of Dinner and an Auction tickets from his desk. Then he walked into the hallway. "Just keep handing out assignments until everything on that list is complete." He waited for her to join him and shut his office door with a resounding slam.

Hunter was standing in the doorway to the chapel. He stepped aside to let Rex pass and then waited for Brooke. They trailed back into the chapel at a much slower pace, allowing the gap between them and Rex to increase rapidly. Finally he walked out the front door, and Brooke sighed with relief.

"That was close," she whispered.

"But we did it without getting caught," Hunter reminded her.

"We haven't been caught *yet* anyway," she muttered.

He reached down to pick up his paintbrush. "Go back to bossing people around. We don't want to draw any attention to ourselves."

As Brooke returned to the podium, she saw Doc and Steamer climb the stairs and leave the building. They needed to get the pictures to Detective Napier. She knew some of Hack's guys were still around, but she felt vulnerable without Steamer and Doc.

She forced herself to munch on the apple even though it tasted like sawdust in her mouth. When she felt like she'd been eating it long enough.

to sell the excuse, she threw it in a nearby paint bucket that had been converted into a garbage can.

She was relieved when Doc and Steamer walked back in. Doc walked along the wall inspecting some of the exposed wires while Steamer tagged along behind him. Brooke handed out assignments, and Hunter pretended to paint for a grueling two hours.

It was nearly nine thirty before Rex and Millicent walked back into the chapel. This time he was all smiles.

"I'm guessing that the dinner went well?" Brooke asked as she handed Millicent the list.

"Stupendous!" Rex proclaimed. "They're running spots about the grand opening on all the local channels tonight and again tomorrow morning. We gave away free tickets to the dinner, and several people promised to attend, which will translate into more publicity. We're riding the wave of success, and nothing can stop us now!"

Brooke fervently hoped that was not true, but she just said, "Well, I guess we'll head home."

"What's the rush?" Rex was still exuberant. "The night is young!"

Brooke looked at her watch. "It's not really that young, and some of us have been doing manual labor while you were being honored at a fancy dinner hosted by local celebrities."

He accepted this blatant flattery as if it were no more than his due. "You're right; it isn't fair. Why don't you let me buy you two dinner at the restaurant of your choice?" Rex suggested. "Obviously Millicent and I have already eaten, but I wouldn't mind having a cocktail. It can be a double date."

Brooke forced a smile. "We aren't dressed for celebrating." She held out her hands to showcase her work clothes. "Besides Hunter and I are refinishing an old antique piano, and we didn't get a chance to work much on it this afternoon."

Rex gave her a condescending look. "There are people you can hire to do that sort of thing."

"It's a labor of love," she replied.

"Oh, your life is painfully boring."

Brooke yawned. "Yes, well, see you tomorrow."

Hunter took her hand and started toward the door.

"Get here early," Rex called after them.

Brooke waved and let Hunter lead her outside. Doc and Steamer were right behind them. No one spoke until they reached their truck.

"So, you gave the phones to Detective Napier?"

Doc nodded. "Your uncle wants us all at Neely's house as fast as we can get there. We'll talk then."

Brooke got into Hunter's car and closed the door. Hunter walked around and settled himself under the wheel. Then they pulled out of the parking lot with Doc and Steamer following close behind in a nondescript pickup truck. Not long ago Brooke would have found this security annoying and intrusive. Now she only found it comforting.

# CHAPTER SEVEN

With Neely gone, nobody was waiting to greet Brooke and Hunter when they arrived at her parents' house. One of Hack's guys answered the door and ushered them inside. The house was quiet and a little lifeless. Brooke led the way into the office, where her uncle and Savannah were waiting. Her uncle was behind the desk, as usual. Savannah was sitting on the small couch, sipping Spriteorade.

"Is the morning sickness better?" Brooke asked her aunt.

Savannah shrugged. "I'll be fine as long as there's not a shortage of Gatorade or Sprite in Nashville."

"Have a seat." Uncle Christopher pointed to some empty chairs near the desk.

Then Doc walked in, still dressed like a city inspector, and pulled up a chair beside them.

Hunter asked, "Where's Steamer?"

"He dropped me off," Doc said. "Now he's on the way to the caterer's place to be trained as a waiter."

"You didn't need any training?" Brooke asked Doc.

"I'm going to bus tables, and there's no training required for that."

Brooke gave Doc an apologetic look and then turned to her uncle. "So Detective Napier has the phones. Any idea how long it will be before we know if there were any stolen coins in the pictures we took?"

Uncle Christopher shrugged. "He passed them on to the FBI. It doesn't seem like it should take too long. We're going to work under the assumption that the FBI sting is on for tomorrow night and plan accordingly. Owl, Hack rounded you up a dress uniform. Hopefully it will fit. It's hanging in Neely's coat closet by the front door."

"Thanks." Hunter didn't look all that appreciative.

Savannah said to Brooke, "And your mother had a dress with matching shoes sent over from a store downtown. They're in your room. If they don't fit, the store will bring a different size to swap out."

Brooke was surprised and a little apprehensive. Not that Neely didn't have good taste, but she tended to treat her daughter like the child she wasn't. So Brooke feared that she was going to find a dress more appropriate for a high school girl than a young woman about to graduate from college.

Sensing her concerns, Savannah said, "The dress is perfect—as long as it fits."

"It's just a dress that Brooke will wear to an FBI sting," Uncle Christopher reminded them. "It doesn't matter what it looks like. Now can we end the fashion discussion and get back to security?"

Savannah gave him a regal nod. "You may."

But before the security discussion could be resumed, Uncle Christopher got a phone call which lasted only a few seconds. As he put his phone away, he said, "Detective Napier's at the back door."

And a minute later, the detective was escorted into the office by one of Hack's guards.

"I just heard back from the FBI," he said without preamble. "There were thirteen stolen coins in the pictures taken by Miss Clayton and Corporal Ezell."

Brooke couldn't resist a little cheer. "Yay!"

Doc patted her on the back, Savannah clapped, and even Hunter managed a little smile.

"So they've got the arrest warrants?" Uncle Christopher asked.

"They're working on that now," the detective told him. "But tomorrow night is definitely a go."

"So we need to finalize our security plan," Uncle Christopher said. "Unless Brooke has decided to skip the dinner, which is what I advise."

"I have to go," Brooke said. "I don't want to, but Rex won't let me out of it."

Her uncle raised an eyebrow, but she didn't elaborate.

"We can secure the area." Doc sounded confident. "We'll have a significant presence inside and out."

Detective Napier said, "Nashville PD will have guys there, uniforms and plainclothes. And the FBI will have a small army on the perimeter."

Her uncle turned to Hunter. "Sit near an exit so if anything goes wrong you can get Brooke out of the building."

"Yes, sir," Hunter replied.

"After the arrests have been made, the police will round up other 'persons of interest' for questioning," Detective Napier told them. "This will include Miss Clayton and Corporal Ezell, but don't be alarmed. It's just a way to keep suspicion from falling on you."

"What about the district attorney, Mr. Shaw?" Brooke asked. "Is he going to be arrested too?"

"Only if he buys a stolen coin from the secret sale," the detective said.

"But he works for Joined Forces!"

Detective Napier shook his head. "We don't have any proof of that."

"So he's just going to get away with his crimes?" Brooke was indignant.

"This is a limited operation run by the FBI to get Lyle Carmichael. We can't expand the scope without risking the whole thing. But," Detective Napier encouraged, "maybe the DA *will* buy some stolen coins."

"Or maybe the police can start a separate investigation of Mr. Shaw and his activities," Savannah suggested.

Brooke sighed. "I sure wish we could get them all at once."

"Me too," Detective Napier agreed. "But knowing there are still more criminals to catch gives me job security."

"Okay, I guess we're set for tomorrow," Uncle Christopher said. "The team will meet again in the morning when Hack and Steamer are here to finalize everything. We won't communicate with Brooke or Owl unless there's a problem."

Hunter nodded, and Brooke asked, "When do you think I'll get my phone back?"

"It could be a long time," the detective said. "I'd go ahead and get another if I were you."

Brooke frowned.

"So are you finished with me, Major?" Detective Napier asked.

"Yes, and thank you for coming."

They all stood and shook hands with the detective.

"Thank you for everything," Brooke told him when it was her turn.

His stained-tooth smile didn't seem as repulsive to her as it once had. "I'm glad you liked my idea."

Uncle Christopher and Savannah walked Detective Napier to the front door. Brooke grabbed Hunter's hand and pulled him up. "Let's go upstairs and make sure my new dress fits."

Hunter's cheeks turned pink. "You don't need me for that."

"Oh, I need you for everything until after tomorrow night," she said. "You have to keep me in your sight at all times, which includes while I'm upstairs." She pulled again, and he took a few reluctant steps toward the office door.

"You don't have to actually come in my room. You can stand in the hallway until I'm all dressed."

Hunter's relief was comical.

Smiling, Brooke led him to the stairs and up to the door of her childhood bedroom. She released his hand and said, "Don't move from this spot. When I'm ready, I'll open the door."

Hunter nodded. "Hurry. I feel awkward standing here."

She walked into the bedroom, where the cheerful purple walls welcomed her. Draped neatly on the bed was the cocktail dress her mother had purchased. Brooke's fears evaporated. There were no bright colors or ruffles. The A-line dress was gray with a black lace overlay, simple and elegant.

With a little squeal of delight, Brooke pulled off her jeans and T-shirt, leaving them in a heap on the floor just as she had when she was a kid. Carefully she slipped the dress over her head. She was able to get the zipper up enough to see that the dress fit perfectly. She was holding her hair up to get the full effect when there was a knock on her door.

"Are you finished?" Hunter whispered.

"Come on in!" she replied.

The door opened hesitantly, and there he was, filling the entire doorframe.

She struck a pose. "So, what do you think?"

He didn't say a word, but his expression spoke volumes. She'd seen that look before—at the resort when they were dressed like a Confederate soldier and his Southern belle. It was admiration and love, a look she'd been afraid she'd never see again.

Fighting happy tears, she walked over and presented her back to him. "Can you zip me up the rest of the way?"

After a moment's hesitation, he complied, his fingers trembling slightly.

When she turned back around to face him, they were standing so close she could feel his body heat. And he was frowning. "You don't like it?"

"No, it's fine," he managed.

"Fine?" she repeated. "Just *fine*?"

"It's beautiful," he conceded a little desperately.

"So you're saying I'm beautiful?" she pressed.

He hesitated for a few seconds but finally nodded. "You're beautiful."

"Even with this wild hair?" She dropped the mass of curls, and they danced around her shoulders.

"I like your hair curly."

Making a mental note of that, she wrapped her arms around his waist. "That's the nicest thing you've said to me since you found out about my criminal past."

He sighed, but he didn't pull away.

"If I'm going to get this kind of reaction from you, I'll have to keep my hair frizzy and wear this dress every day."

His arms settled on her shoulders in the slightest of hugs. And for a few seconds, she was in heaven. But then the moment was broken by her uncle.

"Owl!" he hollered. "Brooke! Where are you?"

Hunter stepped away from Brooke like he'd been scalded. "Up here." He moved to the stair landing so he could converse without yelling. "Brooke needed to try on her dress, and I didn't want her to be alone."

She came up beside him and grinned down at her uncle. "Besides, I needed someone to zip me."

"I stayed in the hallway while she changed," Hunter clarified with an exasperated glance at Brooke.

Uncle Christopher looked from one to the other and then said simply, "The dress looks nice."

"Hunter thinks it's *beautiful*," she informed him.

Savannah joined her husband at the bottom of the stairs. "Hunter's right," she said. "Do the shoes fit too?"

"Shoes?" Brooke repeated. "I didn't see any shoes."

"There's a box up there somewhere." Savannah started up the stairs. "If it's not on the bed, it might be in the closet." When she reached the top, she whispered to Hunter, "You've earned a reprieve, Corporal. You go talk soldier stuff with Dane, and I'll deal with this young lady."

Hunter gave her a look of pure gratitude and hurried down the stairs.

The shoebox was on the floor by the bed. Brooke pulled out a pair of high-heeled pumps that were a shade darker than the dress and had a discreet smattering of rhinestones. There was also a small black clutch purse.

"I like these shoes even more than the dress!" Brooke said as she slipped them on. "I just hope I can walk in them." She took a couple of tottering steps. "I better practice before tomorrow night."

Savannah smiled. "Walk slowly. And I guess Hunter can catch you if you fall."

"Hmmm." Brooke put a finger to her lips. "I might have to fall on purpose."

Savannah shook her head. "You are too much."

Brooke stared at her reflection in the mirror. "I hate to take this off, but I guess I have to. Will you unzip me?" She turned around so Savannah could unzip the dress. Then she carried her jeans and T-shirt into the bathroom and changed.

When she returned to the bedroom, Savannah had the shoes nestled back in the box. Brooke returned her dress to its protective plastic. Then they walked downstairs to join the others.

"I need to put this stuff in your car," Brooke said to Hunter.

He nodded. "I'll get my uniform, and we'll take them both at the same time."

After he removed his dress uniform from the closet, they walked outside. Hunter opened the door, leaned into the backseat, and put the clothes on the hook.

When Brooke saw the dress and the uniform hanging together, her mind flashed back to a similar scene—an antebellum gown beside a coat of Union blue, the costumes they'd worn at the resort. Then she had hoped that one day she and Hunter would be as close as their clothes. Today she was still hoping the same thing.

Hack pulled up to the curb, and they waited by the front door for him to join them.

"You're back," Brooke stated the obvious.

"I am," he said. "I've got your mother and Caroline settled at your grandparents' house, and now I'm starving. Fortunately your mom said for us to eat the leftovers."

They walked into the kitchen, and Brooke opened the refrigerator. She was daunted by the sheer number of food containers stacked neatly inside. "I don't know what to get out."

"Just get out everything," Hack suggested.

Savannah came into the room, followed closely by Doc.

"Are we eating again?" Doc asked.

"Some of you may be." Savannah eyed the food containers with distaste. "I can't eat this late at night."

"I missed dinner." Hunter opened a container of homemade macaroni and cheese.

"Me too." Hack put some leftover ham into the oven. Then he turned to Savannah. "Caroline is all settled in with her grandparents. They were playing Scrabble Junior when I left. She said to tell you hi."

Savannah gave him a smile. "Yes, I just talked to her. She's trying to think of a word that uses both a *J* and a *Q*."

"She'd be better off to just trade in her letters and start fresh on her next turn," Brooke said.

"That's exactly what I advised." Savannah took a seat at the table, distancing herself from the food odors.

"Where's Uncle Christopher?" Brooke asked.

"He just got a phone call from General Steele," Savannah said. "He'll join us as soon as he's through."

"He'd better hurry or there won't be anything left." Hack dished a huge mound of potato salad onto his plate.

Hunter sat down on one of the stools at the counter. "After we eat, we'll head back to Brooke's apartment."

"So soon?" Savannah asked around a yawn.

Brooke nodded. "We need to get some rest. And it looks like you do too."

Savannah smiled. "No matter how much I sleep I'm still tired. It's just a symptom of pregnancy."

The small talk was interrupted by Uncle Christopher's return. He looked grim as he crossed the room to Savannah.

"What's wrong?" she asked.

"The general has a new assignment for the team," Uncle Christopher said. "An emergency."

"How can you leave now?" Savannah demanded.

"I explained that we're scheduled to help with security at the dinner tomorrow night, but he couldn't delay our orders. We're to be at Andrews in two hours."

Savannah stood. "Is that even possible?"

He nodded. "A plane's waiting for us at the Nashville airport right now."

Savannah looked away. "I always hate it when you have to leave, but I really hate it when it's rushed. Since each mission has the potential to be your last, adequate good-byes are important."

Uncle Christopher took his wife in his arms. "I know, and I'm sorry." Over Savannah's head he spoke to his men, "We need to contact Steamer and have him meet us at the airport."

"I'll handle that," Doc said.

"Savannah, do you want to stay here or go home?" Uncle Christopher asked.

"I'd like to go home," she said.

"Hack, I need someone to escort Neely and Caroline to Virginia."

"She just got to your parents' house, and I don't want to cut their visit short," Savannah told him. "Leave them for a few days."

"But that means you'll be alone."

"I'm never really alone when you take an assignment from General Steele." Savannah attempted a smile. "Even with Caroline gone, I'll still have twenty of Hack's guards to keep me company."

Uncle Christopher nodded. "I'm okay with it as long as Hack's guys are there."

"In addition to the regular guards, I can send in my main man, Volt, to stay with Savannah," Hack suggested. "He's the best I've got, and since he assigns personnel for me, he can bring in extra men if necessary. He can also requisition equipment, access money—basically, he's me. While we're gone, whatever Savannah needs, she gets."

"I like the sound of that," Uncle Christopher said. "But if Volt is in Virginia, who will run your security company?"

Hack dismissed this concern. "He can do that from anywhere."

"How soon can he be there?"

"He'll meet us at Andrews and take Savannah back to your house. And he'll make sure the area is secure before they go in."

Uncle Christopher said, "If you trust Volt, I trust him."

"You know I wouldn't leave him with your family if I didn't."

"That's our plan then." Uncle Christopher turned to Savannah. "Can you pack quickly? We need to leave in a few minutes."

"It won't take me long," she promised, moving toward the stairs. "The only thing I really can't leave behind is my supply of Gatorade and Sprite."

Doc closed his phone and said, "Steamer's on his way to the airport."

"What about me, sir?" Hunter asked.

"You stay with Brooke," Uncle Christopher said.

"That leaves us a man short," Doc pointed out.

"The rest of us will just have to take up the slack."

Hunter stepped forward. "But what if you need a sniper? Or a pilot?"

"You've got one arm," Uncle Christopher said. "Do you seriously think you could provide sniper protection for the team?"

"Yes, sir, I do," Hunter responded promptly. "I can shoot almost as well with my left hand as with my right. And as far as flying a plane, well, I'm pretty sure I could do that left-handed too."

Her uncle's expression softened. "I appreciate your willingness and admire your confidence. But you have to stay here, or I'll be so worried about Brooke I won't be able to concentrate on our mission. If I decide we need a sniper or a pilot, I'll request one from General Steele."

Hunter looked mildly reassured.

"What about the dinner tomorrow night?" Brooke asked. "Who will pretend to be a waiter and monitor things from the van outside?"

Her uncle frowned. "I thought you understood that the team pulling out means you can't go to the dinner."

"But Rex . . ."

Uncle Christopher cut her off. "I'm tired of hearing about Rex and how mad he's going to be if you don't do everything he says. Your safety is the most important consideration here. Attendance at that dinner is not an option. You can make up any excuse you like, but before that dinner starts, you are going to leave the call center. I'm going to have to get your word of honor on that." He thought about that and added, "Owl's word of honor too."

Brooke knew there would be severe consequences if she refused to attend that dinner. Rex wanted her there, and he was used to being obeyed. She considered telling her uncle about the baby. He would be shocked, but at least he would understand why she couldn't cross Rex. She felt Hunter's gaze. He knew the choice she faced and was waiting for her to decide.

She opened her mouth, but the words wouldn't come. Her uncle took her silence for acceptance. Hunter was still watching her.

"Doc, call Detective Napier and tell him Brooke won't be at the dinner," Uncle Christopher said. "I don't see how that will affect things for him or the FBI, but I want him to be aware."

"Yes, sir." As Doc was pulling out his phone, he turned to Brooke. "Since you didn't have to use that headache excuse to get the keys to the storage room, you can use that tomorrow night."

"Maybe," she managed, although she knew a headache wouldn't justify her absence as far as Rex was concerned. In fact, she couldn't imagine anything that would.

\* \* \*

Hunter was even more reticent than usual on the drive back to her apartment, and Brooke knew he was worried about the team and their ability to function without him. She had no words of comfort, so she remained silent.

Once they were back in her apartment, they heated up some of the leftovers they had brought from her mother's house. Brooke still didn't have much of an appetite, but Hunter ate with relish—again.

When the meal was over, Hunter said, "I'll clean up the kitchen if you'll play the piano for me while I work."

Brooke was surprised by the request. It was so personal, almost an invitation to remember how they fell in love. "You know this piano is out of tune," she warned a little breathlessly.

His eyes claimed hers. "I don't care."

She was afraid her knees would buckle, so she sat down on the bench. With her fingers hovering over the age-stained keys, she asked, "What should I play? 'Dixie'?"

"No," he said quickly. "Something you've never played for me before."

So she played Mozart and Beethoven and Tchaikovsky and Chopin. After a little while, she got used to the sound of the old piano, and the lack of tuning didn't bother her so much.

It seemed to take Hunter forever to clean the kitchen, and she wondered if he was purposely dragging out the task. But finally he was done, and the concert came to an end.

"Thank you," he said. "I didn't know I liked classical music, but I guess I do."

She shook her head. "Just imagine how much you'd like it if this piano were in tune."

He rewarded her joke with a little smile. "So are you ready to do some tedious piano work?"

"Actually, that sounds fun." She pulled on her gloves. "Here's hoping I don't get any holes in my skin."

When it was time for bed, Brooke watched Hunter make his pallet by the door. Then she walked over to him and whispered, "If you won't take the other half of the bed, will you at least give me a good-night kiss?"

"Brooke," his tone was full of warning.

She ignored it, kissed his cheek, and climbed into bed. Tomorrow they would go back to the call center and work for a while. Then she'd make some kind of an excuse for them to leave before the dinner. The FBI would arrest Rex and his criminal friends. The Nature Fresh case would be closed and its owner appeased. Brooke wouldn't have to worry about being killed or prosecuted. That should be a lot to look forward to. But then there would be no reason for Hunter to stay.

# CHAPTER EIGHT

WHEN MAJOR CHRISTOPHER DANE AND his team arrived at Fort Belvoir, he was briefed on their new mission by his commanding officer, General Nolan Steele. His team stowed their gear on an army transport plane, and by the time he joined them, they were ready for takeoff.

"So?" Hack asked when Dane buckled himself in. "What's our big emergency mission?"

"I'm assuming we're going to be saving the president?" Steamer guessed. "Or maybe somebody robbed Fort Knox? I mean, what else could be worth all this rush and drama?"

"It's not the president or Fort Knox," Dane replied as the plane lurched forward and began taxing down the runway. "An undercover ATF agent has been kidnapped in Haiti."

Hack, Doc, and Steamer all regarded him with the same blank expression.

Hack was the first to recover. "So? What does that have to do with us?"

"We're being sent in to rescue him."

"Why doesn't the ATF go get him?" Doc asked.

"Or the marines or the coast guard?" Steamer added. "There are about ten agencies that should have gotten the call before us."

Dane told them, "The general said we were requested specifically because of our reputation for getting the job done."

"That's what we get for being so good," Steamer muttered.

"Let's just plan the operation," Doc suggested.

Dane opened up a map. "The agent's name is Clemente Alcine. He's an American citizen with Haitian parents who has been working undercover inside the organization of an arms trafficker named Jacques Babineaux, a French national with ties to Al-Qaeda."

"What a fancy name, *Babineaux*," Steamer scoffed. "I hate him already."

"The more you hear about him, the more you'll hate him," Dane replied. "Babineaux is single-handedly responsible for arming some of the largest terrorist groups across the world."

"And why hasn't somebody taken him out?" Hack wanted to know.

"Diplomacy," Dane said. "Haitian officials would be offended if the US accused them of harboring a criminal."

"Even though they *are* harboring a criminal," Hack said with a frown.

Dane gave Hack an impatient look. "I'm just telling you what General Steele told me. The ATF sent in this agent, Alcine, but his cover's been compromised, and we need to get him out before they kill him."

"Wouldn't it be a shame if, during the course of this rescue, Babineaux got caught in some cross fire?" Steamer said.

Dane gave him a grim smile. "It wouldn't be a shame at all. But that's not the kind of operation we'll be running. No shock and awe. It's going to be more of a sneak in and out."

Hack cursed under his breath. "I hate sneaking."

Dane continued, "Babineaux owns a fish plant near the coastal town of Baie de Henne. That's the hub for his arms business."

Steamer wrinkled his nose. "A fish plant?"

Dane pointed to a spot on the map. "It's on the quiet side of the island, a stone's throw from Cuba."

"Do we know how the ATF agent's cover was blown?" Doc asked.

"We do not," Dane answered. He focused again on the map in front of him. "We'll fly to Miami and then catch a ride to Haiti on a coast guard helicopter. We'll walk to the fish plant while it's still dark. And then here's my plan . . ."

For the rest of the flight, they pored over satellite photos and maps. By the time they arrived in Miami, the operation was set.

"Sweet and simple," Steamer approved.

"Once we have Agent Alcine, we'll go back to the beach, where a helicopter will pick us up. No one will be able to prove we were ever there."

"Sounds perfect," Hack said. "Except that we'll be leaving that criminal behind so he can keep selling weapons to terrorists."

"That's someone else's battle," Dane said. "We're just assigned to get the ATF guy without causing an international incident."

"I'm still a little nervous about going into the mission without Owl," Steamer said. "He's our eyes in the sky, our bird in the trees. Running an operation without sniper support is like going in naked."

"I don't like it either," Dane said. "But we don't have a choice."

"We can do this without Owl." Hack didn't seem concerned. "We've worked without him before—when he was flying a plane for VIPs."

"Or we could add another man in Miami," Doc suggested.

Hack shook his head. "Working with a stranger is worse than working shorthanded."

"I agree," Dane concurred. "So it's decided. Now you guys try to rest until we land."

As his team settled down, Dane looked out the plane's window at the black night. He hoped Savannah was sleeping peacefully, but he was afraid she was awake, worrying about him.

* * *

Three hours later Dane and his men were camped in a Haitian jungle near Jacques Babineaux's fish plant. Wearing camouflage and face paint, they blended into the landscape so well they could barely see each other.

"This place is *dangerous*," Steamer hissed. "And I don't just mean because we're a few yards away from one of the world's biggest illegal arms trafficker. I just killed a mosquito that was as big as my fist!"

"Wait till you see the crocodiles," Hack whispered back.

Even in the dim light, Dane saw Steamer's face go pale. "If you don't bother the crocs, Steam, they won't bother you."

The team waited quietly, watching the fish plant and making note of the guard rotations. Dane had just decided it was time to move when his combat phone vibrated. Since General Steele was the only person who had this number, Dane answered quickly. "Yes, sir?"

"Major Dane, this is General Moffett," a familiar, if unpleasant, voice replied. "I'm sorry to inform you that General Steele is ill and has been relieved of his duties. I was assigned to fill in for him."

"Is the general all right?" Dane asked.

"The information that I was given is that his condition is serious but stable," Moffett said dismissively. "My first order of business as your commanding officer is to cancel your current mission. Pull back to the helicopter pick-up area immediately. Your transport is on the way."

"But, sir, we're already in position just a few yards from the fish plant," Dane explained. "We can get the ATF agent and be out in a matter of minutes."

"I said your mission is canceled," Moffett repeated. "Back out now."

"And just leave the agent?" Dane confirmed.

"That is correct," Moffett replied.

"But, sir, we can rescue him and still make it to the helicopter."

"The mission is canceled, Major!" General Moffett's tone had moved past impatient to apoplectic.

"I'm sorry, sir, I can't hear you. Our connection must be bad. If you can still hear me, tell the helicopter we will be at the pick-up point in half an hour." Dane disconnected the call. He looked up and saw all his men watching him.

"What's going on?" Doc asked.

"General Steele is in the hospital, and General Moffett has been temporarily assigned to cover his command."

There were groans all around.

"Not Moffett!" Steamer expressed their collective frustration. "He hates special-op teams in general and us in particular!"

Dane nodded. "Yes, but he's now our CO. He canceled our mission and ordered us back to the pick-up point."

"We're supposed to leave our guy down there?" Steamer pointed at the fish plant.

Doc whispered, "Even though we're right here, just a few feet away?"

"Yes," Dane confirmed.

Steamer said, "Then the ATF agent will die—or worse."

"Probably," Dane agreed. "But those are our orders."

"Little Miss *Moffett* obviously doesn't know who he's dealing with," Hack said with disdain. "We never leave a man behind."

"No," Dane agreed.

Doc said, "So we're going to get him anyway?"

"I'm going to try to get him," Dane said. "The rest of you are going to meet that helicopter."

His men just stared.

Dane waved his hand at them. "Well, go on."

"No, sir," Doc said with respectful firmness. "Where you go, we go."

"All for one and one for all," Hack added.

Dane clenched his teeth. "You know I hate that silly slogan!"

Hack grinned, gold tooth glinting in the Haitian moonlight. "Yes, sir."

"I really want you to go to the helicopter," Dane tried again.

Steamer shook his head. "We can't, sir. You understand."

Dane did understand, but he still wanted his men to retreat.

Hack tipped his head toward the fish plant. "You'll have a better chance of success with our help."

Dane couldn't argue with that. He checked his watch. "Well, if you're determined to throw your military careers away, let's go."

Hack and Steamer crawled forward first. Dane and Doc crouched a few yards back, waiting for them to get into position.

As they watched the men move silently toward the edge of the trees, Dane asked, "Do you think we're getting too old for this, Doc?"

"We're not getting any younger, but we've been on so many of these missions we could do this in our sleep."

Dane sighed. "It seemed more fun in the old days. I loved the challenge and didn't mind taking the risks. Now all that has changed."

"Yes," Doc agreed. "And we're seriously shorthanded. I don't just mean Owl—we're missing Wigwam and Cam."

"And Wes."

"We were a great team, back . . . before."

Doc didn't say "before Savannah," but Dane knew that's what he was thinking. "I can't regret that things are different now."

"No," Doc agreed.

"And we're still a great team, just a smaller, older one." Dane checked his watch one last time. "Okay, it's time for us to join the party."

\* \* \*

Dane and his team approached the fish plant, following their carefully laid out—if hastily assembled—plan. Steamer disabled the generator and entered the dark fish plant by digging under the fence in back. They all moved methodically toward the metal shed where aerial satellite photos indicated the ATF agent was being held.

There were two guards in front of the shed, further evidence that they were at the right place. Steamer and Hack neutralized both guards with minimal noise. The door was padlocked, so Doc and Steamer searched the fallen guards until they found a key. Once the lock was removed, Doc sprayed the door hinges to prevent squeaking. Then they opened the door.

Inside was ATF Agent Alcine. He was younger than Dane had expected, handsome, with light-brown skin and close-cropped hair. He was sitting against the wall with his hands secured behind his back, his mouth covered with duct tape.

Doc crawled over to him and did a quick assessment. "He seems to be in good condition," he whispered.

"We're an army special-ops team," Dane told Alcine. "We've been sent to rescue you. Can you walk?"

Alcine nodded.

"We're going to remove the tape and cut your hands free. Then we're going to get out of here before another guard comes."

The agent nodded again.

Dane yanked the tape off, and Alcine endured this painful procedure in brave silence. After Hack cut the tape that bound the agent's hands, Dane allowed him to stretch and flex his fingers to restore circulation. Then he waved toward the door. "Let's go."

But the ATF agent said, "This place has a huge stockpile of weapons that could be used against American soldiers. We can't just leave it here."

Hack looked annoyed. "We sure can't take the weapons with us."

"We have to do something," Alcine insisted.

"Like what?" Dane demanded.

Alcine pointed to a building about a hundred yards to the right. "The weapons are stored right there. We could blow them up."

"That will reduce our escape time to zero!" Steamer scoffed.

Dane shook his head. "Our assignment was to get you out of here alive. The weapons would be a bonus, I'll admit, but I don't see any way to accomplish that without risking the whole operation. So we're going— *now.*" He turned to his team. "Start moving back toward the jungle. Go quickly but carefully until you reach cover. We'll meet up at the helicopter site."

The team nodded in unison and moved to the fence. Steamer went first, slithering underneath quickly and then crouching as he ran toward the jungle. It took Hack considerably longer to get under the fence because of his size, but soon he too was lumbering toward the tree line. After Doc slipped under, Dane turned to the ATF agent and pointed at the depression under the fence. "Your turn."

The agent didn't move.

"Come on, Alcine!" Dane hissed. "We've got to go now!"

But the young man stood there, seemingly frozen in place. Dane took a step toward him, intending to drag him under the fence bodily if necessary. Then he saw a look on the young man's face that he'd seen only a few times before.

Alcine's skin had turned ashen. His lips were pressed tightly together, and his eyes shone with unshed tears. "I'm sorry, sir," he said. "I know this isn't your fight, and I don't blame you and your team for leaving. But those weapons are my responsibility, and I can't let them be used against inno-cent people. With all due respect, I'm going over there and blowing them up, so help me God." Then he turned and ran toward the building where the weapons were being stored.

For a split second, Dane just stared after the boy-agent in stunned disbelief. He was used to being obeyed. And *he* was usually the one to remind others that duty should come first. Quickly he collected himself and started trudging after the zealous agent.

Doc fell into step beside him a couple of minutes later.

"You saw what happened?" Dane asked softly.

Doc nodded. "He's a brave one."

"Misguided," Dane replied. "But yes, very brave."

Soon they heard Hack trudging up behind them. "Is that boy crazy?" he demanded.

"He's trying to do the right thing," Dane said.

"He's going to get us all killed!" Steamer contributed as he joined the group.

"That's a real possibility," Dane muttered.

Hack added, "Or at least fired."

"Our military careers are over anyway," Doc predicted, "now that General Moffett is our CO. Just by being here, we've disobeyed a direct order."

"Little Miss *Moffett*," Steamer mocked the unpopular general. "I wish I could make him sit on a tuffet—whatever that is."

"Once General Steele is back in charge, our careers—such as they are—will be safe," Dane tried to reassure them.

Doc said, "And Agent Alcine's act of bravery gives me hope for when we're too old to do this anymore."

"Which was when, yesterday?" Hack rasped.

"Quiet!" Dane commanded. He looked in the direction Alcine had gone. "Our best chance of survival is to catch him and formulate a plan for blowing up the weapons. Just storming in there is suicide for sure."

"We should have a few more minutes before someone notices that the guards we took out aren't making their rotations, but not more than a few," Doc said.

Dane looked at the men gathered around him. They'd been with him for almost ten years. They had fought together, bled together, and grieved together. Now they would risk their lives together in what was almost surely a hopeless cause. There was so much to say and no time to say any of it.

"One for all and all for one," Steamer whispered the team's unofficial slogan.

Dane nodded and pointed toward the building of weapons. "Let's go."

They moved ahead slowly, shoulder to shoulder.

"Does anybody see him?" Dane whispered.

Doc answered, "He's ten yards ahead, crouched down beside that stack of wooden pallets."

"How are we going to approach without spooking him?" Steamer asked.

"I'll go first," Dane said. "If he doesn't kill me, I'll wave for the rest of you to follow."

"Now that sounds like a great plan," Hack muttered.

"Do you have a better one?" Dane asked.

"Yes, sir," Hack replied. "Let me approach the rogue agent."

"He's not a rogue agent," Dane argued. "He's a foolishly courageous kid—and less likely to hurt me since I don't look like I want to kill him."

Hack's scowl deepened. "I don't want to kill him, but I'll admit I'd like to knock some sense into him."

"I'm going," Dane said. "Watch for my signal to join us."

Dane didn't wait for his men to object. He approached Alcine silently, and when he was close, he whispered the young agent's name.

Alcine whipped his head around, obviously terrified. "Sir?" he asked when he saw Dane.

"We thought you could use some reinforcements," Dane explained. Then he waved for his team to move up beside them. Once everyone was assembled, Dane asked, "So, do you have a plan?"

He pointed to some fuel canisters. "I'm thinking that if we can fire some flares into those fuel canisters, the weapons should take care of themselves. Do you have flares with you?"

Dane nodded. "We have flares, and that's a good plan except I don't think the fuel containers are close enough to the building to guarantee that a fire will start inside."

"So somebody's going to have to move the canisters," Hack said. "And I guess that somebody is me."

"The missing guards could be noticed at any second," Doc whispered urgently.

Dane nodded. "So we have to work fast. Hack, you go move the fuel canisters and be quiet!"

"Yes, sir." Hack moved off into the darkness.

"Steam, you and Doc take posts on either side of the building so you can warn us if we're expecting company."

"Yes, sir," Doc said.

"I wish we had Owl in the trees," Steamer added.

"Well, we don't. Now go."

They hurried away, staying low and moving silently.

"Alcine, that leaves you and me to fire the flares." Dane handed the young agent two of the four flares from his pack. "We don't have any to waste, so we need to get close and make each one count."

"Yes, sir."

Dane strained his eyes to see in the darkness. Hack was moving the fuel canisters but not all that silently. Steamer and Doc were in their positions as lookouts.

Dane and Alcine moved closer. Finally Hack had both canisters leaning against the building. He even turned one over so fuel was leaking around the door. Hack started making his way back toward them, staying close to the ground. Dane marveled that their barely conceived plan seemed to be working to perfection.

Then Steamer gave an urgent signal.

"Someone's coming," Dane whispered to Alcine. "Now!" They both fired flares at the weapon storage building simultaneously. Just as they'd hoped, the cans of fuel ignited instantly. Within seconds the building was engulfed in flames. There was only one unexpected problem. Apparently in the process of moving the fuel, Hack had gotten some on his clothes. When he crawled away, he left a trail of fuel on the dried grass. So when the fuel ignited, a little path of fire burned straight up to Hack, and soon he was blazing too.

By the time Dane realized what had happened, Hack had stopped, dropped, and rolled. The fire was out, but Hack didn't move.

"He must be hurt!" Steamer called out, oblivious to the dangerous attention he was drawing to himself.

"I'll get him," Dane said. "Steamer and Doc, you take Alcine and go to the helicopter pick-up site. If Hack and I don't come soon, leave without us."

Dane turned and headed for Hack, confident his men would obey his orders. But then he heard footfalls behind and turned to see them all following along.

"You won't be able to lift him alone, sir," Steamer said.

"He's right," Doc concurred.

Dane nodded in resignation. "Come on then. But hurry!"

"Go!" Hack rasped as they approached. "Are you crazy? They'll get us all!"

"We don't leave men behind," Dane reminded him.

They each grabbed an arm or a leg and lifted. Hack stiffened with pain but didn't cry out.

The team started for the fence, and they almost made it. But just as they reached the small trench they'd made, dark clad figures attacked. Holding Hack, their hands weren't free, and they couldn't protect themselves.

Dane felt an arm clamp around his neck, pressing his windpipe and interrupting the flow of air to his lungs. He dropped Hack and fought, but it was too late. He couldn't dislodge the arm. As he lost consciousness, he remembered Doc saying that these missions weren't a challenge anymore. Then everything went black.

* * *

Dane forced his heavy eyelids open and tried to get his bearings. He was lying on a dirt floor in a dark room. His mouth was taped shut, and his hands and feet were bound so tightly that he'd lost feeling in his extremities. With great difficulty he pushed himself into a sitting position, leaning against the wall closest to him. Then he began assessing the situation.

The wall he was leaning against felt like corrugated metal. They were probably in the same shed they had rescued Agent Alcine from. Metal would be marginally easier to escape from than cinderblock. He counted that as one positive thing.

Squinting into the blackness, he searched for the other members of his team. He could see the outlines of three others. All of them were very still, possibly drugged. None were big enough to be Hack. Maybe their captors were keeping the wounded man somewhere else. There was another possibility, but Dane couldn't bear to consider it.

Gradually his eyes adjusted to the scant light, and he was able to tell that the man closest to him was the ATF agent. He assumed the other two were Steamer and Doc, but it was too dark to be sure.

The heat and humidity combined to make the confined space stifling. His clothes were soaked with sweat, and he was thirsty. There was no way to tell if it was still night or if it was the next day. And he had absolutely no plan for escape.

He wanted to blame the ATF agent for the mess they were in, but he knew the fault lay with him. He had overlooked one contingency. Extreme valor.

# CHAPTER NINE

BROOKE SPENT A RESTLESS NIGHT tossing and turning. Every time she woke up, she leaned over the edge of the bed to see if Hunter was still there. He always was.

Each time his eyes had regarded her solemnly as he said, "Go to sleep."

Each time she had smiled and tried to follow his advice. But she couldn't relax. When the Joined Forces dinner was over, Hunter wouldn't have to stay with her. She couldn't bear the thought of losing him, but she couldn't think of a way to convince him to stay.

Finally, just as the sky outside her window was getting lighter, an idea came to her. Then, with a smile on her face, she fell into a deep sleep. She woke up two hours later with Hunter shaking her shoulders. When she opened her bleary eyes, his face was hovering close.

"You sleep like the dead," he whispered.

She noted the dark circles under his eyes. "And you don't sleep at all."

He stepped back. "I made breakfast."

She pushed herself into a sitting position, clutching the top of her flannel Christmas pajamas together. "I have something important to discuss with you. Can we shower first?"

He shook his head. "Breakfast first, shower later."

Since she wanted him to be in a good mood when she made her proposal, she didn't argue. She followed him into the kitchen and saw that he'd made pancakes, along with sausage for him and strawberries for her.

"You really know how to spoil a girl," she told him. "I could get used to this."

"Don't."

"Yeah, yeah." She kept eating.

Once they were through with breakfast and the kitchen was clean, she took him by the hand. "It's time for that shower now."

With resignation and a little trepidation, he followed her into the bathroom. They went through the now-routine process of steaming up the small space. Then she pulled him close, put her mouth to his ear, and whispered, "I came up with an idea during the night while I was thinking about you instead of sleeping."

He ignored her romantic overture. "What kind of idea?"

"Well, there's nothing I can do about the times I have been dishonest in the past," she began. "And at first I thought that meant things were hopeless between us because you could never trust me again."

He nodded.

She frowned. "You weren't supposed to agree with me. Can't you try to be more positive?"

"Can't you hurry? It's getting hot in here." He pulled at the collar of his shirt. "And your hair is growing by the second."

She reached up and ran her hand across her frizzing hair. "You like it curly, remember?"

"It's way past curly," he said. "But forget about your hair. What are you trying to tell me?"

"You can't trust me because I have lied to you in the past."

He nodded warily.

"You're thinking of trust as something that's earned, but it's not always. Sometimes you instantly trust someone you've just met, like a doctor."

"I guess," he said grudgingly.

"And I haven't told a single lie to you in the future."

He narrowed his eyes. "That doesn't make sense."

"I want you to give me the benefit of the doubt, like you would if we'd just met and I was a brain surgeon."

"Brooke . . ."

"Okay, just pretend we're meeting for the first time." She stuck out her hand. "Hello, my name is Brooke, and I promise I'll never lie to you from this moment forward."

He looked at her hand but didn't take it.

"Please, Hunter, give me a second chance."

"I think you want to keep your word, but I'm not sure you can. Exaggerations and little white lies come naturally. You might not be able to stop."

"There's only one way to find out," she pressed. "Put my vow of honesty to the test. If I lie to you again, I'll prove that I can't be trusted. But if I don't lie to you ever again, then you have to trust me."

"It's not that simple."

"It's exactly that simple," she disagreed. "I'm not asking you to think of me as your wife—"

"I don't," he assured her.

She pretended not to hear this disheartening remark. "Or even as a friend. Just think of me as someone you can trust, like a brain surgeon."

He considered this for a second. "You promise that you'll never lie to me again? Not to spare my feelings, not to spare someone else's feelings, not for any reason?"

"I promise," she told him solemnly. "Not even to spare your life—or mine."

He clasped her outstretched hand in his. "Then I accept your challenge. Now let's get out of this bathroom before we mildew."

\* \* \*

Brooke followed Hunter into the living room feeling hopeful and almost happy. Hunter had accepted her challenge. She was determined to keep her word. Maybe things would work out for them after all.

"We've got a little time before we have to go to the call center," she said. "Maybe we can work on the piano?"

He nodded and picked up the roll of steel wool.

Brooke had just put on her gloves when Hunter's phone started ringing. He glanced at the screen. "It's Rex."

"I forgot to tell him I lost my phone," she said, mindful of the cameras.

Hunter scowled and handed her the phone.

She put it up to her ear. "Hello?"

Rex's strident voice came through the speaker. "Why aren't you answering your phone?"

"I can't find it," she replied. "It might be at my mom's house."

"And why wasn't your boyfriend answering *his* phone?"

"We were in the shower."

"Again?"

"We take a lot of showers." She looked over at Hunter and mouthed, *Sorry.*

He sighed in exasperation.

"According to Millicent's schedule, we aren't supposed to be there until nine this morning," she added in their defense.

"Well we might as well throw the schedule out the window!" Rex replied with a hint of desperation. "Millicent broke her ankle! She's at the hospital getting a cast put on, and it's pandemonium around here! We've got flowers being delivered, and the caterer is trying to set up. And *Today* has a camera crew here to do an interview. I can't concern myself with the minutiae, so I need you to come now."

Brooke was not surprised by his dictatorial tone or that he seemed more concerned about the dinner preparations and his *Today* interview than he was about his personnel/public relations director. "I hope Millicent's going to be okay."

"She'll be fine," Rex dismissed this. "How fast can you get here?"

"I don't have any experience as a party planner," she tried. "I wouldn't know where to start."

"Millicent has all kinds of notes, and if you can't figure things out, you can call her. If I don't get things under control, Mr. Carmichael will cancel the auction."

She glanced at Hunter, and he shrugged. "We're on our way," she told Rex.

"Hurry before this situation becomes unrecoverable."

Once they were in the hall, away from prying ears and eyes, Hunter said, "I hate the way he bosses you around."

"After tonight it will all be over."

Hunter punched the elevator button. "I wish I felt more confident about that. Rex is like a bad penny—he seems to keep turning up."

* * *

When they walked into the call center, Rex was waiting impatiently. "You really should be more responsible," he said in lieu of a greeting. "You're not a teenager anymore. You have to keep up with your phone."

Typical Rex. He needed her help, but instead of being nice he was giving her grief.

"People lose their phones all the time," she replied. "Losing a phone is not a sign of irresponsibility or immaturity."

"Well I'm tired of trying to call you and not getting an answer." Apparently he planned to take out his frustrations on Brooke since Millicent wasn't there.

"I can't help it that Hunter constantly wants to take showers. He's obsessed with cleanliness."

Rex scowled. "You can take as many showers as you want, just keep your phone nearby in case of an emergency—like today. And your hair looks horrible again."

She put a hand to her head. "Steam from the shower—again."

Rex looked pained. "Try to stay off camera during the *Today* segment."

"That's a promise," she assured him. "Now tell me what's going on here."

Rex shuddered. "I can't bear to talk about it. Call Millicent, and she can tell you which of the many things going wrong should take priority."

He recited Millicent's number, and Hunter handed Brooke his phone. Millicent was only marginally less panicked than Rex, but at least she had a plan. By the time the call ended, Brooke had an idea of where to begin.

"What did she say?" Rex asked.

"She wants all the flowers in your office with the air conditioner turned up as high as it will go," Brooke replied. "Then she wants me to reassure the caterer and get him anything he needs for tonight."

Rex nodded, looking more relaxed already. "What about him?" he pointed to Hunter. "I've got some touch-up painting he could do."

"I'm staying with Brooke," Hunter said firmly. "Every step she takes, I take. She won't be out of my sight for a second."

Rex smirked. "Sounds like a waste of manpower, but whatever. Now I'll go call Mr. Carmichael and tell him everything is under control."

"That might be a little premature since I haven't actually done anything yet," Brooke murmured.

"I have confidence," Rex claimed. Then he walked into his office.

\* \* \*

The old church was a bevy of disorganized activity. Brooke stared around at the chaos with a feeling of despair. She wasn't sure anyone could pull this together in time for the dinner.

Hunter leaned down and whispered, "I don't mind so much that you blamed our frequent showers on me, but why did you have to say I have an obsession with cleanliness? Couldn't you have come up with a better excuse?"

She frowned at him. "What excuse would you have preferred?"

"I don't know. Maybe something like I have asthma, and the steam helps me breathe better?"

"I wish I'd thought of it. But cleanliness is nothing to be ashamed of."

"Neither is asthma," he muttered. "An obsession with cleanliness makes me seem whimpy."

Brooke was trying to think of a clever response when she saw her reflection in the glass of the call center's new entrance doors. Her long hair seemed to have doubled in volume thanks to their pretend shower that morning. She knew a brush would be of no use, so she twisted the whole frizzy mess into a bun at the back of her head. At least that way it was less visible.

When Brooke and Hunter walked into Rex's office carrying boxes filled with flowers, he raised his eyebrows. "So you've switched from Fuzzy-Wuzzy to schoolmarm?"

"This is my 'Civil War–era' look," she replied with a warm glance at Hunter. "And by the way, Hunter has asthma."

Rex looked perplexed, and Hunter sighed.

"Now, if you'll excuse me, I've got to try and pull this party back together."

With Millicent directing Brooke over the phone and Hunter doing double duty as bodyguard and her assistant, she managed to save the flowers from wilting, keep the caterer from quitting, and generally organize the chaos. And she was able to do it without getting her frizzy hair caught on national television.

Rex was too busy with his *Today* cameo to bother them, which helped.

Finally Brooke stood at the podium that had refused to budge and surveyed the large room. There was a long table right in front of the podium for what Rex called "dignitaries." Obviously he was using the term loosely since tonight that would include a known criminal and Rex himself.

The room was filled with almost a hundred round tables covered with floor-length green or blue tablecloths. In the center of each table was a white vase that would eventually contain a flower arrangement. The Joined Forces logo was strategically displayed in several places around the room, covering holes and exposed wires. Rented place settings of china and crystal stemware gleamed under the room's newly installed recessed lighting. Potted trees were arranged along the perimeter, making the room seem warmer. It looked beautiful.

Hunter's phone rang, and Brooke looked down to see Millicent's name on the screen. "I was just thinking about you," Brooke told her.

"How does it look?"

"Pretty good," Brooke replied. "It will look better once you get here and arrange the flowers."

"Send me some pictures," Millicent requested. "I should be there in an hour. I'm just waiting for the emergency room doctor to release me."

"I'll see you when you get here." She had just finished sending a few pictures to Millicent when Rex rushed in.

"The room looks great!" This qualified as effusive for Rex, so she assumed that his *Today* interview went well.

But Brooke didn't want his praise or his approval. "Tell Millicent. She deserves the credit."

Rex nodded absently. It seemed that the girl was both out of his sight and his mind. "Mr. Carmichael is very pleased that you saved the day. In fact, he's invited you and the corporal to sit at the head table with us at dinner tonight."

Brooke felt Hunter stiffen, but this was not the right moment to tell Rex they wouldn't be attending. She wanted to wait until Millicent arrived, knowing Rex would object less strenuously if he had someone to manage any unforeseen difficulty. So she just said, "That's an honor."

Hunter scowled.

Rex gave her a superior smile. "I just hope you have time to do something about that hair before the dinner."

\* \* \*

Millicent arrived an hour later hobbling on crutches and holding a Taco Bell sack. "I brought lunch! And I ordered yours vegetarian," she told Brooke.

"That was very thoughtful of you." Brooke was genuinely touched. "Thanks."

When they were finished eating, Brooke and Hunter carried their wrappers to the garbage can. "We need to make our excuses and get out of here pretty soon," Hunter murmured.

"I want to wait until the last minute when everything is busy and Rex won't have the time to argue." She frowned. "Well, he won't have *as much* time to argue."

Hunter nodded, and they walked to the podium, where Millicent was standing with her crutches.

"Let's get started on the flower arrangements," she said.

Brooke and Hunter walked to Rex's office and knocked on the door.

"Come in!" he called.

Hunter turned the knob and shoved.

"We're here to get flowers," Brooke told him.

He nodded, and they both picked up a box.

"I'm about to gather some workers to bring coins up from downstairs. I'd ask you to help, Corporal, but that broken arm might make you clumsy, and some of these coins are worth thousands." Rex acted as if he had just denied Hunter a great opportunity.

"I understand," Hunter said.

Brooke would have been amused if she hadn't been so worried that Rex was going to walk into the storage room and realize that the coin boxes had been tampered with. She led the way back into the chapel with her heart in her throat.

Millicent demonstrated how she wanted the flowers arranged in the vases, but Brooke found it hard to concentrate. Her attention was focused on the stairs. At any second Rex might come charging up, spewing accusations.

But when he climbed the stairs, he was just holding a few of the thin black boxes she was now quite familiar with. Several volunteers were behind him carrying similar loads. He arranged the boxes on the two long tables near the podium. And Brooke was able to breathe freely again.

"Now that the coins are out in the open, they have to be under guard at all times," Rex said as a security guard walked over and took up a position beside the table.

Brooke nodded, thinking about all the boxes still downstairs, the ones Rex never intended to be auctioned openly.

Then the caterer came rushing up, distraught because the icemaker wasn't working.

"Can you check on that?" Millicent asked.

With Hunter shadowing her step for step, Brooke went to see what they could do to solve this problem. The caterer was set up in what would eventually become the telemarketing room, and it didn't take them long to determine that the icemaker, rented for the evening, could not be repaired within their limited time frame. So Brooke called an ice delivery company and arranged for fifty ten-pound bags to be sent over immediately. Then, feeling competent, she reported back to Millicent.

The young woman thanked them for helping avert an ice crisis, and they all started arranging flowers. But it quickly became apparent that their flower skills were not up to Millicent's standards.

"This is not going to work," she said, eyeing several tables. "After you put the flowers in the vases, bring them to me. I'll arrange them, and then you can put them on the tables."

This process improved the quality of the arrangements, but it was time-consuming. As they finished the last vase, the band was already warming up. Brooke was pleased when she did the math and realized she wasn't going to have to make up any kind of an excuse to avoid dinner. They had simply run out of time and wouldn't be able to change before the event was scheduled to begin.

Rex walked over and saw her smile. "What's so funny?" he asked.

"Nothing," she rearranged her expression to fit the situation. "In fact, we have a problem."

His eyes narrowed. "What kind of problem?"

"The dinner starts in thirty minutes," she pointed out. "That doesn't give Hunter and me enough time to get home and change. I hate to miss it, but—"

"You're not going to miss it," Rex interrupted. "Your apartment's only ten minutes away. You have plenty of time to get home and put on a dress."

"I'm a mess!" She lifted a frizzy lock of hair for emphasis. "It will take more than ten minutes to make me presentable."

Rex pursed his lips. "I'll delay the dinner a few extra minutes to give you time for that hair, but get back here as fast as you can."

It wasn't exactly what she had hoped he'd say, but it was enough. Once they made their escape, any excuse would do—a flat tire, a headache, or a wardrobe malfunction. She could have used twisted ankle if Millicent hadn't already taken that one. But making up a good lie was the least of her worries. Grabbing Hunter's hand, she pulled him toward the door and freedom.

Rex was watching her, and his eyes had a knowing look—as if he could read her mind. "Just a second." He reached into his wallet and removed two small photographs. He handed them to Brooke. "Be back here in forty-five minutes or these will be on the ten o'clock news." His voice was soft and menacing.

Reluctantly she looked down at the pictures. They were poor quality, probably taken by security cameras. One was of Brooke walking into the hospital in New York, obviously pregnant. And the other was of her walking out after delivering the baby. He'd known all along. She dragged her eyes up to meet Rex's gaze.

"Forty-five minutes," he repeated.

She nodded mutely, feeling foolish. How had she allowed herself to forget that Rex was evil and not just a self-absorbed buffoon?

"We'll be back," she said. She had no choice. Then she started walking toward the door, confident that Hunter would follow.

She made it to the car before she started crying. Hunter opened the door for her but didn't ask any questions, so she knew he'd seen the pictures. They drove the short distance in silence.

As they walked to her apartment building, Brooke wiped her eyes so the protesters wouldn't see her tears.

Once they were in the lobby, Hunter said, "So Rex knows about the baby?"

"Yes."

"At least he didn't make any threats about challenging the adoption."

"He didn't have to make threats; they were implied."

Hunter punched the elevator button. "Eventually you're going to have to stand up to him."

She nodded. "But not tonight."

"We gave your uncle our word of honor that we wouldn't attend that dinner."

She turned and looked up at him. "I have to go, but you don't. You can save what's left of your honor."

"The only thing less honorable than breaking my word would be to let you go back to that dinner alone."

Tears threatened again. "I'm sorry, Hunter."

"It's okay." They were silent for a few seconds, and then he added, "I don't understand why Rex is so determined for you to be at the dinner tonight."

"I guess he just wants to show me who's in charge or torture me," she said. "And he's accomplishing both—for now."

* * *

Hunter paused by her door. "Before we go inside, we need to let Detective Napier know that we're going to be at the dinner after all. It might make a difference in how the FBI handles things."

She nodded. "You'll have to make the call. I don't have a phone."

Hunter dialed the number and explained that they would be attending the dinner despite the fact that her uncle had forbidden it.

"Rex is basically blackmailing Brooke," Hunter said. "I won't go into the details, but she feels she has no choice."

"I see," the detective replied gravely.

"We'll be sitting at the head table with Carmichael and Moreland and the governor," Hunter added.

"Thanks for letting me know. I'll pass this information on to the FBI. And you two be careful in there. We expect everything to go smoothly, but you'll need to be vigilant just in case something goes wrong."

Hunter said, "I understand."

"And I'll be there if you need me."

"Thank you, sir." Hunter put away his phone, and they hurried into her apartment.

"Do you need to take a shower?" Hunter asked, looking at her hair.

"No time for that," she said. "I'll just get my hair wet and blow-dry it."

"You change in the bathroom then, since you'll need water." He handed her the lovely gray dress. "I'll use your room."

She got her things and walked into the bathroom. After one last longing glance toward Hunter, she closed the door.

\* \* \*

Brooke's hair was more manageable after it had been dampened and dried. It was still curlier than usual, but she wouldn't be confused with a poodle. She repaired her makeup and put on the dress, zipping it as far as she could. Finally she slipped on the shoes and faced herself in the small mirror.

The dress and the shoes were perfect. Her hair was adequate. She had hoped to bedazzle Hunter; now she just hoped she wouldn't embarrass him.

Hunter was standing in the living room dressed in full military regalia. He was breathtaking, and that, combined with her tight skirt and high heels, caused her to trip over her own feet.

He stepped forward and put out a hand to steady her. The fabric of his dress uniform was stiff—much like his posture. But through the cloth, the warmth of his arm was familiar and comforting.

"You might not want to let go of me as long as I'm wearing these shoes because if you do, there's a good chance I'll break my neck."

He frowned. "Do you think you should change them?"

"They match my dress!"

He sighed as he zipped her dress the rest of the way. Then he secured her hand against his arm, and they walked as quickly as her high heels would allow toward the door.

On the way to his car, Brooke whispered, "I feel like we're celebrities."

"Going to a dinner where we might get shot."

She smiled. "But we sure look cute!"

He sighed again.

\* \* \*

The sidewalk at the call center was cordoned off with yellow rope. On the other side was a group that consisted of Nature Fresh protesters, members of the press, and curios onlookers. Brooke kept her eyes down and held on tightly to Hunter's good arm until they reached the front door.

Brooke was surprised to see Rex, resplendent in a black tux, standing by the door to greet his guests. A well-dressed man with perfectly coifed white hair and beady dark eyes was there as well.

Rex whistled at Brooke. "I didn't think you'd be able to get that hair under control, but you did!"

"Are you going to introduce me to this lovely lady?" the beady-eyed man asked.

"Lyle Carmichael, meet Brooke Clayton." Then he turned to Hunter. "And this is her bodyguard, Corporal Ezell. But I see he's forgotten his sword."

"Mr. Carmichael," Brooke murmured politely.

The man took her hand and gave her an old-fashioned little bow. "I understand we have you to thank for stepping in and making this dinner happen after Millicent's injury."

It took every ounce of self-control she possessed to keep from yanking her hand away. "I didn't do much of anything," she demurred.

"Beautiful and modest," Mr. Carmichael praised her. "A winning combination."

Hunter followed Brooke inside, but Rex held up his hand when Hack's bodyguards tried to enter. "No one is allowed unless they have a ticket."

Hunter reached for his wallet. "I'll buy them one."

Rex smirked. "Too late, Corporal. At elegant events like this, we don't sell tickets at the door."

Hunter let his hand fall to his side.

"Lock the doors, Rex," Lyle Carmichael said. Then he turned back to Brooke. "Allow me to escort you inside. I believe we're to be seated right next to each other."

As the man pulled her toward the old chapel, Brooke looked over her shoulder at Hunter. After another moment of indecision, Hunter finally left Hack's men at the door and trailed behind Brooke and Carmichael.

The newly remodeled room looked better in the dim light. The tablecloths and the flowers were perfect, creating the elegant atmosphere that Millicent had hoped for. And the room was filled to capacity with paying guests.

Carmichael led Brooke to the table at the front where Mr. Shaw and Millicent were talking with the governor. Millicent introduced the newcomers to the governor. Brooke and the DA exchanged wary nods.

Millicent was pale, and there were dark circles under her eyes. Brooke was sure the doctor had instructed her to rest her injured foot, but instead she was entertaining the dignitaries for Rex—no doubt hoping for praise she wouldn't get. Her dress was reminiscent of a 1920s flapper outfit. The metallic fabric seemed almost fluid as it rippled along her tiny frame. Under other circumstances she would have looked cute, at least. But exhaustion, the cast on her foot, and the crutches had reduced the effect.

As Mr. Carmichael had mentioned earlier, Brooke's name card was right beside his at the table. Thankfully, Hunter was on her other side.

Rex moved to the podium and welcomed all the guests. Then he asked everyone to be seated so the dinner service could begin. The band began playing, soothing old ballads that reminded Brooke of the music from the Civil War resort. A salad was served, followed closely by a variety of rolls. Instead of sitting at the table, Rex moved around the room, speaking to people and acting charming—all, Brooke had no doubt, just to increase the bottom line.

Meanwhile back at the head table, Brooke quickly found that Carmichael was an unpleasant dinner companion. He was loud and pompous and had a tendency to talk with his mouth full. And he flirted outrageously with Brooke throughout the meal. Finally she'd had enough and told him she was married.

"Married?" he repeated.

She reached over and took Hunter's hand in hers. "We're newlyweds, actually."

Carmichael frowned. "Well, I'm sure Rex never mentioned that."

"It probably slipped his mind," Brooke predicted. "You know Rex, if it doesn't involve money, he can't remember it for long."

Carmichael gave her a grudging smile. "That sounds like Rex all right."

For the next few minutes, Carmichael carried on a conversation with Mr. Shaw. Then he stood and said, "If you'll excuse me, I think I'll go sit next to that lovely creature at the other side of the table. Hopefully *she's* not married."

Brooke was happy to see him go. A few minutes later, Rex noticed Carmichael's empty seat. He asked Brooke what happened.

"He preferred to sit by a beautiful single girl instead of an old married woman," she told him.

Rex narrowed his eyes at Brooke. "I thought that was a secret."

"It is," she replied. "I only reveal it to protect myself from legal prosecution and from lecherous old men."

Rex glanced across the table, and his eyes widened. "That's the governor's daughter!"

Brooke pressed a finger to her lips. "Well, you'd better keep an eye on them then."

The woman next to Hunter was a talker and didn't seem to mind that he was making no comments. Brooke's vegetarian plate looked good, but she was too nervous to eat. She noticed that Hunter didn't eat much either. Dessert was a variety of cheesecakes. Brooke chose praline and pretended to eat it until the catering staff cleared all the dishes away.

Then Rex returned to the podium and announced that the auction was about to begin. "But first we're going to hear a few words from our governor."

The governor started toward the podium, waving vigorously at all the potential voters. On his way back to his seat, Rex stopped behind Brooke's chair and slid it away from the table. Leaning down he whispered, "Come downstairs for a minute. I need to talk to you."

Brooke shook her head. "I can't . . ."

But Rex already had a hand at her elbow and was pulling her up.

The governor had reached the microphone and began his speech with a weak joke. The crowd laughed politely. Then he noticed Rex and Brooke standing by the head table. He gave them a questioning look.

Rex smiled. "Excuse us, Governor." Then he tightened his grip on Brooke's arm and propelled her toward the stairs. To avoid making a bigger scene, she didn't resist.

Hunter stood and followed them, looking furious.

Brooke could hear the governor launch into another ill-advised joke as they walked down the stairs.

"I'm sorry to take you away from the governor's speech," Rex said once they reached the lower level. "I know how you love that stuff." He was smiling, obviously pleased that he had gotten his way.

"I hate political speeches, but I also hate being rude. Why couldn't we wait until after the auction to talk?" Brooke demanded.

He looked over at Hunter and then moved a few steps away. "Because I wanted to apologize. I feel terrible about those pictures."

Rex never apologized, so she was instantly on her guard. "Why did you take them?"

"I didn't take them," Rex nearly scoffed. "Mr. Carmichael insisted on doing a thorough background check on all Joined Forces members before he would join. Those pictures turned up while they were gathering stuff on you. Imagine my surprise when I did the math and realized that we had something *special* together."

"We don't have anything together, Rex. A family adopted the baby. It's theirs, not ours."

"The last thing I want is responsibility for a kid, so you don't have to worry about those pictures."

"Then why did you show them to me?"

"I wanted you to know that you couldn't keep secrets," he said. "Not for long, anyway. And I wanted you here tonight. You'd promised, and you were trying to back out."

"You didn't need me here."

"I did. I needed a beautiful woman to entertain Mr. Carmichael."

Brooke couldn't relax yet. It would be like Rex to lull her into a sense of security and then go in for the kill. "Too bad you didn't know the governor's daughter was so attractive."

He grinned. "So you accept my apology?"

Anxious to end the unpleasant chat, she nodded. "Now can we go back to the dinner?"

"We can't interrupt the governor's speech again!" Rex pretended to be horrified by this thought. "While we're waiting, let me show you the rest of the coins." He unlocked the storage room door.

She tried to hold back, but he pulled her inside. The cluttered storage room was now crowded. People were lined up at every table, and there were guards, some with visible weapons, standing along the perimeter walls. Brooke was beginning to be seriously afraid when she felt Hunter move into place beside her. It was still a dangerous situation, but at least she wasn't alone.

"What's going on down here?" Brooke asked as if she didn't know.

"We're having a little private sale for serious coin collectors," Rex replied. Then he turned to the potential customers standing closest to him. "Welcome, folks! I hope you're finding something you like!"

He led her to a table in the back and showed her a couple of rare coins from Spain that were made near the time Columbus came to the Americas. Brooke had no interest in the coins—especially since she knew some of them were stolen—and she didn't like being in the confined space.

"I'm starting to feel claustrophobic. Can we go back upstairs?"

Rex checked his watch. "The governor still has several awful jokes to go."

"So how much longer . . . ?" she began. Then there was a disturbance at the door. They turned to see men wearing FBI vests rush into the storage room.

"Nobody move!" the lead man commanded.

But everyone did. The coin sellers grabbed their wares and rushed to stow them out of harm's way. The customers turned and ran for the exit. Someone hit the light switch, plunging the room into total darkness. Hunter pushed Brooke against the back wall. He absorbed most of the impact as they were buffeted repeatedly by frightened occupants of the storage room.

Then the lights came back on, and Brooke looked for Rex, but he was nowhere in sight.

"All coin dealers stay where you are," the FBI agent announced. "The rest of you may go into the next room where agents are waiting to get your names and other information."

"It doesn't look good that we're down here," Hunter whispered.

"I wonder if that's the way Rex had it planned."

"You think he knew the FBI was coming?"

She shrugged. "The timing seems a little too perfect."

People moved around the agents by the door, ebbing and flowing as they passed out of the storage room and into the kitchen area. Hunter and Brooke followed the crowd toward the exit. They were waiting their turn to talk to an agent when gunfire erupted in the storage room.

"Upstairs fast!" Hunter shouted into her ear.

More shots were fired, and Brooke joined the mass of humanity at the stairs. The FBI agents who had been asking questions in the kitchen were now fighting their way through the crowds, trying to get into the storage room.

Finally she made it to the stairs and climbed them on all fours. She had lost sight of Hunter and couldn't turn her head enough to search for him. Once they reached the landing, the people who had been pressed so tightly against her dispersed suddenly, and she almost fell. Righting herself, Brooke clung to the wall and looked around. The banquet hall was the picture of pandemonium.

People were screaming and running, knocking over chairs and each other in their desperation to get out. The overhead lights were off, but light coming in from the perimeter doors provided enough illumination for Brooke to see the carnage. Uniformed policemen were trying to restore calm, but the genteel coin purchasers had become a self-serving mob.

Brooke searched the teeming throng for Hunter. Was he still downstairs? Had he been pushed outside? She was losing hope when he emerged from the stairwell and hurled himself toward her. She clung to him, happy to be reunited.

Hunter said, "Eventually the FBI will restore order, but it's going to take a while for the exits to clear. And I don't want us to be too close to the stairwell in case the shooters decide to use it as an escape route."

Brooke looked around. "Where can we go?"

Hunter frowned. "Let's try to make it up to the podium. We should be out of harm's way there."

More gunshots echoed from downstairs. "We need to move now!" He took her hand, and they started running.

Another volley of shots was fired as she lunged behind the podium, bruising her elbow and ripping her dress in the process. Hunter knelt down beside her, and his body became her shield.

Gunfire reverberated through the large room, and Brooke saw that the shooters were coming upstairs now. The people who had been bottlenecked at the exits were finally able to surge through. Brooke looked longingly at the now-cleared doors. But with the gunmen upstairs, they couldn't risk crossing the open floor. They would have to cower behind the podium until the shooters were apprehended. Brooke heard the wail of sirens and took comfort in the knowledge that more help was on the way.

The policemen at the doors who had helped the guests exit turned their attention to the gunmen. Soon Brooke and Hunter were right in the middle of the cross fire. Brooke felt the impact of the bullets on the other side of the podium. She pulled Hunter tight. If she was going to die, she wanted to be in his arms.

As the shooting intensified, the noise became deafening. Brooke had accepted that there was no way they were going to leave the room alive. Then she heard someone calling her name.

At first she was afraid it was a heavenly messenger sent to guide her toward the light. But the voice wasn't soft and sweet like an angel should sound. It was strident and a little nasally. "Brooke!" This time the voice was closer, and something poked her on the foot. Did angels poke? She didn't think so.

Brooke opened her eyes and saw Millicent, still wearing her metallic dress, crouching in the choir-robe closet. She was jabbing Brooke's foot with a crutch.

"Millicent?"

"Will you two come on?" she looked aggrieved. "You're going to get killed out there!"

Brooke nudged Hunter and pointed toward the closet. His eyes widened when he saw the girl, and Brooke could tell by the way his body stiffened that he didn't want to trust her.

"If we stay here, we'll die," Brooke said. "Millicent is our only chance."

Hunter nodded with obvious reluctance. He put his good arm around Brooke, and together they lunged away from the relative safety of the podium and into the closet. Millicent slammed the door shut behind them and locked it from inside. Then they scooted to the far back wall behind the row of choir robes. It was so dark Brooke couldn't see her hand in front of her face.

Hunter turned on the flashlight feature on his phone, creating a little circle of light. The noise from the banquet room was muffled by the thick wooden door. For the moment they were safe.

"Thanks," Brooke whispered.

Millicent nodded wearily.

"Does your ankle hurt?"

She nodded again.

Brooke tried, "Do you know where Rex is?"

"He's gone," she said. "He left me behind." She closed her eyes, and tears slipped onto her cheeks.

Brooke understood how painful the end of a relationship could be. She knew the pain would ease with time and that Rex wasn't worth a single tear. But she also knew that telling Millicent those things now would not help. So Brooke just put her arm around Millicent's shoulder and let her cry.

\* \* \*

As suddenly as the shooting had begun, it ended.

"Is it safe to go out now?" Brooke whispered.

"Let's wait a few more minutes to be sure," Hunter urged.

At the prospect of leaving the closet, Millicent dried her tears on her forearm and sat up a little straighter. Brooke moved a few inches away, allowing the girl some dignity.

Hunter leaned close to Brooke and said, "I'm going to assess the situation. Wait here." Then he turned and crawled toward the door.

Brooke followed right behind him.

When he realized she hadn't obeyed his order, he gave her a cross look.

She shrugged. "You're supposed to be at my side constantly. I'm just trying to help you out."

He unlocked the door and pushed it open a crack. Brooke clung to the fabric of his uniform coat as they peeked into the banquet room. The overhead lights were still off, and smoke from the gunfire further hampered visibility. But through the gloom, she could make out a few policemen milling around. Paramedics were rushing all over the large room, treating and transporting the wounded.

A group of people emerged from the lower level, and Hunter tensed. But it was several FBI agents leading a group of handcuffed people. As they passed the closet, Brooke scanned each face, searching for Rex, but she didn't see him. Carmichael was at the end of the line, looking furious.

"So what do you think?" she whispered to Hunter after the FBI agents led their prisoners out of the room. "Can we leave this closet?"

"I think it's safe to get out, but let me go first," he replied. "The policemen are going to be a little jumpy after that shootout, and if we startle them, we might get shot."

"That would be my luck," she muttered.

Hunter opened the door and stepped out into the banquet room. A nearby police officer walked over and asked to see his ID. As Hunter took out his wallet, he told the officer that there were two women in the closet as well.

"I wanted to be sure it was safe before they got out."

The officer checked his driver's license with a flashlight and then stuck his head into the closet. "Come on out, ladies."

Brooke helped Millicent get the crutches balanced under her arms then led her out of the closet. Millicent gave the officer her driver's license, and he checked it as well. When he turned to Brooke, she shook her head.

"I don't have any ID. I had a little purse when I got here tonight, but I don't know where it is now. My name is Brooke Clayton, and Detective Napier can vouch for me."

The officer shone his light in her face. "You're Miss Clayton? The detective's been looking everywhere for you. He'll be very relieved that you're okay." He pulled a radio from his belt and held it up to his mouth. Amid the static and police jargon, she heard him give Detective Napier their location.

While they waited for the detective, Brooke examined the damage to her dress. The skirt was ripped almost to her hip, and she held it closed with her hand. She looked at the bullet holes in the podium and realized that if it hadn't been filled with concrete, she and Hunter might be dead. Then she looked at the closet. And if it hadn't been for Millicent, they might still be dead.

Her teeth started chattering. Hunter took off his uniform jacket and draped it over her shoulders. She let go of her skirt and slipped her arms into the warm sleeves.

"I feel kind of woozy," she told him.

"Hang in there," he said. "This will all be over soon."

Detective Napier rushed up at that point and told them they were going to have to come to the police station for questioning.

"We didn't see much," Brooke said. "We were hiding for our lives."

"We're questioning everyone," he said. "And you might be surprised what you remember. Follow me. I'll drive you personally."

Outside they saw Mr. Shaw in front of the call center, holding what looked like an impromptu press conference. All the reporters and camera crews that had come to cover the auction were now covering the FBI shootout with coin thieves.

Detective Napier whispered, "He's claiming to be part of the sting."

Brooke was offended. "Can't you stop him from telling lies to the press?"

The detective raised an eyebrow. "Are you serious?"

"Well then, arrest him," Hunter suggested.

"Unfortunately I can't do that either." The detective sounded discouraged. "He didn't buy any stolen coins."

* * *

The paramedics insisted that because of her earlier injury Millicent take an ambulance to the hospital to be checked out. Brooke and Hunter rode in Detective Napier's unmarked car to the police station. While he drove he explained the scope of the disaster. Two people had been killed during all the shooting, both employees of Lyle Carmichael, and as many as a hundred people were wounded.

"And it's a miracle it wasn't much worse," the detective added.

"How did that happen?" Hunter asked. "I thought it was supposed to be simple. Just a surprise raid to arrest the illegal coin guys. No shooting, no injuries."

"It was not the FBI's finest hour. You know how it goes sometimes, Corporal. Even the best laid plans can fall apart unexpectedly."

Hunter nodded. "Another thing I know is that Major Dane is going to kill me when he finds out I let Brooke go to Rex's 'Dinner and a Shootout.'"

"You didn't let me do anything," she replied with impatience born of shock. "*I* went to the dinner. You just came along to protect me. And we had no idea there would be a shootout. Besides, we're fine."

"Major Dane will probably be unhappy," the detective agreed with Hunter. "Refer him to me, Corporal, and I'll do the best I can to get you out of trouble."

"Thanks," Hunter said. "But I'll make my own explanations."

When they arrived at the police station, Brooke was sorry to see that a group of spectators had gathered there. They pushed their way inside, and Detective Napier put them in a small interrogation room.

"Get comfortable," he said, pointing to a pair of metal folding chairs. "This could take a while."

Unsteady on the high heels and still feeling a little dizzy, Brooke sat down and snuggled into Hunter's coat. He paced around the room, unable to relax.

She had dozed off by the time Detective Napier returned. "Well, good news, folks. You're free to go for now. You may have to come in later and give a deposition. I'll let you know." The detective handed Brooke her purse.

"Thanks. Did you find Rex?" Brooke asked.

"No. Mr. Moreland seems to have disappeared into thin air."

"At least the FBI got Carmichael," Brooke said.

"Oh yes," the detective agreed. "Maybe the arrest of a crime boss will overshadow the bloodbath that preceded it. And speaking of arrests, Mr. Van Wagoner has retracted his request for a reinvestigation of the Nature Fresh fire. Apparently it's better for him insurance-wise just to leave it alone. So you don't have to worry about any charges being filed. Things worked out for you this time, Miss Clayton, but I strongly advise you to keep your nose clean in the future."

"Yes, sir, I will," she promised.

"So what are you kids going to do now?"

Brooke gave Hunter a warm look. "We're going home."

The detective grinned. "Come on. I'll drive you myself."

"That's really not necessary," Hunter told him. "My car is at the call center if you'll just drop us back off there."

The detective shook his head. "That place is a madhouse, and you'll get yourself in more trouble with Major Dane if you take Miss Clayton back there. I'll take you to her apartment now and have someone bring your car later when things have calmed down."

So they climbed into a police car for the second time that night, but this time they were headed home.

*　*　*

When they arrived at Brooke's apartment, the guard at the door informed them that it had been cleared of all surveillance devices.

"Courtesy of the Nashville PD," the detective told them. "No more cameras. You have your privacy back."

Brooke murmured close to Hunter's ear, "I guess that means your asthma is cured."

He gave her one little nod and then walked through the apartment with the detective to confirm that they were alone.

When the men circled back to the living room, Brooke said, "So I'm all safe and sound?"

"Yes," Detective Napier replied. "I've advised Corporal Ezell to keep the guard at your door and the one downstairs until Major Dane gets back. Even though Carmichael is in jail, Rex Moreland is still at large. So I'd suggest that you lay low for the next few weeks. Maybe you could go to Virginia for a nice long visit with your uncle."

"I can't be gone for *weeks*. I'm about to start my last semester at Vanderbilt," she told him.

"Maybe you could take online classes to finish school?"

"It's hard to take piano classes online," Brooke murmured.

"Especially at the level she plays," Hunter added.

The detective raised an eyebrow. "You play well?"

"She plays extremely well," Hunter answered for her.

The detective pointed at the piano. "Want to give me a demonstration?"

She shook her head. "Maybe another time."

Detective Napier smiled. "Well, I'll leave you two alone then. Be careful, and call if you need me."

"We will," Hunter said as he walked him to the door. "And thank you."

Once the detective was gone, Brooke wrapped Hunter's coat more tightly around her and tried to stop shaking. "This whole night was horrible."

"It was pretty bad," Hunter agreed.

"All that shooting and screaming, people hurt and dying!" She went on, despite the fact that her teeth were chattering. "I don't know if I'll ever get those images out of my mind."

"In time the memories will fade," he said with the voice of experience. "They never completely go away, but it gets better."

She wrapped her arms around his waist, and he allowed the contact. "Will this ringing in my ears go away?"

He rested his chin on the top of her head. "Your hearing should be back to normal by tomorrow."

She clutched two handfuls of his shirt. "I'm so disappointed that Mr. Shaw is not going to be prosecuted. In fact, this successful FBI sting might get him reelected since he claims he was part of it all along."

Hunter shrugged. "We helped the FBI arrest a major criminal. We'll have to be satisfied with that."

"Maybe I should be, but I'm not," Brooke told him. "Mr. Shaw is a public servant! He's supposed to uphold the law and care about justice and liberty and the Constitution. He betrayed the trust people put in him, and now he's going back to his regular life. He'll be sitting around his dinner table eating pot roast, going on vacation, coaching his kid's baseball team, taking his wife out to eat . . ."

"Smiling into the TV cameras," Hunter added helpfully.

"And trying other people for *their* crimes. It's not right."

"This is going to sound cynical and unpatriotic and maybe worse, but the truth is there are some things you just can't fix. It's good that you want to try, but you need to accept that you can't single-handedly change the poultry industry and you can't take enough pictures to get all the criminals arrested and you can't personally end corruption in government."

"And I can't make you forgive me." She fought tears of discouragement.

"I forgive you," he corrected. "What I can't give you is a blank memory."

She released him and reached down to pull off her shoes. "I've got to get out of this ripped dress, put on my pajamas, and go to bed so I can watch you not sleep on your pallet by the door."

"I'll stay out here on the couch tonight since we don't have to keep up the pretense of a loving couple for the cameras."

She couldn't bear the thought of him being so far away. "What if someone comes in through my bedroom window?"

Hunter sighed. "Okay, I'll sleep on your floor."

Satisfied she headed toward her room to change.

\* \* \*

Brooke was more than tired. She was bone weary and emotionally traumatized. So she expected to fall asleep quickly, but she didn't. Curled on her side with the comforter pulled up to her chin, she stared at Hunter. He was lying on his back, his profile backlit by the moon. She thought about how brave he'd been that day. Several times he had protected her at his own expense. She tried to imagine making it through even one day without him and couldn't.

"You're staring at me again," he said from his pallet by the door.

"I can't help it," she murmured. "Does it bother you?"

"I'm getting used to it," he replied. After a few minutes, he said, "We shouldn't have gone to that dinner. Your being there didn't accomplish a thing except to put you in danger. The FBI would have gotten Carmichael anyway."

"I made the decision."

"I could have carried you out of there and locked you in this apartment if necessary," he said. "Your uncle would have thanked me for that."

"You wouldn't take away my free will." It wasn't a question. It was something she knew to be true about him.

There was a brief silence, and then he said, "No, but I'm sorry you had to see all that tonight. And I'm sorry that I've let Major Dane down."

"He'll understand," Brooke said. "He'll be mad, but he always gets over that."

He didn't comment on this but made a rare personal admission. "I'm worried about the team. They aren't safe without me. I'm their eye in the sky." There was no conceit or pride in his statement, just honest concern for his team.

"They'll be back soon," she tried to comfort him.

"I hope so." He turned on his side, facing away from her. "No more talking. Now quit staring at me and go to sleep."

She stopped talking, but she couldn't quit staring. After what seemed like hours, her eyes finally got heavy, and she slept.

# CHAPTER TEN

BROOKE WAS AWAKENED BY THE sound of someone screaming. It wasn't until she felt Hunter's arms around her that she realized those terrified sounds were coming from her own mouth. Her pajamas were damp with perspiration, and her heart was pounding wildly. She clung to him as the last vestiges of the nightmare faded away.

"Are you okay?" he asked gently, his good hand stroking her hair.

She pressed her cheek against his neck. "I am now."

They sat there on the bed, staring out her window at the dark night. Brooke craved the light. It seemed like everything would be better if the sun would just come up. "When will it be morning?" she asked.

"Soon," he murmured. "Just go back to sleep."

"You won't leave me?"

"I'll stay right here until dawn," he promised.

\* \* \*

When Brooke woke up on Sunday morning, she was still wrapped in Hunter's arms. To prolong the moment, she tried to pretend she was still asleep, but he wasn't fooled.

"My arm is cramping," he told her. "I've got to get up."

Reluctantly she shifted her weight so he could escape. He stood there flexing his hand and looking tired.

"I'm guessing you didn't sleep?"

"Not much," he admitted.

"If you don't get some rest, you're going to be no good to me as a piano restorer," she teased.

"I'm not sure I'd be any good to you with that even if I was rested." He turned and moved toward the door. "I'll go make breakfast."

"And I'll go take a shower. A real one—without you."

When Brooke joined him, she was gloriously clean, her hair was straightened for the first time in days, and she was wearing a hot-pink cotton sundress. She felt like Miss America.

"So?" She twirled around to give him the full effect of her improved appearance.

She saw the appreciation in his eyes, but he said, "I was getting used to your poodle hair."

"Hunter Ezell," she said in her best Southern belle drawl. "You know that special hairstyle requires a long, steamy shower. Is that what you're suggesting?"

He put a plate of pancakes in front of her. "I'm suggesting that you eat your breakfast."

She sat at the table and picked up her fork. "Pancakes are almost as good as steamy showers."

He took the chair across from her. His plate was piled with pancakes and sausage smothered in syrup.

As she watched him eat, she said, "I have a favor to ask."

His fork paused in midair. "What kind of favor?"

"Nothing much. It's just that after last night I feel so grateful to be alive, and well, I'd like to go to church this morning. And I know you can't let me go anywhere by myself, so would you come too?"

He was silent for a few seconds. Then he said, "My dress uniform's not fit to wear."

"Your regular uniform will be fine. The service just lasts about an hour. I'm not in the mood to talk to people, so we'll get there right on time and slip out just before it ends."

"What time does it start?"

She checked her watch. "We've got thirty minutes."

He handed her his phone. "Let Hack's guys know, and I'll go change."

\* \* \*

At exactly nine o'clock, they arrived at the building where the small congregation, made up mostly of students, met. It had been a long time since Brooke had attended church, and she expected to feel awkward or out of place, but it felt strangely like coming home. The familiar hymns reminded her of childhood and, therefore, of her parents and brother. So she fought tears during most of the service.

As she'd promised, they left during the closing song, and once they were in the car, she said, "Thank you for coming with me. I know church isn't really your thing."

"I didn't mind."

"Maybe we can go again some time?" She tried to keep her tone casual, as if it wasn't desperately important to her that he make even a small commitment about the future.

He gave her a solemn look. "Maybe."

When they got back to her apartment, she changed into a cute pair of jeans and her favorite shirt.

"You should have put on work clothes," Hunter commented when she joined him at the piano. "You might ruin those."

"I don't intend to work hard enough to risk my clothes." She flashed him a grin as she pulled on her gloves.

After an hour she was tired and hungry, and although she hated to admit it, she was also bored. She looked across the piano at Hunter. He was working his steel wool patiently along the wood grain, lifting off years of lacquer and grime.

"You are so meticulous," she told him. "This old piano is going to be worthy of the Smithsonian by the time you get finished with it."

"Not even close," he disagreed. "But I do find it satisfying to take something old and battered and restore it to its former beauty."

She walked over to him and said, "Well, it's time to take a break from all that satisfaction."

"What kind of break?" he asked warily.

"I need to talk to you for a minute. We can take a pretend shower if you want my hair to curl."

He shook his head. "We can just talk here."

She removed the steel wool from his hand and moved in close. "So, how do you like the new, honest me so far?"

He gave her an exasperated look. "I had to stop working for you to ask me that?"

She nodded. "I want your undivided attention for just a minute. I'm starting to get jealous of my own piano. And my fingers ache."

He sighed. "I appreciate your efforts to be more honest—especially with me."

She was pleased by this response. "And how does that affect our relationship?"

"It doesn't. Right now I'm your bodyguard. When your uncle gets home and releases me from this assignment, we can discuss the possibility of a personal relationship."

Her smile faded. "You make it sound so formal. I love you. You love me. I'm honest now. What more do we need for a successful marriage?"

He considered this seriously. "A successful marriage depends on more than love and trust—things like compatibility, mutual interests, common goals."

"That's baloney," Brooke whispered. "Love is all you need. There's even a song that says so." She sang a few off-key bars.

"How can you play the piano so beautifully when you're tone-deaf?"

She was offended. "I am not tone-deaf!"

He picked up his steel wool pad. "Break's over. Back to work."

"Slave driver," she muttered as she pulled on her gloves.

Her father called shortly after their break to invite them to dinner, so Brooke got another refinishing reprieve. Hunter seemed nervous about the prospect, but Brooke was grateful for the chance to spend time with her dad. When they arrived Raleigh was grilling hamburgers. He had paper plates and buns and condiments, along with a tub of store-bought potato salad, arranged neatly on the picnic table out back.

As they sat down to eat, Brooke said, "Hunter took me to church today."

Her father gave them both a warm smile. "That's good, although I wish you'd come with me. It was lonely sitting there without your mother."

"How is Mom?"

"She's enjoying the time with her parents," Raleigh said. "And I'm gone so much it's selfish of me to want her to be waiting here when I get home, but I do!"

Brooke smiled. Her parents had always seemed so old, and she'd never had a desire to be much like them. But now, as her father described his feelings for her mother, she realized that was exactly what she wanted. If her fondest dreams came true, someday maybe Hunter would be cooking hamburgers for their daughter.

"How's your arm?" Raleigh asked Hunter.

"Fine, sir."

"You don't have to call me sir. I'm not a military man," Raleigh said.

"Sorry, sir." Hunter blushed. "It's a habit."

To save Hunter from more stilted conversation with her father, Brooke asked, "So, Dad, what have you heard from Adam?"

He was only too happy to tell her, so for the next little while, they listened to a glowing account of her brother's exploits in Zimbabwe.

They had ice cream for dessert, and then Neely called. Brooke and Hunter took this opportunity to say good night.

"Oh, Brooke and Hunter are just leaving," Raleigh said into the phone. "Can I call you back?"

"No need to do that, Dad." Brooke kissed him on the cheek. "Hi, Mom!" she called. Then with a wave she took Hunter's hand and led him through the house to the front door.

* * *

On Monday morning they followed what was becoming a comfortable routine. While Brooke showered and tamed her hair, Hunter made breakfast. Then they both ate, and she cleaned the kitchen while he got their piano-restoration supplies set up.

But just as they were about to start work, Hunter's cell phone vibrated. He took off his gloves and pulled the phone from his pocket. "It's Savannah," he said before he answered.

Brooke stayed close so she could eavesdrop.

"Owl, I just saw the news report about the Joined Forces dinner on Saturday night!" Savannah's voice sounded anxious. "They had footage of the gunfire and a list of all the people who were injured! I'm so thankful you and Brooke weren't there!"

Hunter raised his eyes to Brooke's. "I saw the news too, and it did look pretty bad. Have you heard anything from Major Dane and the team?"

"I haven't," she said. "Which isn't unusual."

"No," Hunter agreed. "Communications are limited during a mission."

"But honestly, I'm uneasy in a way I've never been before. Maybe it's just because I'm pregnant," she rushed to add. "Or because I'm here alone."

Now that Savannah needed reassurance, Hunter looked panicked.

"It's okay," Brooke whispered to him. "Just listen."

Savannah continued, "But I can't help feeling like we pushed our luck—that once we knew about the baby, Dane should have told General Steele he was no longer available for covert operations."

"You want him to quit the team?" Hunter asked.

"Yes. And I feel so guilty, but I can't help it. I'm not even sure that he *can* quit. It's such a part of him. But I want him to have a regular, safe job. I want him to be home at night. I'm just so tired of worrying about him all the time."

"I know it's hard," Hunter said.

"I used to think that living my life in constant fear was the price I had to pay for being married to such a great, brave man. But I've changed my mind. Dane has done his share, and so have I. Someone else can do what has to be done from now on. I don't think I can live this way anymore."

"Try not to worry. Everything will be okay."

"I hope you're right." Savannah sounded less confident. "But I can't stop wondering if this uneasiness I feel is a warning. What if Dane really needs help, and I'm ignoring it?"

Hunter was in over his head, and he knew it. He turned pleading eyes to Brooke.

She took the phone from him and said, "Hey, Savannah. It's Brooke, and I've been listening in."

"You probably think I'm a basket case."

Brooke looked at Hunter. "No, I completely understand your concern. Why don't you call General Steele and check on the team? The worst that will happen is you'll seem like an overprotective wife."

There was a brief pause, and then Savannah said, "And I can live with that. Thanks for the advice."

"Anytime," Brooke replied. "Call again if you need me."

\* \* \*

Savannah ended her call with Brooke and immediately dialed General Steele's number before she could lose her nerve. It rang several times and was finally picked up by the switchboard operator.

"I'm trying to reach General Steele," Savannah explained.

"General Steele is on leave," the operator informed her. "General Moffett is handling General Steele's responsibilities now. I can transfer you to his office if you'd like."

General Steele was on leave while he had a team in the field? That made no sense at all. Her chest constricted. "Yes, transfer me, please."

General Moffett was also unavailable, but Savannah talked to his secretary, who informed her that General Steele had suffered a heart attack and was at Fort Belvoir Community Hospital in the cardiac critical care unit.

Savannah felt dizzy and sat down in the nearest chair. "My husband is Major Christopher Dane," she told the secretary. "He's on a mission for General Steele, and I don't know where or when he's supposed to get back or if he's okay."

"Try to remain calm, Mrs. Dane," the secretary soothed. "I'm sure he's fine, but I'll have General Moffett call you when he gets in."

Savannah thanked the woman absently and ended the call. She stared at the phone for a few seconds, trying to decide what to do.

"Mrs. Dane?"

She looked up to see Hack's "main man," Volt, standing in the doorway.

"Are you okay, ma'am?" Volt was a departure from Hack's normal hire. Instead of linebacker-sized, he was short and thin. His skin was very black, and startlingly, he had no hair. No eyebrows, no eyelashes—his head was slick as a bowling ball. She wondered if he'd been through chemotherapy, but he'd offered no explanation, so she hadn't asked.

"General Steele had a heart attack, and another general is in charge of the team."

"Well I'm glad someone's watching out for them," Volt replied.

Savannah shook her head. "I'm not sure that anyone is. Because of the secret nature of the assignments the team is given, there might not be much information about it. And if General Steele can't fill in the new general . . ."

Volt frowned. "The team really could be in trouble."

Savannah took a deep, shuddering breath. "I need to get to Fort Belvoir and talk to both this General Moffett and General Steele."

"I'll drive you," Volt offered.

"Thanks, but you should stay here. If Dane needs to contact us, this is where he'll call."

"I'll have to send a car to follow you," Volt said hesitantly.

She nodded. "Tell them to be ready in fifteen minutes."

\* \* \*

During the drive to Fort Belvoir, Savannah started to second-guess herself. She had never interfered in Dane's military life before, and he'd been on dozens of dangerous missions. She was afraid that when he got home he'd be angry with her. But she was more afraid that if she didn't step in, he might not come home.

So she rehearsed in her mind what she was going to say when she got to the hospital. She didn't want come on too strong, but she wanted to be taken seriously. It was a fine line she'd have to walk. And she hoped her supply of Spriteorade held out so she didn't throw up on anyone.

Once she reached Fort Belvoir, she showed her military ID at the visitor checkpoint and then drove to the hospital. She disliked hospitals, hated being away from Caroline, and dreaded the imposition she was about to become, but her concern for Dane and the team urged her on.

During the ride up in the elevator, she studied her blurred reflection in the stainless steel door. Her hair was too long, her clothes too big, and that bottle of Spriteorade didn't scream, "I'm a force to be reckoned with." Before she lost all confidence, the elevator arrived at her destination, and the doors slid open.

She found Claudia Steele in the cardiac critical care waiting room. The women embraced briefly and then sat on one of the uncomfortable couches.

"How's General Steele?" Savannah asked.

"The doctors have him sedated." Claudia tucked a strand of gray-streaked brown hair behind an ear in a nervous gesture. "They're waiting for the results of some tests, and by tomorrow they should be able to give us a prognosis."

"So he's going to be okay?"

"The doctors are cautiously optimistic." Then, she asked politely, "How have you been?"

"Good." Savannah raised her bottle of Steamer's elixir. "I've got morning sickness, and this is the only thing that allows me to function."

Claudia smiled. "I'm sorry about the sickness, but congratulations on the baby. When are you due?"

"January."

"I guess Caroline is excited?"

"Oh yes," Savannah replied.

"And Major Dane?"

Savannah was growing weary of the small talk and was grateful for the opportunity to introduce the purpose for her visit. "I'm honestly not sure how Dane is. He left with the team on a mission on Saturday. As usual I don't know where they are or when to expect them back. And I'm concerned that without General Steele there to provide support, they might be, well, not getting what they need."

Claudia furrowed her brow. "All of Nolan's duties were assigned to another general." She put a hand to her head. "My brain is mush right now, so I can't think of his name, but I can find out for you."

"It's General Moffett," Savannah provided. "I'm going to see him next, but I was hoping, well, I'm just so much more comfortable with General Steele. Would it be possible for me to see him for a few minutes?"

"No, dear, I'm sorry, but they only allow immediate family members in, and we're limited to five minutes each hour."

Savannah didn't even try to hide her disappointment. "Oh, I see."

A nurse came to the waiting room door. "Mrs. Steele, it's time."

Claudia stood quickly. "I have to go now."

Savannah stood too. "I'm sorry for imposing on you during this difficult time."

"Nonsense," Claudia scoffed. "You and Major Dane are like family. I'm always glad to see you. Good luck with the morning sickness, and try not to worry about Major Dane. Nolan always says he's the best." Then Claudia rushed down the hall for her five-minute visit with the general.

Fighting discouragement, Savannah took the elevator down to the lobby.

* * *

Savannah's next stop was INSCOM headquarters at Fort Belvoir. It was familiar territory, but now she was an outsider. And the stakes were high. Her plan was to go first to General Steele's office. His secretary might be able to give her some information or at least tell her a little something about General Moffett. Forewarned was forearmed.

When she arrived at the door to General Steele's office, she noted that the secretary's desk was empty. During her time in the general's employ, that desk had been manned by the supremely capable Louise, who was now retired. Savannah indulged in a moment of nostalgia as she walked past the desk and into the office. She stopped short when she saw that there were three people inside.

One man was typing on the general's computer, another was going through the papers on his desk, and a woman was standing at an open file cabinet. All were wearing uniforms, which seemed to indicate that they had the right to be there. But they all looked vaguely guilty when they saw her. This made Savannah wonder if they were exceeding the bounds of their authority and taking advantage of General Steele's absence to do some snooping.

"My name is Savannah Dane," she announced to the group. "My husband, Major Christopher Dane, works for General Steele. I'm here to get a report on him and his team."

The man at the computer stood. "I'm General Moffett, and I was assigned to oversee General Steele's workload." He waved at his two companions. "We're doing our best to get up to speed on everything that he had going. Which is no easy task since General Steele doesn't always follow protocol. Things will be different now that I'm in charge."

Savannah felt a tremor of fear. "Can you tell me when Dane's team will be back?"

The woman at the filing cabinet walked over and handed General Moffett a file. He glanced at it and then placed it on the desk. "I can tell you that one of the first things I did when I assumed control was to cancel their assignment and recall them. However, Major Dane refused to obey that order."

Her heart sank.

"So I recalled the helicopter that was waiting to pick them up. When he's ready to come home, he can call me."

"You cut off their transportation?"

"I can't leave a multimillion dollar helicopter and two pilots at risk while Major Dane conducts what is now an unauthorized action," General Moffett said. "Besides, I have to teach them a lesson. There's no room in my command for rogue soldiers who make their own decisions and ignore orders."

She ignored the rogue remark and asked, "What if they can't contact you for some reason? How will they get back?"

"They're resourceful," the general said. "I have complete confidence that they will return. And then I should have their attention when we talk about procedures for future missions."

Terrified for Dane and appalled by General Moffett's attitude, she decided to try begging first. "Please, sir, my husband is a good man and a brave soldier. He has given many years of dedicated service to the army. I don't care if you court martial him once he's back, but please, help him get home. We have a daughter, and I'm expecting another baby." Tears flooded her eyes, which normally would have been embarrassing, but under the circumstances she hoped they would help her case.

"I'm sympathetic to your situation," General Moffett said, although he didn't sound it, "but there's nothing I can do."

"Can you tell me where they are at least?"

He shook his head. "That's classified information."

She abandoned the nice approach. "I'm not going to sit around and just hope for the best," she said. "I'll have to go over your head."

"Feel free," General Moffett invited. "You'll find my immediate superior at 1600 Pennsylvania Avenue. Now if you'll excuse me, I've got work to do."

His arrogant attitude should have made her furious, but instead it just strengthened her resolve. Without another word she turned and walked out of the office. He had just picked a fight with a Spriteorade-logged pregnant woman, and there was no doubt in her mind that he would eventually rue this day.

* * *

While sitting in her car, Savannah called an old friend who had worked with her at Channel 7. He was now a correspondent for CNN, the author of several books, and had a very successful political blog site.

"Hey, Edgar," she said when he answered.

"Hey yourself, beautiful," he responded. "When are you going to give up on domestic life and come back to the cameras that love you?"

"Never," she assured him. "I'm crazy about the domestic life."

"You've been brainwashed!"

"I miss you."

He sighed. "I miss you too—and the good old days when we were idealistic and young. And when you didn't have a husband."

"Actually my husband is the reason I'm calling."

"I should have known it wasn't because you wanted to talk to me."

"Oh, I love talking to you," she assured him. "But right now I need your help." She explained the situation and finished with, "The head of INSCOM is in the best position to help Dane. General Moffett has refused to do that and basically told me that there's no power above him except the president of the United States. I intend to prove him wrong."

"And introduce him to the power of the press?"

"Specifically you," she confirmed. "I'm hoping you can use your blog to put some pressure on the general. I either need to convince General Moffett to help Dane or convince the army to replace him with someone who will."

"Whoa," Edgar said. "You're not messing around."

"I'd call the president himself if I thought he'd answer," Savannah responded seriously.

"And what am I going to say to put pressure on this unpleasant general?"

"We can't mention Dane or the team by name since that might make things worse for them . . . wherever they are." Her voice trembled a little, but she pressed on. "I'd like to start a rumor that people in the Washington community do not believe General Moffett is qualified to run INSCOM—even temporarily. I'm a person, so this rumor is completely true. But it can't be attributed to me."

"Of course."

"If you say you've heard a rumor to that effect, since you have so many contacts, it will be taken seriously."

"I can certainly mention that I've heard this rumor from a reliable source. And I'll even do a little research and see if I can find some facts from General Moffett's military career to give it a little more bite."

Tears flooded Savannah's eyes. Edgar was a very busy man, and this offer would require valuable time. "The more bite the better."

"I'll see what I can do," Edgar promised. "This isn't going to cost me my job, is it?"

"You've already got more money than you can spend anyway," Savannah teased. "And if you're unemployed, I'm sure I can find a spot for you at the Child Advocacy Center."

She heard Edgar chuckle. "You realize that you're making an enemy of a very powerful man? I am too, of course, but I already have plenty of enemies, so I'm used to it."

"General Moffett has left me no choice."

"Okay, I'll do some quick research and then put the rumor on today's blog. And I'll mention the general on my show tonight. So tune in."

"I will," Savannah replied gratefully. "Be sure and spell his name right M-O-F-F-E-T-T."

"I've got it. And it's been good talking to you. Don't wait for a crisis to call me again."

Savannah ended the call feeling confident that she had done the right thing. Her only concern was that the blog rumor and the subsequent pressure on General Moffett might take too long. She really needed to find out where Dane was, and that meant talking to General Steele. So she turned back toward Belvoir Community Hospital. She was going to visit Claudia Steele again, and this time it would not be mistaken for a social call.

* * *

Mrs. Steele was not in the waiting room where Savannah had visited with her before, so she checked with the nurses' station and was informed that the general had been transferred to a private room.

Savannah was pleased to hear this. Not only did that mean General Steele must be doing better, it also meant he would be easier to access. She asked for his room number and was directed to the other side of the cardiac wing.

"Are you a family member?" the nurse asked. "Because only family and people on the approved list can visit."

"I'm family," Savannah said with a smile. Claudia herself had said so just an hour before.

When she arrived at the general's hospital room, she knocked lightly before opening the door. He was asleep in the hospital bed. Wearing a hospital gown instead of his customary uniform, he looked pale and somehow diminished. Claudia was sitting in a chair beside the bed and looked up when the door opened. She stood with a frown and waved for Savannah to follow her back out into the hall.

"Nolan is resting and can't be disturbed," she explained once they had the door closed behind them. "I told you earlier he's not up to having visitors."

"That was when he was in the critical care unit," Savannah reminded her. "Now that he's in a private room, I assumed that the visitation rules wouldn't be so strict."

"Oh, he's far from recovered," Claudia said. "And the doctors want to keep him calm while they determine exactly what happened."

"I just need to talk to him for one minute so I can find out where Dane and his team went."

"General Moffett—"

"Won't help me," Savannah interrupted. "I've just come from there. He has abandoned the team in—wherever they are. I may be forced to organize a rescue myself, and I can't rescue them if I don't know where they are. I hate to bother you again, but the lives of Dane and his team may depend on it. If you don't want me to go in, you could ask him."

Savannah felt that she had presented the situation clearly, and she fully expected cooperation. So Claudia's response shocked her.

"I'm sorry, but none of this can be mentioned to my husband. It would upset him and could cause another episode. At the very least, it will hamper his progress. I can't risk that."

"My husband and his team are at risk," Savannah repeated.

Claudia nodded. "I understand that."

"They accepted this mission at General Steele's request."

"I know, and I'm sorry." Claudia wrung her hands. "But I can't do anything that might hurt his heart. Think if it was your husband. Wouldn't you do anything to protect him?"

Savannah took a step back. "I hope that I wouldn't sacrifice the lives of his men. He wouldn't want that."

Claudia looked away. "I'm sorry. I can't help you."

"You won't help me."

"I have a responsibility to my husband." Her voice was cold and determined. She turned to a passing nurse. "This woman was trying to enter my husband's room without permission. Can you have security escort her out and make sure she doesn't bother us again?"

The nurse gave Savannah a stern look and pushed a button on her radio.

"It won't be necessary to call security," Savannah said, her eyes locked with Claudia's. "I'm leaving." Then she turned and walked away. All her adrenaline was spent. She just felt lost and alone.

As she rode the elevator down to the lobby, Savannah thought about General Steele. He had been like a father to her, and she didn't want to do anything to reduce his chances of full recovery, but she was terrified for Dane. He was somewhere without support from home, and a few words from General Steele could have made all the difference.

Savannah was frustrated by the setback, but she couldn't give up. Somehow she would find a way to help Dane.

# CHAPTER ELEVEN

DANE DIDN'T KNOW HOW LONG he had been staring at the door before it finally opened. The light from outside was blinding, and he covered his eyes as two men hauled him up roughly. His cramped muscles protested, but he kept his balance. He looked back inside just before they slammed the door shut. Doc, Steamer, and Agent Alcine were watching in mutual misery. At least they were alive and seemed unharmed. Now if he could just find Hack.

Dane was dragged across a large open area that consisted mostly of packed dirt with a few patches of well-trampled brownish grass. Bullet casings and broken glass littered the ground, and the smell of rotting fish was almost overpowering.

They took him into a larger building with high ceilings and windows that let in light. Fans suspended from the ceiling whirred, making it slightly cooler. A dozen armed men were milling around the room— leaning against walls, looking out windows, or talking to each other in small groups. The furniture was sparse and unimpressive except for the television mounted on the far wall. It was the largest one Dane had ever seen.

His escorts brought Dane to an abrupt halt. He tried to stand tall and proud. He wasn't afraid, exactly. He had faced death many times and was prepared to do so again. But for years his courage had been partly based on the fact that he had nothing to lose. That had changed. Now he had much to live for. He kept his expression blank.

A man separated himself from the others and approached him. He was average height with dark hair and eyes. He was dressed basically the same as the others, in jeans and a blue cotton shirt. The only distinction was a black shoulder bag. Dane assumed it contained a weapon of some type, maybe a bomb. He had an air of authority that Dane recognized. This was the man in charge, the man he would have to negotiate with.

"What is your name?" he asked in slightly accented but excellent English.

"Major Christopher Dane, US Army," Dane replied.

"It is nice to meet you, Major Christopher Dane." His tone was slightly mocking. "I am Jacques Babineaux, international businessman."

Dane nodded in acknowledgment. "My commanding officer is General Moffett, at Fort Belvoir, Virginia. I request that you contact him and work out a prisoner exchange."

"I will contact your general," Babineaux assured him. "I will tell him that the US Army owes me weapons to replace the ones you destroyed last night."

"I doubt the army will give you weapons, even in exchange for my team. But you could ask for humanitarian aid or money."

"Hmmm," the man said. "Yes, with Americans it always comes back to money."

Dane decided to ignore that remark. "My men need water and food."

Babineaux nodded. "We will take care of that soon. We wouldn't want the rumor to start that Jacques Babineaux is a bad host!"

There were some laughs from the men around the room.

"What is the condition of the injured man, Lieutenant Buchannan?"

"The big man? He has a few burns; some of them on his leg are fairly serious. I had my medic tend to them. He was given antibiotics and painkillers. He will be fine."

Dane was relieved, but he couldn't bring himself to thank the man.

Babineaux spoke to Dane's guards. "Take him back to the shed. Lock him inside but leave him untied. Keep guards around the building. If anyone tries to escape, shoot them. Now someone turn on the news."

\* \* \*

Brooke's hands were covered with wood dust, so she pushed the hair from her eyes with her forearm. "Is it time for lunch yet?"

"Almost," Hunter replied without looking up from the piano surface. They had finished the stripping process and were now sanding, which Brooke found even worse. "Are you hungry?"

"Not really. I'm just tired of sanding."

Hunter frowned. "We don't have to do this. I thought you wanted to."

"I want the piano refinished, and I like the idea of us doing it together. But I don't really want to sand all day long. I was thinking we could go out to lunch or see a movie—or both?"

He put down his sandpaper. "I don't like the idea of being in a restaurant or a movie theater. They're both difficult to secure."

She walked over and picked up the TV remote. "Okay, soldier, you've just sentenced yourself to an afternoon of game shows."

* * *

During the drive home, Savannah's mind was racing. Her trip to Fort Belvoir had been mostly unsuccessful, but at least she now knew for certain that Dane needed help. She also knew she was woefully unqualified to provide it. But there was no one else, so somehow she would find a way. As Dane was fond of saying, failure was really not an option.

When she drove up to the cabin, she thought of the first time she'd seen it. That day she had been driving into the enemy camp. Today it was her home. Dane was her husband, the father of her children, and all the team members were like family.

After a deep breath and a swig of Spriteorade, she climbed out of the car and walked into the cabin.

Volt met her at the door. "Did you find out where the team is?"

Savannah shook her head. "No. General Steele's wife wouldn't let me near him, and General Moffett won't tell me. And to make matters worse, he's called off their transport home."

Volt's eyes narrowed. "Why would he do that?"

"He ordered them to abort their mission, and my husband ignored him. So he basically said they have to find their own way back."

"So what do we do now?"

"I've started a media campaign against General Moffett, and I'm hoping he'll change his mind and bring the team home. Or that the pressure will cause him to resign or get fired. But if that doesn't work, we're going to have to find out where the team is and rescue them ourselves."

"I'll help you all I can," Volt said, "but I'm a little out of my element with army stuff."

Savannah nodded. "We definitely need a real soldier's help. So my next step will be to call the only member of the team who isn't lost."

* * *

Brooke and Hunter were halfway through *The Price is Right,* and she was already bored again. Finally she understood the problem. She wanted Hunter to focus on her. The only time she felt she had his full attention was when her life was in danger or when they were taking a pretend shower.

Deciding it was time for a serious discussion, she turned off the TV.

"Don't you want to see how much she wins playing Plinko?" he asked.

"No, actually, I don't."

He raised an eyebrow at her contentious tone. "So do you want to start sanding the piano again?"

"No, I want you to look at me."

"I am looking at you."

"I mean really look," she said. "I want you to watch me and notice everything I do, the way you did at the resort."

"I want to do the right thing," he said. "Why are you trying to make it harder for me?"

"If by the right thing you mean leave the woman you love over a glorified set of standards, then yes, I want to make it very hard for you."

"Right now I'm on duty. I can't let you distract me because that might compromise your safety."

All her anger evaporated instantly. "So you find me distracting?"

"Very distracting."

She was pleased, but before she could capitalize on this minor admission, his phone rang.

"It's Savannah," he said. Then he answered it.

The conversation was very one-sided, with Savannah doing most of the talking and Hunter occasionally adding a yes or no.

Finally he said, "We'll be there as fast as we can," and closed his phone.

"We're going to Virginia?" Brooke wasn't opposed to this idea. They could use a change of scenery. But then she noticed that Hunter's eyes were even more solemn than usual. "What's wrong?"

"Your uncle and the team are in trouble."

\* \* \*

The next few minutes were a flurry of frantic activity. While Hunter was on the phone arranging transportation, Brooke packed a suitcase haphazardly. She didn't know how long they would be gone or what circumstances they might find themselves in. So she put a little of everything in her suitcase.

When she was ready to go, she found Hunter waiting anxiously by the door.

He said, "We've got to go now."

Her heart thudded. He was not one to overreact. "Are you going to tell me what's going on?"

He took her suitcase and opened the front door. "I'll fill you in during the drive to the airport."

Once they were in the hallway, Hunter conferred with the guard at the door. It was decided that the round-the-clock surveillance would continue while they were gone. And the guard agreed to let Detective Napier know their whereabouts in case he needed to contact them. Then they hurried down to the car.

As soon as they were settled, she said, "Okay, tell me what you know."

"General Steele is the commanding officer who assigns missions to the team. He's the commander of INSCOM—that stands for Army Intelligence and Security Command."

She waved her hand to hurry him along. "I don't care about all the army mumbo jumbo. Just tell me what happened to my uncle and his team."

"General Steele had a heart attack and is in the hospital. General Moffett was given temporary command of INSCOM during General Steele's absence. Apparently he told Major Dane to abort the emergency mission General Steele sent them on. Major Dane refused, and so the team has been cut off as a disciplinary measure."

Brooke frowned. "By cut off you mean . . ."

"The army has abandoned them somewhere."

Brooke's eyes widened. "So what can we do to help him?"

"I'm not sure, but we'll figure that out when we get to Virginia."

* * *

Their flight was short but excruciating since they were both so worried. It was hard for Brooke to think about her uncle in trouble. She had always considered him invincible. Hunter had a rental car waiting for them at the airport in Fredericksburg, and they drove straight to the cabin.

When they arrived, Hunter parked on the gravel driveway in back. Then they walked up to the house together, and one of Hack's men let them inside.

"Mrs. Dane is in the office," he told them like a huge, scary butler.

When they walked into Uncle Christopher's office, Savannah was sitting behind the desk, and she appeared remarkably calm. A small, bald African-American man was pacing in front of the window.

Savannah gave both Hunter and Brooke a quick, hard hug, the kind you give at funerals when everyone is united in mutual grief. Then Savannah pointed to the man by the window. "This is Volt. He works for Hack."

"That's Volt, as in electricity because I'm small but powerful," he told them. "And I more than *work* for Hack. I'm the mastermind behind his very successful security business. I hire, I fire, I handle payroll, and there's not a computer system I can't hack into—even Hack's!" He studied Brooke carefully. "And I assign guards to girls who need protection. So you're the famous Brooke Clayton, eluder of the country's best bodyguards."

"I'm sorry about that," Brooke said. "I've promised not to do it again."

"Hmmm." Volt seemed undecided about her as he turned to Hunter. "And you must be Owl."

Hunter held out a hand. "I am."

Volt accepted the handshake. "I've heard about you too, for better reasons. You stayed back from the operation because of your injury, right?"

Hunter nodded. "And to protect Brooke—since she kept losing her bodyguards."

Volt grinned, and Brooke felt like the butt of a bad joke.

Savannah waved to a couple of empty chairs and asked all three visitors to sit. Once they were seated, she ran through the chain of events up to this point.

"After my conversation with General Moffett, I asked a friend to start a rumor using his political blog and his connections with CNN."

"What kind of rumor?" Hunter asked.

"That people believe that General Moffett isn't qualified to run INSCOM. I hope the pressure will either cause him to cooperate with us or cause the army to replace him."

Brooke was impressed. "You're playing hardball."

"I'm desperate," Savannah replied. Then she pointed to the laptop on Uncle Christopher's desk. "Here's the blog."

Brooke and Hunter read it quickly. The blogger had done an excellent job of combining quotes from notable individuals, facts, and supposition to create a very persuasive article.

"This is great," Brooke told Savannah. "I almost believe it myself."

"That's because it's completely true," Savannah replied a little defensively. "I started the rumor, but General Moffett *isn't* fit to run INSCOM. He deserted an entire team of men to teach them a lesson."

Hunter nodded his agreement. "He deserves everything he gets."

Mollified, Savannah continued, "Edgar e-mailed me that there are already thousands of comments on his blog, and they're getting so many phone calls and texts they can't handle them all. Soon other talk shows will pick up the story, and then we should start seeing some results."

"But if Moffett and the army don't cave?" Brooke asked.

"Then we'll have our own rescue plan ready." Savannah turned to Hunter. "I'm hoping Owl can tell us how to get started."

"Yes, ma'am," Hunter said. "Major Dane always starts an operation by making notes on a legal pad."

Savannah opened the desk drawer and took the top pad off a large stack. "Here you go."

Hunter accepted the legal pad and a pencil. Then he pulled his chair up to the corner of the desk and began to write. "The way I see it there are a few things we'll need to have before we can attempt a rescue. First, we've got to find out where the general sent them."

Volt said, "And that's just for starters. Once we find out where they were sent, we'll need to verify that they're still at this location. To do that you would need serious intel—the really high quality stuff generals have access to and we don't."

"I thought you were a super-hacker who could get access to anything," Brooke said.

Volt held up a hand. "Let me clarify—I can get anything, but the kind of stuff we need can't be gotten without attracting attention. And I'm talking soldiers-at-the-door-with-machine-guns kind of attention. If we're all in jail, who's going to rescue the team?"

"Okay," Savannah said slowly. "So how can we get the information we need without getting arrested?"

"General Steele can't help us because his wife won't let him," Hunter said. "And the new general won't help us because he's trying to prove some kind of point with Major Dane."

"Somebody with a high security clearance in any of the big agencies could probably give us what we need," Volt said. "CIA, FBI, DEA. Do we have friends in any of these places?"

"Doc has a friend at the CIA who's helped us before," Savannah said.

"You got a name?" Volt wanted to know.

She shook her head.

"Then that won't do us any good," Volt said.

Savannah waved her hand. "Okay, we don't want to get bogged down here. Let's assume that somehow I can get the information we need about their location."

Hunter said, "The second thing we need is manpower."

"That's my specialty," Volt said. "Besides our regular guys, I've got a former Green Beret and a retired Navy Seal on my payroll. Both have combat training."

"Can you get them here quick?" Hunter asked.

"Already on their way." Volt flashed him a smile. "I told you I was good."

"Next we'll need equipment and transportation," Hunter continued.

"I can probably take care of both," Volt said thoughtfully. "'Course it's going to depend on where the team is. I can rent a plane, but I don't know if I can get one that will make it to China."

Brooke saw Savannah's face go pale and said, "Hopefully the team isn't that far away."

"Hopefully," Hunter agreed.

"The only other thing we'll need is money," Volt said. "Lots of it. Renting planes and buying guns and other combat equipment . . . well, it don't come cheap. I can access some funds from Hack's business accounts, but without his signature I can't get more than a couple hundred thousand."

"I can get some money," Savannah said. "Will you need more than a million dollars?"

"A million should do it," Volt told her. "It's so nice to work with rich folks!"

Savannah gave him a weak smile. "We're not rich, but my sister is, and I'm sure she'll help."

Hunter said, "The next question is how long do we wait for the blog pressure to work?"

"Not long," Savannah said. "I want Dane and the team home as soon as possible."

Hunter nodded. "Let's plan to be ready in the morning. If General Moffett reverses his decision or gets fired before then, we can always cancel the rescue. If not, we'll be set to go."

"That sounds good," Savannah told him.

Hunter turned to Volt. "Go ahead and start collecting equipment, anything you think we might need. Rent some space at the airport in Fredericksburg and stockpile it there. Line up a plane or two and maybe a helicopter."

Volt seemed pleased. "Now you're talking."

"Savannah, get the financing lined up so he can pay for everything."

She nodded. "Now we just need to get the team's location."

"I'll handle that," Hunter said.

"How?" Savannah asked.

He stood. "I'll go to the hospital and talk to General Steele."

"Mrs. Steele will have the hospital staff block your access to him," Savannah predicted. "She threatened to call security on me."

"I'll work around Mrs. Steele." Hunter looked at Brooke. "Will you come with me?"

She was honored.

Then he added, "I might need you to provide a distraction while I sneak into the general's room."

"We've established that I can be very distracting," she teased him. "And if distraction doesn't work, I can hold Mrs. Steele down while you talk to the general."

"If I thought that was a reasonable option, I'd take one of Hack's men with me."

Brooke scowled, and Volt laughed.

"Before you go, let me give you an untraceable satellite phone. Now that we're at odds with the government, we can't be too careful."

Hunter nodded solemnly.

"There's one number already programmed in," Volt told him. "If you call it, you'll reach me. I can get messages to anyone else. Otherwise it's just like any other phone—camera, flashlight, wake-up call. You can even check your Facebook."

Hunter took the phone and headed for the door. "We'll be in touch."

# CHAPTER TWELVE

JUST AFTER BROOKE AND HUNTER left, Savannah got a call from an unknown number. She pressed accept warily.

"Mrs. Dane?" General Moffett demanded harshly. "I know you're behind the little smear campaign about my competency, and I want it to stop now. How dare you suggest that I'm not qualified to head INSCOM."

"How dare you desert your own team in the middle of a mission," Savannah shot back.

"I can't believe you had the audacity to attack me and the United States Army!"

"Where is my husband?"

"I told you that information is classified."

"If you don't tell me or go get them yourself, you'd better start looking into retirement."

"You are way out of your league here!" He sounded furious. "And let me assure you, your husband's military career is over!"

At the moment that seemed like a small price to pay as long as he came home alive. "Tell me where he is."

Instead of answering, the general hung up on her.

Shaking all over, she looked at Volt.

He said, "Well, that went great."

* * *

Once Brooke and Hunter were settled in the rental car and headed toward Fort Belvoir, Brooke turned sideways in her seat. "So do you have a plan for getting into the general's hospital room?"

"You're going to distract Mrs. Steele while I sneak past the nurses."

"How will you get past the nurses? Only family is allowed. You'd have to claim to be his son or something."

"You've pointed out that I'm not a good liar," he said. "Maybe you could tell the nurses that I'm the general's son."

She glared at him. "I've turned over a new leaf, remember? Besides, how could I distract Mrs. Steele *and* lie to the nurses for you at the same time?"

He sighed. "So you tell me. What should we do?"

"Well, first we have to come up with a specific distraction."

"You could impersonate a hospital employee and ask Mrs. Steele to fill out some forms."

She shook her head. "Ah, amateurs . . ."

"What's wrong with that?" Hunter seemed offended.

"Impersonating a hospital employee won't work—and not just because it would require me to lie. Hospital employees know each other; they wear badges and uniforms. We don't have the time or resources to research everything I would need to know, wear, and do in order to pull that off."

"So what's a better idea?"

She considered this for a few seconds. "I could ask her to take a survey about her hospital experience."

"How is that not impersonating an employee?"

"I'll say I'm a volunteer. Or," she smiled, "a *student* volunteer doing *research*. After all, I am a student. And *volunteer* implies permission from the hospital. And just about anything can qualify as research."

"That sounds good."

"And if someone asks me a question I can't answer, my 'student volunteer' status is a reasonable excuse for ignorance."

He nodded. "What questions will you ask?"

"Things like 'Do you like the food?' or 'Was the temperature in your room comfortable?' or 'Were the nurses nice?'—that sort of thing."

"That takes care of Mrs. Steele, but how will I get past the nurses?"

Brooke pressed a finger to her lips and thought for a few seconds. "You'll arrive at the hospital in uniform and with a folder marked 'Top Secret' or 'For General Steele's eyes only' or whatever the official army jargon is for that kind of thing."

"I think if we just write his name on the folder that will be enough," Hunter said.

Brooke shook her head. "They make this stuff seem more exciting on TV. Anyway, you'll show your ID, and they'll let you in to see him."

"And how is this more honest than pretending to be the general's son?"

"Because we'll stop and buy a folder and write the general's name on it so everything you say will be true."

After brief consideration he said, "It might work."

Brooke frowned. "It will work. You have to believe in it if you want anyone else to. So first you're going to have to get a uniform."

"I have one in my suitcase in the trunk."

She raised an eyebrow. "Now that's what I call being *prepared*."

"Actually it's army policy. Active duty soldiers are required to have access to a uniform at all times."

"Hmmm, I was hoping I was going to get to see your apartment at Fort Belvoir."

"You're not missing anything, trust me."

"I do," she said with a smile. Then she continued, "So now all we need is a file folder and a Sharpie marker. Unless you have those in your suitcase too?"

He shook his head.

"Then give me that fancy satellite phone, and let me try to find an office supply place nearby."

He gave her the phone, and it was, as Volt had promised, easy to operate. She located a Kinko's six minutes away.

After she gave him directions, she asked, "Do you really think I could check my Facebook on here?"

Hunter shook his head with a heavy sigh.

\* \* \*

Savannah heated up a can of soup for lunch and was trying to eat it when Volt rushed into the kitchen. He put his iPad on the table beside her and said, "You gotta see this."

Volt pushed play, and Savannah watched as General Moffett's face filled the small screen. He was standing beside another man on a podium of some kind. The other man tapped the microphone and then introduced himself as Ryker Glenn from the State Department.

"There have been some malicious rumors flying around Washington today, and we want to set the record straight."

There were murmurs from the crowd.

"Accusations have been made regarding General Moffett and his suitability for the command of INSCOM. We believe the source of these rumors is a band of rogue soldiers who went AWOL during a recent operation. They started the rumors in response to the general's disciplinary actions. We want to assure the public that the US Army has complete confidence in the general, and he will continue in this command until further notice."

Savannah seethed as she watched General Moffett standing there with a self-satisfied smile on his face. They had accused Dane of being rogue and AWOL in the same sentence.

Mr. Glenn continued, "We request that all calls to the general's office, the State Department, and the White House cease immediately so we can get back to the business of protecting our country. Thank you."

The general leaned forward and spoke into the microphone. "Yes, thank you."

"Who are these rogue soldiers?" a voice called from the audience.

"What type of disciplinary action has been taken against them?" Another question was hurled at the men standing on the podium.

"Is it true that the general has a drinking problem?"

Mr. Glenn held up a hand. "We came here to issue a statement. This is not a press conference. Good day."

The general and his escort walked away from the cameras.

"Well," Volt said. "So much for getting any help from the army."

Savannah's phone rang almost immediately. It was Edgar.

"Did you see the general on TV?"

"I saw him," Savannah confirmed, close to tears. "I feel like my plan backfired. They're attacking Dane and the team."

"Don't worry, girl!" Edgar encouraged her. "This fight is far from over. In fact, that non–press conference just gave us a bunch of extra publicity. We're having a petition with ten thousand electronically signed names delivered to the White House in an hour calling for the general's resignation."

Savannah put a hand to her heart. "Really?"

"Really," Edgar confirmed. "And the general's incompetence was mentioned on every news talk show that has aired so far today. The ball is rolling, and there may not be a way to stop it. You might actually get General Moffett fired! But don't waste any sympathy on him. I've done a lot of research on his military career, and this is not the first time he's put politics before his men."

"I don't have any sympathy for him," Savannah replied. "But the question is will it all be in time to help my husband?"

"I can't answer that question," Edgar said. "If I were you, I'd have a backup plan."

"Thank you, Edgar."

"I should be thanking you," he said. "I haven't had this much fun in years, and when it's all over, I may be more popular than Hannity!"

# CHAPTER THIRTEEN

HUNTER HAD JUST PARKED IN front of Kinko's when he got a text from Savannah. He read it and then handed the phone to Brooke. She skimmed the text and returned the phone. "So General Moffett is trying to fight back."

"I don't know why he won't just go get the team," Hunter said. "All this drama makes no sense."

Brooke shrugged. "I don't know either, but Savannah said to be careful, and I think she's right. As the only active duty member of the team—and the only one who's not lost—you're vulnerable. Maybe I should try and sneak in General Steele's hospital room while you wait in the car."

"He doesn't know you, and he won't tell you classified information."

She pursed her lips. "I guess that's true. So you'll have to go into the hospital, but please be careful."

He nodded. "I will."

While Brooke shopped for file folders and Sharpies, Hunter took his uniform into the restroom and changed. She had just finished paying for her purchases when he came out—completely transformed.

Brooke stared at him and realized that clichés existed for a reason—men in uniform really were irresistible. As they met at the exit, she whispered, "You look so nice."

He put a finger to his lips. "Don't attract attention." Then he took her hand, and they walked to the car. Once they were driving toward the hospital, Brooke opened the package of file folders and wrote *General Steele* on one of them with the Sharpie marker.

"If I saw this, I would think it was from General Mofffett's office." She held up her handiwork. "How about you?"

"It looks okay."

"High praise!" she said lightly. Then she showed him the survey template she'd found. "It's already printed up with general questions. I might have to adapt a few of them, but it gives me something to go by."

Hunter nodded. "That's even better."

"Now we have one last stop to make before heading to the hospital," Brooke said, scanning the sides of the road.

Hunter frowned. "Why are we stopping again?"

She waved a hand from her chin to her feet. "I look like a piano refinisher. Mrs. Steele will take me more seriously if my appearance is professional."

"You want to go shopping?" he confirmed. "Now?"

"A girl at Kinko's said there's a boutique a couple of blocks up." She saw the sign and pointed. "There it is."

Hunter pulled into the closest parking space and turned off the car. "You're sure this is necessary?"

She nodded. "I have to look the part. Consider it a uniform, like yours."

With a sigh he opened his door.

"You're coming in with me?" she asked in surprise. "While I shop for clothes? I thought after our last shopping experience, you vowed never to go into a store with me again."

"I don't want to," he assured her. "But I can't let you go in alone. It would be a breach of security."

Brooke laughed. "You are a brave soldier!"

As they walked up to the boutique's entrance, Hunter whispered, "Try to keep a low profile. We don't want the people here to remember us."

"Your face is extremely handsome and covered with bruises," she said. "I doubt these folks will be forgetting you anytime soon."

He sighed loudly, and they walked inside.

A zealous salesperson met them the instant they stepped into the shop. Brooke explained her needs and provided her size. Ten minutes later she was modeling for Hunter in an expensive business suit and shoes that matched.

"It's perfect!" the salesclerk enthused.

Brooke frowned at her reflection. "The pants seem a little tight."

The woman studied Brooke's backside and then shook her head. "A size bigger would be too loose." She turned to Hunter. "Doesn't she look fabulous in this suit?"

"She looks great no matter what she wears," was his low-key compliment.

Even though the words had been forced from him, Brooke was pleased. She turned to the clerk. "I'll take it!"

"If you'll bring it to me after you change, I'll put it in a nice hanging bag for you," the clerk offered.

"I think I'll just wear it."

While Hunter paid for her purchases, Brooke sprayed on some perfume from a sample bottle on the counter. Then looking and smelling like a different person, she followed him outside.

"I'll repay you for this," she promised as they walked to the car. She didn't add that it might take her a year, assuming she was able to get her job at the yogurt shop back.

"Don't worry about it." He held the car door open for her. "For the time being, all expenses are business expenses."

"I like the sound of that." She smoothed the luxurious fabric of the suit pants against her legs. "Now head to the hospital but minimize bumps and sharp turns. I need to repair my makeup, and I don't want to lose an eye."

By the time they arrived at the Pence Gate entrance to Fort Belvoir, Brooke was confident about her appearance at least. After Hunter showed his military ID and Brooke showed her driver's license, they were waved through.

Hunter proceeded to the hospital and parked. As he backed into a space near the exit, he explained, "I want to be prepared in case we have to get out of here fast."

They used the satellite phone to bring up a diagram of the hospital and referred to it as they mapped out their plan.

Pointing at the small screen, Brooke said, "Here's the cardiac care floor where I'll lure Mrs. Steele out of the general's room. I'll take her into this waiting area to do my survey. You wait in the lobby until I have Mrs. Steele distracted. Then come up these stairs and into the general's room. It's possible that no one will stop you, but if they do, just say you're from INSCOM and you're delivering something to General Steele."

He nodded.

Brooke checked the time and then handed the phone back to Hunter. "Give me fifteen minutes to get into position and then come up." She put her survey template into one of the unused file folders and got out of the car. She started to walk away and then turned back. "Speak with authority when you talk to those nurses."

"I will."

"And when you get in to see the general, make it quick. I don't know how long I can keep his wife occupied."

"I won't need more than a few minutes."

"And tell him what a weasel his replacement general is," Brooke suggested.

"I'll make time for that."

"Okay, well, wish me luck."

"Luck," he replied.

She wanted to ask for a lucky kiss but knew he'd refuse, and that would put her in bad mood. So she stood up straight and walked toward the entrance to the medical facility. As she entered the cool, mildly anti-septic confines of the hospital, she tried to assume the air of a qualified, experienced survey-taker. Pausing at the information desk to get her bearings, she noted the elevators and their proximity to the entrance—that would soon be her exit.

She took a few deep breaths to steady her nerves. Projecting a calm image was crucial to the success of their plan. The biggest challenge she faced was staying true to her newfound integrity. She was going to have to mislead the nurses and Mrs. Steele, but she couldn't lie outright. This was her chance to prove to Hunter that she deserved his respect.

A clever approach was key because if Mrs. Steele refused to take the survey, they were dead in the water. Her eyes scanned the large lobby area and settled on a gift shop. And an idea came to her. With a smile she walked inside and purchased a small plant potted in a ceramic replica of the hospital. The words Fort Belvoir Community Hospital were displayed prominently along the front, just under a bright purple bow.

Carrying the plant carefully, she headed for the elevators. When she stepped out on the cardiac floor, she looked around slowly. There was a long desk directly in front of her, and hallways leading to patient rooms ran along on each side.

Brooke took a deep breath and approached the desk.

"How can I help you?" a young woman in hot pink scrubs asked pleasantly.

"My name is Brooke Ezell," she responded, her voice quivering a little with this first use of her married, if temporary, name. "I'm a college student doing research, and I have a survey for Mrs. Steele, the wife of the patient in room 203. Would you please ask her to join me in the waiting room? It will only take a few minutes."

The nurse frowned. "What kind of survey?"

"I'll ask her to rate her husband's hospital experience based on several different criteria."

"Is it required? Because I've never heard of student surveys before."

"It's not required," Brooke admitted. "But if she completes the survey, the facilitating nurse, which would be you, gets a hundred dollar gift card. Let me make note of your name so we can send it to you." Brooke checked the nurse's name tag and jotted the information on the top of the freshly printed survey.

There was a little gleam of avarice in the nurse's eyes. "Why Mrs. Steele?"

"Random selection," Brooke replied. "It's your lucky day!"

"Well, okay," the nurse in pink said, no doubt with visions of a gift card dancing in her head. "Wait right here, and I'll get Mrs. Steele."

Brooke stood anxiously by the desk and commanded herself not to fidget. The nurse returned a few minutes later, followed by a small, thin woman with short gray-streaked hair.

Brooke stepped forward. "Mrs. Steele?"

"Yes," the woman responded warily. "The nurse said you needed me to fill out a survey?"

Brooke gave Mrs. Steele a reassuring smile. "I appreciate your willingness to participate. The information I collect may be used to improve hospitals across the country."

"Will it take long?" Mrs. Steele looked over her shoulder. "I don't like being away from my husband."

"It's only a few questions. You'll be back in his room in no time." Brooke led the general's wife to a far corner of the waiting room. "We'll have the most privacy here." She took a seat facing the hallway and motioned for Mrs. Steele to take one opposite her. Once Mrs. Steele was settled, Brooke presented the potted plant. "This is a little gift for you and your husband, a token of appreciation and best wishes."

Mrs. Steele accepted the plant, and some of the tension left her features. "Oh, how nice. Thank you."

"Now for the questions." From the corner of her eye, Brooke saw Hunter pass the waiting room headed toward the nurses' desk. She resisted the urge to watch him and kept her forced smile firmly in place. "On a scale of one to ten, with ten being the most positive and one being the least positive, how would you rate your overall experience since your husband was admitted to the hospital?"

Brooke estimated that she had been asking questions for about ten minutes, and Mrs. Steele was growing visibly impatient. She risked a glance at the hallway. No Hunter. Frowning a little, she repeated, "Could you rate your experience on a scale of one to ten, please?"

"Eight."

"What about the food?" Brooke asked. "On a scale of one to ten, how would you rate the taste?"

Mrs. Steele answered, "Seven."

Finally, after rating the friendliness of the hospital staff as a nine, Mrs. Steele stood. "I appreciate everything the nursing staff has done for us, and I really hope one of them wins the gift card," she said. "But I've been away from my husband for too long. I can't answer any more questions."

Brooke masked her panic with an effort. "I know your time is very valuable, and I can't even begin to tell you how much we appreciate your willingness to participate in the survey. There are only a couple more questions. On a scale of one to ten, how would you rate the comfort of the hospital beds?"

Mrs. Steele took a few steps toward the entrance to the waiting room. "I'm sorry, but really, I can't answer any more questions."

"Can I mark it down as an eight?" Brooke persisted.

Mrs. Steele nodded vaguely then turned and walked to the hallway with purpose.

"Mrs. Steele!" Brooke called out.

The woman turned to Brooke, her eyes angry. "I told you I'm through with this survey."

Brooke nodded. "I understand. I just didn't want you to forget your plant."

Reluctantly Mrs. Steele returned to the corner where Brooke was standing, and the plant exchanged hands. Brooke was desperately trying to think of another stalling tactic—short of tackling the woman and physically holding her down—when she saw Hunter walk by the waiting room entrance headed toward the elevators.

Relieved, she gave Mrs. Steele a genuine smile. "I hope you have a nice day."

Mrs. Steele didn't even bother to respond. She rushed down the hallway with the plant clutched to her chest.

Brooke walked quickly out of the waiting room and ran straight into Hunter.

"Sorry!" she whispered. "I thought you had gone to the elevators!"

His arms went around her in an automatic gesture. "I came back for you."

She clung to him. "I'm glad you missed me, but don't you think hugs should wait until—"

"Brooke!" he hissed. "General Mofffett just got off the elevator. They're going to catch us here. Then I'll be headed for a court martial, and your uncle and the team will die!"

There wasn't time to formulate a plan, so she took the only option available. She pulled him into the women's restroom.

If anything, he looked more distressed than he'd been at the thought of a court martial.

After checking the stalls, she said, "We're alone."

"But what if someone comes in here?"

"If you'll hold the door closed, that won't happen."

He pressed a hand firmly against the door, looking only slightly less alarmed. "This is a nightmare. Getting court martialed for trying to save your buddies is one thing, but sneaking into a ladies' bathroom . . ." He let his voice trail off. Apparently the consequences were too awful to consider.

"Pull yourself together," Brooke hissed.

He looked so pale and shaken she started to worry that he might never fully recover from his two minutes in the ladies room.

"And relax that death grip you've got on this door. I'm going to check to see if the coast is clear." He eased back, and she cracked the door open as an older man with a lot of medals on his uniform walked past, accompanied by two lower-ranking soldiers. Slowly she closed the door.

"He just walked by with a couple of flunkies," she whispered. "We'll give them a minute to get past the nurses' desk, and then we'll make a run for the stairs. If that nurse tells them that the general just received a delivery from a bruise-faced soldier, they'll start an all-out search."

"And if they catch us, your uncle and the team . . ." Again he couldn't complete his sentence.

"They're not going to catch us." After counting to sixty, she pulled the door open and glanced down the hall. It was empty, except for a woman who was walking toward the restroom. "Great," she muttered.

"The general?" Hunter asked.

"No," she said, "but we're about to have company. Just act natural." She took his hand and pulled him out into the hallway.

The approaching woman stopped and watched them with wide eyes. Brooke considered trying to explain, but that would take time they couldn't spare. And there really was no good excuse anyway. So she just gave the woman an apologetic smile as they rushed on by. They descended the stairs as fast as they could. Once they were on the main level, they slowed their pace to keep from attracting attention.

"This place is full of security cameras," Hunter said. "If they're looking for us, they could pinpoint our location in a matter of seconds."

Sobered, she followed him toward the lobby. When the doors were in sight, she felt relieved—until she noticed several MPs huddled near the exit. She knew Hunter had seen them too when he stopped short and pulled her behind the marginal privacy of a large potted plant.

Holding her close he whispered, "We can't let them get us both, so we're going to separate. If I think they've spotted us, I'll draw them off so you can escape."

"No!" she pleaded.

"If they don't stop me, I'll meet you at the car. If they do stop me, go straight back to the cabin and tell Savannah that Major Dane and the team are in Haiti. They were sent to rescue an ATF agent from a weapons dealer who uses a fish plant as his cover. It's near the town Baie de Henne, and the guys might be there. It's a place to start at least."

Brooke's mind skidded from their current dangerous situation to a conversation she'd had with Rex a few days before—when he'd bragged about recruiting a Haitian businessman who owned a whole beachfront town.

"Are you listening to me, Brooke?" Hunter shook her shoulders gently.

She nodded. "It's just a strange coincidence. Maybe it doesn't mean anything, but . . ."

"What?"

"When you mentioned Haiti, it reminded me of something Rex said. He's been working for more than a year to convince a man from Haiti to become a member of Joined Forces, and he recently succeeded. I made plane reservations for him once or twice, and the name of that town sounds familiar. I know there are a lot of people in Haiti and it's probably not the same man, but did General Steele tell you the name of the weapons dealer?"

"Babineaux," Hunter said. "Jacques Babineaux."

The ground seemed to shift beneath her feet. "That was his name," she whispered. "Babineaux."

"Are you saying there's a connection between Babineaux and *Rex*?" Hunter demanded incredulously.

She nodded. "I think so, yes. And that makes me wonder if the team's assignment in Haiti is related to Rex too."

Hunter thought for a second and then shook his head. "We'll figure that out later. Right now we've got to concentrate on getting out of here."

She knew he was right, but her mind was still searching for the piece of the puzzle that would make everything fall into place. It was there, just beyond her reach.

Hunter shook her shoulders. "Brooke, forget about Rex. Go out the front entrance and get to the car quick. I'll cut through the building and take another exit." He gave her a little shove. "Remember, your uncle's life depends on us."

Left with no choice, she tore her eyes away from Hunter and walked stiffly toward the door. One of the MPs providing security looked up and studied her for a few seconds. Then he approached her with purpose.

Brooke tried to think of an excuse for their behavior as the MP got closer. She couldn't come up with anything, so she looked for an escape route. Running would be futile, and it was too late to turn around and search for another exit. The MP was so close now she could read his nametag. *Flanagan*. At least she could put a name to her defeat.

"Ma'am," Flanagan said politely.

She stared at him, unable to speak or move or even breathe.

"Let me get this for you." He leaned forward and opened the door.

Brooke's temporary paralysis faded, her breathing resumed, and she gave him a weak smile. "Thank you."

He smiled back. "Anytime, ma'am."

She stepped past MP Flanagan and out of the hospital's cloyingly serene atmosphere into relative freedom. She gulped a deep breath of warm, humid air. But it was too soon to relax. Walking quickly across the courtyard to the parking deck, she was constantly on the lookout for anyone who might try to stop her. She knew she needed to put as much distance as possible between herself and the MPs. But every step took her farther away from Hunter, who might need her help.

She paused and considered going back. Then she heard a siren in the distance. Hunter might be in trouble, but his life wasn't at stake. She had to give Savannah the team's location. Which meant she had to leave Hunter behind.

Reluctantly she increased her pace to a semi-trot. And as she turned the corner into the parking deck, she glanced back at the hospital and saw two of the MPs rush out. Time was almost up, so Brooke broke into a run.

The rental car was where they'd left it. There were no MPs, but there was also no Hunter. Wiping impatiently at her useless tears, she fumbled with the keys. Once the door was unlocked, she swung into the driver's seat. She turned the key in the ignition, and the engine roared to life. After one last desperate—and futile—look around the parking deck, Brooke threw the car into gear and pulled out with her tires squealing.

Since she was the only car on DeWitt Loop, she felt exposed, but when she made it to Belvoir Road and merged with the traffic, she started to think she might actually get away. With effort she drove slowly enough to avoid attracting attention. She focused on the road in front of her and tried not think about Hunter or what might be happening to him at the hands of the Fort Belvoir military police.

When she reached the Pence Gate, she tensed as an MP stepped out of the guardhouse. She barely breathed as he checked her driver's license. Leaving Hunter was terrible. Leaving him and being arrested by the MPs, rendering her useless to Uncle Christopher, would be unbearable.

She clutched the steering wheel as the MP stepped into the little office and picked up the phone. His eyes met hers briefly. She knew that look—guilt. Then he turned his back so he wouldn't have to look at her. It was all the confirmation she needed. She had to act now.

Out of the corner of her eye, she saw the slightest movement as a hand reached out of the backseat and covered her mouth. Now the MP at the guard shack didn't seem like the most dangerous option.

She let go of the steering wheel and grabbed the hand at her mouth.

"Don't fight me!" a familiar voice commanded. "Drive!"

"Hunter!" she mumbled against his hand. "You're okay. You're *here*!"

He removed his hand from her mouth but stayed hidden on the floorboard of the backseat. "Hit the gas, Brooke!"

"But I might damage—"

"Brooke!"

She jammed her foot on the gas pedal, and the car shot forward, mangling two large orange cones in the process. The MP on the phone reacted with surprise. In her side mirror, she saw him run out of the guardhouse and stand in the street, staring after them. The phone was still in his hand, and two damaged cones were crumpled at his feet.

Then she rounded a corner, and he disappeared from her view along with the rest of Fort Belvoir.

Hunter sat up in the backseat. "Turn left here."

She slammed on the brakes and took the turn wide. The car's wheels screeched in protest.

"Go down two blocks and turn left again." Hunter put his arms out to steady himself in preparation for the inevitable centrifugal force.

"Will the MPs come after us?"

"They only have jurisdiction on the base."

"They might call the local police."

"They might." He pointed up ahead. "Get on I-95, move into the center lane, and stay just under the speed limit."

She followed his instructions. Once they were mixed in with the heavy traffic on the interstate, she looked at him in the rearview mirror. "Why didn't you tell me you were in the car?"

"I couldn't be sure you weren't being watched," he replied. "And next time check the backseat before you get in. I could have been anybody."

She glared at his reflection. "I know you're not trying to say it was my fault you almost gave me a heart attack!"

"Keep your eyes on the road! We won't be any good to your uncle if you have a wreck and kill us!"

She risked one quick glare and then concentrated on driving.

After a few minutes, she asked, "So how was the general?"

Hunter frowned. "He seemed confused, and I thought he was possibly even delusional—talking about how someone poisoned him and caused his heart attack. But now that there's a chance Rex is involved in all this, he may be right."

"Rex poisoned General Steele?"

"Maybe not personally, but the way I see it, there are two options: either everything that's happened is coincidence, or everything is connected."

"And Uncle Christopher doesn't believe in coincidence. So, let's think of what's happened and try to figure out how it fits together. First, Rex recruits a Haitian businessman for Joined Forces. Next, he comes to Nashville and starts converting an old church into a call center."

"Rex insists that you attend the grand opening dinner, which is really a cover for selling stolen coins," Hunter continued. "You help the FBI set up a sting, and the team gets an emergency assignment to go to Haiti and rescue an ATF agent who was working undercover for Babineaux, a

Haitian businessman, which means the team isn't available to protect you during the dinner."

"Then General Steele was given something that made it look like he'd had a heart attack, and he was removed from his command." Brooke continued the list of odd events.

"General Moffett was put in his place, and his first order of business was to cut off Major Dane and the team in Haiti. Then we attend the dinner without proper backup, and we almost get shot."

"And then Rex disappeared." Then one of the puzzle pieces she'd been searching for fell into place. "If these events are connected, there's only one continuous thread that runs between them all. Me." Brooke met Hunter's eyes in the rearview mirror. "Rex is trying to kill me."

Hunter nodded. "It means he's already tried at least twice—with the Nature Fresh fire and the shootout at the dinner. So if all this isn't coincidence, I think it's safe to assume he'll try again."

Fear and sadness overwhelmed her. "But why?"

"I don't know," Hunter said grimly.

"And if Rex tried to kill me at the dinner, that means he knew the FBI was going to raid the auction. He may have even recruited Lyle Carmichael and agreed to the coin auction just so the FBI would have a reason to come in and bullets could fly."

Hunter was frowning. "There's a lot we need to figure out, but right now I need to report on my visit with General Steele so we can set up the team's rescue." He took out the satellite phone and called the only number preprogrammed in.

Volt answered on the first ring. "Owl!"

"I spoke with the general. The team's in Haiti. A town called Baie de Henne"

"Got it," Volt said. "You on your way here?"

"Yes," Hunter replied.

"Good 'cause Mrs. Dane just got a call from her friend at CNN. It seems that some guy is claiming he's got Major Dane's team. But General Moffett refused to pay the ransom. He said our government won't negotiate with terrorists."

Hunter muttered something under his breath.

"Can you do me a favor?" Hunter asked. "It's probably illegal."

"That's my favorite kind. What do you need?"

"General Moffett's phone number," Hunter said. "And I don't mean his office number. I want his cell so I can call right now and get him personally."

"Breaking into the US Army secure database," Volt murmured. "Yeah, that's illegal. It'll just take me a few seconds." True to his word, Volt provided the number less than a minute later.

"Thanks," Hunter said. "Brooke and I will be there soon." He ended the call and then dialed the number Volt had given him.

"Moffett!" the general's voice reverberated through the car.

"General, this is Corporal Ezell."

"Corporal, I know about your unauthorized visit to General Steele's hospital room. You're in a lot of trouble. Turn that car around and come back to the base immediately!"

"I'm just trying to help my team, sir."

"You need to learn your limitations," the general replied impatiently. "We've been in contact with the Haitian government, and they're going to assist us in working out a civilized release of the captives."

"Why can't you just send another special-ops team in there and get them out?"

"We can't start a war over a few soldiers who can't obey orders. With Cuba right next door . . . it's a very delicate situation. And the Haitian government is very sensitive about accusations of illegal activity, and they don't appreciate unsolicited American intervention. They're already upset that Major Dane and his team entered the country without permission. If we go in again under the current circumstances, the international consequences could be catastrophic."

"General Steele told me he was poisoned. He thinks someone set the team up and then took him out so he couldn't help them."

"Those are the ravings of a sick, heavily medicated man."

"I think he's telling the truth, and if you're not involved, you need to find out who is," Hunter said. "And if you are involved, as soon as the team is safe, I'm coming for you." Then he disconnected the call.

"I hate him," Brooke said with tears in her eyes.

"I don't hate him," Hunter said. "I don't care about him or Haiti or their government or Cuba or any international problems a rescue might cause. I only care about getting our guys out."

"How are you going to do that?"

"I'm going to start by doing something I promised myself I would never do." Their eyes met in the rearview mirror.

"What?"

"I'm going to call the president."

"Of the *United States?*" she whispered.

He nodded. Then he put his fingers to his lips. "People are always asking him for favors, and I didn't want to be one of them. But we're out of options." He put a series of numbers into the phone.

His call went through two switchboards, and finally Brooke heard a familiar voice say, "Owl? Is that you?"

She nearly fainted.

"Hello, sir." Hunter always sounded stiff and a little formal, but now he was positively ramrod. "I'm sorry to bother you, but there's a situation here at Belvoir that I think you should be aware of." Hunter went on to explain, with an economy of words, what had transpired over the last few days. He concluded with, "You need to be very careful. Don't fly with any new pilots or go out with any new secret service personnel. When there is a breach of security with one of your pilots, well, there could be a reason."

"I appreciate the warning," the president replied. "And I take threats to our military very seriously. What can I do to help your team members?"

"You can't get personally involved, sir, just in case it doesn't go well. But if you could assign someone with a high security clearance to help us so we'll have access to the intel, we need to arrange a rescue."

"I'll send someone right away," the president promised. "Are you at Belvoir?"

"No, sir," Hunter said emphatically. Then in a more controlled tone of voice, he recited directions to Uncle Christopher's cabin.

"Help is on the way."

"Yes, sir. And thank you, sir."

"Thank *you*, Corporal."

Hunter ended the call and put the phone in his uniform pocket.

"I can't believe it!" she said reverently. "You *do* fly the president around!"

"Not regularly," he told her, "but sometimes, yes. Please don't tell anyone. I could lose my job if you do."

"I won't say a word," she promised. "And isn't it a good thing you can trust me now!"

# CHAPTER FOURTEEN

DANE AND HIS TEAM WERE sitting on the floor in the shed that Babineaux was using as their jail cell. They were huddled in the middle, away from the metal walls that conducted heat from the blazing sun outside. They kept conversation and movement to a minimum to conserve their strength and reduce dehydration.

Suddenly the door of the shed swung open. Dane looked up into the blinding light, hoping it was the guards coming to distribute water bottles. But it was Babineaux who stepped inside. And he didn't have any water.

"Well, I have some bad news for you," he said with false remorse. "I made a very friendly offer to your American government. In exchange for your lives, I asked only for a paltry million dollars—more of an apology than a payment—and ten minutes of live television airtime. And do you know what they said?"

Dane stared back, refusing to be baited into a comment.

"They said no," Babineaux provided. "And not just no. They told the world that you are rogue soldiers who are absent without leave. That you are a disgrace to your country."

He paused, probably hoping for a reaction from his prisoners.

Dane was proud as his men and Alcine looked ahead stoically, giving Babineaux no satisfaction.

Finally their captor lifted his shoulder in an eloquent shrug. "Well, we'll see how they feel about that when I start mailing them your bodies one at a time." He stalked out, slamming the door behind him, and they were left in hot darkness again.

\* \* \*

When Brooke and Hunter arrived back at the cabin, they found Savannah and Volt waiting in Uncle Christopher's office.

"It's about time you got here," Volt said. "We need to get this operation into high gear."

Hunter ignored this. He pulled out a chair for Brooke and then sat beside her. "On the way back, I spoke with General Moffett. He told me that the army was working with the Haitian government to get the team released."

"Do you think we can count on that?" Savannah asked.

"No," Hunter answered with blunt honesty. "It might work eventually, but not soon enough. So I called in a favor from a high-ranking friend, and he promised to send someone to help us."

"How high ranking is your friend?" Volt asked.

Brooke held her breath, waiting for the answer.

"High enough," Hunter replied.

"And what kind of help can they give us?"

"Security clearance for the satellite maps and other intel we'll need to plan our operation." Hunter left it at that.

Volt's fingers drummed against his laptop. "No manpower, equipment, or financing?"

Hunter shook his head. "No. My friend can't help officially."

"We appreciate any help we can get," Savannah said. "Tell us exactly what General Steele said. As close as you can remember."

Hunter took a deep breath and then began his summary. "He said the doctors were keeping him drugged."

"That's true," Savannah interrupted. "According to his wife, they want to keep him calm until they figure out what caused his heart attack."

Hunter continued, "Then he said that someone tried to kill him, but when I asked him who and why, he switched subjects to Major Dane and the team. He asked if they were back, and when I told him they weren't— and that General Moffett had cut them off—he got very upset. He said he never should have sent the team on this mission, that something was wrong about it. He thinks they might have purposely been sent on a suicide mission and that he was given something that made it look like he'd had a heart attack so he couldn't help them."

Brooke's heart clenched with guilt. Hunter put a hand on her arm. She appreciated the gesture of reassurance, but she didn't really feel any better.

"Then he told me they'd been sent to Haiti to rescue an undercover ATF agent who was being held by an arms dealer named Babineaux. He told me the operation took place at a fish plant near Baie de Henne. And he made me promise to get them out."

"But he didn't give you any idea who would want to kill Dane and the team?" Savannah asked, her voice shaking.

"No, but Brooke and I have our own ideas on that subject."

Brooke quickly explained their theory. When she was finished, she added, "It could just be a string of coincidences . . ."

Savannah shook her head. "You know your uncle doesn't believe in coincidence. I'm certain you're right. All of this has been put into motion because Rex Moreland wants you dead."

Brooke spread her hands. "The question is why."

"You can figure out the whys and wherefores after we have our boys back on American soil," Volt said. "I've done some research on Babineaux since your phone call, and he is one bad dude."

"I think Volt's right—we don't have time to investigate Rex and his connection with Babineaux right now." Savannah looked at Hunter. "But in the meantime, we need to take extra security precautions. If Rex wants to kill Brooke, he may try again."

"We'll be extremely careful," Hunter promised.

Volt rubbed his hands together. "Okay, back to how we're going to get the guys out."

"Where do we stand on supplies and equipment?" Hunter asked.

Volt opened his laptop. "I have a helicopter and two planes lined up with a third one on standby. I've got guns and ammo and grenades and surface-to-air missiles and Kevlar suits and MREs and bottles of water and, well, just about anything you could possibly need. Except intel. We don't have satellite pictures confirming that Major Dane and the guys haven't been moved. Without that we could go to all this trouble and still not get them. Or worse, we might get them killed." When Volt saw the look on Savannah's face, he added, "Sorry."

"I want you to speak freely around me," she assured him.

Brooke tried not to sound discouraged when she suggested, "Maybe the ATF will help us since they have an agent involved."

"If the ATF could get them out, they wouldn't have asked the army to extract their agent in the first place," Savannah said. "I don't see any point in involving them."

"And that's a shame too," Volt said. "Because even though the ATF is small as federal agencies go, it has some of the broadest powers. We could really use that kind of clout."

An alarm on Volt's phone went off. He checked it and then looked up with a stunned expression. "Well I'll be a monkey's uncle. Corporal Ezell, do you know an ATF agent named Chu?"

"No. Why?"

"Because she's down at the road and wants the guards to let her come up to the cabin. She said to tell you a friend sent her. It's like we made a wish, and she appeared."

Hunter nodded. "Have the guards escort Agent Chu up to the house."

Volt relayed this instruction, and Hunter walked to the back door to wait for them. When he returned Brooke had to control a gasp of surprise. Agent Chu was not at all what she had expected.

The agent looked to be in her early thirties, small and exquisitely beautiful. Her black hair was cut in a short wedge with two sleek points brushing her porcelain cheeks. Her dark, almond-shaped eyes regarded them steadily. Any thoughts that she was as delicate as she looked were dispelled when she spoke.

"Those imbeciles you've got guarding this cabin kept my gun even after they verified that I am a Special Agent for the ATF. Can you explain that?" She looked around, obviously trying to determine who was in charge.

Hunter stood a little straighter and replied, "I guess they didn't think you'd need your gun in here."

Agent Chu narrowed her lovely eyes at him. "And who might you be?"

"Corporal Hunter Ezell," he replied promptly. "US Army."

Agent Chu's eyes moved to Volt.

He raised both hands in mock surrender. "I'm just a civilian."

"Me too," Brooke added when the agent's eyes fell on her.

"I'm Major Dane's wife," Savannah said when it was her turn. "So I guess that makes me something in between."

Agent Chu looked incredulous. "For the love . . . Corporal, when I agreed to come here, I never dreamed you'd be so woefully undermanned— not to mention a bunch of *amateurs*."

Volt bristled at this remark. "I've got a green beret and a navy seal waiting in Fredericksburg. Along with a helicopter and three planes."

Chu raised an eyebrow. "Well, that does make me feel a little better." She studied Savannah. "I met Major Dane once. He's a good man."

Savannah nodded in acknowledgment. "Yes, he is."

"The agent they were sent in to extract is a good man too." She turned to Hunter. "Since you're the only soldier here, I guess you're in charge?"

"I guess so," he looked a little ill, "though I've never led an operation before."

"Don't admit that again," Chu commanded. "A leader can't show weakness. If you act like you know what you're doing, others will follow you."

He nodded. "Yes, sir, I mean, ma'am."

She put her hands on her narrow hips. "So what is it the army has trained you to do?"

"I'm a pilot and a sniper," Hunter replied.

"Are you any good?" Chu asked.

"Yes." Hunter sounded slightly more confident.

Chu pointed at his cast. "How much will that affect your shooting abilities?"

Hunter shrugged. "Not too much."

"Good," Chu said. "So how can I help?"

Volt answered, "We've got a basic plan, but our main weakness is intel."

"What's wrong with your intel?" she asked.

"We don't have any," Hunter explained. "We, I mean, *I* don't have a security clearance high enough to get military maps of the area and satellite images confirming that the team is at Babineaux's fish plant."

"My clearance is high enough to get you any intel you need, but I think I've brought most everything you mentioned with me." Agent Chu pulled out a sheaf of grainy satellite photographs from a leather satchel. "And I can confirm their location. These photos were taken last night and have been carefully analyzed by an expert. The four heat signatures in this small shed never move more than a few feet. So the chances are better than 80 percent that those are our guys."

"But there should be five heat signatures," Hunter said.

Chu shrugged. "Either there was a casualty or one man is being kept separately for some reason."

Brooke watched the blood drain from Savannah's face.

Agent Chu was either oblivious to Savannah's discomfort or chose to ignore it as she pulled a folded map out of the satchel. "This is a military map of the area. It shows latitude, longitude, altitude, miles, nearest water source, nearest fuel source—pretty much everything we could possibly need to know. So we can use this to plan our routes in and out, drop-off and pick-up spots, etc."

Volt took the maps and scanned them greedily. "Sweet."

"Getting to the fish plant shouldn't be hard," Chu continued, "but getting inside will be a different story. The compound has security cameras, motion detectors, and about a hundred guards. You can't bring in enough troops to overpower them."

"Do you know how Major Dane and the team handled this?"

"I believe they took out a generator, the one that provided power for the surveillance system," Chu said. "Then they dug a hole and went in under the fence. Even if that worked—which I doubt since the rescue attempt failed—using the same ploy again would be suicide. This is no surprise attack. Babineaux has bragged to the world that he's holding Americans hostage. He'll be expecting a rescue attempt."

"You could create some sort of diversion to draw them out of the fish plant," Volt said. "Then slip in and get our guys out while everyone is otherwise occupied."

Chu gave him an impatient look. "Do you think Babineaux is an idiot? Anything that happens near that fish plant will immediately be suspect. We might as well call him and say, 'Here we are!'"

Volt took this scathing reprimand like a man. Then he added, "I guess I should have said a really *good* diversion. We need something that they don't recognize as a part of a rescue attempt or something so cataclysmic they can't ignore it even though they see it for what it is."

"Like what?" Agent Chu demanded.

"What if we created a diversion that seemed like a natural occurrence?" Brooke suggested. "He wouldn't be suspicious of an earthquake or a hurricane."

"Or a tsunami," Volt added enthusiastically.

"We can't create an earthquake or a hurricane." Chu gave Volt a severe look. "And we certainly can't create a tsunami!"

Volt shrugged. "No, but you gotta admit it would be cool."

"I don't mean we could actually create a natural disaster," Brooke said. "But maybe we could make them think something was about to happen weather-wise. That would distract them, right?"

"She said the tsunami is out," Volt replied dismissively.

Agent Chu put a finger to her lips, considering. "Actually, you might have something."

Brooke was pleased.

Volt looked astonished. "The tsunami is back on?"

The agent shook her head. "We can't create a tsunami, but maybe there's a real weather event that we could exploit for our benefit." Agent Chu pointed at Volt's laptop. "Tell me the forecast for Haiti during the next twenty-four hours."

"Chance of rain," Volt read from his computer, "but nothing severe."

"Could we exaggerate the forecast to make it seem like a bad storm is coming?" Hunter suggested.

Volt shook his head. "Based on what I've seen so far, Babineaux is too well connected technology-wise for that to work. If he finds conflicting weather reports, he'll smell a rat."

"And if a hurricane warning is announced in Haiti—a country that was recently decimated by a hurricane—there would be large-scale panic. People might get hurt. We can't be responsible for that. Look for something else we could exploit besides a weather event."

Volt was already typing. "Yes, ma'am. I mean, sir."

Chu narrowed her eyes at Volt. "What was your name?"

"Volt," he supplied nervously.

She shook her head. "Okay, Volt, give me some options."

Volt read from his computer screen. "There's a beauty pageant for senior women in Port-au-Prince on Wednesday."

"What else?"

"A mortician's convention starts tomorrow. Over twenty coffin manufacturers will be displaying their wares."

Chu frowned. "I don't see how that is going to help us distract Babineaux on the other side of the island."

"Maybe the plane carrying the display coffins could fly over the fish plant and mistakenly drop them out of the cargo hold," Hunter suggested.

Volt swung around to face him. "The *coffins?*"

Hunter nodded. "It'd be something they'd have to deal with."

"Hey, that kind of stuff will bring you bad luck, man," Volt warned.

"And we've got plenty of that already," Savannah muttered.

Despite the serious circumstances, Brooke had to work hard to control a giggle.

"Okay, what else do you have besides coffins?" Chu asked Volt.

"A softball tournament, a couple of family reunions. That's about it.

Chu ground her teeth. "For the love . . . we can't catch a break."

"Maybe we could use my idea except without the coffins," Hunter suggested.

"But the falling coffins *was* the distraction," Agent Chu pointed out.

"We could fly in the invasion team, and let them out a few miles from the fish plant. I'll stay on board and fly in close. Then I'll crash-land the plane on that field." He pointed to a spot on the map. "If we have extra fuel on board, it will burn hot and fast. They'll have to use manpower to put it out or risk the whole plant burning down."

Brooke was so terrified she could barely make her mouth form the words, "But Hunter, you . . ."

He turned and put his hands on her shoulders. "I'll parachute out at the last minute."

Brooke leaned against him, weak with relief.

Chu thought for a minute and then nodded. "I like it. Volt, make sure the plane has extra fuel and plenty of parachutes."

"Yes, sir!"

"Now that we have our diversion, we need to come up with our actual invasion plan," Hunter said.

"We will have to approach with extreme caution and be prepared for considerable resistance," Chu warned. "I suggest two teams going in separately. Best-case scenario—both teams reach the fish plant, and we combine to rescue the team. But if Babineaux detects one of us and attacks, maybe the other team can still sneak in."

"I like that," Hunter said thoughtfully. "But as you pointed out, we're undermanned. It will take too long to come up with another team."

"You provide one team, and I'll provide the other," Chu said. "I've already got a group assembled and ready to go."

"They'll work under my direction," Hunter qualified. "This is our op, our team that is being held captive. Your team will be my resource. I have to approve everything they do."

Chu seemed surprised by his assertiveness and not particularly happy, but she didn't argue. "I'll agree to that as long as we collaborate closely."

Brooke hated to interrupt, but there was a question she had to ask. "Agent Chu?"

The agent swung her deceptively beautiful eyes to Brooke. "Yes?"

"If you have a team, do you know why my uncle's team was sent in originally?"

The room was quiet as everyone waited for the answer.

"No," Agent Chu replied. "In fact, I was furious when I found out we'd been skipped over for some army knuckleheads. Do you know why Major Dane's team got the assignment?"

Before Brooke could answer, Hunter spoke. "We have a theory, but no time to prove it now."

Agent Chu nodded. "Then we'll save that conversation for later." She spread the map on Dane's desk and pointed out the proposed drop-off and pick-up sites for both teams. Hunter and Volt studied the map and considered Agent Chu's suggestions carefully. Brooke sat by the window, barely taking her eyes off Hunter. He was going into danger, and she would be separated from him for the first time in weeks. It made her want to weep, but she would not cry in front of the terrifying Agent Chu.

"It's all a little cut and dry," Chu complained. "I'm afraid Babineaux will see right through it. Corporal, you'd better make that plane crash really spectacular if we're going to have a chance of pulling this off."

"Can I make a suggestion?" Savannah asked.

Agent Chu nodded.

"I don't know if this would qualify as a distraction or a solution, but there's something else I think we should try before we risk two more teams. I'm not in the military, but I have been associated with Dane and the team for a long time—during good times and bad."

Hunter nodded his encouragement.

"Is there a point here?" Chu demanded.

"I have a suggestion that I want you to take very seriously."

"I'm always serious," Hunter replied.

"That's true," Brooke confirmed. "I've barely ever seen him smile."

He ignored this. "What's your suggestion?"

"Dane always likes to have a multi-pronged approach."

"We'll have two rescue teams, one more than Babineaux should expect," Hunter pointed out. "That's two prongs."

"And a spectacular plane crash," Volt added. "That's prong number three."

They all ignored him.

"Babineaux offered to trade Dane and his team for a ransom. The army refused, but I'd like to offer to pay the money. I think my friend at

CNN can get him ten minutes of live airtime. If he accepts my offer, we won't have to risk any more lives or crash a plane."

Hunter shook his head. "Major Dane wouldn't want you to have anything to do with Babineaux."

Chu wasn't concerned for Savannah personally, so her objection was more pragmatic. "That would never work. How would you contact him?"

"Volt can get his number," Savannah said. "He said he can find anything."

"If I get the number, can you come up with a million dollars in a hurry?" Volt asked.

"I can handle the ransom money," Agent Chu murmured. "And I'm guessing CNN would be ecstatic at the opportunity to give Babineaux airtime. Imagine the jump in their ratings. But you realize we can't trust this man? He may take the money and keep your husband. Then we're back to square one."

"What if we send the rescue teams with the money," Savannah said. "It would look like they were just a security force to protect the ransom. Then if Babineaux keeps his word and gives us Dane and the team, everyone will fly back home. But if a rescue is still necessary, the teams are right there, ready.

"If nothing else, the ransom negotiations and prisoner exchange will distract Babineaux to some extent," Brooke pointed out. "Along with the crashing plane."

"The more distraction the better," Agent Chu said. "Let's do it."

Hunter shook his head. "Major Dane wouldn't want Savannah involved on any level."

"Major Dane doesn't want to be a prisoner in Haiti either, but he is," Agent Chu replied. "So I think we can put his feelings aside for the moment."

Hunter shook his head and turned to Savannah. "I don't like it."

Agent Chu stepped in. "Corporal, your objection has been duly noted. Mrs. Dane is a civilian and therefore not required to follow your orders. And I outrank you. So let me make a phone call to get the money arranged. Volt, are you working on that phone number?"

"Yes, sir!" he called out.

"Mrs. Dane, call your friend at CNN and see if they'll give Babineaux some airtime. If he resists, tell him we're going to call his competition. That should do it. And get that in writing. Babineaux will probably want proof."

Savannah nodded.

"Let's have everything ready so we can make contact in an hour."

Savannah was already reaching for her phone.

Brooke sat by the desk, watching all the activity and feeling useless.

\* \* \*

Brooke noticed that Savannah's fingers were shaking as she dialed the number for her friend Edgar at CNN. She waited on hold for several minutes, but finally Edgar answered. Brooke wasn't actually trying to eavesdrop, but she was close enough to hear every word.

"Sorry to keep you waiting, Savannah, but I've never been this busy in my life! And my new super-celebrity status is your fault. We're getting so many phone calls and e-mails and texts and blog comments that I've had to hire five new people just to keep up. General Moffett may turn out to be the best thing that ever happened to me."

"I'm glad things are going well for you, Edgar."

"I'm sorry that all this publicity hasn't helped to get your husband back. Is there anything else I can do?"

"Actually there is. I need CNN to give Jacques Babineaux ten minutes of live airtime. It has to be uninterrupted. He says he'll kill his captives if you cut him off early."

"Do you know what he's going to do or say?"

"No, but I'm pretty sure it won't be complimentary of the United States or the army or maybe even Dane himself, but it should be great for ratings."

"I feel bad that I'm benefiting again from your misfortune."

"Just get me that airtime. And I need it in writing." Savannah gave him her fax number and then added, "If your producers don't want to take the risk, I'll call Fox or MSNBC."

"I am a little nervous about getting involved with this Babineaux guy. If he finds out I helped you, he might kill me."

"With all this extra business, I'm sure you can afford to hire some bodyguards."

He laughed. "Okay, but if this works, you have to give me an exclusive interview."

"Deal," Savannah said. "But don't mention my plan on TV or your blog or anywhere else until I get Dane back. If you do, you'll lose your exclusive rights."

She heard him sigh. "You drive a hard bargain, but okay. Be watching for that fax."

The others had been conferring across the room, but when she ended her call, Hunter and Agent Chu walked over.

"What did he say?" Hunter asked.

"He's going to send me a fax confirmation in a few minutes."

"Now if Volt can just get us a contact number . . ." the agent growled.

Volt shook his head. "I've tried six numbers with no luck. Either I get an answering service or no answer at all. It's possible that he only uses disposable phones, impossible to track."

"Well, so much for that plan," Agent Chu said.

Volt lifted a piece of paper from the fax tray. "Here's your confirmation from CNN—though I guess it's worthless now."

Then a thought occurred to Brooke. "If I had my phone, I could give you Babineaux's number."

Everyone turned to stare at her.

"So you *do* know Jacques Babineaux?" Hunter's face was pale, and his voice was barely above a whisper. "All that shock and astonishment, putting two and two together and coming up with the Rex connection was just an act?"

Brooke saw the doubt and revulsion in his face as all the progress they had made over the past few days just slipped away. She felt like her heart would break. "Of course I don't know Babineaux. My shock was completely genuine. But if we're right and Rex knows Babineaux, his contact information should be in the Joined Forces database, which I can access from my phone."

Hunter looked relieved, but that didn't make her feel much better. His reaction proved that he still didn't trust her. Maybe he never would. She turned away. The sight of him was just too painful.

"But since I don't have my phone, I might be able to get Rex's newly deserted girlfriend, Millicent, to give me the information," she told Agent Chu.

"Rex and Millicent—are these people I should know about?" Agent Chu asked.

Brooke said, "They're part of the theory we don't have time to discuss right now." Then she turned to Volt. "I need Hunter's old phone. Millicent's number is in it."

Volt produced the phone, and Brooke scanned through the recently called numbers until she found the one she was looking for. Then she used the satellite phone to place the call. After a few rings, Millicent answered tentatively.

"Hey, Millicent, it's me, Brooke." She tried her best to sound carefree.

"I didn't recognize the number."

"Yes, I lost my phone, so now I'm using this one." She glanced at Hunter, hoping he'd noticed her adherence to the truth. "Have you heard from Rex yet?"

"No." Millicent sounded discouraged.

"Well, I won't keep you long, but I wanted to ask you for a favor. Can you look in the Joined Forces database and get me a phone number for Jacques Babineaux? He's the guy in Haiti who owns the beach and will let Joined Forces members stay for free. Hunter and I need to plan our honeymoon soon, and I thought I'd give him a call."

There was a long pause, and Brooke was afraid the girl was going to refuse. But finally she said, "Sure. Just a minute."

Volt slid a legal pad and a pencil over to her. She picked up the pencil and twisted it nervously between her fingers while she waited.

"Sorry." Millicent was back on the line. "I don't have a phone number for him."

Brooke saw her own disappointment reflected on the faces around her.

"But I do have an e-mail address," Millicent continued. "Will that work?"

"That will be great." She wrote down the e-mail address as Millicent recited it to her. "Thank you so much. And I hope your ankle gets better soon." Brooke was just about to say good-bye when Millicent spoke again.

"Um, I think the police are going to let me into the call center today to start cleaning stuff up. Would you be able to come and help me?"

"I wish I could." It wasn't a lie. Brooke really did feel sorry for the girl. "But I'm out of town, and I won't be back for . . . a while."

"Oh, okay." Millicent accepted this lame excuse politely. "Well, maybe I'll see you around sometime."

"Maybe so," Brooke replied. "And thanks again." She ended the call and slumped into her chair."

"Good work!" Savannah cried.

"Quite impressive." Agent Chu praised, picking the legal pad up with her dainty hands. "Now let's start writing down what you're going to say to Babineaux."

Brooke sat in a chair by the window while the others gathered around the desk.

"We'll keep the first contact simple," Hunter said. "We don't want to give him any information he can use against us."

Agent Chu nodded. "We can always give him more details later."

Savannah sat down in front of Dane's laptop. Her fingers hovered over the keys, trembling a little. Then together they helped her compose a short e-mail.

*Dear Sir. My name is Savannah Dane. You asked for a ransom of one million dollars and ten minutes of television airtime in exchange for the release of my husband and his team. I will pay the money, and CNN will provide the airtime. Please e-mail me back so we can work out an exchange. Thank you.*

"That sounds good," Hunter said. "Respectful enough without groveling."

Agent Chu pointed at the screen. "Send it, and let's see what happens."

While they waited anxiously for a response, they discussed what they would do if Babineaux agreed to an exchange.

"The meet site will be important," Agent Chu said. "If you agree to a place we can't secure, we'll basically just be giving him a million dollars in addition to your husband and his team."

"Or someone else might relieve you of the money before you even see Babineaux," Volt contributed. "Like I said before, Haiti has a pervasive criminal element. In fact, I can't think of a single place in Haiti that I'd consider safe to exchange a million dollars."

"Then we'll have to push for an exchange site out of Haiti, one that we can secure," Hunter said. "Like a bank in the Caymans? Or Gitmo?"

"Babineaux won't agree to either of those locations," Agent Chu said with certainty. "The only place *he's* safe is Haiti. I say we offer the international airport at Port-au-Prince. If we make the exchange right on the runway, in full view, it might meet requirements for both sides."

"Don't kid yourself," Volt warned. "Even the airport ain't secure."

"I never kid myself or anyone else," Agent Chu assured him. "I'm not saying this will work, but it's better than trying to transport money through Haiti in a donkey cart."

"I'll suggest the airport—if he ever e-mails me back." Savannah pushed the refresh button on the laptop for the one hundredth time.

One of Hack's guards stuck his head in the door and asked if Savannah wanted him to order pizza for dinner.

"Who are *you*?" Agent Chu demanded, not even slightly intimidated by the fact that Hack's man was three times her size. "A pizza delivery guy?"

"He's one of the guards assigned to protect me while my husband is gone," Savannah explained quickly.

"Well then, he needs to get back to guarding and quit acting like a short order cook."

The guard was obviously offended.

"We have to eat," Savannah pointed out to Agent Chu. Then she turned to the guard. "Please order pizzas. Hack will reimburse you when he gets back."

With one last glare in Agent Chu's direction, the guard retreated, closing the office door behind him.

Once he was gone, the agent muttered, "This seriously is a mom-and-pop outfit. I've never worked under such unprofessional conditions."

"Usually it's much more professional," Savannah said. "When Dane is here." She pushed refresh again and then pointed at the screen. "He wrote me back," she announced breathlessly.

They gathered around her.

Babineaux had written, *Such a pleasure to hear from you, Mrs. Dane. I understand your frustration with the army of your country. I accept your offer to compensate me for the inconveniences caused by your husband and to arrange airtime on CNN. However, in addition, I require replacements for the weapons that your husband destroyed. A list is given below for your convenience.*

It was signed simply *JB*. Underneath was a daunting list of firearms.

Savannah wiped away a fresh wave of tears. "How in the world can I come up with all those weapons?"

"Tell him exactly that," Agent Chu advised. "You don't know how you can possibly come up with the items on his list but that you'll look into it and e-mail him back. And you need to make sure that he really has your husband."

Savannah glanced up. "How?"

"Ask him something about your husband that he could only know if he is holding him captive."

Savannah thought for a few seconds. Then she said, "Dane has scars, terrible scars, from the time he spent in a Russian prison."

Agent Chu nodded solemnly. "Then ask about the scars."

Savannah flexed her fingers and began typing again. *I need to verify that my husband is actually with you. Can you tell me about his scars?*

Babineaux responded promptly. *I asked your husband to remove his shirt, and I see that he has so many scars on his chest and his back. Which ones would you like me to tell you about?*

"What a relief!" Savannah cried. "We found him. We may not have freed him yet, but this is definitely progress."

"Definitely," Brooke agreed.

Savannah returned to the keyboard. *I can raise the money, but the guns will be more difficult. Can you give me a little time on that?*

Again his answer came quickly. *I will give you thirty minutes. And I'm sure I don't have to warn you that your husband's life is depending on you. No tricks. No games.*

Savannah shot Hunter a worried look, but he nodded encouragingly. "Go ahead and answer him."

Savannah's hands began to type. *I understand. All that matters to me is getting my husband and his team back safely.*

The screen remained blank for several seconds, and Savannah had decided that Babineaux was gone. Then another message appeared in her inbox. *For our next communication, we will use video-messaging. I like to look into the eyes of those I deal with. And perhaps you will even be able to see your husband for a brief moment—as my show of goodwill.*

Below the message was his account information for a video-messaging service.

Automatically Savannah typed *thank you* in the message box.

"Don't thank him," Chu objected. "He's kidnapped your husband and threatened to kill him. Besides, he might perceive that as a sign of weakness."

Savannah backspaced to delete her initial response and typed, *I will be ready in thirty minutes.*

"I know this sounds crazy," Savannah said, wiping at her eyes again. "But I hate that my conversation with Babineaux had to end. It felt like a connection with Dane, and now I'm separated again.

Brooke put her arm around her aunt. "You did a great job. Everything's going to be okay." She noticed that no one seconded her prediction.

Savannah took a deep breath. "Now, Volt, I need you to get me set up for video-messaging in less than thirty minutes. Hunter and Agent Chu, how can we come up with those weapons?"

"You could ask General Moffett," Hunter suggested.

"That would be a waste of breath," Savannah dismissed this idea.

"We could try to buy the stuff on the black market, but that will be expensive and time consuming," Volt said without looking up from his computer.

"Not to mention illegal," Brooke added.

"And immoral," Agent Chu contributed. "We cannot give weapons to Babineaux knowing they will eventually be used on innocent people."

"So what do I tell him?" Savannah asked. "He made that a requirement of the exchange."

Hunter thought for a minute. "Tell him that the army won't help you with guns, and you have no experience in purchasing weapons. Therefore you can't meet a tight time line or guarantee the quality of the arms purchased. Suggest that you'll give him an extra million, and he can buy his own guns."

"Two million dollars," Savannah murmured. "Can you handle that, Agent Chu?"

The agent sighed. "Hand me a phone."

# CHAPTER FIFTEEN

DANE WAS DREAMING. HE WAS on the bridge at the cabin, fishing with Caroline. She smiled at him, her eyes so much like her father's. It was almost like he was looking at his old friend. He loved them both—the father and the child.

Then Savannah came walking toward them from the house. She was smiling and carrying a small baby in her arms. Dane strained his eyes trying to see this child, his child, the one he would never meet. He wanted so badly to know if the baby was a boy or a girl, but his vision blurred.

He tried to ask Caroline, but he couldn't make his mouth form the words. She rattled on about fishing and rainbows, oblivious to his distress. He turned back to Savannah and waved, but the baby was still hidden from view. Frustrated he tried to stand. And then he woke up. He was in the hot, dark shed at Babineaux's fish plant. And the other men were watching him with concern.

"Is something wrong?" Doc rasped.

"Just a dream," he replied softly.

"Do you think Hack's okay?" Steamer whispered.

"I don't know," Dane answered. "Babineaux said he was only wounded, but that could be a lie. We have to accept that he might be dead."

Agent Alcine looked miserable. "I'm sorry, sir."

Dane replied, "You were just doing your job as you understood it."

The ATF agent didn't look reassured.

Dane turned his head. "Steam, you doing all right?"

Steamer responded, "I've never been this filthy in my life."

Dane almost smiled. "If you're worried about cleanliness, you're okay."

Then they heard footsteps approaching the door. The chains and padlocks on the door rattled, and finally it was thrown open to expose a guard. He stepped in and grabbed Dane by the arm.

"You are to come with me to see Monsieur," he said.

He proceeded to half drag Dane across the open area and into Babineaux's house. This time the arms dealer was sitting in a large recliner in front of the huge television, sipping something brown. It was iced, and the sight of the condensation on the outside of the glass made Dane's mouth water.

"Forgive me. I know it is rude to drink in front of a guest," Babineaux said. He didn't sound sorry, and he continued to sip his drink.

Then he reached into his black shoulder bag, and Dane wondered if he had been summoned to his execution. But when Babineaux removed his hand, it was empty, as if he just wanted to reassure himself that the weapon was there and ready.

"It has been a terrible day for you," Babineaux began with false sympathy. "I know you must feel bad that you were captured by your own ineptitude. Then your government refused to help you. And even worse, they slandered your name on television for all the world to hear."

Dane was careful not to react, but he did feel rejected and abandoned. He guessed that Babineaux's purpose for this visit was to torture him.

"Your country does not value your life," Babineaux droned on. "However, your wife feels differently."

Dane's heart pounded painfully. Savannah.

Babineaux continued, "She has offered to pay a million dollars and has arranged ten minutes of television airtime. She is a resourceful woman, your wife. You should be proud of her."

Dane didn't respond. He couldn't trust his voice.

"My next communication with her is going to be through video-messaging," Babineaux went on. "I brought you in so you can see her. Never say I'm not romantic."

Dane was conflicted. He didn't want Babineaux talking to Savannah, but the chance to hear her voice, to see her face, was irresistible.

"I've always been a fool for love," Babineaux said with a smile. "I get that from my French father."

Dane refused to be goaded.

"I've always been practical too though. I get that from my Lebanese mother. She never knew when she might be thrown out of her home, robbed, beaten, or imprisoned just because of who she was. So now I'm going to use your wife's love like a weapon."

Dane just stared back.

Babineaux turned to one of the several guards in the room. "Tape his mouth up." He waited until this was accomplished. Then he said, "Now it is time."

Dane watched with dread and anticipation as Babineaux typed into the computer's keyboard. A picture of his office back in Virginia filled the big flat screen on the wall. He could see his chair, the photographs on the wall, a picture Caroline had colored for him. It all looked so ordinary. It was hard to believe he was far away, captive, and unlikely to ever be there again.

Then Savannah came into view as she sat in his chair and faced the computer screen.

"Hello." She sounded nervous. She sounded wonderful.

Dane's reaction was too emotional to hide completely.

Babineaux noticed. "Ah, love," he mocked softly. Then he turned his attention to his computer. "Good morning, Mrs. Dane. As I promised I'm going to let you have a quick glimpse of your husband."

He tilted the laptop slightly so the camera could capture an image of his prisoner. Dane turned away. He didn't want Savannah to see the tears in his eyes.

"Dane!" Savannah cried. He heard the distress in her voice and knew he must look as bad as he felt.

He turned back toward the computer and gave her a nod of reassurance. It wasn't much, but it was enough. The panic left Savannah's face, and she settled against his desk chair.

Babineaux turned the laptop away from his prisoner. "I'm sorry that your husband can't talk to you right now, but you have confirmation of his condition."

"Yes," Savannah replied carefully.

"Have you arranged for my replacement weapons?" Babineaux pressed.

"No," she replied, obviously still shaken from the glimpse of her husband. "The army won't provide them. I considered trying to buy them from someone else, but I don't have contacts in those circles nor time to develop any. Since you already have sources, my proposal is that I give you an extra million dollars and let you buy your own replacements."

Babineaux's eyebrows shot up. "You *are* clever! And I will accept your deal. Two million dollars in cash—one-hundred-dollar bills grouped in hundreds. I'll want to verify the amount, of course."

"Of course," Savannah replied.

"And ten minutes of live airtime on CNN. I presume you have proof of this arrangement."

Savannah held up a piece of paper. "This is the fax I received from CNN. Can you read it or would you like me to fax it to you?"

"Attach it to an e-mail and send it to the address you used previously. Then I will close that account, so don't get any ideas about sharing it with your authorities."

"No, I won't," she promised.

The sound of her voice was exquisite torture. Dane wondered if she was still feeling sick and drinking Spriteorade. He wondered how it was possible to love someone as much as he loved her.

"I am gathering the money now and can have it ready tomorrow morning. I've rented a plane and arranged to fly into the Port-au-Prince airport a little before noon. I propose that you be there with my husband and his team. We can make the exchange on the tarmac in full view of everyone at the airport for both our protection. Then we'll fly away, and you'll have your money."

Babineaux considered this for a few seconds and then nodded. "I will agree to your delivery proposal but not your airport of choice. I'd prefer something smaller and less regulated. Let's say the one in Port-de-Paix."

Savannah looked to her left, presumably checking out this modification with someone else. Then she nodded. "Okay, I'll change the flight plans."

"And one more condition," Babineaux said. "I insist that you bring the money personally."

Dane tried again not to react, but once again he failed.

Babineaux enjoyed his reaction and was smiling as he continued, "Your presence will be an extra bit of insurance against American trickery."

Dane listened tensely. He was sure Owl was helping Savannah and would make her refuse this ridiculous condition. He waited, anxious yet confident that she would say the right thing, the safe thing.

Then she replied, "I'll accept that condition. I will see you at the airport in Port-de-Paix tomorrow at noon."

And Dane felt as if the whole world had fallen in on top of him.

\* \* \*

When the video call ended, Brooke watched as Savannah put her hands over her face and sobbed. Hunter gave her a couple of awkward pats on the back and then looked to Brooke for help. She crossed the room and drew Savannah into an only slightly less awkward hug.

"You did great!" she praised.

"He accepted our terms, basically," Hunter added.

"And your husband is alive." Agent Chu cut to the heart of the matter.

This seemed to make Savannah feel better. She wiped her eyes and squared her shoulders. "Okay, now what?"

Hunter tapped his pencil on the legal pad in front of her where he had written, *Say NO*. "Why did you agree to deliver the money when I plainly instructed you not to?"

"I want my husband back, and Babineaux made it a condition. I had to agree."

"And now we've got to figure out a way around that condition," Hunter said. "If I let you deliver two million dollars to a known terrorist and Major Dane survives, he'll kill me." Hunter winced, obviously regretting his choice of words. "I didn't mean . . ."

"I know what you meant," Savannah assured him. "But we can't give Dane's feelings priority over his life."

Still determined, Hunter changed tactics. "You have to think about Caroline and your baby." He waved vaguely at her midsection. "Major Dane and the team are already at grave risk. If Babineaux gets you too, well . . . you don't want your kids to be orphans."

Brooke was horrified. "Hunter!"

"It's okay," Savannah said. "I understand the risks, but I did what I thought I had to do. And even if it was wrong, it's too late to change it now."

Agent Chu stepped forward. "She really didn't have a choice, but that doesn't mean she will actually make the delivery. Any woman could do it. I could do it if I wear a blond wig."

Savannah laughed humorlessly. "That's ridiculous. Babineaux has seen me face-to-face, and we don't look anything alike!"

"Then we'll find an agent who resembles you more than I do," Chu persisted.

"We don't have time for that." Savannah was growing impatient.

"I could do it," Brooke said softly from her seat in the corner.

All eyes turned to her.

Nervously she lifted a lock of her hair. "Now that I've gone blonde, I look a little like Savannah. We're the same basic height and build. If I wear this new suit"—she pulled on the lapels of her expensive jacket—"I could probably pass for her. At least for a few minutes, especially if Babineaux's attention is focused on the money."

"With the right hairstyle and makeup, you could pass for Mrs. Dane," Agent Chu agreed. "We can fit you for a Kevlar vest . . ."

Hunter was shaking his head. "No way. We'll find an agent or a soldier or someone else who is trained for dangerous situations."

"It's unlikely that we'll be able to find anyone that looks this much like Mrs. Dane on such short notice." Agent Chu waved toward Brooke.

"I want to do it," Brooke added, "so there's no reason to find anyone else. All of this is because of me, and I should do what I can to fix it."

Agent Chu frowned. "This is your fault?"

"More of that theory we aren't discussing."

"We might have to make time for that discussion soon," Agent Chu remarked. "Everything seems to come back to it."

"Anyway, I'll deliver the money in Savannah's place."

Hunter put a hand on her arm and pulled her toward the door. "Can I talk to you for a minute? Alone?"

Brooke shook his hand away. "You can talk to me, but you can't drag me. And just for a minute. I've got a secret mission to prepare for." With that she turned and stalked out of the room.

She walked through the living room and out the front door of her uncle's cabin. The porch overlooked the creek where the sun was setting. Brilliant colors from the sky reflected in the water below. It was like a painting—almost too beautiful to be real.

She heard Hunter come up behind her. He was stepping harder than necessary, almost stomping, in an obvious indication of his displeasure. As if she needed a hint.

She crossed her arms over her chest and turned to face him.

He looked even more furious than when he found out she'd lied to him, and her determination wavered. Then she reminded herself that a few minutes before, he had believed her capable of friendship with the kidnapper and illegal arms dealer, Jacques Babineaux. That was enough to strengthen her resolve.

"You can't go to Haiti," he said. "I have experience in this type of thing, and believe me, you're not prepared for it."

"I'm not going into combat. I'm just delivering a ton of money, and you'll be right there beside me. What could go wrong?"

"Everything! Babineaux is an international criminal!"

"Don't yell at me, or I'm going back inside."

He took a deep breath as if he were dealing with the most annoying person on earth. Then he continued more calmly, "I understand that you want to help your uncle and protect Savannah, but you'd be putting your life at risk."

"I know."

"You say that like it's nothing." Then his eyes narrowed. "Did you stupidly volunteer for this just to get an emotional commitment from me?"

She gasped at his audacity. "You're almost as egotistical as Rex," she accused. "And no, this isn't about you. I *stupidly* volunteered to help my uncle because he's helped me so many times. And he wouldn't even be in Haiti if it wasn't for me." She glanced back at the creek. "But since I've vowed to be completely honest with you, I'll admit that I wouldn't mind if my bravery made you love me a little more."

He shook his head. " Brooke . . ."

"Hunter . . ." she returned in the same exasperated tone.

"I'm serious."

"Oh, I know," she muttered.

"I'm sorry I said that about Babineaux. It was a mistake. When you offered to get his number, it took me by surprise, and I just . . ."

"You just don't trust me." She turned back to him. "You've been trying to tell me that it's not something you can control. Now I understand. But this whole discussion is a waste of time. The ATF can't find someone else in a few hours. I'm not just the best choice—I'm the *only* choice."

Hunter continued to argue. "You're an untrained civilian, and your participation puts not only your life at risk, but the whole rescue operation."

"It's a risk everyone else seems willing to take," she pointed out. "Except you. Why is that, Hunter?"

He stared at her, silently fuming, for several seconds. Finally he said, "Because your uncle charged me with keeping you safe."

"Is that your best argument, really?" she demanded. "That you just want me alive so you can feel like you did your job?"

"You know that's not the only reason I want you to stay alive."

"Either you're my husband and you have something to say about what I do, or you're my bodyguard and have no say whatsoever. Which is it going to be?"

This time he was the one who looked away. "I told you I'm not ready for marriage."

"Employee it is." Then she turned and moved toward the door. She went slowly, hoping he would stop her, but he didn't.

When she walked back into her uncle's office where the others were waiting, Agent Chu demanded, "Well?"

"I'm going," Brooke said.

"I don't know how to thank you." Savannah pulled her into a hug.

Agent Chu gave Brooke a nod of approval and took out her phone. "Let me tell my team it's a go."

Hunter walked in and sat in the corner chair as far away from the others as possible. Apparently this was his way of showing that he had not agreed to this portion of the plan.

Agent Chu ended her call and said, "My team will leave for Miami tonight."

Savannah looked worried. "Now explain to me how all of this is going to work."

Chu turned to Hunter. "Corporal, can you fill Mrs. Dane in?"

Hunter stood and joined the group around the desk. "My team will fly into the airport at Port-de-Paix with the money. And Brooke," he added reluctantly.

Agent Chu noticed the tension and looked between them briefly before saying, "I'll bring my team in on a military transport. It's a regular flight that makes deliveries each week to our embassy there, so it shouldn't draw particular notice from Babineaux."

"Your team won't be at the airport when the money arrives?" Savannah asked.

"We'll be there, but we'll stay out of sight. Depending on how things go, we'll either leave with the corporal's team or head to the fish plant."

"I'm trying to be optimistic," Savannah said. "I really hope he exchanges the money for the team."

"I believe in realism," Chu replied. "I hope the exchange happens too, but I can't count on that. We're playing a deadly game of chess with a cold-blooded killer, and all we can do is match his moves."

Savannah shuddered. "I just want Dane and the guys back safely."

The AFT agent frowned. "Extracting Major Dane, his team, and our agent is the top priority, but recouping the money is a close second. We can't finance terrorist activity."

"After we safeguard the team, we can help you reacquire the money," Hunter offered.

Agent Chu smiled. "It's good to know some army pansies got our back."

"Not *just* army pansies," Volt corrected without looking up from his laptop. "Our team has a navy seal too."

Savannah gave him a weak smile.

Hunter sighed.

The agent pulled out her phone. "I've got a few more calls to make. The rest of you go eat."

They left Agent Chu making phone calls and trudged into the kitchen, but only Volt felt like eating.

"Man, this is good pizza!" he said as he pulled another piece onto his plate. "You folks are missing out."

Brooke gave the pizza covered with sausage and pepperoni a look of distaste. "I'm a vegetarian."

"And I've got twenty-four-hour morning sickness," Savannah added.

Hunter gave no excuse for his rare lack of appetite. He just stared out the window at the creek.

"Spriteorade, anyone?" Savannah offered, holding up the mixture. "This is a fresh batch."

"No, thanks," Brooke declined. Hunter just shook his head.

So they sat in uncomfortable silence until Agent Chu walked in.

"Corporal, as you requested, I've lined up a couple ATF agents to fly your plane," Agent Chu announced.

Brooke looked at Hunter and raised an eyebrow. "I thought you would be the pilot."

"Not with one arm," Hunter said pointedly. "I accept my limitations and don't want to risk the operation."

"Corporal Ezell will have another assignment," the agent said. "Much more important."

Brooke's heart sank. Hunter only had one other exceptional talent besides flying planes. She dragged her eyes up to meet his. "You're going to be a sniper?"

"First and foremost, I'll be your bodyguard—which may be the hardest assignment I've ever had."

Brooke stood and put her hands on her hips. "If guarding me is so hard, I'll take the navy seal *or* the green beret. Heck, I'll even take an ATF pansy!"

Agent Chu's eyes widened. "Whoa."

Savannah gave her a weak smile. "Just a friendly spat."

Brooke concentrated on Hunter. "And let me make one more thing clear. I'm going into this with my eyes open. I know the risks, and I accept them. If I get hurt, it's on me, not you."

Hunter seemed unaffected by her outburst. "Major Dane gave me responsibility for your safety, and he's the only one who can release me from that obligation. So I won't be able to switch assignments with anyone—including a pansy. I'm just following orders."

"Oh, I know that." She turned away so he wouldn't see the tears in her eyes. Unfortunately that brought her face-to-face with Agent Chu.

"This"—the agent moved her finger between them—"whatever it is . . . won't be a problem during our operation, will it?"

Brooke controlled her emotions with effort. "No."

The agent looked at Hunter. "Well?"

"You know how I feel about Brooke's participation," he said. "I think it's a problem for many reasons."

"Are you saying I need to find a replacement for you?" the agent demanded.

"You can't replace me," he said. "I'm in charge of this mission."

"Then put your personal feelings aside, Corporal," Agent Chu said firmly. "We need Miss Clayton, so she's part of the team."

Hunter nodded without enthusiasm.

Agent Chu seemed satisfied. "Now let's put the finishing touches on this plan. What else needs to be done?"

"We'll need your credentials to get flight plans into Haiti approved at such late notice," Hunter told her.

"I'll call the airport."

Volt polished off another piece of pizza. "You still want the helicopter I reserved, or do you have one of your own?"

"We'll use yours," the agent replied.

"And how are we going to handle the plane that we plan to crash and burn in Haiti? Get extra insurance?"

Agent Chu shook her head. "That would be fraud. Either the army or the ATF will reimburse the rental company."

"Suits me." Volt stood and wiped his hands on his jeans. "Then the next order of business is communications. Follow me back to the office so I can give you all satellite phones—except Owl. He already has one."

They returned to the office. Volt pulled out a box of phones and distributed them.

Agent Chu examined hers. "So this phone can't lose service?"

"Theoretically, no," Volt replied. "I haven't tested them personally. They're pre-coded and supposedly untraceable, but I wouldn't use them more than you have to. And, of course, all other phones are to be left here."

Agent Chu put her phone on the desk and then looked at Brooke.

"The Nashville police have mine," Brooke explained.

Agent Chu shook her head. "I can't wait to hear this story."

While the others were going over final details, Savannah took Brooke upstairs and gave her a quick makeup and hairstyling lesson. Brooke watched closely so that she could duplicate the process the next day.

Finally Savannah was satisfied. "There," she said as she studied Brooke in the mirror. "That's as close as we are going to get."

"Do you think it will fool Babineaux?"

Savannah pursed her lips. "For a few minutes probably. Try not to get too close to him."

When they got back downstairs, everyone except Hunter expressed at least some degree of approval over Brooke's altered appearance.

Then Agent Chu said, "We've got the whole operation mapped out, complete with approved flight schedules and timetables and preferred routes and alternate routes. It's a good solid plan."

"I'm satisfied that we're as ready as we can be," Hunter said. Then he handed a key to Volt. "I want you to take Savannah to my apartment at Fort Belvoir and stay there until we get back."

"I'd rather stay here," Savannah said.

"Please don't make me worry about you," Hunter requested.

Savannah caved immediately. "Of course I'll go if that's what you think is best."

"I'll follow them to Belvoir and then meet up with my team," Agent Chu offered. "Just to ease your mind, Corporal."

He nodded. "I appreciate that."

Savannah said, "I'll go pack a bag."

* * *

When it was time for them to go, Savannah hugged Brooke tightly. "Saying thank you seems so lame, but I do thank you!"

"I know," Brooke replied. "There is something you can do for me while we're gone. It's only vaguely related to the rescue plan, but it's important to me."

"Anything," Savannah promised.

"When Hunter and I went to the hospital to see General Steele, I told a nurse she would receive a hundred dollar gift card if she allowed me to give a survey to Mrs. Steele. Since I'm trying to be honest now, I don't want that to be a lie."

Savannah smiled. "Do you have her name?"

Brooke recited it. "She works on the cardiac floor of the Belvoir Community Hospital. You can have it sent there. I'd do it myself, but, well, it's probably better if I take care of it before I go rather than waiting, just in case."

Savannah waved this aside. "Consider it done."

"Let's go!" Volt hollered.

Brooke and Savannah walked out onto the porch together. "This is it then," Savannah said. "I'll be worried sick until it's all over."

"You just keep sipping that Spriteorade and let us worry about Uncle Christopher."

Savannah's lip trembled as she pulled her wedding ring off and handed it to Brooke. "You need to wear this. Babineaux will expect you to have a ring on, and it might bring you luck. My life has certainly been a lot happier since your uncle gave it to me."

Brooke slipped the gold band on her ring finger.

"If something goes wrong—" Savannah continued, "and he's not going to come home, please tell him that I love him."

"He knows," Brooke whispered.

Unshed tears glittered in Savannah's eyes. "I want him to hear it one last time."

Brooke nodded. "If something goes wrong, I'll tell him."

"Mrs. Dane," Volt called in a warning voice. "You don't want me to leave you!"

Savannah gave Brooke a final hug and walked down to Volt's car.

Brooke heard footsteps behind her and turned to see Hunter, followed closely by Agent Chu.

"Well, I guess that's it, Corporal."

"Yes, ma'am," Hunter replied.

"Yes, *Agent Chu*," she corrected. "Don't ever *ma'am* me again." The agent walked toward the lead car and then turned back. "See you two in Haiti."

Brooke smiled. Hunter did not.

"Tomorrow," he confirmed.

Brooke watched them leave from the porch. Hunter stayed on the ground. Once both sets of taillights disappeared, Brooke went inside, climbed the stairs, and walked to the guestroom. Changing into her Christmas flannel pajamas, she curled up on the bed and closed her eyes.

Thirty minutes later Brooke sat up, accepting that she couldn't sleep. She walked over to the window and looked out at the creek, now bathed in moonlight. Hunter was standing on the bridge.

She watched him for a few minutes, strong yet solitary. He'd said some harsh things, and she had every right to be mad at him. He deserved to stand there all night, alone and friendless. But the next day held no guarantees, and she didn't want what might be their last night together to be wasted in anger. So she walked downstairs and out the front door.

Hunter saw her coming and watched her approach with something between trepidation and suspicion.

She stopped on the bridge a couple of feet away from him. Leaning forward to rest her arms on the sturdy railing, she remarked, "It's quiet tonight."

"Yes."

"I never really got this place. I mean, I didn't understand why Uncle Christopher loved it so much. But I think I'm starting to. It's a tiny spot of tranquility in an insane world."

"Yes."

"Are you nervous about tomorrow?"

"I'm anxious to have it over with."

"I'm nervous," she admitted. "I'll go ahead and say it before you do—impersonating Savannah should be a piece of cake for me since I'm such an accomplished liar."

"I wasn't going to say that."

"Well, it's true. And for once, maybe my aptitude for dishonesty will be put to good use."

They were quiet for a few minutes. She inched closer to him, still not touching, but she could feel the heat rising from his arm. She wanted to put her hand on his, to let him know she had forgiven him for treating her like a job and refusing to admit he loved her. But she also wanted him to make the first move.

Finally she said, "I called the adoption agency and warned them that Rex might try to make trouble for the baby."

"That was probably wise."

"And I was thinking that we should let Detective Napier know about the connection between Rex and Babineaux. He might be able to help us figure out why they want me dead."

"I already called him," Hunter replied. "Mostly so he'd know where we were and not start an all-out search. But I mentioned the thing about Rex and Babineaux too."

"It's a shame that we'll be so close to Babineaux, but we won't be able to capture him."

Hunter didn't say anything, but his arm tensed.

She turned and stared at him. "What?"

He gave her an impatient look. "Why do you think Agent Chu asked if I could still shoot with a broken arm? Making sure that Babineaux never sells another weapon will be my job."

Brooke's lungs tightened, and she felt a little breathless. "You're going to shoot him?"

He turned away. "If I get the chance."

Brooke returned her gaze to the moonlit creek. It didn't seem quite as tranquil anymore.

Hunter sighed and moved his hand away from hers. "You should go back to bed and at least try to sleep."

She turned toward the house. "Are you going to sleep on my bedroom floor?"

"Tonight I won't sleep at all," he said, his eyes still on the moonlit creek.

# CHAPTER SIXTEEN

BABINEAUX KEPT DANE IN THE house with him all evening, taunting him about Savannah's decision to deliver the ransom money.

"Did you hear that we are going to have an important visitor tomorrow?" he asked one of the guards. "Major Dane's wife is coming to bring me some money, a lot of money."

The guard responded in French. Unfortunately for Dane, his grandmother had taught him to speak that language, so he understood every filthy word.

"Of course, I have no intention of giving Major Dane up. He is much too valuable. I already have a bidding war going between several groups who have scores they want to settle with him. The two million from his wife will just be a little bonus."

"The wife might be worth some money," the guard proposed in broken English. Obviously he wanted Dane to understand him. "Unless you decide to keep her."

Babineaux laughed. "I've always been partial to blondes."

Dane felt desperate and helpless. He knew Savannah would do anything to save him, but all he wanted was for her to stay where she was safe, far from the grasping hands of evil men. If only there was some way to let her know, to convince her that coming here would be worse than letting him die.

He turned away from Babineaux and his guards. Looking out the window, he felt taunted by the aqua blue water. Freedom was just a few feet away, but it might as well have been a million miles.

\* \* \*

The next morning Brooke got up after only a few hours' sleep. She hadn't made up with Hunter the night before like she'd hoped. Being at odds with each other was not a good way to start what would certainly prove to be a difficult day.

She put on the bullet-resistant vest Agent Chu had given her and then dressed in her new suit and shoes. She applied her makeup and fixed her hair the way Savannah had taught her. Finally she stared at herself in the mirror. To a stranger she could probably pass for Savannah at a distance. Feeling she'd done all she could, Brooke walked downstairs to meet Hunter.

He was standing by the front door and looked up when he heard her coming.

She spread her arms and asked, "Well, do you think I look like Savannah?"

Instead of answering her question, he said, "It's not too late to change your mind."

"Yes, it is. Now let's get to the airport."

When they arrived at the airport in Fredericksburg, Hunter called Volt, and he talked them through to the hangar he had rented. The plane was there, packed with equipment they might need and extra fuel.

They introduced themselves to the green beret and navy seal, named Bosh and Sheffield, respectively. The pilot and copilot were busy going through their preflight checklist.

At exactly nine o'clock, an armored car arrived. A nervous man who said he was a bank executive watched as four large suitcases with built-in rollers were removed from the truck. Hunter checked the suitcases to make sure they did actually contain money. Then they loaded the cases onto the plane.

The interior of the plane was set up with six rows, each two seats deep, on both sides of a narrow aisle. Brooke sat in the first seat she came to—front row next to the aisle. The suitcases full of money were stacked right in front of her and secured with thick straps. Bosh and Sheffield sat at the back of the plane. Hunter was in full soldier mode now. He went up to the cockpit to confer with the pilots, checked the plane, and checked the weather—all while ignoring her.

Brooke tugged on the jacket of her suit, which was bunching up around her bullet-resistant vest, and pretended not to notice his cold-shoulder attitude.

The engines roared to life, and the plane started rolling across the tarmac. Hunter left the cockpit and sat in the front row across the aisle from her. She needed some reassurance and wished they weren't fighting. She glanced over at him, hoping for some sort of encouragement, but he was studying maps and timetables and diagrams. So she turned toward the window and waited for takeoff.

The gentle motion of the plane lulled Brooke to sleep, and she was only awakened when the pilot announced their approach to Port-de-Paix. She sat up straight and checked her seat belt. Hunter was staring out the window, watching their descent. *Probably critiquing the pilot's landing*, she thought.

She turned to her own window as the plane touched down smoothly. While they were still taxiing, Hunter stood and unstrapped the money-filled suitcases. He passed one to Bosh, one to Sheffield, and one to the copilot. He kept one for himself and stood beside the door, waiting.

When the plane came to a complete stop, the pilot came out of the cockpit and spoke to Hunter. "They're expecting a thunderstorm, so we need to get back into the air as soon as possible."

"This shouldn't take long," Hunter replied. "Keep the engines running, and be ready to take off at a moment's notice."

The pilot nodded as he pushed the door open.

Brooke looked out at the ground below. Dark clouds hung low, and the wind whipped at their clothes. Ground crews were rushing around securing planes and transferring luggage in anticipation of the impending rain.

They only had to wait for a few minutes before a yellow Jeep with dark-tinted windows pulled out of a hangar on the far side of the airport and approached them, dodging the ground crews and other vehicles along the way. Hunter tensed, and Brooke moved closer to him.

The Jeep stopped a few yards from the plane. The passenger-side door opened, and a man wearing jeans and a light-blue shirt stepped out.

Hunter turned to her. "Stay here where they can see you, but don't go down the steps."

She nodded, not sure she had enough air in her lungs to actually speak.

Then she watched Hunter, Bosh, Sheffield, and the copilot walk down the plane's metal steps to the tarmac, their suitcases bouncing along behind them. The man from the Jeep met them halfway.

After a short discussion, the man motioned toward his vehicle. The door opened, and two men got out. One was dressed, like the first man, in blue. The other was Hack.

Brooke gasped. His mouth was taped, and his hands were tied behind him. His clothes looked scorched, and his left leg was wrapped from knee to ankle in thick white gauze.

Brooke instinctively stepped out onto the landing, which earned her a scowl from Hunter. She clasped the railing on the steps and stayed where she was. The first man began counting the money, and Hunter peeled the tape off Hack's mouth exposing cracked, dry lips.

"Are you okay?" Brooke called.

Hack nodded. "Just need water."

She stepped back into the plane and returned with a bottle of water. She tossed it down to Sheffield, who handed it to Hack. He drank it down in seconds.

"More."

Sheffield smiled. "Hold on there, sir. Let that one settle for a minute."

It seemed to take the driver forever to count the stacks of bills. It was hot and incredibly humid. The bulletproof vest made it worse, and sweat rolled down Brooke's back.

Finally the man finished his count and approved the amount. "The money is good," the man said in heavily accented English.

"You aren't Mr. Babineaux." Brooke was certain.

The man smiled up at her. "No, no. Monsieur Babineaux, he ask me to get the payment for him. And now our business is completed."

Hunter looked at the huge yellow vehicle and frowned. "Where are the other men?"

"It's just me," Hack rasped.

"Where is my husband?" Brooke took another step forward, playing her part as Savannah. "I paid the ransom for all of them!"

The driver flashed her one of his insincere smiles. "Monsieur, he say you come to visit him and talk more about it." The man held a hand up as if to help her down the steps. "Come! I will take you to your husband!"

Hunter moved to block the way. To his men he said, "Let's get out of here. Now!"

"Madame!" the man called. "If you don't come, the Monsieur, he will kill your husband! Don't you want to save him?"

Brooke stared down helplessly.

"Come with me," the man beckoned. "Your husband is anxious to see you!"

Brooke blinked back tears of frustration as she retreated inside the plane. The men dragged Hack up the steps and deposited him on the first row of seats. Then the pilot began taxiing down the runway as Hunter struggled to get the door closed.

Brooke looked out the window as Babineaux's men dragged the suitcases toward the Jeep.

"Get your seat belt on!" Hunter told her as he worked his way back to his seat. The plane left the ground, and the pilot fought to maintain control. Finally they leveled off and everyone relaxed.

Sheffield cursed like a sailor, appropriately. "They double-crossed us!"

"We were expecting that," Hunter said. "But it's still a disappointment."

"At least we got Hack," Bosh pointed out.

"We gave them the money," Brooke said. "So they won't really kill Uncle Christopher and the other men, will they? They'll just demand more money or something?"

Hunter's expression was tense. "I don't know what Babineaux will do."

Hack stretched his injured leg out across two seats and told Sheffield. "Give me another bottle of water now or you're fired."

The former green beret handed his boss a bottle of water.

Hack drank it in seconds and then asked, "You got any doughnuts?"

"No," Hunter said. "We have some crackers."

"That'll do." Hack accepted several packs of crackers and ate them two at a time. "I'll take another water and something for pain."

"I'm a medic," the copilot said. "Corporal, if you'll switch places with me, I'll see about his leg."

Hunter took the empty seat in the cockpit while the copilot knelt in front of Hack. "There's a first-aid kit in the bathroom." He gestured toward the back of the plane.

When no one else made a move, Brooke said, "I'll get it." She rushed to the tiny bathroom and unhooked the first-aid kit from the wall. Then she brought it to the copilot, who was unwrapping the gauze on Hack's leg.

"What happened?" the copilot asked.

"Gasoline burn," Hack told them. "They've been giving me antibiotics, so it's not too bad."

"It needs to be washed to get the dead skin off," the copilot told him. "But that'll have to wait until we can get you to a hospital."

"So what's the real plan? I know you didn't seriously think Babineaux was going to just hand the team over for a couple million bucks."

"No," Hunter said over his shoulder. "We didn't think this would work."

"But we had to give it a try," Brooke added.

"There's an ATF team here too," Hunter continued. "They're responsible for getting the money back, so they'll follow that yellow Jeep to the fish plant. We're going to land in a clearing up here and let you guys out."

"After you drop us off, what are you going to do?" Hack asked.

"Fly in close to the fish plant, parachute out at the last minute, and crash the plane by the western wall. We have extra fuel onboard, so it will burn hot and fast."

"That's your diversion?"

Hunter nodded. "If we can down the plane just right, they'll have to address the fire even if they realize that we're trying to draw manpower away from their prisoners. Otherwise the whole place might burn down."

"Then the ATF team will come in from one side, and our guys will come in from the other?"

"Yes," Hunter confirmed. "We'll provide cover fire while they get Major Dane and the team. Then they'll cover our retreat as we run for the jungle. Once we reach the trees, we'll turn around and return the favor. A helicopter will pick us up a couple of miles down the beach, and we'll get home fast."

"Not bad," Hack told him.

"We know we're going to be outmanned, but we're counting on the fact that we're better trained and better motivated."

Hack looked at the copilot. "Did you say you had some painkillers?"

"Yes, sir," the copilot replied.

"Well, you'd better get me some. My leg is killing me."

The medic passed Hack a bottle of pills. Hack read the label and then shook two tablets out onto his palm. "Water!" he called, and Sheffield provided another water bottle. Hack tossed the pills into his mouth and washed them down.

Hunter told the copilot, "You'd better keep a close eye on how much medication he takes so he doesn't end up unconscious."

Hack grinned and tossed the medicine back to the copilot. "It would take more than two little pills to knock me out. But I could use a shot of antibiotics. I don't trust that stuff Babineaux was giving me."

The copilot prepared a syringe and plunged it into Hack's massive leg.

Hack grimaced in pain and then addressed Hunter. "Babineaux knows you're coming, so don't count on the element of surprise. In fact, I think he wants you to come. It's almost like that's why he kept us—to get attention. And you're going to be more than outmanned, you're going to be *seriously* outmanned."

Bosh laughed. "And what's worse is I'm the only real soldier on the team. All that's left is a sailor, a pilot, a copilot, a wounded man who can barely walk, a sniper with a broken arm, and a girl."

Hunter muttered something under his breath that she didn't even try to hear.

"Sailors are better than soldiers any day!" Sheffield objected.

Hack frowned. "That brings me to an important question. Why is Brooke here, and what are we going to do with her during the rescue attempt?"

"Babineaux demanded that Savannah deliver the money personally," Brooke explained. "So I'm impersonating her."

"That answers one question," Hack said. "What about the other one?"

"We can't take her near Babineaux," Hunter said. "But we can't leave her alone in the woods either."

"She can't parachute out of a crashing plane, so she'll have to stay with the ground team. We'll take her as close to the fish plant as we dare and leave her in a secure location until the shooting is over. That's the best we can do." Hack didn't look happy. "But she can't be dressed like that." He waved a hand from her head to her toes. "If we walk through the Haitian jungle with a gorgeous blonde, we might as well paint a bull's-eye on our backs."

Hunter gave Brooke a critical once-over. When his eyes stopped at her high heels, he sighed. "There's gear in the back. Find the smallest camo fatigues and put them on. Pick a pair of boots. Wash off your makeup and put your hair under your hat—anything to make you look less like a girl."

"And more like a soldier?" She was mostly teasing.

"You're *not* a soldier," Hunter told her emphatically. "You're a *liability*."

"Hey!" Hack objected. "Watch that name-calling. And remember that since you and I are both wounded, some people would consider *us* liabilities!"

"Hunter's in love with me," Brooke explained. Hunter looked horrified, but the other men were listening with keen interest. "But he doesn't want to be. So sometimes his frustration presents itself as hostility."

Hack's eyebrows rose. "Well, whatever emotional state *Hunter* is in, he'd better address ladies with respect when he's in my presence. You got that, Corporal?"

"Yes, sir," he muttered.

Brooke took a deep breath and addressed the group. "I may not be a soldier, but I think I can be more than a liability. Now if you gentlemen will excuse me, I've got to try to make myself ugly."

"Medic!" Hack called out. "I need more painkillers!"

"I'll try to make you more comfortable," the copilot said. Then he handed Brooke the first-aid kit. "Since you're going to the back, would you mind returning this?"

"I don't mind at all," she assured him. Then she headed toward the bathroom. As she walked down the narrow aisle, she heard Hack ask, "Who's going to call Savannah and tell her we don't have Dane?"

Hunter sighed audibly. "I guess that will be me."

*   *   *

Brooke dug through the box of camouflage fatigues until she found a pair of pants and a shirt in men's size XS. She also found the smallest pair of boots, a backpack, socks, and a belt.

The bathroom was so small there was barely enough room for her to stand, let alone change clothes. She returned the first-aid kit to its hook on the wall then took off her suit, folded it neatly, and put it into her backpack. It was unlikely she would ever wear it again, but it had sentimental value. Hunter had purchased it for her, and she had some fond memories of that day they'd spent together—Kinkos, the boutique, the hospital ladies' room. She smiled and then felt tears sting her eyes.

Putting her emotions aside, Brooke gave herself a sponge bath with tiny paper towels and water from the little sink. Then she put on the fatigues, which were still too big. Fortunately she had the belt, and after adding a new hole with the scissors from the first-aid kit, she was able to cinch it tight enough to keep her pants from falling off.

Once she was dressed in the baggy camouflage, she looked at herself in the tiny mirror. She looked exactly like what she was, a girl wearing a soldier's clothes. She wanted to blend in with the men. She wanted to follow Hunter's instructions. She wanted to stop being seen as a burden.

She scrubbed off her makeup, causing mascara to collect in two matching smears under her eyes. The look was somewhere between football player and zombie, but it definitely was not girly. So she left it. Next she took some brown eye shadow and rubbed it all over her face, hoping to simulate dirt. It was an improvement, but not a total transformation.

Trying to think of anything else she could do, her eyes moved to the first-aid kit. Through the clear plastic lid, she could see the small pair of scissors. She fingered a lock of her shoulder-length blonde hair. It was skillfully cut, professionally highlighted, and definitely girly. And suddenly she knew what she had to do.

She opened the first-aid kit and removed the scissors. Then she pulled up a clump of hair, positioned the scissors, and stared at her reflection in the mirror. Her hand trembled a bit, but her resolve was firm. Slowly she closed the scissors. From that point on, she was committed, so she continued cutting until her head was covered with short blond tufts. It was gappy, and she knew her mother was going to cry when she saw it. But the short hair definitely altered her appearance. At a glance she might be mistaken for a small man. And there could be no doubt that she was all in.

The time had come to face the others. She shrugged on her backpack and walked out of the bathroom with her head held high.

The men looked up when they heard her coming, and their faces expressed varying degrees of shock. She planted her feet firmly on the floor and steadied herself by putting a hand on the backs of the seats on either side. There was a brief, slightly awkward silence.

Finally Sheffield said, "Girl, you are the *truth*."

There were murmurs of agreement from the rest of the guys—except Hunter.

Hack gave her a weak smile. "If I didn't know it was you, I wouldn't know it was you."

Hunter was still staring. Brooke couldn't tell what he was thinking and tried not to care.

"So when are we landing?" she asked.

"Right now," the pilot said. "Everybody needs to get into a seat and prepare for a rough ride."

The plane began a steep descent, and Brooke took a couple of involuntary steps forward before she could steady herself. She plopped into the nearest seat and strapped on the seat belt. Then she clutched the armrests as the pilot brought the plane closer and closer to the jungle below. She closed her eyes as the plane skidded into a clearing and came to a hard stop.

Hunter took off his seat belt and stood. "Let's move quickly."

They worked together to remove the weapons and equipment they would need for their rescue mission. Once they were finished, Hunter walked over to the pilot. "So you're clear on what needs to be done?"

He nodded. "I'll wait here as long as I can. If I feel like it's not safe, I'll get in the air. And I'll be watching for your message that you're ready for me to drop this plane in a ball of fire."

"You're sure you don't want me to do it?" Hunter asked.

"I'm sure Agent Chu wants me to do it," the pilot replied. "And there's no way I'm going to cross her."

Hunter gave him a little smile. "We'll see you at the fish plant then. Try not to get your parachute tangled up in the trees." Then he rejoined the rest of the group.

They were collecting their gear when a text came. After Hunter read it, he passed it to Hack. Then they faced the group with equally grim expressions.

"The guys in the Jeep didn't take the money to Babineaux at the fish plant," Hunter told them. "Instead they're headed toward Port-au-Prince—maybe to put it in a bank, maybe on a boat, maybe they're stealing it. But whatever their intentions are, the ATF team had to stay with the money. We're on our own against Babineaux."

* * *

The mood was solemn as they moved out. Hunter let Hack set the pace, and he walked steadily, if not very quickly. He was obviously in pain, but he didn't complain. Brooke was worried about him and could tell that Hunter shared her concerns. He checked on the big man often, and during their first stop, he put together a makeshift crutch out of a tree limb and a T-shirt.

"Thanks," Hack said when it was presented to him. "I think I can make it, but if that changes, you'll have to leave me behind."

Hunter shook his head. "You know that's not an option."

"It absolutely *is* an option," Hack disputed. "I don't mean leave me forever, just for a while. You can pick me up on the way back."

Hunter's expression was stubborn, but he didn't argue.

"How long will it be before we get to the fish plant?" Brooke asked.

"About an hour," Hunter replied.

"Shouldn't we wait until dark?" Brooke asked.

Hunter said, "Babineaux has infrared cameras and heat sensitive equipment, so he doesn't need light to see us. Darkness would only be a disadvantage for us."

Hack looked over at him. "Tell me you brought your Mr. Fantastic suit."

Hunter made a face but nodded. "I brought it."

"Then it's probably time to suit up," Hack said.

"The rest of you keep walking," Hunter requested. "I'll change and then catch up in a few minutes." He moved off into the dense foliage.

"Why does he have a Mr. Fantastic costume?" Brooke asked.

"Not a costume," Hack corrected. "A suit made of spun glass and wool fibers. It controls his body temperature emissions and blocks infrared imaging, so he'll be invisible to Babineaux's surveillance equipment. And it's camouflaged, so it's nearly invisible to cameras as well. It's a lot like the outfit Mr. Fantastic wears, so I tease him."

Brooke looked toward the woods where Hunter had disappeared. For the first time in a while, she felt sorry for him. She was sweating in the light cotton fatigues and couldn't imagine wearing a wool suit.

"Babineaux will see the rest of us approaching, but he won't know about Owl," Hack was saying.

"Why doesn't everyone wear invisible outfits?" she asked.

"Because nobody else has one," Hack replied. "Owl's is a prototype that hasn't been approved for manufacture yet."

There was a slight movement behind them.

Hack looked over his shoulder and smiled. "Here's our secret weapon now."

The suit Hunter had on was almost gummy in texture and clung tightly to his slim frame. Brooke could tell he felt self-conscious, but she thought he carried off the Mr. Fantastic look quite well. She didn't tell him that though, since they were mad at each other.

At the next stop, Brooke helped Hack rest his leg on a fallen tree trunk. Then she brought him a protein bar and a bottle of water. Once she'd done all she could for him, she sat quietly and listened while the men revamped their plan, taking Agent Chu and her team out of the equation.

"Hack will have to stay in one stationary location. We'll give him lots of ammo, and he can just shoot."

"Brooke could do that too," Hack suggested.

Hunter shook his head. "I want her completely out of the action."

"We don't have that luxury," the copilot said. "At least let her shoot at the plant to provide cover."

"I'm not very experienced with guns," she warned them, "but maybe I could hit something."

Hunter shook his head. "If she's shooting, she'll draw return fire. Arming Brooke will be our absolute last resort."

Bosh said, "We were down to our last resort as soon as we found out that ATF team won't be coming to the party."

"Once we free Major Dane and the other guys, we'll have more help," Hunter pointed out.

"Take Babineaux out quickly if you can," Hack said. "Without him, his men may run—or at least they won't fight with as much enthusiasm."

"If we could eliminate Babineaux, that would make everything simpler," Hunter agreed. Then he stood. "Rest time is over."

And they were moving again.

# CHAPTER SEVENTEEN

DANE GROANED WHEN THE DOOR opened, and he saw the guard reaching for him. Staying in the oven-like shed was better than being tormented by Babineaux. This time, instead of taking him straight to the main building, the guard took him to a row of shower stalls and handed him a thin towel and a small bar of soap.

"You stink," the guard said by way of explanation.

Dane couldn't deny that. He longed to be clean again, even just for a little while. So he took his shower, and when he was through, he found a pair of jeans and a shirt waiting for him. Reluctantly he put them on and stepped out into the open area where the guard was waiting for him.

When they walked into the main building, Babineaux greeted him enthusiastically, as if Dane were an old friend instead of a tortured prisoner. "Welcome!"

Dane stared back silently. The man was obviously insane.

"Oh, this is going to be a fun evening!" Babineaux was clutching his little shoulder satchel as usual. "Come in, come in! Make yourself comfortable!" He waved toward a chair, and Dane sat down. The guard took up a position right behind him.

"I trust you feel better after your shower?"

Dane nodded. "Will my men be given the same privilege?"

"Even as we speak!" Babineaux assured him. "This is going to be a very special evening, and I want everyone to look their best."

"The ransom has been paid?" Dane didn't want to ask, but he had to know.

"Ah, yes, your wife delivered the two million dollars this morning. And in exchange I gave her your big man with the hurt leg!"

Dane was glad to know that Hack was alive and safe. But there was a dark side to this knowledge. If Babineaux only gave her Hack, Savannah would try to get the others. "Where is my wife?"

"She is with the small group of men who accompanied her on the plane. They are walking through the jungle toward us."

Dane's mind was racing. Why would Owl bring Savannah with him on a rescue mission? They had to know it was a trap. They had to know that Babineaux was just toying with them and eventually all the prisoners would die. If they brought more people in, they would just increase the number of casualties.

"It is somewhat insulting, don't you think?" Babineaux continued. "That they would come here with such a small group and think they can take my prisoners?"

Dane stared straight ahead.

"But I'll let you in on a little secret. For years people underestimated me. They thought, *Jacques is just a small fry*, as you Americans say. *He is not enough to worry about.* So they left me alone, and my business grew.

"But then your country noticed my success and tried to take from me what is mine. They steal my shipments, interfere with my communications, coerce my government into harassing me, and even file lawsuits against me. I am forced to hire an army of lawyers. My patience was at its limit. And then they add the final insult—they send an inexperienced ATF agent, a child really, to infiltrate my ranks. It was one insult too many. They wanted to make me look like a fool. So I had to teach them a lesson. I kept their agent. And who looks like a fool now?"

Dane didn't respond and kept his expression blank.

"Your government thought, *Jacques is too stupid to see this boy for what he is. He will let us steal information from him that we can use for more lawsuits. He will spend his entire fortune on legal fees.*" Babineaux wagged a finger at Dane. "But that was a mistake, you see. They underestimated me. I used the boy to feed them false information for almost a year. You cannot imagine the weapons I have transferred without interference because the Americans were looking in the wrong direction.

"But sometimes it is inconvenient to have a spy in your camp. You have to watch every little thing you say. So I was planning to shoot the boy—he deserved no less—but I have an American friend, and he suggested that we arrange a 'rescue' instead. He said it was to my advantage for the Americans to think that they had outwitted me. Then they would underestimate me again in the future. So he arranged for your little has-been special-ops team to be sent in."

Dane absorbed the pain of this revelation without flinching. But his mind was racing. Who had betrayed them?

"So we were waiting for you," Babineaux continued. "My men watched your helicopter land. We saw you camped in the jungle and crouched on the edge of the fish plant. We allowed you to disable our generator and dig the trench under our fence."

Dane's eyes widened slightly.

Babineaux smiled. "This surprises you? You thought you slipped in here, to my compound, without my knowledge? It could never happen. I let you come."

Dane felt like a fool.

"If you would have just taken the boy, you would be home now with your family. But no, you had to destroy my weapons. And not quietly, but in a huge way, so that all my enemies would know that the great Jacques Babineaux had been defeated by the Americans. But I will be the victor yet, and the world will have no doubt. Before this night is over, I will make you pay a high price for your foolish mistake."

One word echoed in Dane's mind. *Savannah.*

Babineaux raved on, "So today, Major, you help Jacques Babineaux come out of obscurity! This day will be talked about for many years. I will be a legend. They will probably write songs about me, maybe make a movie even. Perhaps the actor from *Iron Man*, Mr. Downey Jr., can portray me. I think we resemble slightly, no?"

Dane refused to answer.

Babineaux laughed. "But we can't start the party yet. We have to wait for your wife to arrive."

\* \* \*

Brooke continued to trudge through the dense jungle with the team until Hunter stopped them. "We're only a mile from the fish plant," he said. "We'll eat and rest for a few minutes. Then we'll prepare for our final approach."

The copilot distributed MREs, and Hack ate with relish. "I'm feeling better," he claimed. "This medicine must be working." When he thought they weren't looking, he popped two more pain pills into his mouth. "And this food is delicious."

Hunter turned to the copilot. "If he thinks MREs are good, he must be doped up. Are you monitoring how many of those pills he's taking?"

The copilot shot Hack a nervous look and then shook his head.

Hack laughed. "I'd like to see him *try* and take these away from me."

"They are habit-forming," Hunter reminded him.

"If I get addicted during this hike, I'll check myself into rehab when I get home. But right now I've got to move, and the only way I can do that is to take these pills."

"He'll be okay," copilot said. "Dependency-wise anyway. But he may be doing irreparable damage to that leg."

"I'll worry about that when I get home too," Hack said. "If I make it home. And if I don't, the condition of my leg won't matter."

No one even attempted to argue with this logic.

Brooke poked at the inedible food in her MRE and thought about the upcoming confrontation. It was possible that none of them would survive. If so, she needed to make peace with her bodyguard. She threw her food in the trash sack provided by the copilot and approached Hunter.

"Can I talk to you for a minute?"

He looked around at the others, who were all watching with interest. "Just for a minute." He pointed to some trees a few feet away, and she followed him there.

Once they were alone, she said, "Before we go and face whatever's going to happen at the fish plant, I just want you to know I am sorry I upset you. I did what I thought was right, but I wish we could have been in agreement about it. And I love you. I always will. Whether my life ends in a few hours or when I'm an old lying woman."

He looked at her for a few seconds. Then he nodded.

"Is there anything you want to say to me?"

"Two things."

She felt a glimmer of hope.

He pulled a small gun out of his pocket and handed it to her. "You said you know how to shoot this?"

She stared at the gun, mute with disappointment.

"Take it and use it if you need to."

She checked the safety and then slipped the gun in her pocket. "What's the second thing?"

"There's a good chance this won't end well," he told her solemnly. "So when we get close to the plant, I'm going to put you in a safe spot, and

I want you to stay there—no matter what happens. If it looks like none of us are coming out alive, push the number one on your phone, and the helicopter will come for you. Promise me you'll do it. Don't let Babineaux have the satisfaction of getting you too."

"I will." Then she waited for a kiss or a hug or even an attaboy.

But Hunter just nodded and walked back to his team.

\* \* \*

Dane was beyond panic, beyond terror, almost beyond feeling. Babineaux hadn't killed him physically . . . yet. But the hours of mental anguish had taken their toll. It was all surreal now, as if he was watching a movie or watching someone else's life self-destruct.

"Your rescue team has moved into range of my infrared cameras," Babineaux announced with delight. "Now we can watch their arrival. Each little dot represents a person." He pointed at the huge television, where the views from six cameras were displayed.

Dane was so drained it wasn't even hard for him to remain emotionless anymore.

"We will keep an eye on this smallest dot," Babineaux continued. "It must be your wife. I am particularly anxious to welcome her."

All his buried emotions came crashing back. The pain and fear were worse than he remembered, and Dane nearly staggered under the weight of it. He considered begging. He knew Babineaux was expecting it. He also knew it would not work and might even make things worse. So Dane just stared at the smallest blob on the screen as it moved steadily closer.

"I have found that loyalty is a very rare trait among you selfish Americans," Babineaux was saying. "The fact that these men are willing to risk their lives in a futile attempt to save you is touching. It's too bad they are about to die for their efforts."

Dane stared at the screen, almost wishing Babineaux would shoot him and end the misery.

Then the crazy man clapped his hands. "Oh, how I love a surprise!" He pointed to the display from the camera on the far right. "Look, the cavalry has arrived!"

\* \* \*

Brooke watched the dark clouds rolling in as the team made final preparations for their attack on Babineaux's compound. It wasn't raining yet, but it would be soon. The men painted their faces and loaded their backpacks with extra ammo. Just as they were about to move out, Hunter got a text.

Brooke watched as he read the message and then saw the relief on his face. "Good news for a change?" she whispered.

He nodded. "We won't have to do this alone after all."

There was a slight rustle in the brush behind them, and out stepped Agent Chu. The tiny woman was a complete contradiction dressed in full combat gear, beauty meets beast, a flower hard as nails. She was truly a sight to behold.

"I hope I've died and gone to heaven because, lady, you're my kind of angel," Hack whispered reverently.

Hunter had to smile a little at that. "Hack, meet Agent Chu of the ATF. Alcine is one of her guys, and she's assisting us with the rescue."

Hack frowned. "I thought the ATF team followed the money."

Agent Chu motioned for her team to join her, and several agents slipped quietly out of the brush to stand beside her. "We called in the Haitian government. They arrested Babineaux's flunkies and agreed to safeguard the money. They'll probably steal it, of course, but at least we don't have to worry about it going to terrorists. And I felt like being here was more important. Your team is as solid as a few soldiers and one sailor can be, but there's no way you could take on Babineaux alone."

"We appreciate your help," Hunter told her.

"I've never been so glad to see a woman in uniform!" Sheffield quipped.

Agent Chu turned and stared him down.

"Sorry," he mumbled and moved out of her line of sight.

Brooke noted that he didn't even seem tempted to call her 'ma'am.'

The agent's eyes landed on Brooke, took in her altered appearance, and gave her a nod of approval. "You might make a soldier after all."

Brooke smiled. "I really hope not."

"Do you want to take command here?" Hunter offered the agent.

Agent Chu scowled. "Thanks. As if ditching our money detail wasn't enough to get me fired, you want to put my name on this—*Chu's Last Stand*."

Hunter shrugged. "If we pull it off, you might get promoted."

She considered this. "If we pull this off, we'll all share in the glory regardless of who's in command. Now where are we in terms of implementation?"

"The pilot is waiting for a message from me, and then he'll fly to the fish plant and crash the plane," Hunter said.

"I'd go ahead and send that message," Chu advised.

Hunter pulled out his phone and sent the text. "Hack's mobility is limited, so we'll put him behind the rocks on the edge of the forest with lots of ammo. He can provide cover while my team blasts open the front gate and fights their way in."

"And while your team and the fire have Babineaux's men occupied, my team will come around back, cut our way in through the fence, and free our prisoners," Chu verified.

"But look before you shoot," Hack cautioned. "I wouldn't put it past Babineaux to dress our guys like his guards. He's just that sick."

"Thanks for the warning," Agent Chu said.

"And I'll be in the trees, waiting to get a shot at Babineaux."

Agent Chu tipped her head toward Brooke. "What are you going to do with G.I. Jane?"

"I'm going to leave her hidden in the trees," he said. "I've given her a gun."

Agent Chu turned to Brooke. "You know how to use it?"

"Yes."

"We're not playing games out here. If you come under attack, shoot to kill."

"I understand."

"Okay then," Hunter said. "Let's do this."

The ATF team left first since they had to work their way around to the back of the fish plant. Hunter told the men to get into position and wait for him. "I'll join you after I get Brooke secured."

Once the men were gone, Hunter took Brooke to a small copse where three large trees were growing close together. He helped her to climb into the small space between the trees and sit.

Crouched on the damp ground, she wondered if she'd made a mistake. When she volunteered to be Savannah's substitute, it had seemed so right. But if they had listened to Hunter and brought a trained agent, the team would have an extra person who could actually contribute, and Hunter wouldn't be distracted by concern for her safety.

There wasn't time to tell him all the things she was feeling, so she just said, "I'm sorry."

"It's going to be okay," he assured her. "You stay here no matter what. Promise?"

"I promise, but you know I can't be trusted. So you'd better come back quick."

"Seriously, if something does happen to me, call the helicopter and get out of here. Once you get home, take our marriage certificate to General Steele. He'll help you apply for my survivor benefits."

She grabbed his hands and held them tight. "You have to come back! I'll never get my piano ready for the Smithsonian without you."

"I won't leave that piano at your mercy," he said with a little smile. Then he pulled his hands free and moved into the jungle.

After his departure, all Brooke could do was sit in her tiny circle of trees and worry.

\* \* \*

Dane stood in front of the huge television with a guard on each side. Every muscle in his body was tense as he watched the dots move forward.

Babineaux pointed to the dots that represented the second team, approaching the fish plant from behind. "Come to me!" he coaxed. "Come!"

"Please, let everyone else go and just kill me." Dane knew it was a waste of breath, but he had to try. "There's no reason for so much loss of life."

"Ah, life." Babineaux opened the black case on his shoulder.

Dane braced himself, expecting their captor to pull out a gun and shoot him. Instead Babineaux removed a bottle of pills.

"Life is so fleeting, so fragile. And all you Americans can do is look for ways to prolong it. But I was raised with the understanding that life is often short, and the important thing is to make sure you are remembered when you're gone." He put two pills into his mouth and swallowed them without water.

Dane watched this process with confusion.

"I have accomplished many things, but as we discussed earlier, my achievements have gone mostly unnoticed. Tonight I will be given ten precious minutes of international airtime to introduce myself. Jacques Babineaux—an entrepreneur, a financier, and a man with cancer."

Dane was so astonished by this revelation that he spoke before he could stop himself. "Cancer?"

"To you that must seem like a curse—something to be fought against, complained about, wept over. But it is foolish to resist the inevitable. The knowledge of my impending death has given me focus, determination, and incredible freedom. Nothing can kill me. I'm already dead!"

Dane looked away, refusing to acknowledge the tasteless joke.

"This invaluable knowledge allowed me to get all my affairs in order and even pick my successor. You remember the helpful American I mentioned earlier? He will take over my arms business. I find that a beautiful irony, don't you?"

Hopelessness washed over Dane. Usually he was pitting his skills, his intelligence, his experience against someone who wanted to live. Babineaux couldn't live, and this presented a problem that might be insurmountable.

"So tonight I will have a farewell party in the courtyard where the cameras are ready to transmit the event to the entire world. We'll have special guests and fireworks and a speech."

Several guards entered the room herding Steamer, Doc, and Alcine toward Babineaux. Like Dane the other prisoners were dressed in jeans and blue cotton shirts. Their hands were also taped behind them, and they were trying to look stoic despite the discouraging circumstances.

Then the ground shook as an explosion rent the air. "Let the fun begin!" Babineaux cooed. He looked up at the camera view that showed the flaming fuselage of a wrecked plane. "I must say I'm unimpressed with the diversion your team created. The blaze is so small that it will only require a few men to contain it."

Dane stared at the burned plane and hoped that no one was inside when it crashed.

Then Babineaux said, "Ah, this is the moment I've been waiting for."

Dane's eyes followed the direction of his finger to a small dot that remained still while the others moved forward toward the fish plant.

Babineaux pulled a radio from a clip on his belt and pressed a button. "Send Juan now." Then he returned his attention to the dots. "I must say that your rescue team's approach is very military and organized. Not imaginative—but what can be expected of Americans? Their biggest mistake was leaving your wife in a safe place, away from the action. Now she sits there alone, unprotected. They made it so easy for us."

"Please!" Dane cried out. He knew Babineaux wanted him to beg, to shame himself in front of his men. He didn't want to give the man any satisfaction, but he couldn't help himself. "I'll do anything!"

Babineaux's laughter echoed through the room. Then he said, "I've heard enough from Major Dane. Give me some tape!"

A guard promptly provided a big silver roll. Babineaux tore off a long piece and pressed it against Dane's mouth. Once the tape was secure, he leaned close and whispered, "I'm going to tell you a little secret, Major."

Dane leaned away from Babineaux's stale breath and pretended disinterest.

"Tonight's fireworks are actually explosives, enough to blow up the whole plant and half the town. A sniper in the trees will detonate them on my signal. Now that's what I call going out in a blaze of glory!"

Dane lunged at his captor, but his taped hands hampered him, and Babineaux sidestepped the attack attempt with ease.

The guards rushed forward. One grabbed Dane by the arms while the other slammed a fist into his stomach. He almost welcomed the physical pain. Anything was better than his mental anguish. Babineaux was going to kill them all—maybe hundreds of people—for nothing but vanity.

Babineaux smiled. "Don't act so surprised, Major. You had to know that you would never leave here alive." Then he turned and spoke to the guards. "Take them into the cellar until the shooting stops. Once we have the intruders rounded up, everyone meet in the courtyard."

As the guard dragged him from the room, Dane kept his eyes on the helpless dot on the TV screen. *Oh, Savannah*, his mind screamed. *Why did you come?*

\* \* \*

Hunter reached the area he had chosen for his role in the attack. It was as close as he dared get to the fish plant. He checked out the surrounding area and then climbed up slowly, hampered by his broken right arm. When he reached the top of the tree, he looked out, pleased with his choice. He had a full view of the front of the fish plant. He had placed himself between Babineaux and Brooke. It was all he could do.

He smeared his face with camo paint and put on a helmet covered in fake leaves. Once he had his weapons lined up and ready, he watched for signs of his team's approach. Nothing yet.

And then it began to rain. It was just a light drizzle, but enough to put out what was left of the diversion fire. If the weather got worse, it would be a real problem—affecting his visibility and accuracy. He tried not to worry about that as he sat back and blended into the tree, invisible from the human eye, infrared cameras, and heat sensors. He would get his moment. And he would be ready.

* * *

Brooke sat huddled in her safe space. There was an enormous spiderweb above her head, and the web's owner was in the center, mummifying an insect. She kept her eyes on the spider, hoping she wouldn't become the next victim. Gunfire in the distance startled her from the morbid display. The battle had begun.

Soon she could smell smoke, and the gunfire intensified. For long minutes at a time, there was no break in the ear-splitting cacophony. She wanted to think positively, but it was hard to believe that anyone could survive with so many bullets flying. The sounds and smells of destruction were so distracting that Brooke didn't see the man coming. Dressed all in black, he dropped down from the trees above and yanked her up. Then he hauled her from her safe spot into the tropical forest.

When her feet touched the ground, Brooke tried to pull free, but his body was like cement, his arm strong as a vise. Kicking, clawing, and biting—none had any effect.

He stripped the gun from her hand and threw it on the ground. Then he dragged her toward the fish plant as if she weighed nothing. She was helpless and tears of shame filled her eyes.

The man stopped abruptly and reached down to open a trapdoor. He carried her inside and closed the door behind them. They were in total darkness as he hurried her through a narrow tunnel. Finally they reached a door that opened into a large room. It was dimly lit and sparsely furnished. A huge television dominated the space, covering almost an entire wall. Several armed men were milling around, and they all looked up when Brooke stepped in.

One man separated himself from the others and walked over to her. Brooke recognized him from Savannah's video-messaging session. He was Jacques Babineaux. And he was smiling at her.

"Ah, Mrs. Dane. You look worse for your time in the jungle, I must say. But no matter. I'm sure your husband will be happy to see you anyway."

She couldn't have responded if she wanted to since her captor's vise-like arm was pressed so tightly against her throat.

Babineaux put a hand to his ear as the once-constant gunfire diminished into scattered bursts. "It sounds like the shooting is almost over. Come this way."

The man who had kidnapped Brooke transferred her to Babineaux's control. His hold was much weaker, and for a second Brooke felt encouraged. Perhaps she could overpower him. Then she felt the knife at her neck.

"Hold very still, Mrs. Dane," Babineaux advised. "A single wrong move could result in your *accidental* death."

Brooke took shallow breaths and tried to remain calm. They walked outside into the courtyard she had seen in the satellite photographs. There were several bodies crumpled on the dry grass, but she was relieved that none of them were wearing military fatigues. The exterior surfaces of the surrounding buildings were riddled with bullet holes. An overturned Jeep was on fire. Broken glass and splintered wood carpeted the ground.

"Bring in our uninvited guests, please!" Babineaux shouted. His voice, with its French lilt, was so lovely. Somehow it made his cruelty seem worse.

Several guards walked in through the gate, each dragging a member of the rescue teams. Sheffield, the navy seal, was a bloody mess and almost certainly dead. The green beret, Bosh, was also severely wounded. The guards dumped them onto the ground like bags of garbage.

The pilot and copilot both entered the courtyard under their own power, but three of Agent Chu's agents were carried in and dumped beside Sheffield and Bosh. It took two guards to drag Hack in. The bandage on his injured leg was saturated with blood, and he now had a shoulder wound as well. He didn't move after they threw him down. Brooke was terrified that this time the big man really might be dead.

Agent Chu and the final two members of her ATF team were brought in last. Agent Chu was calm and brave, even in surrender, and Brooke's respect for the small woman grew.

"Now," Babineaux said. "Please bring out our prisoners."

More guards emerged from a set of stairs built below ground level. They were escorting her uncle, Steamer, Doc, and a young man she'd never seen before, presumably ATF Agent Alcine. All of them had their hands taped behind their backs. It was the saddest sight Brooke had ever seen. Tears filled her eyes and spilled over onto her cheeks.

Her uncle glanced up, as if he just had to look. His eyes widened slightly when he saw her standing in Babineaux's grasp instead of his wife.

His eyes conveyed his love and appreciation. And for the first time in a long time, Brooke felt like a good person.

There was no doubt in Brooke's mind that Babineaux intended to kill them. But since Hunter was not among the captured, there was still a glimmer of hope. She willed herself not to look toward the trees. If he was alive, she would not give him away.

Uncle Christopher took a step forward, but his guards pulled him back roughly.

"Major, apparently you didn't notice this knife I have against your wife's throat. If you move again, you'll be shot, and she will die." He looked around the courtyard. "That goes for the rest of you too."

After a short pause to let this threat sink in, Babineaux turned his attention to Agent Chu. "So, you're a DEA agent?"

"ATF," she replied. "Why don't you let Mrs. Dane go, and we'll settle this between soldiers."

"How foolish would that be? To go to all this trouble to get her here and then just let her go?" Babineaux asked.

Agent Chu shrugged. "Only cowards kill defenseless women."

"Brave words," Babineaux sneered insultingly. "If you still have a few men in the woods, and you're thinking they can rush us while my attention is directed toward the television cameras, well, that would be a mistake. I have a sniper in the trees, and he is searching the area with infrared binoculars. He will find any stragglers, and he will shoot them."

Brooke's heart pounded. If Hunter was still alive, he would certainly try to save them. And when he tried, the sniper would shoot him. There wasn't any hope after all.

Babineaux turned to a man behind him. "Tell CNN we are ready to begin our ten-minute broadcast. And remind them what will happen to these survivors if they cut me off early." Once the man had gone, Babineaux told the guards, "If anyone tries to disrupt my speech, shoot them." Then he dragged Brooke into the center of the courtyard under a bright spotlight.

The man assigned to notify CNN came running back. "You're live in thirty seconds!" he said.

Babineaux cleared his throat and counted under his breath. When he reached thirty, he began to speak. "Welcome to our many viewers from across the world! My name is Jacques Babineaux, and you are attending, through the miracle of technology, my farewell party. A few months ago, I was diagnosed with an aggressive form of cancer. I will be leaving this life soon. But before I go, I wanted you to know a little something about me.

"But first, I guess I should introduce my guest," he said as if they were at a dinner party. "This is Savannah Dane." He glanced down for a minute and then began a discourse about his life and his philosophies.

Brooke was standing on her tiptoes to keep the knife from cutting her skin. But finally her trembling legs gave way. Being flat-footed was a great relief to her legs, but she felt blood trickle down her neck and dampen the collar of her borrowed fatigues. It had been a while since she'd prayed regularly or even felt close to God. But in that moment, she closed her eyes sent a plea heavenward. *Please let Hunter be alive, and please help him stop this madman.*

# CHAPTER EIGHTEEN

HUNTER WAS MOVING CAREFULLY THROUGH the underbrush, leaving behind his perfect vantage point—the tree where he had been able to see almost the entire fish plant. But Babineaux had captured Brooke and, with some kind of sick sixth sense, had chosen to gather his captives in a small area of the courtyard that Hunter couldn't see from his perfect tree.

So he had abandoned his location and headed east, desperate to get back up in the sky. He wanted to run at breakneck speed, but he had to pick his way carefully to keep from attracting attention. His Mr. Fantastic suit made him nearly invisible to the naked eye, infrared cameras, and thermal sensors. But it didn't hide the trees and branches that he disturbed when he walked by.

He had heard Babineaux taunting Major Dane and the team. He had threatened to kill Brooke if they rushed him. He claimed to have a sniper in the trees and a fireworks show.

Hunter knew that by leaving his original location he was risking discovery. The other sniper posed the biggest personal threat for him. He might run straight into the sniper—or worse, climb the same tree. There may be no way to stop a massacre inside the fish plant. But he had to try.

He had located another tree that would give him the sight range he needed. Hunter was only a few feet away when he froze. Right ahead was a man dressed all in black. He was standing still, as if he'd heard something he couldn't identify. Hunter stayed crouched behind a tree. The best option would be to wait and let the man move on. But that option took time, and he didn't have any to spare.

So he waited until the man was facing away—which would gain him an extra split second—then launched himself. The man spun, saw the blur that was Hunter, and braced for the impact.

As they collided, Hunter's weight dragged them both to the ground. Hunter used his cast like a club and hit the man's head repeatedly. The man was stunned but put his arms around Hunter and clung tightly. This prevented Hunter from escaping or from using his cast again. Hunter was forced to return the lethal embrace to keep his opponent from flipping him over and gaining advantage.

His first thought was to maintain his superior position and wear the man down. But after a minute of the intense standoff, he knew that would not work. One-armed, he wasn't strong enough to wait out the other man. It became clear that he was going to have to kill his enemy and move on, or the team, and Brooke, would die.

He rolled slightly to his left side and waited for the man to parry. Once the man was committed to an evasive maneuver, Hunter rolled back to the right, freeing his good arm. He put his hand around the man's thin neck and gave it a twist. The man went limp, and Hunter pushed him aside. Then, forgetting about motion detectors, he ran for the tree.

This climb was more difficult than the first one. He still had all his equipment, but now it was wet, and he was winded. Finally he reached a branch high enough for him to see the gathering in the compound. He settled in with the tree's thick trunk at his back for support and braced the rifle against a branch. His lungs screamed for air. His muscles were cramping. His hands were slippery. Raindrops stung his eyes. But he could see Brooke.

Squinting to clear his vision, he looked through the scope of his rifle. He kept his gaze on Babineaux and tried not to let Brooke's awful chopped-off hair or bleeding neck distract him. He had to take out the sniper out first, and then he would shoot Babineaux.

The odds of him making two such difficult shots were negligible under good conditions. Once he factored in his broken arm and the rain, his chances were probably close to zero.

But he'd been born with a remarkable gift for shooting accurately at long range. He'd won many awards. He'd been praised and envied. And he'd always wished that his talent was something else, anything else. He hated shooting. He hated killing. Now in order to save many lives, he would have to make not just one impossible shot but two. He was calm and surprisingly confident. It was the one thing he'd always been able to count on.

\* \* \*

Brooke had lost track of how long Babineaux had been ranting. She'd also lost the feeling in her feet, and her neck had been strained for so long she was sure she'd have a permanent crick.

Finally, with his voice hoarse from so much talking, Babineaux said to the cameras, "And so now, it is time to bid you farewell. I will conclude my remarks, and then there will be a magnificent fireworks display."

At this announcement, Uncle Christopher tried to step forward, but again his guards held him back. Brooke wondered what would happen next. Would Hunter shoot? Would the sniper shoot? Would Babineaux slit her throat and end her participation in the drama? No one moved, and for a few seconds, it seemed that time stood still.

Then, inexplicably, Agent Chu broke from the ranks of her team and ran at Babineaux. She only made it a few feet before a shot was fired from the trees, and she tumbled to the ground. She lay on her back, her face toward the sky, her beautiful eyes open and sightless. A pool of blood formed behind her head and slowly grew.

Brooke sobbed, and Babineaux seemed a little startled by the agent's brave, if senseless, act. He said, "Well, my television viewers, that was not part of my script. A little bonus, I guess you could say."

Then two shots, fired in rapid succession, pierced the night. Instantly the pressure was gone from Brooke's neck. Babineaux staggered backward, and with a weak little salute toward her uncle, he fell.

"Get down!" someone yelled as more shots were fired from the trees, taking down several of the guards.

As Brooke dropped to the ground, gunshots continued from the trees with amazing accuracy. The surviving rescue team members moved into action, engaging their guards in hand-to-hand combat, and soon the rescuers were armed.

Brooke picked up Babineaux's knife and crawled toward her uncle. She cut the tape that bound his hands. He reached up and pulled the tape off his mouth, but he didn't thank her.

"Get over there by that building before you get shot!" He waved toward a bullet-scarred shed a few feet away.

She ignored him and cut the tape from Doc's hands.

Once his hands were free, Doc grabbed the knife. "You'd better take cover before your uncle strangles you." Then he turned to help the others.

Brooke crawled to the shed, avoiding dead bodies and broken glass along the way. Once she was crouched there in relative safety, she turned her gaze to the surrounding trees. Somewhere in the foliage was the man she loved. And a broken arm combined with driving rain had not prevented him from saving them all.

With Babineaux dead, most of his men seemed to lose their will to fight, and they either surrendered or ran for the jungle. As soon as the Americans had the area secured, Uncle Christopher rushed over to Brooke and pulled her into a bear hug.

"Are you okay?"

"I'm fine," she assured him.

"There's still a risk of stray bullets, so stay here," he told her.

Her uncle assigned Doc and the copilot to assess the injured. Doc went to Hack first, and as he knelt beside the big man, Brooke watched anxiously. When Doc asked the copilot for his first-aid kit and began field dressing Hack's shoulder, she took it as a good sign. Her relief was tempered by the fact that many others were not okay. Her eyes skimmed over the bodies of Sheffield and Bosh to land on Agent Chu. The young agent Alcine removed his shirt so he could partially cover her body. Brooke felt a chill that had nothing to do with the rain.

"Steamer!" Uncle Christopher called.

"Sir?" The man from Vegas ran up, slightly out of breath.

"Babineaux's fireworks are really explosives. The sniper would have detonated them if Owl hadn't shot him. They still pose a danger, so we need to clear the area immediately. I'll tell some of the people who live near here so they can evacuate the town. You round up a couple of vehicles that aren't shot to . . . well, that still run."

"Yes, sir!" Steamer trotted off in search of mechanically sound vehicles, and her uncle hurried to the gate, where a few brave townspeople had gathered to see what was happening. Brooke followed him and listened while he gave them custody of the guards, who were now prisoners, and asked them to get medical care for anyone who needed it. Then he encouraged them to keep away from the fish plant until the explosives were removed.

With help from Agent Alcine, Steamer found two Jeeps and a pickup truck. They parked them near the front gate and loaded the bodies. Agent Alcine and the only other survivor of the ATF team insisted on moving Agent Chu themselves. Everyone else stood by respectfully as they lifted her small form into the back of the truck. Brooke saw Bosh and Sheffield in the truck bed, lying side by side. There would be no more arguments between them about what branch of the armed forces was best.

Steamer pointed at Babineaux and asked Uncle Christopher, "Sir, what are we going to do about him?"

Her uncle stared for a few seconds and then said, "Leave him there in the mud."

After the wounded were situated in the Jeeps, Uncle Christopher gathered everyone else around the vehicles and addressed the group, "This has been a difficult day for us all. We've seen some of the worst human nature has to offer—and some of the best. We will forever be grateful for the opportunity we've had to work with these heroes." He put his hand on the back of the truck. "Now everyone get into a vehicle. A helicopter is waiting for us a few miles up the beach."

Uncle Christopher turned to Brooke. "Climb into the first Jeep, backseat, right behind Hack."

She did as she was told. Doc and Steamer sat on either side of her, and Uncle Christopher slid under the wheel. Brooke grabbed the seat in front of her as the vehicle lurched forward. It felt good to leave the fish plant behind them. Now if they could just find Hunter and get out of Haiti.

"Anybody else got a cell phone?" Uncle Christopher asked. "I need to call home."

"I have one," Brooke pulled her phone from the pocket of her rain-soaked fatigue pants and handed it to her uncle. "I hope it's water resistant."

Her uncle took the phone and dialed a number quickly. "Savannah!" he said when the call was answered. "Yes, I'm fine. We all are. Don't cry. We'll be home in no time."

When he ended the call, he passed the phone back to Brooke. "I'd better concentrate on my driving. It would be a shame if I killed us all now."

Brooke couldn't muster even a small smile. The road was treacherous and unfamiliar. The rain had been replaced by fog, and Hunter still hadn't joined them. She wouldn't allow herself to consider the possibility that something had happened to him.

"Hack," her uncle said.

There was no response.

"Hack!" her uncle called, louder this time.

"What?" Hack demanded. "Can't a guy get a little sleep around here?"

"I need you to stay conscious until we get to the helicopter."

As they came out of a sharp turn, the fog lifted, and they saw a figure standing in the middle of the road. He was tall and wild-eyed. The paint on his face was streaked by rain. He was wearing a helmet covered with fake leaves and a futuristic bodysuit that clung to his muscular physique. His damaged, filthy cast showed through the several rips in his right sleeve, and a high-powered rifle was slung over his left shoulder. He was magnificence meets terrible.

"Hunter!" Brooke cried his name.

Uncle Christopher slammed on the brakes to avoid a collision. The Jeep skidded sideways in the muddy street, and the second vehicle had to turn sharply to avoid them.

Awakened by the near collision, Hack cursed under his breath. "Couldn't you find a less dangerous way to join us?"

Hunter didn't defend himself. All his attention was focused on Brooke. He walked to the side of the Jeep, reached over Doc, and lifted her out.

His eyes did a detailed reconnaissance of her face. "You are the most beautiful sight I've ever seen!"

She felt a little hysterical. "You wait until I look like this to give me an unsolicited compliment?"

He fingered the blood on the collar of her fatigues. "He hurt you."

She raised a hand up to the cut on her neck. "It's not bad."

"I love you."

She smiled. "I know."

Then he pressed his lips to hers. His fingers tangled in her short hair.

"Two soldiers in full camo—including face paint—kissing on a jungle road," Steamer said finally. "That's something you don't see every day."

"Get in," Uncle Christopher yelled. "If that helicopter gets tired of waiting for us, we'll be stranded again!"

Hunter lifted Brooke back into the Jeep and then sat in the rear. "Ready!" he called.

Uncle Christopher took him at his word. He put the Jeep into gear, and they went careening off down the road.

Brooke held on tight as her uncle drove along the beach road. He was driving fast, obviously trying to put as much distance as possible between them and the fish plant. As they neared the meet point, they could hear sirens.

"It looks like the Haitians got the word about Babineaux and his explosives," Doc murmured.

A few minutes later, they arrived at the clearing where the helicopter was waiting. They transferred the wounded first, the bodies second, and then the healthy climbed on board. Agent Alcine and the other ATF agent chose to sit in the back by their fallen comrades. Brooke sat behind the pilot, and Hunter took the seat next to her.

She couldn't stop staring at him. And the words he'd spoken kept repeating in her mind. *I love you.* It was what she had waited to hear for days now. Maybe she had finally overcome the past.

Uncle Christopher made sure everyone was on board before he took the seat beside Hack. "Where are you taking us?" he asked the pilot.

"Airfield in Miami," the man replied.

"Can you call ahead and have some ambulances waiting for us?" Uncle Christopher requested.

The pilot nodded. "That shouldn't be a problem."

As they rose into the night, several police vehicles roared into the clearing. Uniformed men jumped out and ran toward the helicopter, shouting and waving their arms.

"I guess they want to ask us a few questions about the mess we left at the fish plant," Doc remarked.

Uncle Christopher shook his head. "We don't have time for that." He looked at the pilot. "Let's go."

As the pilot lifted the helicopter off the ground, the Haitians closest to them aimed their guns and fired.

"Owl!" Uncle Christopher pulled the side door open a few inches.

Hunter swung the rifle off his shoulder and dropped to a knee in one smooth motion. He fired a couple of harmless shots out the door. The policemen took cover, and the pilot was able to complete their ascent. Uncle Christopher closed the door, and Hunter returned to his seat.

\* \* \*

During the short helicopter ride to Miami, Brooke and Hunter didn't talk much. They were content just to sit beside each other, their grimy hands clutched together. Uncle Christopher spent most of his time making calls on Brooke's phone and pacing in the small open space near the pilot.

"General Steele is doing better," he reported after one call. "And apparently General Moffett is taking early retirement."

Brooke smiled. "You'll have to ask Savannah about that."

Her uncle raised an eyebrow as he made another call. He arranged for two planes to be waiting for them in Miami. One would take his team to Nashville, and the other would take the ATF team to Washington, DC.

The next call was to the ATF and involved body transports, funeral arrangements, and posthumous medals. Everyone was subdued when he ended the call.

Mindful of the ATF agents in the back, Brooke turned to her uncle and asked, "Why did Agent Chu run at Babineaux like that? If she'd waited just a few more seconds, Hunter would have . . ."

A look of profound sadness clouded his features. "If Agent Chu hadn't acted as she did, we might all be dead now. Owl had to pinpoint the location of the other sniper and take him out before he could shoot Babineaux. I tried to draw his fire, but the guards held me back. Agent Chu realized what had to happen and sacrificed herself."

Brooke pressed a hand to her lips.

Uncle Christopher turned to look out into the darkness. "She was a remarkable soldier."

Finally as the city lights came into view, the pilot said, "You're going to have to take your seat now, sir. We'll be on the ground in five minutes."

Without a word Uncle Christopher returned to his seat. Once he was strapped in, he told them, "It seems that a friend of Owl's has a VIP plane waiting for us in Miami."

"How VIP?" Hack wanted to know.

"As VIP as it gets," Uncle Christopher replied.

Steamer whistled. "I *knew* you flew the president around!"

"Don't make me shoot you," Hunter said without a trace of humor.

* * *

Once they touched down in Miami, everyone waited while the injured and deceased were transferred to waiting ambulances. Then they waited for the two remaining ATF agents to climb out of the helicopter and board the plane to Washington, DC.

Agent Alcine paused by the door and looked back. "I don't know what to say," he told them finally.

"Nothing needs to be said," her uncle's voice sounded a little gruff. "You did your job, and we did ours. Now the world's a little safer. That's the way it should be."

Alcine nodded. "Thank you, sir." He jumped down out of the helicopter and hurried toward the waiting plane.

Brooke watched while Hunter climbed out of the helicopter. Once he was on the ground, he turned back to help her. It took Steamer, Doc, and Uncle Christopher to get Hack out. They tried to put him in an ambulance, but he refused to go to the hospital in Miami.

"I'm not missing the chance to fly on the president's plane!" Hack said. "I'll get checked out by a doctor in Nashville."

"It's not the president's plane," Hunter corrected mildly.

Hack frowned. "Yeah, yeah, yeah. You said you didn't fly the president around either, and now we *all* know that ain't true."

They carried Hack inside the luxurious plane and laid him across two of the plush leather seats surrounding a large conference table. In the middle of the table was a tray of deli sandwiches, a variety of soft drinks, and a plate of cookies.

When Hack saw the food, he said, "I think I might cry."

"Man, this is nice." Steamer settled into a seat beside Hack. "Major, you think the army would buy our team a plane like this?"

"I'm pretty sure, no." Her uncle selected a sandwich and sat down heavily. "So enjoy it while you can."

The pilot stepped out of the cockpit to speak to them.

"Hey, Corporal Ezell," he said. "How does it feel to be a passenger today? Hunter shrugged. "I'll let you know after I see how well you fly."

The pilot laughed and then spoke to the others. "Ordinarily I have a flight attendant, but since this was an unscheduled flight, I'm on my own. I thought you might be hungry, so I ordered this stuff from a deli in the airport."

Hack picked up a sandwich. "If I could stand up, I'd kiss you."

"You'll have to excuse him," Hunter said. "He's lost a lot of blood and taken an entire bottle of painkillers."

"It's been a while since we've had anything to eat." Steamer picked up a chocolate chip cookie. "And these look delicious."

"Who do we owe for this?" Uncle Christopher asked.

The pilot smiled. "It's on the house. And for your convenience, there are phones and iPads built into each console."

"Are you kidding me?" Hack exclaimed as he opened the console closest to him. "Seriously, we gotta ask the general for an equipment upgrade."

The pilot pointed to a large screen on the wall. "And the iPads are synced to this TV if you want to watch a movie or FaceTime with your families."

"Very impressive," Uncle Christopher said. "Thank you."

"I'm glad to have you aboard. We'll be taking off in a few minutes, so everyone keep your seat belts on."

"Will that interfere with my Internet connection?" Hack asked as he bit into a sandwich.

"No," the pilot replied. "You should be good. Now I'll let you folks eat, and I'll get this plane in the air."

Uncle Christopher waited until the pilot returned to the cockpit before he turned to Brooke. "Okay, what happened between Savannah and General Moffett?"

"I really do want her to tell you the details," Brooke hedged. "But in a nutshell, she went to see him, he refused to help you, so she started a media campaign against him that included blog articles, press conferences, petitions delivered to the White House, and—apparently—General Moffett's early retirement."

"Wow," Steamer commented. "Remind me not to get on your wife's bad side."

"What all the media pressure didn't do was make General Moffett change his mind about rescuing you and the team," Hunter said.

"So we broke into General Steele's room at Belvoir Community Hospital," Brooke added. "Hunter pretended to deliver a top secret document while I forced the general's wife to take a fake survey."

Her uncle raised an eyebrow. "You broke into the hospital?"

Hunter looked embarrassed, and Brooke shrugged. "Sorry, I'm on this new honesty kick, and I can't help but tell the whole truth."

Hack looked at Hunter. "I don't see how you can argue with that."

"We didn't exactly break in," Hunter amended. "I just had a short, unauthorized visit with General Steele. That's when we found out where you were."

"Anyway." As Brooke reclaimed control of the conversation, the plane started rolling toward the runway. "I know everyone's feeling a little euphoric since we just survived certain death in a miraculous fashion, but there's something we need to discuss with you. Something important . . ."

"Go ahead," her uncle encouraged.

Now that she had everyone's attention, she wasn't sure where to begin. Brooke looked at Hunter, and he picked up the explanation.

"There's a connection between Rex Moreland and Babineaux."

"What kind of connection?" her uncle demanded.

"Babineaux was a member of Joined Forces," Hunter said. "Rex has been to his 'town' in Haiti several times."

"Are you kidding me?" Steamer cried.

"I wish," Brooke muttered.

"Start at the beginning," Uncle Christopher said. "Tell us everything."

"We didn't figure this out until just before we came," Brooke prefaced, "but this is I how I think it went." She glanced at Hunter. "Feel free to correct me if I misspeak."

"I will," he assured her.

Brooke cleared her throat and launched into the sordid story. "Rex started visiting Babineaux back when he and I were still together. I remember making airline reservations for him once, possibly twice; I'm not sure. He told me a few days ago that Babineaux had joined the group and was donating a lot of money to the cause. He had also offered free beachfront accommodations to fellow members. I didn't think anything about it until Hunter said you and the team had been sent to Haiti. And when he mentioned Babineaux, well, I knew for sure."

"That we'd been setup?" Doc guessed.

Hunter nodded. "It's been about Brooke from the start—the Nature Fresh fire, the shootout at the grand opening dinner—"

"What shootout?" her uncle demanded. "You weren't at the grand opening dinner."

Brooke took a deep breath. "We were there. I'm sorry. I guess I need to go back a little further in this story."

She told them about her pregnancy, Rex's reaction to that news, and her decision to give the baby up for adoption. When she saw the sadness and compassion in their eyes, her voice faltered.

So Hunter picked up the dialogue. "Brooke had no contact from Moreland for almost a year. But she worried that he would find out about the baby and make trouble. That's why she didn't tell anyone."

"And because I didn't want my parents and family to suffer for my mistakes," Brooke added, determined to be honest. "When Rex came back into town, I felt so vulnerable. I went along with everything—his insistence that I help with the grand opening, the media interviews—to protect the baby."

"But Rex already knew about the baby, and when she tried to back out of the dinner, he pulled that out as his ace in the hole," Hunter told them.

"He had pictures, and Brooke felt she had to go. So we went to the dinner even though we'd promised we wouldn't."

"You gave me your word of honor," Uncle Christopher reminded him.

"Yes, sir," Hunter acknowledged. "But you also entrusted me with Brooke's safety. She was going to the dinner, and so I decided the most honorable thing to do was to protect her while she was there."

"And it's a good thing he went," Brooke inserted. "Because Rex took me downstairs, where they were having the illegal coin sale, just before the FBI arrived. We thought it was just an unlucky coincidence."

"Carmichael's guards started firing at the FBI, and we were right in the middle of it. It's a miracle she wasn't killed," Hunter said.

"Rex slipped out of the storage room just before the guards started shooting," Brooke added.

"Leaving you conveniently in the area when the bullets started flying," Hack muttered.

"We believe the team's emergency assignment to Haiti was just a ploy to get all of you out of the way and make me more vulnerable."

"Babineaux pretty much confirmed that," her uncle said. "He told me he had an American friend who arranged to have the team sent in to get Alcine."

"Rex was friends with Babineaux," Steamer said. "Why doesn't that surprise me?"

"So we know he's tried to kill me twice," Brooke said. "We suspect that he opened the Nashville call center and allowed the illegal coin auction just so he could tip off the FBI about Carmichael and guarantee that bullets would fly during the dinner. But there are several things we don't know. Like why Rex wants me dead."

"You must pose a threat of some kind to him," her uncle said. "Can you think of anything you knew or saw, maybe back when you and Rex were . . . together?"

She shook her head. "No, nothing."

"Maybe it's because you knew about his connection to Babineaux," Doc suggested.

"I wasn't the only person who knew about that. Millicent knew, and he hasn't tried to kill her."

"Yet," Hack said morosely.

"Keep trying to remember," her uncle encouraged. "There must be something."

"What else don't you know?" Hack asked.

"We don't know how Rex got the team assigned to Alcine's rescue mission," Hunter said. "Or how he poisoned General Steele."

"Getting an army special-ops team assigned to extract an undercover ATF agent would require a lot of string-pulling and a high security clearance," Doc said. "There has to be a trail."

"And in order to poison the general, someone would have to have close access to him," Steamer added.

Hunter said, "We don't know if General Moffett is a part of the conspiracy to kill Brooke or if he was just used by someone else."

"If he was in on it, why did he cancel our orders?" Dane asked. "Babineaux said the plan was to let us rescue Alcine and lull our government into complacency."

"Then maybe he wasn't in on it," Doc said. "Or maybe he just wanted to protect himself. If anyone discovered the irregularities of the operation, he could say he noticed the same things and tried to cancel it."

"But the most important thing we don't know is the current location of Rex Moreland," Hunter said. "We haven't had any direct contact with him since the grand opening dinner fiasco."

Hack leaned up on one elbow. "And as long as Rex is free, he poses a threat to Brooke."

"A serious threat," Hunter agreed. "The police have a warrant for his arrest, and we told Detective Napier our suspicions. I don't know if he's been able to learn anything new while we've been gone."

"We obviously need to talk to Detective Napier," Uncle Christopher said.

Doc nodded. "And maybe General Steele, if he's well enough to handle the stress."

"I'll call Detective Napier and see what he thinks." Uncle Christopher pulled out the satellite phone he'd borrowed from Brooke.

"Why talk on the phone when you can do it face to face?" Hack typed onto his built-in iPad, and a ringing phone appeared on the wall-mounted screen. "This way we can all talk to him."

While they waited for Detective Napier to answer, Steamer asked, "Are these really the best sandwiches in the world, or do they taste so good because I'm starving?"

"The sandwiches are good," Doc allowed. "But most anything would seem delicious to us right now."

"Here we go!" Hack announced, and a second later Detective Napier's face filled the large screen.

"Hello, everyone," he greeted. The television screen seemed to accentuate his flaws—the mussed hair, the deep wrinkles, and the dark circles under his eyes.

"The gang's all here," Hack told him.

"Your hair," the detective said when he saw Brooke. "Wow, I hardly recognized you."

She rubbed the top of her head. "Every time I need to disguise myself, I cut my hair. Next time you see me, I'll probably be bald."

"I hope you won't need to disguise yourself again anytime soon," he said seriously.

"Hey, detective," Steamer called out. "Have you visited any good doughnut shops lately?"

"Pretty jovial for someone who's just been through a near-death experience," the detective replied.

Steamer cleared his throat. "I couldn't resist the cop humor."

"Enough with the jokes," Uncle Christopher said firmly. Then he addressed the detective. "Brooke and Owl told you about the connection between Rex Moreland and Babineaux? And about their theory that our emergency assignment to Haiti was part of Moreland's continued determination to kill Brooke?"

Detective Napier nodded gravely. "Yes, and I agree with the theory, but proving it is another matter."

"We understand that, and we're only seriously concerned about two things," her uncle continued. "We want to find out who got us assigned to the Haiti operation, and we want to get Moreland into police custody so we don't have to worry about any more attempts on Brooke's life."

"I don't have the resources to find out who arranged for your team to be sent to Haiti. General Steele may be able to help you, but an investigation like that will have to be handled discreetly."

"You mean it looks bad for the government to admit they have crooks and murderers in high places?" Hack growled.

"There are crooks and murderers everywhere," the detective replied cautiously. "But yes, the government has to protect its own integrity. It's a matter of national security."

"Whoever set this all up is responsible for the death of several ATF agents," Hunter said. "We can't let them get away with that."

"No," Uncle Christopher agreed. "I'll talk to General Steele and see what we can do."

"If we find Moreland, he can tell us who helped him set things up," Doc pointed out.

"Finding Rex Moreland is my number-one priority," Detective Napier assured them. "We've dedicated a lot of resources to it but so far haven't turned up anything. Moreland hasn't been seen or heard from since the night of the grand opening dinner. Apparently he's gone into deep hiding."

"Or maybe he left the country like Freddo," Brooke murmured. "It might help to check and see if any money's missing from the Joined Forces accounts. I would ask Millicent, but I've already stretched her tiny little bit of goodwill to the limits."

"Who is Freddo?" the detective asked.

"Freddo Higgins ran Joined Forces after Rex went to California," Brooke explained. "A few months ago, he cleaned out the Joined Forces contribution account and moved to Mexico."

"Let's not lose focus here," her uncle warned. "We're looking for Rex, not Freddo."

"If the police can't find Moreland, we may have to smoke him out," Hack said.

"And what do you think would be compelling enough to make him throw caution to the wind?" the detective asked.

"The only thing Rex cares about is money," Brooke said. "And if he already cleaned out the Joined Forces accounts, he may not need any more."

"There's no such thing as too much money," Detective Napier murmured. "Especially if he's going to be hiding for a while."

"So if we're going to set a trap for him, it needs to involve money," her uncle said.

"It will have to be something he won't see straight through." Doc sounded skeptical.

"What if Freddo were to contact Rex and say he wants to give back the money he stole?" Brooke suggested.

"There are two huge problems with that idea," Hack countered. "We don't know where your friend Freddo is, and why in the world would he want to give the money back?"

"We don't have to find Freddo," Brooke explained. "We can impersonate him."

Hack laughed. "Waste of time! Moreland knows what this Freddo guy looks and sounds like. We could never fool him."

"It would be very difficult," Doc said more gently.

"Not if we sent him an e-mail from Freddo," Brooke persisted. "If it came from Freddo's old e-mail address, continuing a thread that Rex started, that would make it seem authentic, right?"

"A reply?" Hack murmured thoughtfully. "That does give it built-in credibility."

Brooke started to feel hopeful. "So are we going to try it?"

"Why not?" Hunter said. "If Hack can get into the guy's e-mail."

Hack shrugged. "Unless he's a computer genius, sure."

"Freddo isn't any kind of genius," Brooke said.

Hack sat up a little straighter. "Then give me an e-mail address."

"Are you okay with this, detective?" her uncle asked. "We won't be messing up your investigation?"

"Go ahead," Detective Napier said. "Freddo isn't part of the current investigation, so there's no risk of tainting evidence."

They used another iPad to pull up Brooke's e-mail. She scrolled quickly through the past few months until she came to one from Freddo. "Here, in February he sent me this e-mail about the chicken march."

She gave the address to Hack, and he worked for a few minutes. Then he shook his head. "This fake keyboard is killing me. I need a laptop."

"We don't have a laptop," Uncle Christopher pointed out. "If you can't use an iPad, we might have to wait and do this when we get to Nashville."

Brooke was disappointed.

"I don't like the idea of Brooke being in Nashville with Rex still on the loose," Hunter added. "Can't you keep trying with the iPad?"

"It's delicate work, and if I hit one wrong key, the system will freeze me out."

"So much for that then," her uncle said. "Once we get to Nashville where Hack has access to a laptop—"

"Hey!" Hack looked more cheerful. "I could call Volt and let him tiptoe through the computer code for me. He's almost as good as I am."

"He said he was better," Brooke teased.

"Well, let's give him a chance to prove that." Hack dialed a number, and in seconds he was talking to Volt. A few minutes later, Hack nodded. "He's in. What do we want to say?"

There was some discussion, some back and forth, and even an argument. But finally they decided on a simple message. Replying to an e-mail Rex had sent to Freddo the previous year regarding nonprofit tax forms, they wrote, *Hey, Rex, it's been a while. Sorry that I left without saying good-bye. Things have been going good for me, and I'd like to return the money I took. From what I've seen on the news, it looks like Joined Forces could use it. I'll be passing through the Nashville area tonight, and I can meet you—maybe behind that old church you were trying to turn into a call center. Or someplace else. Just let me know. Freddo*

"I like it," Steamer said. "Humble, repentant, anxious to make amends."

"How often does Rex check his e-mail?"

"He used to check it every time he got a notification," Brooke said.

Uncle Christopher nodded. "Send it."

Hack relayed the command to Volt and then reported, "It's done."

"If we get a response, I'll impersonate Freddo at the sting tonight," Steamer volunteered.

"*If* we get a response, our participation will be over," Uncle Christopher stated firmly. "One of Detective Napier's guys will meet Rex and arrest him."

"And if Moreland doesn't respond?" Hunter asked.

"It's still a police matter," her uncle insisted. "We'll take Brooke to Virginia and keep her safe until they arrest Moreland."

Brooke could tell Hunter wasn't a fan of this approach, but he didn't argue.

Uncle Christopher said, "Hack, tell Volt to monitor that e-mail account and let us know if he gets a response."

"I will," Hack replied.

"And we'll keep you informed, detective," her uncle added.

Detective Napier waved, and then the big screen went blank.

# CHAPTER NINETEEN

When the pilot announced that they were making their final approach into the Nashville airport, Uncle Christopher said, "When we land, I need to get to Neely's house. Savannah and Caroline are there waiting for me. Doc and Steamer, will you guys get Hack to the hospital?"

"I want to go to Neely's house too," Hack objected. "I can see a doctor tomorrow."

"You'll get your wounds taken care of first." Her uncle's tone was firm. "That's an order."

Hack shrugged. "Okay, but explain my absence to Caroline. I know she'll be disappointed I'm not there."

Brooke laughed. "As long as Hunter's there, Caroline will be happy. I think he lets her beat him at Scrabble Junior."

"We all let her beat us at Scrabble Junior," Doc said.

Brooke stared back at them. "And here I thought you were all pictures of integrity."

The iPad in Hack's console pinged, and after checking it, he looked up with a grin. "Rex responded. He's agreed to meet 'Freddo' at the call center tonight to pick up all that money."

* * *

When they walked into the terminal, an airport worker with a wheelchair was waiting for Hack. Brooke and Hunter stood back while Uncle Christopher convinced the big man to sit in it. Then they moved through the airport with Brooke in the middle of their little group as a precaution against possible attack.

Her uncle had arranged for two rental cars. Steamer and Doc loaded Hack into one and headed for the hospital. Uncle Christopher climbed behind the wheel of the second car. "Let's head to Neely's house," he told Brooke and Hunter.

"My car's in the long-term parking lot," Hunter said. "I'll go pick it up and meet you there."

Brooke took hold of Hunter's good arm. "I'm riding with Hunter."

Her uncle nodded. "I'll follow you both."

So Brooke and Hunter walked to the parking lot with Uncle Christopher's rental car creeping along behind them.

When they were in his car, driving to her parents' home, they finally had a few minutes to themselves. Brooke half expected him to recant his declaration of love made in the heat of battle. But he didn't.

She glanced in the mirror and said, "My mother's going to die when she sees how I look. I'm serious—she won't be able to handle this."

Hunter offered her an olive green, army-issue handkerchief. "You can get a little of the blood off your neck at least. And maybe some of my camo paint off your face."

Brooke worked on her appearance for a few minutes but finally gave up. She returned his hanky and said, "You might want to work on your own face. Believe it or not, you look worse than me."

"I need to keep both hands on the wheel, so I'll worry about my face later." He stuffed the handkerchief in his shirt pocket.

"Maybe my mom will be so glad to see me alive she won't care that I'm hideous." Brooke rubbed her scruffy hair. "At least that's what I'm counting on."

"Your hair isn't bad."

"If you like this haircut—that I gave myself with first-aid scissors in the bathroom of a plane—then I know for sure that you're in love with me!" she teased.

"That's never really been the question," he responded with typical seriousness. "I just wasn't sure I could *live* with you. We're so different."

"Honest and dishonest," she provided. "Social and antisocial."

He didn't disagree. "But when I was sitting in that tree and Babineaux had a knife to your throat, I finally understood. I thought I could approach marriage like I have everything else in my life, with cold, clear deliberation. I thought I could resist love if we're not compatible. But the truth is no matter how much you lie—"

"I don't lie anymore," she inserted.

"It doesn't matter if you're a reformed liar or a criminal or if you interrupt me right in the middle of the most important speech of my life." He glanced at her. "I love you, and that's not going to change. I want to be with you—I *have* to be with you, even if that means visiting you in jail."

She smiled and said a little tremulously, "Can we make an exception to the no-touching-while-driving rule? Because I really need to hug you right now."

\* \* \*

Her parents were waiting at the kitchen door when Brooke and Hunter walked in from the garage. As Brooke had feared, Neely burst into tears.

"I'm sorry about my hair, Mom!" Brooke apologized. "Please don't cry. It will grow back."

Neely wrapped Brooke in a desperate hug. "These are happy tears! I'm so glad you're okay! And I'm not worried about your hair."

Brooke leaned back. "Really?"

"I'm not worried because tomorrow I'm going to take you to the best stylist in Nashville and get it, well, professionally adjusted. And maybe they can give you a facial too." Her eyes dropped to Brooke's hands. "And a manicure."

Brooke spread her arms wide. "Hunter likes my new look!"

She heard him sigh.

Neely raised her eyebrows.

"You're the cutest soldier I've ever seen," her father said as he pulled Brooke into a hug.

"You can't believe them," Neely warned her. "Only your mother will tell you the hard truths. And you, young lady, are a sight."

Brooke laughed as they walked into the living room, where Savannah and Uncle Christopher were sitting on the couch. Brooke returned Savannah's wedding ring, and Savannah expressed her effusive and tearful thanks.

Uncle Christopher gave them an occasional wink during this lengthy process, but mostly he just watched Savannah talk, as if he couldn't bear to take his eyes off her. Theirs was the kind of relationship she wanted to have with Hunter. They hadn't made it yet, but she hoped someday they would.

When the never-ending thank-you was finally completed, Caroline came in from the kitchen and asked Hunter to play Scrabble Junior.

"I can't play tonight," he told her. "I have to take.Brooke home. She needs a bath."

Caroline wrinkled her nose. "You need a bath too."

"Caroline," Savannah said in obvious embarrassment.

Hunter smiled. "It's true."

"You're welcome to stay here tonight," Neely offered. "Hunter could stay in Adam's room."

"I want to go home," Brooke declined. "I'll be more comfortable in my own bed. And besides, I have a piano there that needs refinishing."

"Thank you for the offer, Mrs. Clayton—" Hunter said.

"Neely."

"Neely," he corrected himself. "But unless Major Dane thinks it's a security risk, we'll go back to Brooke's apartment."

"As long as a couple of Hack's guys follow you, it should be fine." He lowered his voice and added, "Especially since Rex is meeting the police right about now."

"You'll call us when they have him in custody?" Hunter requested.

"I will," Uncle Christopher promised.

Caroline frowned and asked, "Where are the other guys?"

"Hack's in the hospital because he hurt his leg," Uncle Christopher said. "Steamer and Doc are there with him, and they'll bring him home tomorrow."

"Well, it was good to see everyone," Brooke said, "but we need to go and get cleaned up."

"You won't stay and eat dinner with us?" Neely asked.

"We ate on the plane," Brooke explained. "But I'll come back tomorrow, and we can go out to lunch before I get my hair fixed. How does that sound?"

"Good," Neely replied.

"And while you're getting fixed, Hunter can play Scrabble Junior with me all day!" Caroline said.

Brooke raised her eyebrows at Hunter and whispered, "That's what you get for being a reverse cheater."

* * *

When Hunter pulled up in front of her apartment building, Brooke was pleased to see that there were no Nature Fresh protesters or news vans or television reporters waiting for them. Maybe things were finally going back to something like normal.

Still, Hunter waited for Hack's men to park behind them before he opened the car door. Then all the men surrounded Brooke as they hurried into the lobby. Once they were inside, one of the guards stayed by the front door while the other went to cover the rear exit. Brooke and Hunter took the stairs up to her apartment.

When they approached her door, the guard stationed there stood a little straighter.

"Welcome home," he said.

Hunter nodded. "Everything quiet here?"

"Yes, sir."

Then Hunter realized they didn't have keys. "Do you have a kit I can use to pick this lock?" he asked.

The guard reached into his pocket and produced a small case. "Yes, sir."

Seconds later the door was open, and Brooke stepped inside.

"Wait!" Hunter objected as he returned the lock-picking kit. "Let me go in first."

She stepped back and let him precede her into the living room. He flipped on the lights and did a quick walk-through, assuring himself that the apartment was empty. Then he motioned her in. Everything looked the same as when they had left. She rubbed her hand along the freshly-sanded surface of the piano. It was good to be home.

Hunter closed the door. "We need to talk."

"Yes," she agreed.

"I don't want your parents to think we're just living together."

"They know you're here on assignment from my uncle, and I'm sure they trust that you are behaving like a complete gentleman," she assured him.

"We could just tell them that we're married."

A few days earlier, she would have been thrilled by even this lukewarm proposal, but now the words made her a little sad. "I don't want to just tell them we're married. My mom has been mentally planning my wedding since I was born. I can't cheat her out of the opportunity to put some of those thoughts to good use."

"So do you want to tell them we're engaged?" Hunter asked. "Your mother could plan . . . whatever, and we could have another ceremony."

Brooke was looking for the right words when the lights flickered and went out. "Great," she said. "The weather's not bad, so a breaker must have tripped."

"Where's your breaker box?" Hunter asked.

She pointed down the hallway. "The closet with the hot water heater."

Hunter skirted the piano and walked to the hallway. Out of habit, Brooke followed. He opened the closet door, and Brooke used the satellite phone to shed some light on the panel.

"The breakers aren't tripped." He leaned closer to the wall, squinting at the panel.

"What else could it be?" She looked over his shoulder.

"Nothing good." His voice was low and full of dread.

Brooke processed this information. The lights were out in her apartment, and it wasn't because of an electrical problem. Then there was a thud at the front door followed by a crash as the door flew open and slammed against the wall. Two shadowy figures stepped inside the apartment.

Hunter tried to sweep her behind him, but the hot water heater made it impossible to maneuver in the small closet.

"Rex?" she whispered. Even though her logical mind knew it was foolish, her heart still held out hope that she could reason with him.

But the voice that spoke did not belong to Rex. "Don't move," the first figure said with a heavy Southern accent. It was a genteel voice, one a plantation owner from a long-extinct civilization might have used. "I've got a gun," he added as if they thought this was a social call.

"Mr. Shaw?" Brooke whispered.

"Let me guess," Hunter said. "It's been you—not Rex—all along."

"I needed a front man," Mr. Shaw replied. "And Rex was perfect, too conceited to even imagine that someone might be manipulating him."

Brooke found this new, terrible knowledge staggering. "You're Babineaux's American friend," she whispered. "You hired someone to send my uncle's team on a suicide mission. You tried to kill me—*twice!*"

Brooke's eyes were adjusting to the dim light, and she saw Mr. Shaw nod as he walked around the piano to stand just a few feet away. Then he spoke over his shoulder without taking his eyes off of them. "Mr. Sperry, drag that dead bodyguard inside and close the door."

Brooke was disappointed—but not surprised—to see that Sperry was Mr. Shaw's partner in crime.

With some effort Sperry got the guard into the living room and pushed the damaged door shut. Then he took up a defensive position a little bit behind Mr. Shaw.

"Why?" Brooke asked.

"In order for me to take over Babineaux's illegal arms business in Haiti and maintain my regular life here in Nashville, I had to eliminate all connections between myself and Monsieur Babineaux." Mr. Shaw sounded almost bored.

"I didn't know there was a connection between you and Babineaux," Brooke cried, overwhelmed by the senselessness.

"I went on one of Rex's trips to Haiti a year ago. You made my plane reservations. I've had the airline's records sanitized, of course, but eventually you might've remembered."

She felt Hunter shifting slowly, trying to get himself between her and Mr. Shaw.

"Did the police arrest Rex?" she asked, desperate to delay the inevitable.

Mr. Shaw smiled. "No, Rex didn't go to the call center, although he was fooled by that clever e-mail ploy. I, on the other hand, was not fooled. I knew Freddo didn't send that e-mail because I killed him months ago. The stolen money is in my investment portfolio—Microsoft stock, I think. Anyway, Rex is down in the parking lot behind the wheel of his rental car with a bullet in his head. It will look like he killed the two of you out of jealously and then took his own life. And that will tie up all my loose ends."

With that he raised the gun and fired. The shot was silenced, just a pop, and it went wild, hitting the hot water heater instead of one of the intended victims. The reason for the missed shot became clear when Brooke realized that Mr. Shaw and Sperry were grappling for control of the gun.

Hunter lunged forward and knocked both men to the floor. While trying to avoid being scalded by the hot spray from the water heater, Brooke looked for a way to help Hunter without making things worse. But their tangled feet, sweeping back and forth in the small space, prevented her from even leaving the closet.

Then another shot was fired, and Brooke flinched, but the bullet embedded itself harmlessly in the wooden lid of her old piano.

"Help!" she tried. Then a little louder, "Help us!"

And miraculously help came, but from an unexpected source. The 'body' of the dead guard that Sperry had dragged in resurrected itself and joined the fray. But he only succeeded in breaking the one-handed grasp that Hunter had on Mr. Shaw. The district attorney pulled free, pointed the gun, and shot the guard again. The large man toppled back to the floor with a heavy thud.

Then Shaw turned the gun toward Sperry and squeezed off a shot. Sperry clutched his midsection and fell.

Hunter raised himself into a crouch as Mr. Shaw swung the gun toward him.

"I am so tired of dealing with you people!" the DA complained. There was a trickle of blood running from his mouth, and he wiped it with the back of his hand. "You're making me late for my wife's birthday dinner!"

Panic welled up inside Brooke. Their lives would end here. She would never know what the future might hold. She couldn't bear it. "No!" she screamed and tried to hurl herself at Mr. Shaw. But Hunter caught her and pulled her down beside him.

Then the splintered door slammed open again, and a voice said, "Drop your gun, Shaw." It was Detective Napier, old, fat, and rumpled, in a perfect policeman stance.

Mr. Shaw swung his gun toward the detective and fired. Detective Napier fired as well. Shaw's bullet lodged itself in the wooden doorframe an inch from the detective's head. Detective Napier's bullet struck the district attorney squarely in the chest.

Mr. Shaw looked surprised as his fingers went slack and the gun fell from his grasp. He pressed a hand against the wound in a feeble attempt to staunch the blood. It just oozed between his fingers and dripped down his hand. He staggered and dropped to his knees.

Brooke couldn't look away. She was frightened by how much she wanted him to die. Mr. Shaw pitched forward onto the floor and lay still. Then Hunter took her hand and pulled her out of the closet.

"Call an ambulance!" he yelled to Detective Napier.

"Got some on the way," the detective replied as he circled around the piano and checked Mr. Shaw's neck for a pulse. Then he moved to the bodyguard.

Hunter was leading Brooke toward the front door when Sperry reached out and grabbed her ankle.

"Wait!" he gasped. "I need to tell you . . ."

"Come on, Brooke." Hunter pulled her arm.

But she resisted. "He tried to help us," she reminded Hunter. "He's unarmed and injured, so it won't hurt to talk to him." She knelt beside Sperry; a mixture of warm water and blood saturated the legs of her pants.

"I really didn't know he was going to kill you in that fire," Sperry whispered weakly. "I knew he was going to try again when he told me to come with him here. I had to let him try so you'd know, but I wasn't going to let him hurt you."

"Thank you," Brooke said as sirens approached. "You saved my life." She glanced up at Hunter and Detective Napier. "All of you."

Hunter tugged on her arm. "Let's move out of the way so the EMTs can get in here."

She couldn't argue with that, so she stood and followed him into the dark hallway. Detective Napier was right behind them.

"Are the lights out in the entire building?" she asked.

The detective nodded. "Apparently Shaw cut the electrical lines."

Other residents ventured out of their apartments to see what was going on. More policemen arrived. When the paramedics got off the elevator with stretchers, Hunter led Brooke over to a corner where they would be out of the way. For the next little while, there was constant traffic in the hallway, made more confusing by the lack of light.

Finally Detective Napier came over and stood beside them. "The guard Shaw shot is going to be okay."

Brooke was profoundly relieved.

"Rex Moreland's body was found in his rental car, dead from an apparent suicide."

"Shaw killed him and planned to make it look like he shot us and then himself," Hunter said. "It would have worked if you hadn't gotten here when you did."

The detective made a face. "When Moreland didn't show up at the call center to collect his money, I got a little worried. I knew you had plenty of security, but I decided to come by and check on you myself." He wiped the sweat beading on his forehead. "I'm getting too old for this."

The paramedics wheeled the stretchers by, and Brooke looked away. She didn't want to see Mr. Shaw ever again, not even his lifeless body.

Detective Napier continued, "You can't stay here tonight."

Brooke glanced back at her ruined front door. "No, I don't think I can stay here ever again."

"Come on," the detective said. "I'll take you home."

Brooke knew he meant her parents' house, and although she was dedicated to her independence, tonight she didn't argue. They walked with Detective Napier out to his unmarked police car, passing two ambulances and several squad cars along the way.

"The press hasn't shown up yet," the detective said, "but they will."

Anxious to be gone before that happened, Brooke increased her pace.

\* \* \*

When they reached her parents' house, she invited Hunter in.

He shook his head. "I need to go make a statement at the police station."

"Don't you need a statement from me too?" she asked the detective.

"You can come in and take care of that tomorrow," he said.

Hunter walked her to the door. "I'll see you in the morning." He kissed her gently.

She nodded, too exhausted and emotionally drained to argue.

# CHAPTER TWENTY

BROOKE WOKE UP THE NEXT morning in her childhood bedroom, with the cheerful purple walls. She was stiff and sore, scraped and bruised—all reminders of her traumatic experiences over the past few days.

She knew her parents were worried about her, so she allowed them to fuss. Her mother served her breakfast in bed and fluffed the pillows repeatedly while her father talked of closure and counseling and hope. Finally she'd had enough.

"All right," she said. "I appreciate all the pampering, but Hunter will be here soon so I'm getting up."

Her father gave her one last kiss. "I'll go on to work then."

"I'll walk you to the door," Neely told her husband.

Once they were gone, Brooke found some sweatpants and an old T-shirt emblazoned with a peeling picture of her high school mascot. Then she did what she could with her hair, which wasn't much. Finally she put on a little makeup, hoping she was one of those women who actually looked good bald. She wasn't.

There was a knock on the door, and then Neely stuck her head in. "Are you doing okay?"

"Fine, Mom," Brooke replied. "It seems so quiet. Where is everyone?"

"Doc's at the hospital with Hack," Neely reported. "He had the first of several skin grafts this morning, but he's doing fine. Steamer went back to Las Vegas. Your uncle took Savannah and Caroline home. And of course, your dad's at work. Now let's go downstairs and wait for Hunter."

Hunter arrived midmorning. Brooke met him at the door, and their arms went around each other. After a few seconds, he stepped back and studied her. "You look okay."

"Thanks." She looked at his nice new cast, his old bruises, and his new ones. "Your face is still a mess."

He gave her a little smile. "I know."

Brooke laced her fingers through his and led him outside. "Let's sit on the deck so we can talk for a while."

They sat on the swing in the shade and, for a few minutes, just enjoyed the peaceful summer morning and each other's company.

Finally he said, "It will take a while for everything to really sink in and even longer to deal with it. You might think you're fine, but you might not be."

She cut her eyes over at him. "You're starting to sound like my father. He wants me to go to a therapist."

"That's not a bad idea."

"I'll go if I think I need one, but I'm okay for now."

They were quiet for a few more minutes, and then he said, "So are we planning a second wedding?"

She turned in the swing so she could see him better. "I've been thinking a lot about life and love and us."

"I'm sensing a 'but' here," he said. "Does that mean you don't want to have a second wedding?"

She shook her head. "Just listen. What I have to say is important, and it takes all my concentration to talk without exaggerating anything or slipping in a little white lie."

He sighed.

"Back before, when you were trying not to love me, you said that a successful marriage depends on many factors besides love—compatibility, mutual interests, and common goals. At the time I thought it was just an excuse, but now I don't."

She paused to be sure he was paying attention. When he nodded she continued.

"I've watched other couples that I think have successful marriages, like my parents, Uncle Christopher and Savannah, even Mrs. Steele and the general. And I think it's true. Marriage is about more than just love."

"So you don't want to stay married to me?"

"Hunter! Please, just listen and quit trying to analyze every word I say!"

"I'm listening," he said, his expression more solemn than normal.

"I know we love each other, and we might be able to build a good marriage on only that. But I want a great marriage."

"Just tell me what you want, Brooke. I can't stand the suspense."

"Everything about our relationship so far has been rushed and, in some cases, forced. I want us to take some time to enjoy each stage—courtship, engagement, marriage, and honeymoon."

He still looked a little unsure, but he nodded. "Okay."

"At first I was so desperate to keep you from leaving me that I was willing to have you on any terms. Now I want to be sure you *choose* me. I don't want you to just settle because circumstances threw us together."

"Brooke—"

"I'm not fishing for compliments or trying to coerce a commitment out of you," she assured him. "But I want us to be able to look back at this stage of our lives fondly. When you're ready, I want you to buy me a ring and then surprise me with a proposal. I want to pick out a wedding dress and walk down the aisle on my father's arm. I want to exchange rings and share real vows with you." She paused for a deep breath. "And I don't want my memories of our wedding day to include the Aloha Ice Hut."

He winced. "That was pretty bad."

"A legal necessity is not the way to start a successful relationship."

"So where do we go from here?"

"We can date," she said. "We can go to fancy restaurants, and you can whisper into my ear . . ."

He stared back blankly.

"Okay, well we can go out to eat and get to know each other better," she amended. "We can set some goals and share our beliefs. Then when you like me, as well as love me, you can propose to me."

"The whole get-down-on-one-knee thing like in the movies?"

She nodded. "Definitely. Maybe wearing your dress uniform. And a sword. Then my mother can go into an ecstasy of wedding planning. We'll have a nice little ceremony with lots of pictures that we'll be proud to show our children."

"How long will we date?"

"A few months at least. That will give me time to finish school and decide what to do with my life. I'm also going to revisit the adoption of my daughter."

"You want to contest it?"

"No, I can't do that to the adoptive parents. They trusted my word and have spent the last year loving and caring for her. It would be wrong to break up their family just because my circumstances have improved. But I would like to ask for some communication with them. Maybe they'll send me pictures and updates . . ." She dragged her eyes up to meet his.

He nodded solemnly. "That's a great idea."

She relaxed.

"So are you finished?"

She nodded.

"Is it my turn now to tell you how I feel?"

Nervously she nodded again.

"The way I see it, we've been married for almost a week, and so far I've slept on the floor, and we've only taken pretend showers." He pulled her to her feet. "I say we need to start making up for lost time."

Her eyes widened, and her lips parted. "Hunter?"

He gave her one of his rare smiles and leaned close to whisper, "Mrs. Ezell, I believe it's high time I took you on a date."

# ABOUT THE AUTHOR

BETSY BRANNON GREEN CURRENTLY LIVES in Bessemer, Alabama (a suburb of Birmingham). She has been married to her husband, Butch, for thirty-five wonderful years. They have eight children, two daughters-in-law, three sons-in-law, and thirteen grandchildren. She is the LDS Family Services representative for her stake and works at Hueytown Elementary School. She loves to read when she can find the time and enjoys sporting events—especially if they involve her children or grandchildren. Although born in Salt Lake City, Betsy has spent most of her life in the South. Her life and her writing have been strongly influenced by the town of Headland, Alabama, and the many generous, gracious people who live there—especially her ninety-five-year-old grandmother, Grace Vann Brannon. Her first book, *Hearts in Hiding*, was published in 2001. *Danger Ahead* is her nineteenth novel for the LDS market.